The Pleasures of Time

The Pleasures of Time
Two Men, A Life

by

Stephen Harold Riggins

INSOMNIAC PRESS

Edited by Richard Almonte
Copy edited by Adrienne Weiss
Cover designed by Mike O'Connor
Interior designed by Marijke Friesen

National Library of Canada Cataloguing in Publication Data

Riggins, Stephen Harold, 1946-
The pleasures of time / Stephen Harold Riggins.

Includes bibliographical references and index.
ISBN 1-894663-46-2

1. Bouissac, Paul. 2. Riggins, Stephen Harold, 1946- 3. Gay men—
Biography.
I. Title.

HM479.R54A3 2003   305.38'9664'0922   C2003-900714-6

The publisher gratefully acknowledges the support of the Canada Council, the Ontario Arts Council and the Department of Canadian Heritage through the Book Publishing Industry Development Program. We acknowledge the support of the Government of Ontario through the Ontario Media Development Corporation's Ontario Book Initiative.

Printed and bound in Canada

Insomniac Press
192 Spadina Avenue, Suite 403
Toronto, Ontario, Canada, M5T 2C2
www.insomniacpress.com

The Canada Council | Le Conseil des Arts
FOR THE ARTS | DU CANADA
SINCE 1957 | DEPUIS 1957

ONTARIO ARTS COUNCIL
CONSEIL DES ARTS DE L'ONTARIO

Mozart combines just enough of this touch of pleasurable sadness with the easy cheerfulness and elegance of a mind lucky enough to take in what is agreeable.
—Eugène Delacroix

As bamboo shadows sweep the stairs, no dust is stirred; as the moonlight penetrates the pond, no ripple is made on the water.
—Huanchu Daoren

After having admired the most lovely tulip under the magnifying glass of the Haarlem gardener, one still loves the little bouquet of forest violets: simple flowers, but gifted with an enduring perfume.
—Jules Combarieu

Table of Contents

Preface

I share the opinion of James Boswell, my eighteenth-century model of a tireless biographer, that private conversations are the most absorbing side of literary life. Conversations disappear with little trace unless stubborn and persistent witnesses make it their goal to record—sometimes secretly— what others are saying. When I began writing this book, I was a graduate student in Sociology, still uncertain whether I had chosen the right field of study. In fact, a whole decade passed before I realized I had indeed made the right decision. I wanted to turn the eyes of an archivist upon my life with Paul Bouissac, upon ourselves and our friends. I wanted to write a book that would give as much attention to the obscure as to the famous, where the philosopher Michel Foucault and the composer John Cage could rub shoulders with people they never met but would have enjoyed. Most of all I wanted to document the surrealist vision and Buddhist philosophy of my partner. I began the diary which is the basis for this book on November 20, 1972.

The Pleasures of Time is a journal of love, friendship and domesticity, a collection of shards and remnants from two seamless lives. Paul was already thirty-five years old when we met in 1969. I grew up in the comparative affluence of 1950s and 60s America; he, in the sombre and insecure France of the 1940s and 50s. In comparison with the wild, exotic Otherness which he appreciated so much in the circus, I lived in what seems to me a profoundly straight world, one shaped by Midwestern unpretentiousness. In theory, of course, Paul could record his life better than anyone else. Yet I knew he was disinclined to revisit his past, especially when it required reliving some tense personal failures.

At first I kept my diary a secret from him. I trained myself to remember what Paul said long enough to make copious notes out of sight. Later, I also interviewed him. It might seem odd that I formally interview a person with whom I was to live for more than thirty years. But my Samuel Johnson was probably less cooperative than the original. (A comparison is difficult because we know Johnson's reactions through the writings of his biographer. Sometimes Johnson helped Boswell; at other times he subverted his project.) Paul resented my gathering personal information because he felt it undermined the trust in our relationship. When he spoke to me in confidence, he never knew whether or not it would end up in the public record.

What made writing this book such a compulsion for thirty years is that all of the motivation had to come from me. Paul was either hostile or indifferent. He is afraid of the past's power to "vampireize" the present. All too often I had to discover the gaps in his history and correct the errors. Paul complains that my quest for information makes him feel like a cornered animal, eaten alive, an animal preserved by a taxidermist: "All my artistic endeavours have been done in order to disappear. I try to erase my traces." Such remarks are partly an exaggeration to entertain dinner guests, but they contain more than a kernel of truth. Apparently, I have tested his belief that nothing matters.

As an outsider, I'm fascinated by the elitist student subculture he experienced in Paris in the 1950s. Paul just wants to forget it. On the other hand, when he speaks about his childhood and youth his eloquence is remarkable. He recommended that I rewrite this book as a novel. How many people would read it then, he wonders sarcastically. He accuses me of insensitivity when I prod for information or ask him to decipher letters handwritten in French. I have been very patient. But it is also true that at certain times I simply did not see the "pain and trauma" I am told I caused, as legitimate grief. Remembering the pleasures of time should not be such an ordeal. I am unsympathetic to the very idea of living only for the moment. In his opinion, my book captures a mere ten per cent of his life. I might have captured eleven per cent, I respond, if he had been a better pack rat, kept closer ties with youthful friends and agreed to more interviews with journalists.

Most of my formal interviews took place in my windowless office in St. John's, Newfoundland, when Paul visited during university holidays. I chose a windowless office to avoid looking out on Canada's capital of rain and fog. Trying to gauge Paul's moods and catching him during receptive moments have never been easy. A few interviews were conducted by telephone when he could be coaxed into participating. On these occasions I was in St. John's and Paul at our shared home in Toronto. Paul thought that writing about him had therapeutic value for me in my Newfoundland isolation. He also claims that the best sections of this book are the ones in which he is never mentioned.

Acknowledgements

In completing this book I would like to acknowledge the assistance of a number of people, who in many cases are not specifically named in the text: Judy Adler, Richard Almonte, Jeffrey Chan, Wayson Choy, Jack Der, David Diallo, David Gilmour, Richard Hendrickson, David Higgs, Volker Meja, Khoa Pham, David Smith and Ken-Shung Yong. But above all, I am indebted to Rosemary Clark-Beattie, who understood better than I did how to turn a formless diary into an actual book.

Paul Bouissac feeding a giraffe,
Bouglione Circus, 1960.
Photographer: Terry Clayton

Paul Bouissac, age 16, 1950.

The Debord Circus: Michel Gabereau, Paul Bouissac and Gérard Debord, 1965.
Photographer: Kenneth Eliot. Appeared in *Maclean's*, June 5, 1965

The Circus Is His Kingdom

In his autobiography *The Circus Is My Kingdom* the French circus director and animal trainer Firmin Bouglione describes a certain Madame Ilonka. At some point in the 1950s, we are told, her awe-inspiring act with thirteen Persian bears opened the program of the Bouglione Circus. So frightening was this act that it made even professional trainers shiver. Other than carrying a knife under her belt, Madame Ilonka did not wield any of the weapons that trainers normally use to protect themselves in the ring. Instead, she intimidated the bears with her bizarre voice, "a sort of constant guttural vibration." She had learned the language of bears from her husband, also an animal trainer. Transgressing the accepted rules of gender and marriage, she continued to work with the very animal that had killed him.

Madame Ilonka was then a forties-ish Eurasian woman who spoke French with an accent that was difficult to place. She possessed a formidable technique as an animal trainer, which she was reluctant to share with others. The typical Western European trainer, she maintained, thought of bears as costumed actors riding tiny bicycles and balancing on teeter-totters. In language that anticipated the rhetoric of today's animal liberationists, she insisted that:

> Bears are the great lords of the forest. They are the equals of people. [Where I come from], they live in the garden, near the temples, under the cedars. Bears are the stern gods of the night. They render their judgements. They know. Bears are just. Many secrets are written in the book of their souls.[1]

With the aid of astrology, Madame Ilonka probed the minds of her bears, whose destinies and luck in love, she believed, were determined by the heavens. As a result, she was convinced that ten years earlier one of the bears had decided to murder her and was just waiting for the right moment. Near the end of her time with the Bouglione Circus, she also began to complain about nefarious magnetic waves that made the circus's location inauspicious. This was the only sign that Madame Ilonka might be planning to leave. Three trucks—two full of bears—a mobile home, and the trainer vanished one day without a trace.

Le cirque est mon royaume (to use the French title) is supposed to be Firmin Bouglione's autobiography. In fact, the entire book, including the acknowledgement in the foreword thanking the ghost writer for his assistance, was written by the future French professor Paul Bouissac. It appeared in 1962 when Paul was twenty-eight years old. When he accepted the manuscript for publication, Georges Roditi, literary director at Les Presses de la Cité, had cautioned Paul, "You'll have to add some women to your story. Other than women no one has time to read such books." Bouglione did not believe in presenting women in the ring as wild-animal trainers. He thought they would not react aggressively enough when confronted by danger. So Paul invented Madame Ilonka with the help of two of the officers with whom he completed his military service in the Air Force, Captain Pimpaneau and Commander Bordes.

For the rest, the book is based on lengthy conversations with Firmin Bouglione (1905-1980) that occurred during lulls, when nothing was happening in the circus, or while sharing coffee or dinner with the family. Firmin genuinely liked Paul. The circus director had the sort of popular wisdom of someone who had great familiarity with animals. Before agreeing to sign the contract for publication, Bouglione had asked Paul to read the manuscript aloud to his brother Joseph, whom he knew had a good sense of what information would best serve their artistic interests. Firmin Bouglione, himself, *may* have skimmed through the manuscript, but that was about the extent of his detailed knowledge of its contents. Years later the story of Madame Ilonka was still a source of puzzlement to him. He had no idea what people were talking about when they asked for recent news about the female animal trainer who used astrology to understand her bears.

The fact that Madame Ilonka never existed did not disturb Firmin's brother in the least. He knew the autobiography was fiction embedded in truth. And it was the fiction that he appreciated most. The circus is famous, after all, for taking liberties with the truth. He told Paul that if he himself tried to pull such exaggerated tricks, people would not believe him. Soaring aloft into the realm of fiction and taking the crowd with him, Paul had beguiled the public when he worked as a barker for the travelling zoo which was part of the Bouglione Circus. This is what gave him status among the Bouglione family. The ideal barker invents, elaborates and omits like a novelist.

Despite Paul's warning that the story of Madame Ilonka is a mystery worthy of the novels he ridicules, it is rarely unbelievable. Rereading the passage in response to my questions forty years later, Paul laughed and said: "This is the most credible part of the whole book. I should do more of this."

◆　◆　◆

Born in the city of Périgueux, France, in 1934, Paul Bouissac is best known in North America as an authority on the circus. Although there is a tradition in France of artists and intellectuals finding inspiration in the circus, in the 1970s when Paul established his reputation as a scholar, the only people who wrote seriously about the circus were either amateur historians or journalists. Paul changed that. His master's thesis for a degree in Classics at the Sorbonne was titled "Circus Animals for Parade and Training in Roman Amphitheatres." His Ph. D. dissertation on the measurement of gestures was motivated in part by a desire to record accurately the gestures of performers in the ring. He wrote the first book, *Circus and Culture*, that uses semiotics to decode the social and political messages conveyed from the circus ring. His work as a circus impresario would constitute only a footnote in circus history, although an exceptionally interesting one. His theoretical contribution, on the other hand, is a lasting legacy.

Paul exalts the circus at the expense of the theatre. The circus is not, he argues, a culturally peripheral institution mired in the popular aesthetics of the past. It is a mirror reflecting the social conditions of its society, a crucible in which cultural codes and rules are combined in new ways and a key to understanding the language-like patterns of non-verbal communication. Paul approached the circus with a theoretical sophistication that is rare even today. He studied with the anthropologist Claude Lévi-Strauss and the semiotician Algirdas Julien Greimas and associated with the group of people who later came to be called the Paris School of Semiotics. His writings on the circus blend concepts from semiotics, narratology, structural anthropology and ethnology. In the words of Sally Banes, a performance art critic for the *Village Voice*, Paul makes the circus "supremely intelligible. And when an art begins to make sense while continuing to surprise you, you get hooked."[2]

Paul disapproves of the way North Americans see the circus as entertainment for children. Circus performers secretly dislike audiences of children because they are not sophisticated enough to appreciate their skill and artistry nor the subtle messages as sublime "professional deceivers"[3] that they communicate from the ring. For this reason I hesitate to begin by writing about Paul's childhood interest in the circus. But it is important to point out that he grew up in the 1930s and 40s when France was still largely a rural society and enjoyed closer contact with domesticated farm animals than French children experience today. However, rural life was for him a playground. He has spent his entire life in cities. He talks about building miniature circuses with a persistence and inventiveness that recall the puppet shows and filmmaking experiments of the adolescent Jacques Demy as they are depicted in Agnès Varda's film *Jacquot*. Paul made hundreds of little statues of circus performers in cardboard, paper, and clay from the soil of the farm. When he was ten, he thought of training the old donkey on the farm to do circus tricks. Snails were turned into circus artists. He says he took these ideas very seriously.

◆ ◆ ◆

Paul first read Alain-Fournier's novel *Le grand meaulnes*, translated into English as *The Lost Domain* and *The Wanderer*, for a French course he was teaching at the University of Toronto.[4] The plot of the story is melodramatic, but what makes this novel from 1913 still worth reading is the way Alain-Fournier conveys in such vivid detail the tastes, smells and sights of the countryside in the 1890s. Fifty years later modernization had not yet completely transformed rural life. There is also a brief eruption of the circus in this sedate novel which pleases Paul. Typically, when he draws autobiographical parallels with the novel, he distances himself from his past:

When I read the opening chapter of *Le grand meaulnes*, it brought me back to the time of my childhood. I don't want to say it is a pleasure of nostalgia because I dislike very much the state of dependency that is attached to childhood. I have no idealization of childhood. I am much happier now than at the age of fourteen. I look forward to being happier in ten years. But these sensations, and they really are sensations, are associated with a mixture of pleasure and sadness. For this reason they moved me. I don't like to be moved by these types of things. In my opinion it takes the brain a lifetime to emancipate itself from the conditions of its development.

Le grand meaulnes is set in the region around Châteauroux where Paul's maternal grandparents had their roots and spent all their lives. As a boy, Paul heard stories about the childhood of his relatives. In the late 1940s he visited the area on bicycle. He felt that the regions of Berry and Périgord were his two homes. He also claims his mother had romantic notions about farming because she was raised by a wet-nurse on a farm in the village of Etréchet, near Châteauroux:

In the family context in which I was brought up everything was predictable. I remember when I was in Paris doing my military service I visited several times a friend of my aunt, who had published a book on astrology, a woman who had character. I was telling her about my desire to join the circus and become a wild-animal trainer. And at the same time I was telling her about my plans to write a thesis on the translation of Greek philosophers into Arabic and then into Latin. She said something like "I don't understand how you have all these ideas when I think how conservative your parents are. Between you and me, they are really 'pot au feu.'" Pot au feu means pot roast. In French it is the standard bourgeois dish. It is not anything fancy. It is the good old bourgeois values with their lack of imagination, lack of risk, lack of everything—or so she said. I was a young soldier in uniform. She may have just been flattering me.

The novel's lost domain is a decaying castle. From the age of about three to fifteen (1937 to 1949) Paul grew up in a similar environment on a hill overlooking the city of Périgueux. The family moved from the industrial edge of town to this higher location because their doctor suggested that country air would be good for the children. Although his father did not want to move, his mother was delighted about the prospects of living in a castle then owned by the Countess of Roffignac. It must have been very beautiful in the late-eighteenth or early-nineteenth centuries. By the time the Bouïssac family moved there the fountains were in ruins, covered by thick bushes; the alleys for riding were overgrown. But there was still a tennis court, a functioning farm with cows, pigs, chickens, rabbits, an orchard and a vineyard. The tenants on the main floor made pâtés and fois gras preserves in a factory which was set up in the former stables.

It was for me acres and acres of wonders and mysterious places. We were not castle people, if I can say that, because my parents only rented the top floor of the castle, which was actually just under the roof. It was an apartment made of the former rooms of the servants, which had been connected with each other. There were eight rooms, one after the other. My own room was in the eastern tower. Above that apartment there was a huge attic full of mystery, bats, dusty old furniture, boxes and an enormous stuffed tiger. To reach our floor we had to walk up four flights of marble stairs.

When you grow up in a space which is unique, you develop a sense of uniqueness. There was not a single classmate who had this kind of home, except for a couple of aristocrats who were coming from their castles in the back country. We were in a castle without being aristocrats. The windows were opening on all the city and the river. We had the most beautiful view of Périgueux of anyone who lived there. But we didn't have drinking or running water. We had to walk down to the bridge to get drinking water from a fountain. There was running water in the apartment at only one sink. But it was coming from a well and it was undrinkable. It was just water for washing. There was no hot water. So there was a lot of things which were unusual in terms of discrepancies between us and the house. We did not have any servants. Only Léonie Maze, the cleaning lady, who was coming regularly and had become a part of the extended family.

In the castle there was a lot of mystery as there is in the lost domain of *Le grand meaulnes*, frightening things, ghost stories. There was a tomb of Countess Nordsguld in a remote part of the park. Although there is no one-to-one correspondence with the novel, there is nonetheless the fact that this huge milieu was a space of freedom for me and a space of intense sensations and impressions, and closeness with nature. I was one with that space. The park. The farm, the woods—all that was my territory.

There was a great variety of snails in the park. I was catching fancy snails. I was building little trapezes and I had the snails in miniature boxes like travelling cages. If you put a snail on a hanging string, the snail automatically climbs up it. If you put a snail on a trapeze, it will cross it. Sometimes we were catching snails for food, when it had been raining at the right season, going into the bushes and picking up snails. But I was picking the nice ones for my circus. I remember also that I decorated them.[5]

When Paul reached early adolescence, his paternal grandmother died and his father decided to move back to the family home at number eight rue Philippe Parrot. This was an unassuming row house built directly on the street. Not a sliver of grandeur. The relocation, which Paul bitterly resented (he cried the night they moved), is symbolic of the social decline which is a prominent theme in his family stories. When there were so many beautiful places to live in this 2,000-year-old city, it was even more difficult for Paul to accept the fact that his father—keenly aware of his economic constraints—had chosen to live in such an uninteresting house in an undistinguished street.

By 1970 Castel Fadèze had been abandoned. Later, it was made inhabitable but at the loss of the upper storey where Paul's family had lived. The most obvious change was the division of the park and farmland into small lots for suburban homes. Although many of these houses were attractive, the real estate developers maximized their profits by allowing houses to be built up to the very edge of the castle. In 1997 when Paul and I visited Périgueux together, it was difficult for him to locate Castel Fadèze. It was lost among its neighbours because of the alterations to the roof. Castel Fadèze was still an impressive home, but it had lost its magic. It seemed to Paul like a nouveau riche reinterpretation of a castle, an odd quotation out of place, with a swimming pool instead of fountains. It was no longer the kind of residence a ghost would inhabit.

◆ ◆ ◆

Lunch in Saint-Cloud in the spring of 1978 with Paul's childhood friend Alain Ohrel, then a *sous-préfet*; Ohrel's mother; and the juggler Christian Marin. The stories told at lunch included a tale about Paul training the Ohrels' little dog Taillac. At the age of fourteen Paul taught Taillac to jump on command in numbered hoops and to climb and descend—head-first—a small vertical ladder that was strapped to the edge of a metal table. He even sewed dramatic costumes for the dog out of remnants of old fabric.

Paul enjoyed showing off his skill as a trainer by strolling along a beach of the local river with Taillac following on his hind legs.

Unfortunately, Alain Ohrel's parents gave the dog away when it became a pest. Taillac would pull clothes off the clothesline and ascend the dining room "buffet à crédence" (a sideboard buffet). The farmer who acquired Taillac was surprised to see it climb a ladder at night to sleep in a hay loft. The climbing dog was the talk of the village.

◆ ◆ ◆

Once I asked Paul to explain to me what was so appealing about the circus. For many people it is just a synonym for vulgarity and excess. He responded that when he was a child the circus had embodied a parallel universe, "everything" denied a little boy in a small provincial town in France. He did not think there was anything strange about his reaction. Thousands of people had similar experiences. There are still people in France, and in the rest of the world, who react like he did. Paul gave me this account of the first circus which crossed his path.

Every year during the Second World War there was at least one circus that came to Périgueux, Cirque Bureau. It was very famous. The only large animals it had were horses, but it had all the prestige of the circus. The triviality of the name was completely offset. There was no link between an office or a desk (bureau in French) and the Cirque Bureau (the name of a circus family). We knew the names of some of the horses and so on. For instance, Roxane, the dancing grey mare. My mother would take us there or my grand-father, her father, who was sometimes living with us during the war. My grandfather was of the generation that saw the golden age of circuses in France. He had memories of Buffalo Bill coming to Châteauroux. He was a good little bourgeois who would not have missed a big circus coming to town.

Actually, the first time I saw a circus I think I was taken there by my grandmother, my father's mother. That was just before the war. I must have been four or five. I have a vague memory of that first experience, not a memory of the spectacle, but of the situation, an unusual experience given the background of the ordinary life of a city for a four year old.[6]

The Bouglione Circus, 1957-1962

The impression a reader might form of Firmin Bouglione from *Le cirque est mon royaume* is that he was a cautious and hard-working man who was naturally curious about animal behaviour. His knowledge seems to be encyclopaedic. The book begins with Bouglione retelling a series of stories from his youth of dramatic experiences with dangerous animals. The next section opens with Bouglione trying to imagine why rats in the Middle Ages might have followed a pipe player. Bouglione rejects the idea that the music played by the piper was supernatural. Either some notes corresponded with signals the rats themselves made when communicating with each other or the pipe player had secretly trained them. The photographs in the book show a portly man presenting tigers and panthers while dressed in a gentleman's suit. He claims that his father had been the first wild-animal trainer to present an act in a formal dress suit.

Firmin Bouglione was actually rather shy and inarticulate, Paul says. His memory could be faulty. Candid remarks in print about his youthful rowdiness were not appreciated because he was anxious to protect the public image of his circus. Firmin enjoyed taking liberties with the truth, like his brother Joseph. One of his best yarns was that he had outwitted journalists by convincing them he had harnessed lions to a plow and trained them to work in the fields.

In his youth Firmin Bouglione was a sort of poker-faced joker. But he could be very extreme in his practical jokes. I told you that he had a skin disease. Part of his skin was discoloured. Once it happened that a woman, who had heard my story that the discolouring was actually scars due to fighting with wild animals, came to the circus and expressed her sympathy to him. He looked at her and said: "Oui, ma pauvre dame. You don't know what it is like. You would never believe from which part of my body they took the skin they grafted on my face." He was doing that to people who looked respectable.

People in the circus were telling me stories about how sedate Firmin Bouglione had become with age. They were saying that when he was younger he went once to a pastry shop in a small French city. Pastry shops are always supposed to be a bit elegant and snobbish. They make all these fancy cakes for special occasions, always very clean. Lying on the shelf or the counter was a beautiful tray of cream cakes. Bouglione pretended to accidentally put his hand in the cakes and splashed them around, shocking people, while profusely apologizing. He tried to clean up the mess but purposefully made an even greater mess, knocking down big cakes. At the end he would generously pay for everything. It was just a way of having fun.

These were the types of stories which had entered the folklore of the circus. People were still laughing about them decades later. Probably they were inventing part of the stories. The Bougliones had gigantic proportions in the eyes of the people who knew them or who were gravitating around them. They had a reputation for being immensely rich.

The sisters Marthe (1879-1962) and Juliette (1881-1949) Vesque were commercial artists who illustrated scientific books and drew models for the Sèvres porcelain factory. But their passion was the circus. Their drawings and diary are unrivalled as a record of the circus in France from about 1900 to 1940. Accustomed to mainstream public entertainment, the Vesques were shocked by the behaviour of the Bougliones when they entered the circus business.

For instance, the Vesque sisters say in their diary that in Versailles when the circus came to town the Bouglione riders were entering the bistros with their horses. They were riding horses like you see in Western films. Horses are nervous and very jumpy when they are in an unfamiliar place. The Bougliones were making them jump and enjoyed startling people. But at the same time making history because such things had never been done in France. It was not a part of everyday life to make a big splash in a city by entering a café on horseback. The Bougliones were flamboyant people. Their circus was always unique in France because it had a flavour of unruly poetry, majestic informality, or an overpowering, pungent spontaneity. One of my friends used to say: "It had colour. It had atmosphere."[7]

♦ ♦ ♦

Dimitri Maximov, a Ukrainian from Yalta, is a former circus conductor and composer who liked to bet on horses. For the *tiercé* his favourite numbers were 5, 8 and 9. He usually gambled on lucky numbers rather than on the names or talent of jockeys. Maximov once worked at the Cirque Pinder or Cirque Amar, if Paul remembers correctly, but at the time they met at the Bouglione Circus he was too old to conduct and was employed as a cashier at the Bouglione travelling zoo and Winter Circus. Paul calls him the "factotum" of Firmin Bouglione and his wife. Maximov helped them in countless ways, doing errands, and teaching music to their daughter Gypsy.

Maximov loved to work as a cashier when Paul was the barker because visitors were often so captured by his stories that they forgot to pick up their change. More importantly, Maximov reinforced Paul's delight in mystifying people. A mystifier tries to make people believe exaggerated and unrealistic tales.

Maximov was a bit crazy and surrealist and carefree. He was always making nonsense jokes. He was someone who had a certain degree of education, if only because he was an educated musician and composer. But when he was younger he was a sort of playboy, probably very attractive, with Slavic charm, and had a reputation as a womanizer. Firmin Bouglione himself was also a great mystifier.

Paul is so skilled in fooling people that it can be difficult to convince them that he is merely joking. One of his adolescent school friends was jealous of Paul's ability to speak as an equal with sophisticated adults and capture their attention. Another friend, Michel Viala, called on Paul's help when he found himself drafted into the navy in unpleasant circumstances. He remembers Paul saying: "It's not difficult to mystify an admiral."

I was telling all sorts of stories as a barker. For instance, Firmin Bouglione had a skin disease which made discoloured patches on his skin. Whenever he would walk by, I would switch my speech to the story of Firmin Bouglione capturing lions in Africa with his own hands, struggling bare-handed with the lions, and being inflicted with terrible wounds on his face.

There was in the zoo a worker, an old man, who was a vague cousin of theirs (the Bougliones). His nickname was "le grand Belge." I never knew his real name. He used to nap after lunch on the bales of straw in the elephant tent. Once we placed near him a glass jar with some big flies in it. I was saying to the public that under the elephant tent "you will see the former terror of the Congo, 'le grand Belge,'" who did all sorts of feats that I invented. "A man in front of whom a whole continent was trembling. This great, courageous man has been reduced to nothing by the tsetse flies. You will see him deeply asleep next to the flies." That was mystification. I told people "You can poke him and you can see he has no reaction any more." He used to be startled and would jump up when they poked him. He could not understand what people meant when they talked about the flies.

We were producing thousands of inside jokes and people in the circus were having a lot of fun doing it. For instance, when visitors asked Maximov "what is there in the zoo?" he would say "chickens, rabbits, flies, fleas"—or all sorts of fantastic animals that were not there. He had a strong Russian accent, looked at them with these deep blue eyes, at the same time laughing a little bit. He was always a little tipsy. He had a sort of smile, and looked at them as if he were saying "what do you expect?" As an outsider, he thought the crowd was dumb. Of course, he was purposefully misinterpreting their questions. They were usually legitimate questions, but he was playing with the questions and transforming them.

I was sometimes announcing the "giant spiders of South America, 'les araignées jockeys, les tarentules d'Amazonie,'" which were being trained to ride horses. Sometimes you had naive visitors who would come back and say: "We didn't see the spiders! Where are they?"[8]

♦   ♦   ♦

For circus performers to capture and hold the attention of audiences, Paul theorizes, the barker who introduces sideshows or live acts should tell stories which exaggerate the risks and perils to come. The stories need to be open-ended in order to build tension. Circuses require good barkers because so much of the uncertainty is staged through talk. Emphasizing the professionalism of performers in controlling risks is not the best way to reach a mass audience.[9]

There is an autobiographical side to such ideas. Paul thrives on taking professional risks. He entertains paradoxical ideas just to see where they lead, and simultaneously undertakes too many challenging projects. Since some of these are bound to fail, he says it is vital to have alternatives. One in four is a success.

♦   ♦   ♦

Riggins: One of the differences between the way you and I react to the circus is my intolerance of fear. I do not like being frightened. As long as high wire artists have a net or they are attached by a safety cable, I am happy to watch. If lions have been trained to act like lambs, so much the better. But I am not entertained by someone risking his or her life. I would rather stare at the ground and ignore the performance, if this is what I perceive they are doing.

I am not certain what would be the best way of discussing this topic, but I thought that maybe you could illustrate your opinions by talking about Henri Dantès or some other performer from the Bouglione Circus. Taking risks and arousing fear in spectators are important components of many circus acts. Why should this be appreciated?

Bouissac: Henri Dantès was a very interesting stage name because it evoked Edmond Dantès, a popular hero of Alexandre Dumas' book *The Count of Monte Cristo*. Heinz Honvelhman was his real name. His nickname in the circus was Hans. It was a typical German romantic name for the French.

Dantès was very elegant and daring in the ring. He was too young to be tainted by memories of the war, but the fact that he had such a classic French name as a performer was perhaps to offset his German appearance. The first time I saw him was probably in 1956. He was about two years older than me. I went to the Porte d'Orléans, one of the places in Paris where the travelling Bouglione Circus performed last at the end of its touring season. That was probably in October or November. I was so enthused by his act the first time I saw him that at the intermission I went to the zoo to speak to him. Dantès was feeding the lions as he used to do after the show. I told him how wonderful I found his act. But he hardly paid attention.

Later in the winter the friend of a friend, with whom I had been on a student trip to Morocco, told me his sister was acquainted with one of the Bouglione daughters. The name of this friend was François Lepine. He was the son of a famous medical researcher. The Bouglione daughter was named Madonna. There were four brothers. She was a daughter of the eldest Bouglione brother, Alexandre, who had died prematurely.

François Lepine invited me and Madonna Bouglione to a party at his parents' place. I told her that I would like to work in their circus. She promised to introduce me to her uncle, Firmin Bouglione. Sure enough, some time later I went to the Winter Circus and she introduced me. I asked him if I could join the circus. Firmin said I could come work in the summer. I just had to get the information about the itinerary to know where to find them.

Riggins: Since you came from a family that had no connections with the circus, was it easy to convince Bouglione to hire you?

Bouissac: I didn't have to plead to work for them. Circus owners always have problems with the stability of their basic workers, people constantly joining and unexpectedly dropping out. It's very disruptive for circuses when someone who has been given a task quits unexpectedly. So they would welcome a student that seemed reliable. After that, when I was returning to the circus I kept talking to Firmin. That's when I met Dantès more personally, also through Madonna. At this point Dantès was very nice and friendly. He did not remember having met me before. But suddenly I was associated with the management of the circus. Very likely I was introduced to Madonna Bouglione as a serious student and this was conveyed to Dantès. When exams were finished that year, sometime in June 1957, I took the train to Morlaix in Brittany. I arrived in the morning and immediately went to the circus to look for Firmin Bouglione and Dantès and get on the payroll. I was assigned to the travelling zoo.

Riggins: We have gotten sidetracked from my original question. Let's go back to the topic of fear. Why should spectators enjoy the staging of fear in the act by Dantès?

Bouissac: Dantès was the embodiment of the circus hero. He looked vulnerable, younger than his age, and he was taking many risks. He was always dressed in white. He was not scratched very often. But sometimes if he raised the stakes by working too close to his animals, he would suffer scratches which would draw blood. The audience could see the blood. He had all this sort of suicidal prestige which is one of the fascinations of adolescence. And everybody in the circus was focused on him. He was an intense womanizer, a mode of life which was well served by his heroic status.

Riggins: You used an interesting phrase, "suicidal prestige which is one of the fascinations of adolescence." I assume you are referring to boys rather than adolescents in general. Are fear and the staged arousal of fear life-enhancing? Isn't this what is troubling about the daredevil aspects of the circus?

Bouissac: François Mauriac used to publish an editorial every week in, I think it was the *Nouvel Observateur*. Mauriac wrote some very laudatory lines about Dantès. Mauriac said Dantès looked as if he were coming straight from Eton College in England because he looked so proper. When I went to Germany in the late 1980s to meet Rolf Lehmann, the circus photographer with whom I had been in touch by mail for some time, we talked about our circus memories. Lehmann agreed that Dantès was the last of the heroic wild-animal trainers of this period of the circus which was coming to a close under the pressure of a shift in attitudes towards animals. Lehmann told me he had never again seen anything like the act for which I was for a time the cage attendant. How lucky!

Riggins: What was unique about his act that other trainers could not imitate?

Bouissac: It was Dantès' personality, the risks he was taking for the sake of the artistic value of the show, the staging, the speed, the natural choreography, the elegance of his gestures. You could never forget that it was a fight for life. Dantès wanted to have everything completed in seven minutes. One of my tasks was to monitor the speed of the act with a stopwatch beside the ring. If he was completing a part of the act twenty or thirty seconds late, I was making a sign so he would try to accelerate and make up for the lost time.

Riggins: This seems, though, more like an unpleasant stereotype of German punctuality rather than something that contributes to the aesthetics of the act.

Bouissac: If a lion act is too slow, it can quickly become boring. The spectators start noticing things which are counterproductive from the point of view of the show. A very fast pace takes the spectators breathlessly through the act. The spectators are in a way grasped at the beginning of the act and then taken over by the drama and the tempo. Only at its conclusion can they breathe freely.

It didn't look like a contrived piece of art. It was so artistic that it looked entirely natural. The lions were doing all these routines, constantly roaring and jumping. And at the same time there were brief moments of calm, perfect stillness. I described the act in great detail in *Le cirque est mon royaume*. Actually it was the first circus act I ever described. I knew it by heart.

The lions were César, Thompson, Sudan, Royal and Blackie. Blackie was the nice one. At the end, after having "fought" with these lions, Dantès lay down on the ground in the middle of the roaring lions. He had nothing for protection except one whip in his right hand. He was calling the lions by cracking the whip toward them. He was making them rush toward him and lay on top of him. First, he had one lay on his legs, one on his thighs, and one on his belly. And then I think he had one lay next to his feet. The fifth one was coming more calmly and laid on his chest. That was the nice one. It was very dramatic when the last lion was walking toward his face. The audience did not know that this one was very tame. You could see the tension. The lions up to that point had been constructed as extremely ferocious. He had all these lions laying on top of him and suddenly he would make a slight move and they would all jump up and return to their seats. Of course you can do this act with tame lions, but if the audience has the impression that they are like sheep, it does not have any effect. That so little time elapsed between the moment when they were roaring, jumping and attacking, and the time when they appeared momentarily subdued was the merit of the speed of the act. There was an alternation of ferocity [with] moments of harmony so that this part of the act was a sort of climax.

In the middle of the act Dantès sat on a chair and made these ferocious lions lay down at his feet. The good one was coming to his back and putting its paws on the same seat, resting its chin on his shoulders. This was forming a kind of scene or composition. There was a contrast between a fast dynamism, aggression, fights and brief moments of perfect composition when all these forces seemed to converge toward stability and harmony.

At the same time it was a very classic act because there was nothing superfluous in it. Nothing like Clyde Beatty, for instance. Dantès was never holding a chair or an iron bar or anything like that. He only had a whip and a stick. There was a minimal manipulation of accessories, but when he manipulated them it was done with a tremendous energy and strength, lifting the stools and throwing them to the side when he was finished. There was no dead time in the act. Even functional gestures, like moving a stool from one site to another, were built into the act. Each part of the act was flowing into the other. You understand how that can build something aesthetic?

Riggins: Yes. Other than keeping time, what was your contribution to the act?

Bouissac: Dantès' act was the first one on the program at the Bouglione Circus. When I was working there, one of my tasks was to check to see that all of the stools were in the right position for the opening. The stools had been placed by the circus hands. They put them more or less where they should have been but not exactly at the right spot. For me, my work was like a religious ritual. The implements were almost sacred.

Riggins: Your last remark sounds like something the juggler Christian Marin would say.

Bouissac: Yes. Dantès resembled Christian Marin in the sense that he was entirely consumed by his art; he was doing things for his own pure satisfaction. The last time I saw Dantès he was performing at Bouglione's Winter Circus. He was presenting an old Bouglione tiger act. In this act there was a mature rough tiger. At one point in the act Dantès was making the tiger cross the ring walking on its hind legs. This is something that many people do. But usually most trainers do this act with a young tigress. When I saw Dantès, I realized he was working in a different manner. He was provoking an attack from the tiger. As the tiger was dashing for him, he confronted it in order to force it to rise on its hind legs. This is a movement tigers make when they fight with each other. He was staying close enough to sustain the provocation while moving away. He would progressively withdraw, but not until the tiger had crossed most of the ring on its hind legs as a way of attack. He would suddenly increase his distance and the tiger would fall back on its four legs. Then he would chase it back to its seat or to the exit.

After the show I went to see him. While we were drinking, I told him "You do something wonderful." I told him how much I appreciated this passage, which probably lasted thirty seconds or less. And then he had a broad smile. He said "Ah, you have seen that" as if he was in front of someone who had been able to appreciate something that nobody sees. After that he got very sad and he said: "You know I do that for myself because I realize that not even my boss appreciates it. The audience doesn't appreciate what I am doing because they don't understand it." He knew that for the public a tiger walking across the ring on its hind legs was nothing but a classic routine. The way he was doing it was a masterpiece that was so perfect nobody saw it. You see what I mean?

Very often when circus artists reach a high degree of artistry, they lose their commercial appeal because they refuse to produce cheap effects. They work into their art many nuances and subtleties, performing in an apparently effortless manner as if it were casual, something of a very high complexity or audacity. It does not communicate to the audience; it remains unseen. Sometimes when artists who do tricks with very easy effects talk about their act or this particular part of their act to people who know about circus art, they have a way of apologizing by saying: "Well, I know it is cheap. But it is what the public wants."

In this thirty-second sequence with the tiger I saw an achievement of Dantès' artistic life which he was doing at high risk and for his own artistic satisfaction. What was making it such an instance of utmost artistry was that everything had to be right, the timing as well as the level of energy. I would say that both he and the tiger were engaging in a ritualized mutual aggression rather than in Pavlovian conditioning. There had to be a coincidence of fast biological rhythms for the two organisms to perform simultaneously this dance of life and death.

The Debord Circus, 1964-65

Frank Rasky's article about the Debord Circus in *Maclean's* magazine is titled "The Professors' Wonderful Circus" in reference to the sixteen university professors that Paul convinced to invest in his enterprise.[10] To coax a wild-animal trainer into collaborating, Paul named the one-ring show after his business partner Gérard Debord, whom he knew from his days with the Bouglioues.[11] The journalist appreciated Debord's "bone-crushing handshake," his biceps that bulged like the muscles of a blacksmith, as well as the fresh claw marks and scars on his chest.

> Debord wanted to do something on his own. The idea of going to America to start a circus was thrilling to him. . . . I had seen him in the cage when he was eighteen years of age. At that age, Firmin Bouglione had trusted him to present a large number of tigers, maybe sixteen or eighteen tigers. Firmin was not someone who would have put him in the cage, if he had not trusted him to stay alive. Debord had been properly trained by Firmin.
> Debord was not from a circus family, but from a military family. He was a dropout or a runaway who had joined the circus in his mid-teens. He was a difficult character. But he had the "mystique of the trainer," this tradition in France of the great lion trainers which Henri Dantès embodied. They were like saints to people, half saints, half heroes. Debord was someone who was young enough to start a new circus. He had the energy. It is not easy to find a lion trainer who will say "yes, I will go with you to start a circus," especially if there is no money to start with.[12]

Paul was the chief executive of the Debord Circus, fundraiser, visionary and ring-master. In addition, there were two multi-talented performers, Max Bertei and Michel Gabereau. After a successful career as a flying trapeze artist, Bertei had turned to juggling, clowning and dog training in his golden years. Michel Gabereau, an audio-technician and amateur magician, had met Paul when they lived in the same student residence on Rue des Fossés St. Jacques in Paris. Gabereau was in charge of the sound and lighting equipment of the show.

The spectacle opened with an animal act, ponies and horseback-riding monkeys that were trained and presented by Debord. Next, Bertei juggled with cigar boxes. Debord presented trained bears. Gabereau did a magic act: pulling a rabbit out of a top hat; turning a rabbit into a dove; making scarves appear, disappear and change colour. Bertei's dog act, a parody of a bullfight in which the dogs wore artificial horns on their heads, was the virtuoso element in the spectacle. Gabereau and Bertei did a comic sketch dressed as tramp clowns. The finale was Debord's lion act. The Debord Circus travelled throughout southern Ontario during the summer season of 1965 along with the King Shows, Canada's largest travelling carnival.[13]

Paul refers to this as his experimental circus. In retrospect it is viewed as a kind of participant-observation experiment. The article in *Maclean's* is proof that from the outset Paul had grandiose visions of artistic innovativeness because the journalist draws parallels with the best European models, the Moscow and Knie circuses. With obvious exaggeration, Rasky also calls Paul "Canada's leading circus impresario." I suspect that the lasting impression was not the spectacle, but Paul's eloquence and humour in talking about his future intentions.

I am definitely *un circophile*—or what North Americans call a "circus nut." But I am not enamoured of the American-style circus, the three-ring mass production, full of cracking whips and pratfalling buffoons and plenty of hoopla. I prefer the personalized specialty act. Mine is a one-ring theatre, where the clown is a sensitive actor who can move you to tears or laughter, and the animal trainer is a quality *artiste* in intimate rapport with his friends of the jungle. You might define the American circus as a big drum. My kind of circus is a fine viola.[14]

Given Paul's audaciousness, his own impulse to use hyperbole and the optimistic, nationalist spirit that existed in mid-1960s Canada, it is not a surprise that he suggests acts loaded with Canadian symbolism and comedy:

My ambition next season is to train a Canadian beaver to build a house on stage. I'd have Canadian wolves race in chariots pulled by Canadian reindeer. Why not? If the Moscow Circus can train a Russian fox and a rooster to put on an act together, why shouldn't we develop typically Canadian circus talent?[15]

The day after the journalist noted these remarks he returned to the headquarters of the Debord Circus, located on a tobacco farm near the improbably named town of Utopia, Ontario, not far from Barrie. As Paul swept the floor of the musty, unheated barn, he offered more quirky ideas:

"Perhaps later in the season we can train an elephant to play chess," [Paul] reflected, with a swish of the broom. "Perhaps mount a giant anteater, a spotted Dalmatian dog, and a leopard together on a pyramid. For comedy, we'd have monkeys riding piggyback on top of real pigs. And for music, we could hire a genuine Canadian Salvation Army brass band. They would be *sensationnel!*"[16]

◆　◆　◆

Paul was always trying to find some angle to his circus which would attract the media. The lion Malika and Debord shared a cage on a float in a Grey Cup Parade in Toronto. Malika, on a leash, appeared at a poolside party given by the author Pierre Berton. The event was caught by a *Globe and Mail* photographer. There was also the time Paul invited reporters to see the new anteater. It died before they arrived. Paul had to convince them it was hibernating.

Entertaining after-dinner stories about the Debord Circus—even if accurate—are a kind of selective attention that grossly distorts the actual experience of the partners. When there was no time to make long-range plans, not even middle-range plans, the reality was at times a true nightmare. In response to my persistent questions decades later Paul talks about "these stupidities" and this period of "always being on the edge." He claims, however, that he coped rather well because he was younger and more reckless. Here—with some ironical asides thanks to the retrospective memories of Gérard Debord and Paul—is a catalogue of crises, some small, some with potentially catastrophic consequences.[17]

Gérard Debord, the banker Jim Parkinson and Paul went together to New York to buy bears from an importer located near the port. Parkinson was the brother of one of Paul's female students, who heard about the Debord Circus in her French classes. Parkinson had a bit of money to invest and was instrumental in negotiations because he understood the mentality of businessmen and was a native speaker of English. The importer had advertised in a professional magazine for people working in circuses, fairs and carnivals. When the buyers arrived at the store, they discovered a pet shop selling poodles, parakeets and parrots. They were taken to another floor where the advertised Himalayan bears were kept. The bears were too young for training. Debord thought they were four or five months old, maybe younger. He wanted animals over one year old because he hoped—unrealistically—to present them in the circus within six months. Finally, the Debord partners decided not to buy anything, but they did take the importer's advice to visit a private zoo in New Jersey offering bears for sale of the right type and age.

They reached the zoo in New Jersey at closing time. No one was there except a manual labourer. Parkinson told him they wanted to have a quick look at the animals before returning to make some purchases. The employee let them in and talked off the record about the stock. Parkinson left a tip. The next morning they discovered the "employee" was the owner. That they could be so easily fooled was an indication of their naiveté.

Debord knew enough about animals to see through some other schemes. They were shown a lioness supposed to be gentle and trainable. Since Debord had already presented lionesses in an act, he could see that it was a castrated male, not a bona fide female. After that the owner of the zoo behaved in a more professional manner. He realized he was in front of a man of the trade. Debord was captivated by a female tiger. He actually knew tigers better than lions. But the owner would not sell this one, saying "You're young. I don't want to cause you harm by selling this very dangerous animal." When a wild animal becomes unmanageable in a circus, it is frequently sold to a zoo where it will have little direct contact with humans. The Himalayan bears, Milord and Max, appeared to be fine. The partners bought them. There was also a lion cub that tempted Debord. The cub was too young, maybe five or six months old, but he decided to buy it as well. Arrangements were made to pick up the animals the following week. With only one car, the Debord Circus could not afford to cash and carry live animals.

Debord had been an apprentice in welding and was going to a do-it-yourself garage in East Toronto to construct transport cages for large animals out of steel and thick wooden planks. A few days after returning from New York two of the cages were ready. They rented a trailer which they hooked to Parkinson's car. Debord and Parkinson went to New York alone because Paul was teaching full-time that week. The bears were easy to transport. The lion cub was in the back seat in a wooden crate. The cub was fierce and excited. It was destroying the cage from the inside. To be driving with a wild lion in the back seat, even though it was small, made Parkinson very nervous. Never before had he been near lions. The cub was named Zizi in honour of the French dancer Zizi Jeanmaire who was performing then in Toronto. Paul asked their lawyer, Hector Howell, to see if he could convince Jeanmaire to christen the cub. Either she was not interested or did not have time. But the name stayed.

Alone in his steel cage in the barn, Zizi would rush for the bars and growl at people. When food was brought, he would wait in the back of the cage until no one was near, rush for the food, and retreat from people as far as possible. Debord thought he had made a mistake in choosing Zizi. He was impossible. One day Paul noticed the cub seemed to be attracted to the lion Malika (princess, in Arabic) and suggested Debord put them together. Debord eventually took the advice. Almost immediately Zizi became as tame as Malika, so tame that Debord was letting both of them loose and played with them in the barn. It amazed Paul to see how quickly the character of Zizi changed. Later, however, as Zizi matured he reverted back to his old intractable self.

Another lion, named Caesar, was found in Rockland, Ontario, at a private zoo. The owner had bought the lion from the Detroit Zoo. Once the Rockland Zoo had gone bankrupt, the owner disappeared. The Detroit Zoo was probably only one of several businesses which had claims on his property. The Humane Society was called. They knew how to take care of raccoons, but not lions. The small Riverdale Zoo in Toronto might have housed the lions. But all the spaces were occupied. This gave the partners of the Debord Circus another media opportunity, presenting themselves as saviours of wild animals. They returned to the farm in Utopia with Caesar in a crate.

In the end the Detroit Zoo was more interested in the crate than the lion. "A lion is a strange item," Paul commented. "Sometimes you need one and it's really not easy to find it. But once you have a lion, it can be difficult to dispose of. A lion is not something you just discard." Caesar was trained by Debord despite being over four years old. Paul tried to interest reporters in photographing Debord with the lions. Caesar did not seem to be vicious or aggressive. He had what Paul calls a straightforward character that matched Debord's psychology.

Three very young black bears were purchased at a game farm in the Catskill Mountains. One was a little female named Pucelle (virgin, in Latin). The name of the second was Gamin (kid, in French). The third was a very sweet character called Jimmy. The winter before the bears were fully trained, Paul managed to get a contract for a show at the coliseum of the Canadian National Exhibition in Toronto. It was a sort of Christmas show put together by one of the Garden Brothers. Only two bears needed to be transported to Toronto. But four had to make the trip (two Himalayans and two black bears) since the Debord Circus did not have spare cages. One black bear was left in a cage in the barn. It was not possible to mix the species in the same cage. The truck they had purchased had at that point only a frame. Debord was going to build the rest in a few weeks. They had to push the steel crates on the truck and tie them with ropes. So that the bears would not freeze, wooden panels were fixed around the cages. Driving was risky. Debord was afraid the ropes would come loose and the bears fall off. He was not looking forward to a bear hunt in Toronto. Every time he turned a corner, he had to stop and make sure the ropes had not shifted. The show went reasonably well. The bears did not do much, though. It was not a particularly impressive first performance in a space as big as a coliseum. But some audiences, just happy to see wild animals, can be forgiving. A few days later Debord had to reweld the cages because he noticed that some of the bars were coming loose.

Twice animals escaped from their cages in the barn in Utopia. Once the cage attendant, Peter, forgot to lock the sliding door of the cage holding the lion, Malika. She pushed it open when nobody was in the barn. Fortunately, the barn doors were closed and the Shetland ponies were in a sort of shed against the barn. The door between the stable and the barn was also closed. The lion lay down on a bench in the workshop. It was easy for Debord to bring her back to the cage because she was used to playing with him in the barn. The mean Himalayan bear, Max, who could not be trained because he was too bad-tempered, escaped and climbed up into the beams of the barn. It took Debord a long time to throw a lasso around his neck and bring him back to his cage. At one point in the middle of the night Debord was so concerned about recovering Max that he telephoned Paul in Toronto. Paul had Debord leave the telephone hanging so he could follow the action at a distance. It was a tense moment. Paul was going to trigger an emergency plan, if he heard nothing from Debord for a while.

Debord wanted a rare lion with a black mane. In response to their advertisement a small zoo in Scranton, Pennsylvania, offered a Nubian lion at a low price. The mane did not look as if it had been artificially darkened. But the animal was too young to be trained, about a year old. Debord was reluctant to buy a lion that appeared sickly. Paul put pressure on him because he thought it looked like a nice animal. At least it was collar-broken and had been raised by hand. The day after it arrived in Utopia, Debord had to call the veterinarian, a Dr. Darling. The lion (named Hoggar after the mountains in the Sahara Desert) was suffering from pneumonia and required expensive medical care and antibiotics. The barn was too cold for a sick lion. Debord put it behind the couch in the trailer where he lived. Hoggar was very quiet. But, of course, he was a lion. Debord slept next to him, fed him, and cleaned up after him.

Visitors sitting on the couch jumped whenever Hoggar growled. The only visitor not frightened was Paul's student Sarah Willen (a fictitious name). She kept cool and was thrilled to have a lion next to her. All this made wonderful stories later on. Friends who visited Utopia on weekends fantasized when talking about the experience: "We were having tea and cookies in the trailer. Suddenly there was a piercing growl from a huge lion. . . ." Their stories had epic dimensions that led to a lot of folklore circulating among Paul's colleagues at Victoria College.

At some point when the bear cub named Jimmy became sick, the director of the Riverdale Zoo was consulted. In the middle of the winter he refused to drive to Utopia, but was willing to examine the cub in Toronto. Jimmy had to be taken to Paul's apartment on Bedford Road in downtown Toronto. Late at night Michel Gabereau drove the car. Paul was in the front seat beside Gabereau. Jimmy and Debord were in the back. From a distance a young bear can be mistaken for a German shepherd. So none of the motorists on the highway that night realized what kind of creature was in the car beside them. Nor did the landlord, Alexander McDonald, realize what was living above him for a few days. On occasion Paul can be surprisingly sentimental about animals, a reaction heightened in this case by financial concerns. "When you have sick animals like this," Paul told me, "you are constantly concerned about their health and well-being. Actually, the owner is obsessed with them. You are constantly looking to make sure they are in good shape and stress-free."

That weekend some colleagues from Victoria College went to Paul's apartment for dinner. Jimmy was allowed to come to the dining room. He ate morsels of food from their hands. After that, for the rest of their lives, they talked about having dined at the same table as a bear eating ice cream on Bedford Road.[18]

◆ ◆ ◆

Sarah Willen was one of the free spirits who was attracted to the Debord Circus. A recent immigrant to Canada, she enrolled in a night class in French. Paul, not yet thirty years old, was her instructor in his first year at the University of Toronto. Because the subject was conversational French and many of the students were adults, the instructor and students learned more about each other than in most university courses. Willen had studied at the University of Moscow, but was working as a secretary in Toronto. Paul liked her humour and her tendency to make fun of the staid Toronto of the early 1960s. They shared a European background. Paul convinced Willen to return to university. He thought she should enter a Ph.D. program because she was certainly more intelligent and lively than many college-level language instructors he knew. She eventually earned a Ph.D. and became a professor of Slavic languages.

In a letter to Paul, Willen recalls her ordeals with his shoestring operation some fourteen years earlier. Her first meeting with the Himalayan bears of the Debord Circus was in late November or early December, 1964:

> You managed to get at some Xmas tree celebration a walk-on part for the bears. I was supposed to walk out with them, Gérard watching in the wings. On the way there you kept telling me how mild and tame the bears were. On arriving we were met by a very angry Gérard with a bandage. She bit him. It was a she. He kept

calling her choice names—feminine ones. He took a look at me, a look at the bears and my chance for appearing on the stage with bears was forever lost.

The farm outside Barrie. The first time I drove there it was a sleety February day. You and I bought meat at de Groot's and then you said we had to deliver it to the farm. I'd never before driven on the highway, the 400 overpass was just then built. Somehow I found my way. There were a lot of trucks on the highway. To change lanes I would come out at a forty-five degree angle, pass the truck, then back to my lane another forty-five degrees, sometimes even sharper. The car would tilt and shake. The truck drivers would blow their horn. You were trying to doze off and would wake up every time with a jerk. Then there was the time the ponies arrived. It was bitter cold. Was it the same winter? You had a lot of animals by then, in their cages in the big barn. The truck with the ponies arrived. It backed into the barn. The ponies were led down. The animals in their cages were holding their breath, watching what was going on. One of the ponies refused to budge, crossed its hind legs and stood firm. Two people were pushing, one was pulling. The animals got very excited, gripping the cages and silently watching. Then we had lunch in the trailer. The little lion was sick and tied to the back of the trailer on a short rope. In the middle of the trailer was the stove on which a piece of steak was cooking. The lion kept pulling the rope towards the stove. Behind the stove was a bunk bed. It was so cold that we climbed with our boots on to the bed, and there we had our meal, Gérard complaining that his bed will be full of crumbs. The lion, straining at the rope, was watching us.

Then it was spring. I drove you to Yorkdale. I had a green suit on. You complained that it was bad luck. Yes, things didn't quite work out. You were very poor then. The animals had to be fed. You told me that all you could afford to eat was potatoes. Your shoes needed soles. They had a carnival across from Yorkdale and you had a tent with the animals. . . . One day, after rehearsal, before the performance, Gérard was having a bath. [My husband] came in from work, heard the splashing in the bathtub and asked who was there. "The lion tamer," I answered. [My husband] lifted his eyebrows and walked out to the garden. Was this the time we drove to the very respectable suburbanite in Bramalea?...You wanted him to sponsor the circus. You made a very good pitch. He didn't buy. No, I did not have my green suit on. By then I had dyed it black.

Willen agreed to sell tickets for the circus in May in Brantford, Ontario. Not wanting to alarm her husband, she gave him some pretext about visiting the farm of a friend's sister. Rather than drive herself she asked a fellow student to take her. The trip was uneventful, although she later discovered the student had been jailed for indecently assaulting women. After finding a hotel room she went to the carnival site where the circus was supposed to appear and waited:

> The stalls neighbouring the site for the circus were very solicitous about my fate and the fate of the circus. It got dark. Still no circus. I went back to the hotel, not far from the fair. Strange goings on in the hallways—half undressed women, men, noise, running around after each other somewhat puzzled me. Then people knocking at my door alarmed me. I took my little bag and went back to the fair. It was after eleven and at the coffee stand a general meeting took place. Nobody had heard from the circus. I had other job offers. I was asked to join the fair entertainers union, was told about the advantages of belonging to it, both social and material. Still no circus. . . . Then one of the men, I don't quite remember whether he was a barker or a shooting gallery owner, offered to drive me to Toronto. By then it was midnight and this seemed the best solution. On arrival in Toronto I took a taxi home and explained to my husband that an epidemic among the poultry made my stay at the farm unwelcome. . . . (March 15, 1978)

Last minute glitches had delayed the loading of the equipment and animals in the three trailers. The circus had its premiere two days later. Willen was supposed to have introduced the show.

◆   ◆   ◆

On August 11, 1965 (three months after the performances in Brantford), the lions from the Debord Circus were seized by officials of the Ontario Humane Society when one of its trucks broke down on highway 401 near the town of Woodstock. Officials thought that the six lions were underfed and so they filed two charges of neglect.[19] Debord later testified in defense of the circus, saying that the officials had misperceived the condition of the lions. The animals had missed only one meal, due to the breakdown of the truck, not from wilful neglect. Debord did not believe that fasting for one meal would have any detrimental effect on them. Animals often go for long periods without food in the wild. In most circuses and zoos they are put on a fast one day a week.

◆   ◆   ◆

Riggins: Why wasn't your circus able to make enough money to survive longer than this one summer?

Bouissac: There never was any significant money. We did not have any capital to start with. We could establish the circus only because so many things were made by hand by Debord and I could talk people into buying shares in our company. I was convinced that our youth, energy and luck would eventually bring success to our enterprise. Many people thought there was a market for this sort of exotic family show. Our dedication and skill was obvious to anybody visiting our winter quarters. Debord started building things after he arrived in Toronto, before moving to the barn in Utopia. He welded four individual animal cages at a do-it-yourself garage. When Debord arrived, we did not have more than fifty dollars. I had my account at the Toronto Dominion Bank where Al Ross, the professor who had recruited me to Victoria College, also had his account. He became the first shareholder of the Debord Circus Ltd. Ross went with me to talk to the manager to see if they could lend us some money, maybe a thousand dollars or something like that. But the manager at this bank wouldn't cooperate. So I closed my account, and opened one at the Canadian Imperial Bank of Commerce where the manager agreed to lend us the money to establish a circus. But it was a very small amount. His name was Mr. Geddes.

With this money we started renting the barn. But we were helped at the start by Jim Parkinson. He was a banker in a small city in Ontario. I think it was through him that we found the barn. At the beginning he was to be a partner, but after a while he understood how tough, how difficult it was, and took off. He had bought one of the trucks. When he left, we had to pay him back. After we had incorporated the company, there were a few things which we could buy in part by selling shares.

Riggins: Didn't you tell me once that the Algerian War had a detrimental effect on Debord?

Bouissac: Because of his know-how with animals, Debord had served in the military as a dog trainer. He fought in Algeria where he had many traumatic experiences. I thought I could get along with Debord as well as when we knew each other at the Bouglione Circus. I did not realize how much he had been traumatized by the war. Before he was quite sober. He was following Firmin Bouglione's rules. Bouglione rarely drank alcohol and believed that a trainer should abstain. Since then Debord's personality had changed somewhat. This occasionally created problems.

Riggins: Was the circus made unstable by disagreements between the partners?

Bouissac: This is the type of thing I don't want to dwell on. Because the circus didn't work financially as well as anticipated, the partnership showed strains. Michel Gabereau took off in the middle of the season. The trainer and the magician definitely did not get along. The day when we were deprived of Gabereau's station wagon and we had to hire a driver every time for the big truck, the whole operation became very fragile. There was a huge semi-trailer with all the equipment and the ponies, another little truck for the bears. Debord was driving the six lions and the house trailer which was hooked behind the lions' truck. I was in the station wagon with Gabereau. Bertei used his own station van. There were three convoys. So every time we moved we had to hire two casual drivers. The day when we did not have the station wagon to monitor the move, and we were not in communication with each other, there would be tremendous problems. None of these trucks was second-hand but fourth-or fifth-hand. We knew they could run for only a few months. If a truck broke down, we had to rely on hitchhiking to get help. Mobile telephone did not exist yet. It was a nightmare.

Riggins: What would you do differently, if you could repeat the experience of establishing a circus?

Bouissac: Probably when we started I was idealizing things too much. My flaw was not perceiving all the potential problems. I overlooked a lot of practical aspects and was just looking at the goal, investing a lot of energy in the goal. You get a vision and immediately invest your energy toward the implementation of that vision. Sometimes reality bends. Sometimes it brutally resists.

The Circus of the Century, 1976-78

The Circus of the Century was inspired by a musical expression of Dante's *Divine Comedy*—François Bayle and Bernard Parmegiani's *Paradise*. Paul and I heard it at a concert of electroacoustic music in Paris in 1974. Paul's knowledge of classical music is limited, but he enjoys concerts of contemporary music. While listening to *Paradise* it dawned on him that "clusters of crystalline sounds travelling in space" would be a wonderful accompaniment for a flying trapeze act.[20] A poetic description of the piece is provided by Chion and Reibel in their book *Les musiques électroacoustiques*:

It is a piece made of "rapid musical flashes coming from an unmovable substance, immune to time, and whose subtle grains escape the senses little by little." In order to situate these musical ecstasies, we would say that by opposition to the strong and free drifts of the "gliding musics," they are animated by a quivering, a continual shuddering, as if one could not stop trembling in the fear that this instance of bliss will disappear in the next second.[21]

In Paris in June 1976 I met the German curator Jörn Merkert who was in France doing research about the sculptor Julio González. When I introduced Jörn to Paul at the Café de Flore a week later, Paul told him about his dream of using avant-garde music and art to reinvent the circus. Merkert thought this was such an exciting idea that within a few days he suggested they introduce it together to the people planning the 1978 Berlin Festival. The proposal was completed in Toronto six months later, on January 17, 1977 (Paul's forty-third birthday). All of the ideas are Paul's, although he did utilize Merkert's personal relationships with artists. The opening section of the proposal deplores the capitalist nature of Western European circuses which impedes creativity:

If we consider the circus's long history, we can observe that it has continuously transformed itself by integrating into its system the technological advancements and the artistic achievements of its contextual cultures. However, those transformations have always been consistent with the fundamentals of its unique art in as much as it has never been alienated by the new elements it has used: electricity, nylon net (cage), electronic sonorisation, introduction of the bicycle and the car, cosmonautic style, musical themes, to mention only a few, have been organically incorporated to the point of becoming a part of its "language." However this "natural" process of symbiosis between the circus and its cultural context has always been relatively slow and occasionally awkward, because of economic considerations and lack of innovativeness on the part of its professionals. . . . It is also the case that the introduction of new technologies is generally motivated by economic pressure because the circus, which is an art to its audience and to most of its artists, is a profit-oriented business to most of its financial backers and directors. . . .

Artists and directors usually rely on small companies or individuals for the making of their costumes. Some major circuses have

---

their own designers and workshops. The general principle is to obtain the maximum effectiveness and resistance for a minimum price. The costumes reflect the economic status of the artists as well as their personal taste. Some choices are real successes; but more often than not a technically good act is aesthetically impaired by the type of costumes used. The same remark can apply to the music selected. It reflects the limited musical knowledge of the performers or the mediocrity of the second-rate composers who specialize in custom-made music for circus artists. It is usually beyond the reach of a circus man to benefit from the art of outstanding contemporary designers, painters or composers. However, there is nothing in the art of the circus as such which should prevent such collaboration.

The proposal is illustrated with four hypothetical acts, which I can outline in more detail than in the submission, relying on Paul's unwritten intentions. The first was a technological innovation for the Washington trapeze, a single hanging trapeze for a solo performer who does feats of balance. The performer Paul had in mind was Gérard Edon (Mr. Silky in the ring) who presented physically demanding feats of balance on the Washington trapeze in a refined and understated manner.[22] Paul wanted to give Edon the possibility of inventing a Washington Trapeze which could swing in a figure-eight arc. Edon had never tested the technology that might make this possible, but he thought it could be done with a hollow bar containing some kind of liquid. Electroacoustic noises, perhaps by François Bayle or Bernard Parmegiani, would be the accompaniment.

The submission alludes to a "clown well-known for his musical abilities" who would perform Luciano Berio's "Sequenza V" for solo trombone. Written in homage to the clown Grock, this is a comic piece that combines theatrical gestures with instrumental and vocal actions. The clown would also introduce new musical instruments commissioned from the Baschet brothers. By the time the proposal was written François Baschet had agreed to take part, but Bayle and Parmegiani had not been contacted. Paul hoped to entice the clown at the Blackpool Tower Circus, Charlie Cairoli, to be the trombonist. Cairoli was one of Paul's favourite informants for his research.

The third act was a team of foot jugglers who would use decorated props and costumes, perhaps by the Op-Art painter Victor Vasarely, and perform to the minimalist, hypnotic music of a composer such as Steve Reich. Paul had the three Castor brothers in mind. With their feet, the Castors juggle large rubber balls and other objects including the smallest brother rolled up into a ball. Later, Paul asked Ursula Sax to design props for the Castors. She is another personal friend of Merkert. Sax was known for sculptures in wood and metal, usually intertwined lines that are purely abstract, but some suggest landscapes and people flying or dancing. The fourth act was to consist of wild animals rarely seen in circuses (perhaps wildebeests, antelopes or moose). Music would be written specifically for each species using the rhythm of its gait. There was also a fifth act which Paul had envisioned but did not mention in the proposal because it was impractical. This was a recreation of the trapeze act of Barbette, a male transvestite who was a star in Paris in the 1920s. Professor Gilbert Bleau, who had gathered information on Barbette in the hopes of writing a book, was willing to serve as an historic adviser.

In conclusion, Paul cautioned that composers, artists and other professionals from non-circus backgrounds should not allow their "poetic" concept of the circus to determine their work. Instead, the project should give everyone the time to acquire a sophisticated understanding of the circus arts that can only come from close interaction with the performers. "It is believed," Paul concluded, that such an event "would be a landmark in the history of the circus."

♦ ♦ ♦

In June, 1977, the contract was negotiated in West Berlin with festival organizers. As a result, the circus became the theme of the 1978 festival. It was decided that The Circus of the Century would take place at the New National Gallery, near the Berlin Wall, over a period of six days. Paul was given a free hand, except for the constraints posed by Mies van der Rohe's ultra-modern building: no heavy animals, no high wire acts. According to the verbal agreement of June 28, a budget of 135,000 marks was promised for all of the expenses plus Paul's honorarium. In addition, it was implied in conversations that more money might be available in the future. Jörn was given the task of assembling an art exhibition on the theme of the circus at the New National Gallery. An exciting time of preparation seemed to lie ahead. Although plans were discussed about inviting some classic one-ring circuses, it is no exaggeration to say that The Circus of the Century would be the highlight of the upcoming festival.

During the weeks that followed Paul became obsessed with the project. Even he was surprised by how much it captured his attention. His mood rose and fell. He feared he might not have the opportunity to perfect his creation. In retrospect, the title "The Circus of the Century" was surely a mistake because it made such grandiose claims. In July we had dinner at an Italian restaurant in the Chelsea district of London with Eduardo Paolozzi, one of the pioneers of Pop Art in Britain, and an adoring female friend. Paolozzi was acquainted with Jörn, whom he called "the nicest man in Germany," and it was initially Jörn who suggested that Paolozzi might be an inspiring collaborator. Paul asked Paolozzi to design the costumes for the opening charivari, a sculpture from which clown-acrobats jump, and the free-standing ladder act that would immediately follow. Paolozzi said he was delighted by the invitation. He enjoyed the circus and looked forward to taking part for the sheer pleasure it would bring him. But he also hoped to contribute something meaningful to the men and women who made the circus live.

While scouting for performers from July 5 to August 23, Paul travelled to Blackpool, Amsterdam, Zurich, Luzern, Geneva, Blankenberge, The Hague, Albertville and London. He visited the Knie, Blackpool Tower, Annie Fratellini and Althoff Brothers circuses; and attended a three-day clown festival in Blankenberge, Belgium. Paul gave the VIP treatment to people who were susceptible to its charms. He wined and dined the directors Pierre Etaix and Annie Fratellini at the most expensive restaurant in Albertville. Paul served as an intermediary between the tightrope walker Philippe Petit and the festival. Realistically, stars flashed in the eyes of some of these people only because they saw money and fame. So Paul had to get beyond their feigned interest in order to nurture his own artistic ambitions. In justifying his travel expenses to festival organizers he wrote:

> I would like to emphasize the fact that it is sometimes necessary to visit some persons twice or more because a great part of the success of the project depends on their being fully convinced of its feasibility and thoroughly enthusiastic about this new concept of "Circus und Kunst." This means that I have to engage in a go-between strategy which requires a good deal of sweet talk and energy.
>
> The target of this first phase is to bring together in convenient places, toward mid-September, teams of acrobats, composers and artists so that they can study the practical and concrete aspects of each endeavour. I am confident that something interesting will emerge from this enterprise (No date, apparently late August, 1977).

The American composer Charles Boone was recommended to Paul by organizers at the Berlin Festival. After Boone was contacted, he asked for more information about the nature of his commission for some percussion music. "What instruments could I use? I prefer very simple, classical ones:

snare drums, bass drums, cymbals, tom-toms etc. That's about all." Boone suggested that Paul listen to "Raspberries," a piece of his for three drummers. "I imagine anything I would do for your project would be somewhat like this older piece" (August 22, 1977). Even more interesting than "Raspberries" is Boone's piece "Shunt," written during the following months and probably closer to the piece Boone would have composed for The Circus of the Century.

A Tentative Program for The Circus of the Century (Early August, 1977)

Director: Louis Dedessus le Moutier, father of the foot jugglers, the Castors

Master of Ceremonies Petit Gougou (Alain André)

Musical overture: Juan Allende-Blin.

1. Charivari: Ten performers from the École Nationale du Cirque (Paris) presenting somersaults, jumps, feats of balance and humorous acrobatics.
Ten costumes and one statue by Eduardo Paolozzi.
Music by Charles Boone.

2. Free-standing ladder: Alexandre Bouglione.
One costume, three ladders and an illuminated floor by Eduardo Paolozzi.
Music by Charles Boone.

3. Dog act: Eddie Windsor (Douglas Kossmayer) and Lolla Basset.
Electronic music or musical reinforcement from a small orchestra.

4. Trapeze: Valérie Granier-Deferre.
Contemporary harp music.

5. Juggler: Chris Christiansen (Christian Marin).
One costume and accessories by Hajime Kato.
Sound-producing props made by the Baschet Brothers.

6. Comedians: Rolly and Ary.
Musical reinforcement from a small orchestra.

Intermission

7. Foot jugglers: The Castors (Toly, Charly and Eddy Dedessus le Moutier).
Three costumes and accessories by Ursula Sax.
Electronic music by Bernard Parmegiani.

8. High-school Horse: Carmelitta Miazzano.
Musical reinforcement from a small orchestra.

9. High wire Walking: Philippe Petit.
Accessories and electronic sounds by the Baschet Brothers.

10. Clowns: Pierre Etaix and Annie Fratellini.

11. Washington Trapeze: Gérard Edon.
Accessories and electronic music by François Bayle.

12. Finale: the Charivari acrobats wearing Sri Lankan masks; all of the performers salute the audience.
Music by Charles Boone.

Alternative ideas proposed in late July: (1) An animal act involving a pig, a chicken, and a rabbit or a cat. (2) Musical clowns, including Dimitri, playing innovative instruments or Berio's "Sequenza V." (3) The clown Dimitri doing short gags between the acts of other performers.

Two types of performers appear on this tentative program. Some are young, in the early stages of their career, apparently receptive to new ideas. The others are well-established and tend to have personal ties with Paul. Either they are good comedians or they present a conventional circus act with classic purity. Paul hunted for an exuberant master of ceremonies, speaking German with a French accent, similar to Joel Grey in the musical *Cabaret*. He thought he had found an ideal person in Petit Gougou.

> While the audience finds their seats, the room is dimly lit. Then, officials make their inaugural speeches under a spotlight which isolates them either at their seats, or at another location, depending on where they want to speak. In my opinion it would be a good thing to have the Mayor of Berlin speak from his seat and [an administrator from the Berlin Festival] to answer him and address the audience from the right side of the artists' entrance so that the sacredness of the ring is preserved.[23]

A blackout was supposed to follow. Then a burst of music and special lighting effects that would fully illuminate Paolozzi's decorations. The musicians' costumes, if not by Paolozzi himself, would at least complement his decorations. Asking the Chilean-born composer Juan Allende-Blin to write the overture was a diplomatic choice, to please an administrator at the Berlin Festival. A pupil of Messiaen at Darmstadt, Allende-Blin had written, among other things, a piece called *Open Air* and *Water Music* for an experimental instrument that suggests an ultra-modern calliope.

The technical innovation for Alexandre Bouglione's free-standing ladder act was going to be clear plastic ladders. Eddie Windsor had already worked in such nightclubs as the Moulin Rouge, introducing his dog Lolla Basset as a great star. Actually, Lolla has been trained to make fun of him by doing either nothing at all or the opposite of what he announced to the public. Valérie Granier-Deferre is the daughter of Annie Fratellini. At age nineteen she was presenting a graceful trapeze act, which Paul thought would be the "poetic moment" of the first part of the show and would be accompanied by contemporary harp music.

Chris Christiansen was another young French performer. The innovation for his act was juggling objects that produced "clusters of crystalline sounds" as they were propelled through the air. The Baoding iron balls used by the Chinese in hand reflexology show the idea is feasible. The Japanese-French artist and long-time friend of Paul, Hajime Kato, had accepted the commission for Christiansen's costume. A champion bicycle rider, Kato was known in Paris for dynamic abstract paintings that resembled crystals flying through space. Carmelitta Miazzano was presenting two horses in succession doing the steps of classic Haute École. Dressed as a North American Native, she rode without a saddle. For The Circus of the Century Paul was not going to change the nature of the act, but he wanted Miazzano to ride in the nude. Although neither the two horses nor the rider were classic beauties, they had character, he thought. Their movements were so well matched that removing all intermediaries between the woman and her horses, as well as the right lighting and music, would transform the act into a "unique expressionist masterpiece." Both Annie Fratellini and Pierre Etaix were good comedians as well as talented musicians. Their act was a succession of "subtle gags with surrealistic flavour." The dramatic conclusion was Gérard Edon on the Washington Trapeze. The Sri Lankan masks used in the finale were to come from the private collection of the anthropologist Bruce Kapferer who had indicated his willingness to have them displayed in this sort of processional event when Paul had met him at a Wenner-Gren Foundation symposium in Berg Wartenstein in Austria.

◆ ◆ ◆

Pervasive anxiety about the commitment of the festival staff in West Berlin began to surface even before a less speculative program could be worked out. It was not clear why they were so hopeless. When Paul returned from the clown festival in Blankenberge (July 26-28), he was furious at the festival liaison officer, a refugee from the undemocratic regime of the German Democratic Republic, who had been assigned to him. He had not been encouraged in school to learn to speak English or French fluently. Unfortunately, Paul cannot speak German except for a few phrases he typically uses as jokes. The liaison officer appeared to be imprisoned in an authoritarian mindset. Paul interpreted his actions as Prussian arrogance worsened by incompetence.

The Circus of the Century was in danger of being stillborn. Festival organizers did not sign Paul's contract until August 30, more than two months after their gentleman's agreement. Time was slipping away without individual contracts being issued. Soon all of the good performers would have finalized their plans for the summer. Paul was not sure what was happening. He tended to imagine conspiracies. But perhaps festival staff were simply not capable of mounting shows from scratch. Trying to maintain contact with the organizers over the distance that separated Paris and West Berlin did not help. When Paul's contract finally arrived in the mail, the subsidy had been reduced to 105,000 German marks plus 15,000 marks for his personal expenses and a modest honorarium. This was an insufficient amount of money given Paul's ambitions for the project. The Circus of the Century started to be scaled down to the rank of a "chamber circus."

Nearly three months passed between Paul's first request to be reimbursed for his preliminary expenses and the arrival of the cheque, although it was promised every time he telephoned. Because he was paying all his expenses out of his own pocket, we began to have financial problems which he kept secret from me. He was even late in paying the rent for our apartment in Paris. If the organizers were this inefficient at the outset of the project, what was going to happen later when delicate scheduling was required? That was the most nagging worry.

Finally, on November 28, Paul wrote the Berlin Festival saying that he was withdrawing from all of the events. The letter was a bluff. Paul hoped his "apparent withdrawal" (as he said privately) would force the organizers to furnish a new liaison officer and a more generous budget. Paul had talked about mailing the letter earlier, but felt that he had no alternative except to wait until the cheque arrived that covered his preliminary expenses.

The more insightful letter of November 28 is the one he sent to Eduardo Paolozzi. Paul kept from Paolozzi the truth about his high-stakes gamble with the organizers:

With great regret I eventually decided last week to withdraw from the Berlin Festival. You can imagine how much it cost me to make such a decision after almost six months of passionate work. But I find it impossible to battle day after day against ill will, bad faith and incompetence. I make, of course, an exception for our friend who is unfortunately unable to control the situation and suffers as much as we do from…fishy intrigues and double dealings.

…I hope to see you some day in Paris. When I have recovered from the current depressed mood, I will try to work on another project to be submitted to another institution. But when and which? Any ideas?

The author of a history of the Ballets-Russes has written eloquently about a renaissance of the circus he was anticipating as early as 1936. Convinced that the artistic possibilities of the circus were underrated, Prince Peter Lieven wrote: "It is the branch of art which is on the brink of a renaissance. All it needs is a leader, and creators, who will raise it back to its true level as a great and noble art."[24] Yet in 1977 in West Berlin—for whatever reason—the time was not yet ripe for a renaissance of the circus.

In the afternoon after mailing the protesting letter to Paolozzi, Paul and I went to see an exhibition on Diagilev's Russian Ballet at the Centre Culturel du Marais in Paris. It was a poignant and sad visit. Earlier, Paul had enjoyed thinking of himself as "the Diagilev of the circus." This unhappy and incomprehensible experience with the Berlin Festival he calls "the tragedy of my life."

♦ ♦ ♦

In response to Paul's letter of resignation Paolozzi wrote on December 12 that he was sorry that the project had been cancelled because he was looking forward to "working out some ideas" with him. We'll never know what these ideas could have become, but a joint creation between the two men seemed to promise so much. In the opinion of one critic, Paolozzi thrives on the inspiration and technical advice provided by other people. Paul rarely suffers from a paucity of ideas, which he generously offers to friends and acquaintances. Paul, however, is more comfortable associating with younger people and Paolozzi is ten years his senior.

Both Paolozzi and Paul think of themselves as outsiders. Paolozzi was raised by Italian immigrants in Scotland in a tough working-class district of Leith. Paul's feelings of marginality in France and Canada are pervasive. The two men are invariably attracted to whatever is new, including the most recent technology. They celebrate eclecticism and share an intense amateur's interest in the natural sciences. Paolozzi's favourite magazine at one time was *Scientific American*.[25] Although neither would apply to himself the label "surrealist," its example of rebellion inspires them. Surrealism sharpened their wit, a prominent element in Paolozzi's art as in Paul's writings. To many people, the circus is at best a lowbrow form of art. Disrespect for elite culture is even more prominent in Paolozzi's early collages that borrow imagery from pulp fiction and advertising. For the artist, designing costumes and props for a circus would have been a logical extension of his life-long interest in the officially lowbrow.

◆ ◆ ◆

Jörn had earlier thought of this project as "our dream." He had worried about building up dreams "which are soap-bubbles instead of crazy-wonderful-utopic-realistic ideas" (January 31, 1977). The phrase suggests that Jörn was thinking of The Circus of the Century in terms different than Paul's. Of course, Paul owed him a full explanation for his withdrawal, which was not a rash decision. In early December, Paul and I went to Monaco to the premiere circus festival in Europe where Prince Ranier annually awards the equivalent of the Oscars. Upon our return to Paris, Paul at last wrote to Jörn, indirectly calling attention to what had been lost for the Berlin Festival:

We have just returned from Monaco where we attended a series of circus shows of extraordinary beauty. The word "sublime" is not too strong to describe them. Although the Principality is either a nest of eagles or vultures of international finance, the sun is warm and the landscape very agreeable. I met Marja Keyser there. She also came, with a group of people from Holland, to attend the festival. There were groups of Americans, Germans, British, etc., very rich people and ordinary people. Such as the 21-year-old mechanic whose acquaintance I made two years ago, and who each year takes a week of holidays at this time of the year in order to attend the festival.

I talked a long time with Miss Keyser about the Berlin festival. In the absence of any official letter coming from the festival, she has stopped preparing an exhibition. She absolutely shares my opinion that enthusiasm cannot take the place of organization for a project of this magnitude, and that it is now too late to do anything in good conditions. She, like me, has other professional obligations, as do the other possible collaborators. Even if we were ready to consecrate *all* our free time, there are limits to what one can do in these conditions. She therefore wants to inform you that you cannot count on her. She won't directly communicate this because she has never received any official letter (a letter you told me would be sent to her in July!) and she cannot decline an offer which has never been formally offered. She is very deeply disappointed because of everything this signified to her and because of the work she has done since July....

The reasons for my refusal to continue some kind of collaboration with the festival include both the fact that the situation in [early] December 1977 was as catastrophic as far as performances were concerned as well as the exhibitions and the catalogue because of the absence of organization on the part of the festival and the museum, and that *nothing which was promised me has been done*. Naturally, what caused me to make this decision—as I explained to Eckhardt—is the attitude of G.P.—because I feel capable of struggling against the absence of organization if the heart and trust remain true—but not against crafty bad will. I enclose copies of my last correspondence with Eckhardt. I find his letter very hypocritical, after his behaviour since the summer!

Let's turn the page and not talk any more about it. However, I would be grateful if you make sure that my name is not associated with the festival in any way—and that the ideas which I have submitted are not used without my authorization. Moreover, I have officially registered the manuscripts and the correspondence associated with the project "Circus of the Century" in order to legally guarantee my rights.

However, I am not abandoning the hope of realizing one day, by some other means, this project which is dear to me. But I am not undertaking anything before next year. For the moment, I must resolve the problems caused by this defeat— which is for me a personal tragedy—and make up for the delay in my university and literary work.

We very deeply hope that our friendship will survive this test. But I am sure that you understand my position which is caused by a rational analysis of the situation and not by emotional reactions—although the result is for me a serious emotional shock. I hope that you will—soon—spend a few days with us, who still love you.

Ploop! Ploop! Paul (December 15, 1977).

◆ ◆ ◆

Charles Boone's lengthy response to Paul's letter about the cancellation was considerate. Their contact had been superficial and by mail. Boone admits that he had earlier been the victim of a similar experience, the "Berliner Disease." Boone places the blame on endemic problems in West Berlin rather than on individual organizers. He resided in Berlin for two years thanks to a fellowship funded by the German government. More than a year before his tenure began he received an official invitation to compose a piece for the 1975 festival. Another letter was waiting for him at his arrival in June saying that the piece would not be performed:

> Naturally, I was very angry about this and [Eckhardt] promised me a performance of the work at a later date. Now it is more than two years later and the piece remains unperformed, in fact, unfinished because I was so disturbed by this business. I found that this sort of thing is not at all uncommon in that town, having been promised several performances that have not taken place. One large piece of mine has been scheduled and postponed four (!) times during the past year. It is presently scheduled for a concert this coming spring, but I am doubtful that it will transpire. At first this kind of thing is annoying but when it happens in one place so consistently it becomes almost amusing.

Boone concluded by writing that because of his knowledge of the Ballets-Russes, he felt he understood what Paul was attempting to accomplish. "You have some exciting plans and I hope you will have the opportunity of carrying them out in the not too distant future. . . . [The project] sounds to me like quite an adventure, and a good one too." (January 16, 1978)

◆ ◆ ◆

In the spring and summer of 1978 Paul tried two other venues, first in Paris and then in Bonn, for resurrecting The Circus of the Century. A proposal was submitted to the Beaubourg Museum of contemporary art, an organization whose official goal is to democratize the fine arts. The first meeting, on January 13, produced nothing tangible. Alain Ohrel, then a high-ranking national administrator, wrote to the director of the museum. The result was a second meeting, a polite, no doubt politically-motivated display of interest, far short of the kind of commitment required to get the project off the ground. The third meeting in June was exasperating and humiliating. The museum administrator barely understood the short proposal. When a person has an idea that is ideally suited to an institution's goals and which flatters French culture, it is infuriating to be forced to exert pressure to have the idea taken seriously, let alone implemented. Jean Millier, President of the Beaubourg Museum, did say in a condescending tone in a letter to Ohrel that Paul's project was compatible with the goals of the museum:

> It is true that many painters, musicians, writers have been interested in the "world of the circus" and that some contemporary artists are not indifferent to this theme and their encounter in a broad context constitutes a long-term goal that is not devoid of interest. (June 27, 1978)

After making up his mind to withdraw the project in protest, Paul called an acquaintance who worked at the museum. You're too sensitive and impatient, he complained to Paul. Taking this man's advice, Paul never bothered to contact the museum again. The proposal may still be gathering dust in some obscure archive.

The second attempt was more half-hearted. Paul reconnected with an old German friend, Hans Daniels, who had been elected Mayor of Bonn. They had drifted apart over the years for no particular reason other than distance and diverging careers. Daniels suggested presenting the circus at a summer-long gardening exhibition and fair in Bonn. Paul planned to name the circus "The Paolozzi Circus" as an enticement to attract Eduardo Paolozzi. But after all of the other failures Paul did not have the heart to pursue his dwindling dream any further. In academia it is easier to achieve one's dreams.

◆　◆　◆

The catalogue for the circus exhibition at the 1978 Berlin Festival refers in a perfunctory manner—as Paul insisted—to the origins of the theme of the festival: "The initial idea for this exhibition comes from a suggestion made by Professor Paul Bouissac of the University of Toronto, who is one of the outstanding circus researchers and who in his work often takes unusual paths. For that reason it is all the more unfortunate that we could not get him to participate in this project."[26]

Paul had recommended inviting Marja Keyser, a librarian at the circus archives of the University of Amsterdam, to help assemble the art exhibition

on the circus. Keyser had impressed Paul when he visited the archives to
find illustrations for his book *Circus and Culture*. Despite Paul's withdrawal
from the project and Keyser's own misgivings due to the inefficiencies of
the festival office, she decided to participate when she sensed the curator's
desperate situation:

> On Monday I went to the Museum where [Jörn] told me the news
> that after it had been in the newspapers that there would be no
> catalogue for lack of money, a commercial publisher had said he
> would like to publish one at his own risk, on the condition that all
> texts and photographs would be ready by the end of the week. And
> [Jörn] had accepted—madness of course, but as you have seen, the
> book justifies his decision. The material for the exhibition was
> quite satisfying, although of course there were gaps, but the large
> number of beautiful nineteenth century prints allowed these to be
> filled in with photographs. Seeing that one could make a good and
> interesting exhibition with it, I decided to collaborate, and I spent
> the rest of the day working, getting acquainted, and thinking of the
> big problem of writing my part of the catalogue text....
>
> Although when in Amsterdam I was sometimes angry when
> promised letters didn't come until much later, I now can under-
> stand this. The problems you had with the contracts for the show
> were of course different, mostly caused by the Festival people. But
> as I say, I have never seen anyone working so hard, [as Jörn] with
> the catalogue, and the illustrations and the proofs, and with all the
> difficulties of the organization and hanging such a big exhibition in
> so short a time.
>
> Dear Paul, I hope you are not angry because I finally took part
> in the Berlin exhibition. I know (and mind, [Jörn Merkert] knows
> too) that although the exhibition (I don't talk about the show) is
> good, it is not the highlight you had in mind—far from that. Just
> know that I still respect your reasons for withdrawal, and that I
> think them justified. You had a responsibility towards friends,
> colleagues and artists to be engaged that cannot be denied. When
> I finally did the historical exhibition I had just myself to consider.
>
> ...If the organization in Berlin had been better, your dreams
> about the new and beautiful performances would have become
> reality; when one knows how it could have been, there can only be
> sadness.... (September 28, 1978)

◆ ◆ ◆

All hope had not been abandoned. The last time Paul publicly talked about his own plans to reinvent the circus was to the performance art critic for the *Village Voice* in 1980.[27] A personal letter from the Italian composer Sylvano Bussotti is evidence of Paul's last significant effort to motivate a modern composer to write for the circus:

> I was also sad not to be able to meet you in Toronto! Anyway I am still a little sick. So many misfortunes and complications have kept interfering with my life for the last three years.
>
> I thank you very, very much for your book [*Les demoiselles*] and the extreme attractiveness of your project for which you will always find me passionately available. I look forward to receiving news from you about its development as it happens—from a practical point of view—and I hope to soon have an opportunity to meet you. Please excuse the brevity of this reply. (I found upon my return to Italy a huge backlog of problems to solve and I must finish a new work to be premiered next month.)
>
> I assure you of my friendship and sincere gratitude. (November 8, 1978)

◆　◆　◆

By the 1990s the circus as an institution had evolved. People were talking about the "new circus." The defining characteristics were the construction of the show around a story or theme, the absence of trained animals and the rejection of death-defying acrobatic feats. In this sense The Circus of the Century, despite Paul's experimental aesthetic, was squarely within the classic tradition of European one-ring circuses in which there is a unified style combining all of the elements of a performance. Paul certainly appreciates the creativity of the new circus but thinks its tendency to tell stories is excessive, a sort of "semiotic overkill." Paul enjoys watching trained animals perform and included even exotic animals in The Circus of the Century. He has a high tolerance for watching reckless acrobatic acts. Although they were not the most significant element in his planned program, it did include at least three daring high wire and trapeze acts. The Circus of the Century was not a marriage of theatre and circus. Nor was there ever any pretence that it would function like a hippie commune or a family cooperative. To sum up the difference: The Circus of the Century was more elitist. It was a circus conceived by a French intellectual.

Examples of the new circus include Le Cirque de Barbarie and Le Cirque Aligre in France, Circus Roncalli in West Germany, Circus Lumière in Great Britain. In Canada there is Le Cirque du Soleil; and in the United States the Big Apple Circus, the Pickle Family Circus and Circus Flora.[28] This was a more European than American phenomenon, but eventually even Ringling Brothers and Barnum and Bailey followed the trend. Its models sprang from diverse sources. The narrative side was due in part to the propagandistic quality of shows produced by the Moscow Circus, which occasionally toured Europe and North America to great acclaim. It was also the achievement of middle-class students of the theatre and performing arts. They had the benefit of a more artistic education than was characteristic of older generations of circus performers, who tended to be from more impoverished backgrounds. The Mitterrand government in France established a circus school open to the public, thereby undermining to some extent the power of circus families who had jealously guarded professional secrets. Also, the new generation was more comfortable with television and skilfully used the media to advance their careers.

Unfortunately, Paul was only a spectator observing the new talent.[29] As I write, there is a remote possibility that something comparable to The Circus of the Century may be realized in Japan. During one of Paul's visits to Tokyo he asked the British composer Thomas Adès at a reception following a concert if he had ever thought of writing music for the circus. Shocked at first by the startling question, Adès floundered but then quickly responded: "No...but...why not?"

Notes

1 Firmin Bouglione, *Le cirque est mon royaume,* Paris: Presses de la Cité, 1962, 301.

2 Sally Banes, "Reading the Circus/And You Thought it was Just for Fun," *Village Voice,* May 26, 1980, 37.

3 Paul Bouissac, "Behaviour in Context: In What Sense is a Circus Animal Performing?," *Annals of the New York Academy of Sciences,* June 12, 1981, Vol. 364, 21.

4 Alain-Fournier, *The Lost Domain,* Trans. Alan Pryce-Jones, London: Oxford University Press, 1959.

5 Paul Bouissac interviewed by Stephen Riggins, February 15, 1996.

6 Paul Bouissac interviewed by Stephen Riggins, October 27, 1995.

7 Paul Bouissac interviewed by Stephen Riggins, February 16, 1994.

8 Paul Bouissac interviewed by Stephen Riggins, March 10, 1994.

9 Paul Bouissac, "The Marketing of Performance," in *Semiotics and Marketing,* Jean Umiker-Sebeok, ed., Berlin: Mouton de Gruyter, 1987, 396-398.

10 Frank Rasky, "The Professors' Wonderful Circus," *Maclean's,* June 5, 1965, 18-19, 35, 37-40.

11 Bouglione, 129-132.

12 Paul Bouissac interviewed by Stephen Riggins, October 27, 1994.

13 The itinerary of the Debord Circus, Ontario, 1965: May 7-15, Brantford. May 17-22, Windsor. May 24-29, Sarnia. June 8-12, Toronto (Greenwood). June 13, Toronto (Yorkdale Plaza). June 16-19, Toronto (Dufferin St. & Highway 401). June 21-26, New Liskeard. June 29-July 3, Sault Ste. Marie. July 6-10, Espanola. July 13-17, Timmins. July 19-22, Sudbury. July 31-August 2, Windsor. August 4-5, Leamington. September 14-18, Welland.

14 Rasky, 37.

15 ibid.

16 ibid, 39.

17 This entry is based on a personal recording Gérard Debord made for Paul Bouissac in the mid or late 1970s and on interviews Stephen Riggins made with Paul Bouissac in February 2001.

18 Pierre Léon has published a short story which is a thinly disguised depiction of the Debord Circus in *Les rognons du chat,* Vanier, ON: Les Editions L'Interligne, 1999, 59-65. In English the title would be *The Kidneys of the Cat.* Paul suggested he might retaliate by writing *The Chameleon's Prostate.* Paul dismisses the author as "Le Douanier Léon de la litterature."

19 In "Debord Decision Reserved," *The Daily Sentinel Review* (Woodstock-Ingersoll) reported that:

> Hector M. Howell, of Toronto, one of the owners of the Debord Circus, acting in defence of Debord said that the testimony showed that the animals had gone only for a short period of time without food, as they were never fed on Sunday at any time.
>
> The animals were normally fed in the evening so they only missed one meal he said, and that was due to the breakdown, not wilful neglect.

Debord testified that missing a meal would not 'particularly affect' the animals.

Clipping in the possession of Paul Bouissac, no date. See also "Circus Faces Counts as Animals Seized," *The Daily Sentinel Review*, Woodstock-Ingersoll, Ontario, August 11, 1965, 1 and "Circus Animals Held Pending Care Assurance," *The Daily Sentinel Review*, Woodstock-Ingersoll, Ontario, August 12, 1965, 9.

[20] Paul Bouissac, "Detailed Outline of the Circus Programme (Without Mention of Costumes and Music)." Undated manuscript for The Circus of the Century, 9. In the possession of Stephen Riggins.

[21] Michel Chion and Guy Reibel, *Les musiques électroacoustiques*, Aix-en-Provence: INA-GRM Edisud, 1976, 92.

[22] Paul Bouissac, *Circus and Culture: A Semiotic Approach*, Bloomington, IN: Indiana University Press, 1976, 30-32.

[23] Paul Bouissac, "Item One/Musical Opening." Undated and unpaginated manuscript for The Circus of the Century. In the possession of Stephen Riggins.

[24] Peter Lieven, *The Birth of the Ballets-Russes*, New York: Dover, 1973 (1936), 315-316.

[25] Frank Whitford, "Inside the Outsider," in *Eduardo Paolozzi: Sculpture, Drawings, Collages and Graphics, Catalogue for an Arts Council Exhibition*, Stamford, Lincs.: J.E.C. Potter & Sons, 1977, 14.

[26] See *Zirkus Circus Cirque*, Nationalgalerie Berlin. 28 Berliner Festwochen, 1978. Ausstellung vom 9. 9. bis 5. 1. 1978. Oberhausen: Verlagsgesellschaft Greno, 1978, 11.

[27] Sally Banes, "Reading the Circus/And You Thought it was Just for Fun," *Village Voice*, May 26, 1980, 37.

[28] See Ernest Albrecht, *The New American Circus*, Gainesville, FL: University Press of Florida, 1995.

[29] Paul Bouissac, "The Circus's New Golden Age," *Canadian Theatre Review*, Vol. 58, Spring 1989, 5-10.

View from our apartment, Rue
de Grenelle, Paris, 1983.
Photographer: S.H. Riggins

Paul Bouissac, early 1970s.

The Old Opossum's Bad Apples

Capturing the truth of Paul Bouissac's mystifying novels is like trawling for catfish with a gourd, to quote an old Zen saying. It seems this elusive even to the most sophisticated readers. A critic for *Le Monde* writes in a review of his first novel, *Les demoiselles*: "The art of Paul Bouissac is that of a litotes expanded into a literary narrative."[1] A litotes is an ironical understatement, an affirmative expressed through a negative. It is bound to be confusing. The humour in *Les demoiselles* is reminiscent of Nabokov, an author Paul has never read, and the obscure meanderings of Robbe-Grillet. The French poet James Sacré writes that the two spinsters, who are the central characters, seem to have "curiously stepped out of Robbe-Grillet's *Last Year at Marienbad*. The story revolve(s) around a sort of emptiness or almost around something (what secret?) rather than nothing."[2]

Two interviews and some of my diary entries may help solve the haunting little mysteries of Paul's stories. Revealing information about his literary intentions and the real world sources of his stories makes the novels more interesting, although they may lose some of the open-ended ambiguities and silences which Paul appreciates. I won't make the waters phosphorescent, but I cannot avoid muddying them a bit. I also note that Paul frequently dodges questions about his creative writing, divulges information piece by piece, and my knowledge of French is less than perfect.

◆ ◆ ◆

November, 1973. We have travelled from Paris to Lugano so Paul can interview the Swiss clown Dimitri at the Knie Circus. We spend the morning strolling along the lakeshore. Winter roses are in bloom. Paul asks me to take photographs of an elaborate ornamental gate in the park by the Municipal Museum.

"Will you take a picture of that metal gate from here?" Paul asks.

"It's too far away," I say. "You can't see the details well."

"Will you take the picture anyway? I want two pictures. One with me standing before the gate and one without me."

"What for? You won't be able to recognize anyone from this distance."

"Just take the pictures."

"But it's a stupid idea."

"Take them anyway and use the edge of the shadow there and the crossing of these two tree limbs so the pictures are identical."

"The sun is shining from the wrong direction."

"Anytime I ask you to do the least little thing for me, you refuse. Either you're too shy or you can't do it perfectly or you're too lazy."

"All right! I'll take the photographs. But I'm not going to use the crossing of the tree limbs as a guide."

◆ ◆ ◆

If Paul had told me that he wanted to use these photographs as documents for writing his third novel, I might have been more cooperative. The photographs are supposed to illustrate Buddha's ideas about futility and the transitoriness of the self. There is an incident in the novel in which a character looks for a photograph of the gate to prove a person's existence. But the character finds only the photograph without him. Paul did not explain the story to me in Lugano because he thought I was too immature to understand. Probably, he was right. He has shown the photographs to friends and asked them if they see a difference. No, some replied.

Paul wants to write a book in which he plays intellectual games with readers by setting up expectations—using the commonsense certitudes of everyday life or the conventions of novels—and then subverting them. In this case one of the expectations is the unity of the self. At the start of the novel there are three characters, whom readers naturally assume to be three different people. Midway through the book readers abruptly learn that each character is actually two people. For instance, when Mr. Léon-Orsay goes to pick up his photographs, the sales clerk asks if he wants the portraits of Mr. Léon or Mr. Orsay. Three characters swell to six by the middle of the novel, shrink to three at the end. To fool readers Paul has to make sure that Mr. Léon-Orsay has all of the attributes and memories of both men.

Les demoiselles

Paul gave Jean C. an autographed copy of *Les demoiselles* with a dedication that refers to Jean's interest in Russian icons and the religious sect called the Doukhobors: these icons disguised as icons behind which are hidden sweet, beautiful bodies. ["Ces icônes déguisées en icônes derrière lesquelles se cachent de doux beaux corps."]

◆　◆　◆

The plot of *Les demoiselles* cannot be summarized properly without giving away the surprise ending. All one can say is how it begins—with the arrival of two spinsters in a provincial French town. The spinsters appear to be paragons of virtue but are associated with foul play. The narrator is a self-appointed sleuth who tries to uncover their identity, apparently out of idle curiosity rather than a desire to combat evil.

   Les demoiselles adheres to several of the conventions of traditional detective or mystery stories. The plot is full of twists and turns. It opens with an enigma about wrong-doing and ends with a revelation. There are hijinks, farce, colourful rogues. Fracturing the storyline with rapid shifts in time and place as well as philosophical reflections functions to prolong the suspense. On the other hand, readers are puzzled for varying periods of time, about the what, who, where, when and how of events. Orderly expositions are the exception. Nor was characterization one of Paul's interests. The plot lacks an unerringly penetrating detective who solves every riddle. The sleuth keeps his wits about himself, but his appearance is another mystery. He is never described or given a name. His gender is ambiguous, but evident in the use of masculine adjectives. The sleuth, "I," is the only character who has an inner life, most obviously in his unrequited love of "you." Instead of "you" always being the same person, his identity may constantly change and represent nothing more substantial than moments of impossible happiness.[3] The novel is not devoid of truths about human nature but readers are unlikely to remember which character states these unflinching truths given the interweaving of several stories. Ultimately, the sleuth is the creator of the enigma he solves.

While writing *Les demoiselles* Paul rented for a while *une chambre de bonne* near the Place de la Bastille. It was an inexpensive apartment, but he could see through a skylight the statue atop the fifty-two meter column designed by Alavoine Père to commemorate the Revolution of 1830. The statue is a *génie*, supposedly representing "liberty that takes flight, breaking chains and spreading enlightenment."[4]

> This was the last place where I lived before I was drafted into the air force [during the Algerian War]. When I received money, a fellowship from the government, I could afford to live in my own room, not in a shared apartment as I had earlier. But that year I did not do any work at all because I had never been free before.
>
> It was a pleasure to see the statue. I could see it in the frame of my little skylight if I twisted my neck a bit. All I could see was the statue and the sky. The statue was very beautiful in the changing light of the day, in the winter as well as in the spring and summer. It shone in rainy weather. For me, it was an image of hope and freedom. I even wrote a two-line poem about the statue: "Un petit génie ailé, était-il l'amour ou la liberté?"[5]

◆　◆　◆

At the bar of a British pub near Place Danton, just off Boulevard Saint-Germain, an attractive, ascetic-looking man tries to come to terms with the death of a friend. Charles (not his real name) talks to any stranger who will listen. But sadly, Paul is the only sympathetic dreamer at the café on that wintry night. Charles' friend worked as an assistant for an artist, was in love with him, and felt that he was exploited. (Committing suicide over something this insignificant is incomprehensible. It cannot be the whole story.) Charles feels guilty because he introduced his friend to the man who in his opinion bears much of the responsibility for the tragedy. Charles angrily says he wishes he had murdered his friend. At least then he would know why he passed away.

◆　◆　◆

Charles resembles the kind of characters Paul likes to invent in his novels—men who have "le charme propre à tout ce qui est à la fois jeune, vague et incertain."[6] Less charitably, some might be called bad apples.

If I were to situate Charles socially, I would describe him as a somewhat sophisticated gay male who lives "unrealistically" on the fringes of conventional society. He lives, as well, on the fringes of a world of petty criminals and male prostitutes. There is a soft and defenseless air about him, however. He seems to enjoy social isolation, as if he were complete in his solitude. The only photograph he carries in his wallet is that of a pet dog; in the subway he holds his hand up in mid-air as though grasping an imaginary pole for support. Charles has no interest in accumulating more money than the amount necessary to dress attractively, in used or moderately priced clothes, and to frequent popular sidewalk cafés in fashionable Saint-Germain-des-Prés, where he may spend a few dollars a night. He patronizes the Brasserie Lipp, Picasso's favourite many years ago.

♦ ♦ ♦

We invite Charles to celebrate his birthday at the restaurant of Paul's cousin, Le Mange Tout, 30 rue Lacépède in Paris. Charles looks a few years older than the 29 he claims to be. He was trained to make optical lenses as a profession, he says, but decided to become an artist after viewing an exhibition by the surrealist Max Ernst. Charles felt that Ernst had stolen *his* ideas. He supports himself now by working as an assistant for an artist who exhibits torn posters as art objects.

The torn posters are a kind of "found art," salvageable at any location in Paris where posters are rapidly glued on top of one another rather than stapled. When vandals tear strips off them, they unwittingly create abstract designs and puns by exposing pieces of the posters underneath. Commercial and political advertisements are thus transformed into abstract art or into jokes and counter-messages. In either case an anonymous creative force, the accidental collaboration of pedestrians, takes on the character of nature itself and subverts human intentionality.

One evening Paul came home laughing about Charles looking up in the air while walking along the sidewalk. The night before, Charles explained, he had torn strips off some of the posters and was looking to see if pedestrians had pulled on the loose ends and "improved" the designs. In reality the creation of these vandalized posters is not as spontaneous as the theory proclaims. Charles consciously thinks of their visual qualities when he makes the initial selection. While they are stored in his apartment, he modifies some of them.

Charles is so comfortable around Paul that he makes silly jokes. As a pun on his family name, he jokes that he does not have to create art. He is art itself.

◆ ◆ ◆

Three posters from the May Rebellion of 1968 once hung in our Toronto apartment. One was an anonymous lithograph, "Power to the People," showing in a primitivist style a band of joyful red demonstrators beside an overturned symbol of authority, a policeman in black. The second was Cascella's lithograph "Proposal for a New Flag" that depicts black anarchist and red socialist suns kissing. The third, Zao Wouki's purely abstract poster with the message "Vivants d'abord." Freely translated, it reads: "Save the Living First."[7]

Paul became so irritated at Giscard d'Estaing, whom he saw as corrupt, snobbish and without ideas, that in 1981 he registered to vote for the first time in his life to cast a ballot for Mitterrand in the Presidential election. Although more sympathetic to the Left, he remains aloof from politics, an attitude consistent with one of the characteristics of the New Novelists, their rejection of politically engaged literature.

The philosopher Michel Serres, four years Paul's senior, writes that disinterest in politics is typical of their generation marked first by the horrors of the Second World War and then by the French colonial wars in Vietnam and Algeria. "Our active politicians come, more often, from the preceding or following generations.... My generation was formed, physically, in this atrocious environment and ever since has kept its distance from politics. For us power still means only cadavers and torture."[8]

◆ ◆ ◆

From a visit to Blackpool, the English seaside resort, Paul retains a mental snapshot of Michel Viala's spectacular physical beauty in the early 1960s—Michel walking on the beach in the wind and sun in the prime of his youth. The character named "le petit Hippias" is a rather realistic, and sometimes unflattering, portrait of Viala, a maker of animated films. He and Paul have been friends since their school days in Périgueux. Years after the novel appeared in print I asked Viala if he recognized himself in *Les demoiselles*. The fact he had not perceived he was a model says a lot about the liberties which Paul took with the truth.

When Paul and I visited Blackpool in July of 1974, I felt overwhelmed by its ugliness and coarseness: a short, stocky imitation of the Eiffel Tower on the roof of a building; the tacky "illuminations" on the beach—cut-out plywood trees sprouting light bulbs. Viala, more philosophical, laughed at everything. To these French tourists, it was hilarious that the inhabitants of Blackpool failed every time they tried to make something beautiful.

During the same visit Paul and Viala resided with a British family in Wigan. Paul had known the family since living in their home a few years earlier as a high school exchange student. Embarrassed by Michel bursting into laughter in the middle of meals, Paul explained his behaviour as a French way of showing his happiness. In fact, Viala was making fun of British customs. Consistent with this is the remark in *Les demoiselles* that le petit Hippias should succeed as an artist because he has enough "insolence" not to let people overlook him. Although his teachers might think he is a bit retarded, he is smart enough to despise their instruction.[9]

Hippias Minor and *Hippias Major* are early Socratic dialogues by Plato, named after the Sophist philosopher, Hippias of Elis, who was Socrates' interlocutor.[10] Paul has never explained why he was so taken by these dialogues. But it is easy to see parallels with a novel in which truth and falsehood are so difficult to disentangle. At the beginning of both dialogues Socrates teases Hippias, presumably the stance Paul is assuming in the novel with respect to his friend. Socrates and Hippias of Elis debate the difference between rhetoric and truth, how liars differ from truthful persons, and the morality of unintentional crimes. The sophists taught rhetoric to anyone willing to pay. Thus, they were supposed to have been more concerned about how an audience reacted to a statement than with its accuracy. Hippias is strongly opinionated, but unable to counter sound arguments. Socrates is less certain about the truth. The parallel here is that Viala, once a member of the Communist Party, has more consistent political views than Paul does. The concluding sentence of *Hippias Minor* begins, "inconsistency is to be expected in me...."

◆ ◆ ◆

My early interpretations of *Les demoiselles* were rejected by Paul when he complained that I was overlooking the nuances of irony and distance. He tells absurd stories. Crazy things happen, but the characters define them in ways that make them personally comprehensible. The narrator reports the speech and thoughts of others, making the bizarre compatible with bourgeois commonsense, while at the same time dissociating himself from them. The technique which allows him to do this is free indirect style

("style indirect libre"), a blend of a character's own thoughts and those of a person who reports them. The transition from one speaker to the next is almost imperceptible.

His example of irony is a story about the grandmother of his school friend, Jean-Gérard Nay. A devout Catholic in old age, the grandmother had a number of set phrases for any circumstance arising in life. One of these was that God grants people different states of grace including special help for extraordinary circumstances, "grâces d'états." A person facing tough circumstances with inner fortitude presumably benefits from this type of spiritual help. Grace is a touchy subject in Catholic theology since people have tortured and flayed each other over different interpretations of its meaning. It became a joke shared by Paul and Jean-Gérard, who used it inappropriately. If there was an enormous dessert for dinner, they did not need to worry about how they were going to eat all of it: "Il y a des grâces d'états."

◆ ◆ ◆

Charles still goes to Saint-Germain-des-Prés. He has changed little during our fifteen-month absence from Paris, although his financial situation appears more precarious. He has stopped salvaging torn posters from the streets and refuses to get any kind of paid employment, but still manages to wear fashionable-looking clothing. Except for the out-of-date lapels, his sport coat looks new. Last summer he was evicted by his landlord for failing to pay his rent. Charles then began living at hotels. He says he enjoys the impression of being on vacation.

Some days even the cheapest hotels were more than he could afford. When he was absolutely destitute, he slept on the roof of the science faculty at Place Jussieu. He enticed men by promising a spectacular panoramic view of central Paris.

◆ ◆ ◆

Poverty forces Charles to accept stolen money from his acquaintances. He talks about Greece where life and the climate are more humane than in Paris. But he was once fired by a Greek fisherman who employed him because he threw "blue lobsters" and "lobsters with sad eyes" back into the ocean. He claims he was so moved by a sunset in Greece that he ejaculated.

◆ ◆ ◆

Charles strolls among the crowds on Boulevard Saint-Germain with someone he just picked up. Exuberant gestures punctuate his talk about the
Pyramids. Two days ago he quit his job at a hotel and has been more or
less happily drunk ever since. When we last saw him, he had found the
man he hoped would be his lover for life. Shortly afterwards this man
deserted him, stealing everything of value in his room.

◆ ◆ ◆

Last night we met Charles at Saint-Germain-des-Prés and he accompanied
us to Montparnasse for a beer at the Café Le Sélect. Recently, he decided
that surviving the winter and finding a job required better clothes. The
only way of raising the money for new clothes was by writing bad cheques.

Well-dressed in a sports coat, he went to a bar in Le Pigalle where
some teenage boys robbed him because they mistakenly assumed from his
appearance that he was wealthy. He handed all of his money, a hundred
franc note (the equivalent then of about twenty American dollars), to the
handsomest boy in the group. This led to jealousy and bickering because
the boys could not agree on how to divide the money. They solved the
dispute by buying Charles a beer and pocketing the change.

Charles hesitates to criticize people who engage in petty crimes, even
when he is the victim. He believes the high rate of unemployment in
France and the low minimum wage give some people no alternative.

Le Sélect rekindles painful memories. Charles talks to us about being
here on a cold night with the torn-poster artist and the friend who committed suicide. They left the café drunk, but still managed to climb over
the fence that encloses the Luxembourg Gardens. While walking along the
stone rim of the pond, Charles was pushed into the icy water by his friend.
Soon the friend began to worry that the wet clothing would make him sick
and rushed him back to his apartment. The friend made a fire under the
bed to keep Charles warm, igniting the mattress. He had to throw water
on the mattress to extinguish the flames.

◆ ◆ ◆

During the winter Charles began working at night loading merchandise
on trains, certainly not a satisfying occupation. Working so hard is tiring
and destroys his interest in art and in socializing. He is unusually quiet
throughout dinner. Last year he was employed for about six months, the
longest he has worked in some time. This includes a series of temporary

jobs, one of which was moving an exhibition at a famous Paris museum. Among the pieces he moved were torn posters by his former employer.

◆ ◆ ◆

Charles is back in his usual cheerful spirits. He cunningly negotiated a bank loan using torn posters as collateral. How many banks outside France would accept torn posters as a guarantee for a loan?

◆ ◆ ◆

The truth is that I never liked Charles very much, although I understand the impact on Paul of the circumstances of their meeting. So these are second-hand stories, filtered through Paul's eyes, and unintentionally remote from lived experience.

◆ ◆ ◆

At 76 rue des Saint-Pères in the seventh arrondissement Mlle. Marie-Louise Haumesser kept a boarding house for people from affluent families who were in Paris completing their studies. In *Les demoiselles* the character Creüze is based in part on this woman, who is remembered by Paul and his future colleague David Smith as extraordinarily patriotic and traditional. The presence of cats in the apartment is also a prominent theme in their stories. At the time Paul was staying with Mlle. Haumesser she was once dismissed from a hospital to die in peace at home. Paul made her bed assuming it would be her deathbed. However, she recovered. For a few years in the early 1960s Mlle. Haumesser's ex-boarders kept in contact through a grandly titled "Société Internationale des Haumesseriens," which consisted primarily of personal memories and a mimeographed address list. The most common names on the list are American and Egyptian, although there are also people from France, England, Belgium, Switzerland, Lebanon, Iraq, Venezuela, Tunisia, Argentina, Holland and Colombia. In French the word "creuse" means hollow. As the origin of a fictitious name it may suggest the hollowness of bourgeois values. Several crucial conversations in *Les demoiselles* take place in Creüze's salon. She meets a fanciful end. Alone in her apartment, she falls dead from a heart attack. After five days her starving cats devour her face. The novel's narrator-detective considers her to be both cruel and admirable.

◆ ◆ ◆

Paul needed help in presenting the manuscript of *Les demoiselles* to publishers. When he was in Canada, the person who played this key role was the historian Jean-Claude Allain, who was working on Paul's behalf as early as the autumn of 1969. He and Paul had met at the Lycée Lakanal and were close friends for a few years. It was Allain's grey cap which Paul borrowed when he followed the footsteps of his medieval forefathers in making the three-day walking pilgrimage from Notre Dame cathedral in Paris to Notre Dame in Chartres.

The elitist student subculture of the Lycée Lakanal, its practical jokes and nicknames, is reflected in their letters. Allain addresses Paul as Jean-Jacques or J. J. (for Rousseau); Paul addresses Allain as Denis (for Diderot). The signature in Allain's letters is usually Paul's nickname for him, "kouniklos"—rabbit, in Greek. They disagreed on politics and literature. Paul thought Allain was too enamoured of law and order. Because there was a historic Prefect of the Police whom Allain especially admired, Paul sometimes referred to him jokingly as the "préfet" and to his wife as the "préfète." In one letter Allain is frank that he knows little about modern literature but thinks that in his boorish (Boeotian) opinion *Les demoiselles* really should be divided into paragraphs and chapters like conventional novels before it is submitted to publishers.

Their classmate at the Lycée Lakanal who was the first to succeed artistically and in the media was the feminist Hélène Cixous. By 1970 she had already won the Prix Médicis for her novel *Dedans* and had written extensively in the most prestigious Parisian newspapers and magazines. They turned to her for help because of her connections with publishers. On February 21, 1970, Allain wrote to Paul giving the substance of a long conversation with Cixous. Allain withheld from her the complete history of their negotiations with publishers, telling her that Gallimard had refused the manuscript but not alluding to Tchou's rejection. In Allain's words, Cixous praised the "stylistic perfection and erudite knowledge of language and culture" that *Les demoiselles* represented. "It does not belong to the genre of the Nouveau Roman but demonstrates by its art, its technique and even by its cultural and sociological reference, the legacy of the classic novel. It has no chance now of being published by Grasset, Gallimard or Seuil."

Allain went to so much trouble helping Paul find a publisher that he even retyped a few pages of the manuscript which he thought had too many handwritten corrections. They had typewriters with identical fonts. Allain also gave *Les demoiselles* to an unnamed acquaintance whom he considered an authority on modern literature. Allain was concerned that this person not suspect that Paul Bouissac was his own pseudonym. The acquaintance found the first thirty or forty pages difficult to read because of the ambiguities of the story and the "over-polished style." But eventually he concluded that these apparent liabilities proved to be effective means for holding the reader's attention. Despite the deeply pessimistic story and its ironical and paradoxical elements, this reader was touched by the "quest of the I." However, like Cixous, he was not optimistic about publication. To the extent that *Les demoiselles* resembled a Nouveau Roman, it might be difficult to publish even with Editions de Minuit.

February 3, 1970, the critic and editor André Dalmas wrote Paul that in his opinion Tchou had not actually rejected *Les demoiselles* because its catastrophic financial situation had prevented its proper evaluation. He wanted Paul's permission to give the manuscript—this time officially—to Le Mercure. "Do not fear anything, not even silence," he reassured. March 31, an employee of the "service des manuscrits" of Editions Albin Michel wrote that they were declining to publish *Les demoiselles*. Allain's correspondence of May 6 reports that he had contacted Dalmas. From their conversation he had formed the opinion that it was a bad time to publish novels in Paris either for financial reasons or because of uncertainties due to the necessity of renewing the genre. He thought the prospect of being published before the end of the year was "near zero."

Nonetheless, more encouragingly, Allain and Dalmas invented a "little scenario" that would allow them to present the manuscript to Editions de Minuit. Since Dalmas and Jérôme Lindon, the head of Minuit, were not on good terms, Dalmas could not give the manuscript to him in person. They decided that Allain would take the manuscript to Lindon. Dalmas would write a letter recommending publication so that it would not be lost amidst a mountain of unsolicited manuscripts. One worry was that Lindon did not need at that time another writer working in the tradition of the Nouveau Roman. The authors to whom he was already committed were in mid-career and the novelty of the genre had worn off. To promote authors unknown to the reading public might be perceived as an unnecessary expense unless they were doing something strikingly different.

◆ ◆ ◆

To a foreigner, Midnight Editions (Editions de Minuit) might sound like the name of a publisher of pornography. The reference is quite different, however. The company was founded during the Nazi occupation of Paris when it was necessary to print in secret at night. The major figure in the history of Minuit, Jérôme Lindon, became affiliated with the company after the war but was initially hired in part because of his teenage activities in the Resistance. By the time of his death in 2001, Lindon was considered one of the three most important French publishers of the twentieth century (along with Gaston Gallimard and Bernard Grasset). Lindon is remembered in particular for supporting the apolitical Nouveau Roman movement as well as socially engaged writers. He agreed to publish the unknown Samuel Beckett when every other company in Paris rejected him. Despite Editions de Minuit being a small independent company, Lindon could count among his authors two recipients of the Nobel Prize for literature, Beckett and Claude Simon. Books published by Minuit also received illustrious prizes, such as the Goncourt, European, Renaudot, Fémina and Médicis.[11] *Le Monde* praised Lindon for making "rebellion—against fashion, conformity, power—a rule of his life."[12]

Paul did become a "Midnight novelist." The contract to publish *Les demoiselles* with Minuit was signed on July 9, 1970 and the novel appeared in October of the same year, disproving his friends' pessimism. That some readers are reminded of Robbe-Grillet should not be a surprise. He was a literary advisor to Editions de Minuit for twenty-five years beginning in 1955. *Les demoiselles* was originally titled *Le voyage à Tanger*. But Lindon did not like the title. Jean-Gérard Nay, with whom Paul had discussed the novel in the early years of its composition, often referred to it as "your spinsters." So Paul immediately suggested to Lindon that they call it *Les demoiselles*. November 6, Allain wrote that he had received two copies. "I flatter myself thinking that they are the first, still smoking copies which left the press." He grumbled again that "nothing had been done to aid the public" by inserting breathing space in the manuscript. As Paul had requested, one copy went to Hélène Cixous "avec un mot ambigu."

◆ ◆ ◆

The term "Nouveau Roman" was invented by Robbe-Grillet and Lindon in 1957 following an article in *Le Monde* by Emile Henriot who was reviewing recently published novels. Henriot did not know what to call their odd style and simply referred to them with the vague term "new novel." Robbe-Grillet and Lindon capitalized it. Much of the theory was invented later.[13] Most critics divide the history of the New Novel Movement into two phases.[14]

The first ("phenomenological") phase covers the 1950s and early 60s. Cixous was too categorical in rejecting the label Nouveau Roman for *Les demoiselles*. There are parallels with both Robbe-Grillet and Nathalie Sarraute. For example, some of the characters in *Les demoiselles* are mythomaniacs. The conventional wisdom others use to make sense of their oddities is patently simplistic. The ambiguous qualities of the spinsters undermine the reassuring provincial world they inhabit even more than do their crimes. However, it is true that the book does not explore the mechanisms of human consciousness. Psychological realism was never one of Paul's preoccupations. Nor does *Les demoiselles* contain Robbe-Grillet's meticulous and objective descriptions of objects. (The "thing-oriented" quality of Robbe-Grillet's and Ponge's writing did influence Paul. He later inspired me to write sociologically relevant descriptions of interior decoration.[15])

The second ("structuralist") period of the New Novel Movement is the decade beginning in the late 1960s. To some extent, *Les demoiselles* resembles the most famous novels of this era because it is about the process of reading and writing. The novel is supposed to be "confusing, merging, ambiguous," Paul tells me. He consciously wanted to make readers "work to discover the wisdom in the text" by erecting barriers to facile under-standing for the same reason Zen monks give nonsensical answers to legitimate philosophical questions. Go find the meaning of life yourself is the answer. He does let readers in on his game by planting signposts in the text, for instance, writing about how he amuses himself by juxtaposing texts as if making verbal collages. "Nonetheless, everything has a meaning whatever order is adopted."[16] Despite the stylistic difficulties of the book, incentives to continue reading are scattered throughout it, including a wicked sense of humour and bizarreness. Most of the jokes make serious points. They are evidence of his "Buddhist leanings." By frustrating readers *Les demoiselles* intentionally questions the intelligibility of the world. As one of the characters in his second novel protests, how can people expect rationality on a planet that floats in air?

♦　♦　♦

Personally, I think the most satisfying way of reading *Les demoiselles* is to disentangle the hoard of stories by creating one's own electronic version. After the book has been scanned by a computer, it can be easily divided into conventional paragraphs and chapters. Readers will make the breaks in different places, but the result should be less maddening than trying to make sense out of the original. In my case this required enough strength of character to ignore complaints that "you're ruining my artistry."

An organist who wants to play for services in a village church will find that he or she cannot just be a musician. There must be a personal life for the congregation to gossip about. Without exception, in the absence of information locating the organist in some social structure, churchgoers will invent it. Readers do the same thing with characters in novels. If they encounter unrealistically vague characters, they will use their common sense, the conventions of literature and what they know about the author to invent the missing information. Knowing so much about Paul, I may not be his ideal reader. I instantly turn *Les demoiselles* into autobiography. For me, the sleuth is always Paul, a hip and gay version of Agathe Christie's Hercules Poirot. In real life some people also play games with Paul, because of his accent and appearance, pretending he is Poirot. Usually, he plays along.

Umberto Eco ironically defines semiotics as "the discipline studying everything which can be used in order to lie."[17] It may be no accident that in *Les demoiselles* Paul blurs the distinctions between truth and fiction, male and female, self and other, narrative stages, even human and animal. Having a sleuth or a detective as a main character could also be related to semiotics. A detective is a skilled reader of signs.

The world of cardboard characters Paul depicts might illustrate the perspective of the sociologist Erving Goffman who revealed the cynical, self-conscious impression management of face-to-face interaction. The novel is also a comically absurd version of Harold Garfinkel's eth-nomethodology in that readers discover just how easy it is to invent common sense explanations for practically any mystical and cryptic occurrence. The following scene is an example. It occurs at a party given by the spinsters. At this point in the novel there is no reason to think that part of the story has been kept from readers. Thus, the comment that the sleuth should remember his or her own story is incomprehensible. The reference to Liverpool is also puzzling. No one has previously mentioned the city. "They" could be anybody, the party's hosts or the novel's characters in general:

(Farizio) wanted to know, if he dared be inquisitive at this point, why I did not better situate the action of my novel. I protested that the novel did not belong to me and besides the story might be true. He thought I had not understood his question and insisted I remember my own story, specifying that they worked at a con-struction site in Liverpool, which was, my god, a very peculiar place which did not resemble any other and he detected in me a stubborn hatred of the picturesque which went as far as making me refuse to use the direct style in reporting the simplest dialogues. I sent him back to his meringues by saying that as long as one finds the unstable balance at the point which is neither place, he will think all cities are alike. He protested. The debate seemed fine to him. He talked about having his eyes blindfolded, and to strengthen his argument, handed me his handkerchief. I took it, then gave it back to him. He saw that it was very dirty and remembered that he had perfumed it outrageously. He quickly hid it in his pocket, having the impression that people were watching, and suddenly left us. The evening ended in confusion; Farizio's perfumed handker-chief…made people uneasy.[18]

♦ ♦ ♦

From the tone of *Les demoiselles*, readers might imagine that the author is a middle-aged man disillusioned about love and preoccupied with human suffering and the transitoriness of life. Much of the writing was actually completed when Paul was in his early and mid-twenties, long before the book was published. In French fiction of the 1950s and 60s, homosexuality tends to be presented by gay authors as an "open secret."[19] But as far as *Les demoiselles* is concerned even this seems an exaggeration. It might be more accurate to say that this story about deception easily lends itself to a gay reading.

Gay readers are likely to impute special significance to the gender ambiguities of some of the major characters. We immediately see what might be implied by the narrator's enjoyment of his "passions noctam-bules," which is to "rôder" or to prowl along the banks of the Seine. That appearance is a misleading clue to reality is hinted in many incidents. Portraying the title characters as maidens is illogical. Not only are both of them elderly, one is a widow. The older maiden wears a wig and has a profile which people consider "dur et grave."[20] The younger one is unable to produce a birth certificate, a requirement for marriage, and gives an improbable explanation for its loss. Some characters wonder how the sisters could be related when they do not look alike.

The narrator does not share the opinion of some other characters that a marriage between a retired, one-legged colonel and a much healthier, younger woman is inappropriate. He judges the relationship in an inclusive manner that would encompass gays and lesbians: "Far from consecrating a crazy and blind passion, (this union) seals a wise and enlightened love."[21] Another example of an event that can be interpreted as a coded reference is the narrator's observation about the wedding and the nuptial parade through town: "No dance, no alcohol, all the fes-tivities were in people's hearts and they had the modesty not to reveal anything."[22]

Are these coded references to homosexuality, recognition of the deception and impression management inherent in social life, or tongue-in-cheek mockery of people's tendencies to gloss over the obvious oddity of things? Probably all three. But I think the first is the least important to the author. This would be consistent with Paul's politics, both now and in the heyday of gay activism. He has never been a member of a gay organization nor participated in demonstrations. He feels it is enough for lesbians and gays to live openly in committed relationships, whose nature is apparent to friends, relatives and neighbours. Edmund White notes in his book about Paris, *Le Flâneur*, that homosexual French writers and philosophers have been very reluctant to become involved in the identity politics of the gay movement. Ironically, French novelists such as Proust, Gide, Cocteau and Genet were pioneers in gay literature. This tendency to refuse the labels of a ghetto is also evident in Paul's creative writing. According to White: "For the French any subgroup of citizens is a *diminishment* of human equality."[23]

Juvenilia and Literary Theory

Paul's early writings, composed between the ages of about twelve and twenty-two, include poetry and four short plays he hopes no one will ever see. The first play is a sort of clown act, which seems to have been destroyed or lost. Paul no longer remembers where he got the idea, but probably from a circus act. The theme is a time machine that rejuvenates old people. Like the sorcerer's apprentice, the operators of the machine lose control of their own invention. Paul was encouraged to write this comedy by a teacher at the Institution Saint-Joseph in Périgueux, Jean Bever, co-author of several vaudevilles on military themes and a man of the world. Bever was not a priest but a married man hired by the school rather late in life. Paul remembers Bever smelling in class like cat urine. As the owner of one or two dozen pet cats, Bever boasted to his students that he and his wife were compiling a dictionary of cat language. It was not unusual for class assignments to be returned with food and coffee stains from the café Bever frequented, the Café de Paris. Paul believes Bever was the author or co-author of a potboiler called *La belle-mère enragée* (The Rabid Mother-in-law). Bever often digressed from the lessons and talked about life, cats and his plays. He also gave students more worldly tricks for remembering the Greek alphabet and vocabulary than the priests did. Despite the teacher's limitations, Paul credits Bever for fostering his students' creativity. He edited Paul's first play before its performance.

Paul's first and second plays, which had religious themes, were both performed at the Institution Saint-Joseph as part of money-raising events. The unperformed third play, *Tasu*, includes one character whose name, spelled backwards, is the family name of a friend in Périgueux who committed suicide as an adolescent. Jean-Gérard Nay believes that this death contributed to a spiritual crisis in Paul's life and helps explain his nihilism. Yet, this is precisely the kind of autobiographical subject which Paul refuses to discuss because he does not see it any longer as significant. While labelling people can obscure as much as it reveals, the change in Paul's religious views over a period of several years might be described as an evolution from conservative to liberal Catholicism on the way to a philosophy that is agnostic and Buddhist. It is worth noting here that in high school Paul was runner-up for the Prix Léon Authiat, a prize for students in religion named in honour of a graduate of the Institution Saint-Joseph who was killed in the First World War.[24]

As far as I know, the only surviving play is the last in the series of four. Its title, *Berg*, was the nickname of a German student in Paris who was part of Paul's circle of friends. Paul's mother sought advice from a local priest about his juvenile interest in writing plays. Paul interprets this as a sign of his mother's cultural naiveté. Perhaps it is. But there are also events in *Berg* involving murder and insanity which would worry many parents. For me, it is not a pleasure to read *Berg*. Although it anticipates some of the themes of the later novels (existentialism, the fantastic), the dialogue tends to lack the inventive humour of *Les demoiselles*. One exception, a sign of the comic wordplay that would follow, is the character named The Dictionary of Transcendental Homonyms. The following excerpt might give a flavour of the existentialist themes in *Berg*:

Grave: Berg, one can always despise humans and prefer music instead but that does not deny the fact that one always dies in the arms of other people, on the ground, and that it is always the hand of another person which shuts our eyes.

Berg: Why do you think about such things? It isn't worth the trouble thinking about people so much, and believe me, if they are capable of this last gesture, it is because they can't stand the white eyes of the dead. People commit endless mistakes and faults. They are stupid beyond words.[25]

◆ ◆ ◆

The staff at the Institution Saint-Joseph in Périgueux, the private high school Paul attended, included a priest who had a cult status: Father Jean Sigala (1884-1954), a recipient of the Legion of Honour for bravery as a front-line chaplain in the First World War. Sigala was wounded in 1916 and again in 1918. Volunteering as a chaplain in 1939, he still thought his rightful place was on the front lines. A few months later he was imprisoned by German authorities for three months before returning to his old teaching position. Sigala, a so-called "red priest" in a locality where priests tended to be conservative or apolitical, established the local cell of a clandestine Resistance group called "Combat." Of the eight founding members, five were killed; three returned from concentration camps. Arrested by the Gestapo on February 18, 1944, Sigala was among the prisoners at Dachau who were freed by American soldiers on April 29, 1945.

I first encountered Paul's tribute to Sigala forty-seven years after it had appeared in print in a little booklet. Paul had never mentioned it. That Paul was the only student from the last year of Sigala's career who was either asked to write a eulogy or who volunteered this task is significant. It says something about his teachers' perceptions of his Christian faith and his literary skills. Paul's tribute read in part:

> We received in our class the instruction of a man, not a textbook. We had the priceless opportunity of being among his last students, after the Resistance, after Dachau, and of hearing his words which were not futile. Perhaps we will never fully know what we owe him, but we are grateful to him for awakening us to a more con-scientious, more manly and more Christian life.
>
> Should we recall our teacher standing at the lectern in class? Should we recall his voice when we knocked at his door? Should we say how we were welcomed? And recall his simplicity and his affection? These are still alive in our memories. May we remain faithful to them forever![26]

I showed the letter to Paul. At first he dismissed it, complaining that I was sweeping up dust from under the carpet. The religious sentiments in the page-long letter, he said, do not reflect his real self but his social envi-ronment as a teenager and the conventions of obituaries and eulogies. He was twenty years old at the time of Sigala's death. Paul claimed that his real self only emerged later. He said that he had never been "captured" by Sigala. Nor was he the teacher's pet.

If Paul's disdain for the sentiments of 1954 seems brutal, it should be remembered that he does not dismiss Sigala's political activism but rather his unsophisticated religious views and a type of patriotism which he feels is out of place now in a multicultural Europe. In class Sigala did not dwell on his political activism, although he did talk about Dachau. How the patriotism and Catholicism of such a well-educated man could survive horrendous experiences on the front lines of battle remains a mystery.

Paul had already read Montaigne by the time he was a pupil in Sigala's philosophy class and had some familiarity with the French tradition of religious skepticism. In Paul's eyes Sigala had found the truth in Thomas Aquinas, and tried to dogmatically impose it on others. Paul objects to the way Sigala had an answer for every question. At university Paul discovered how much philosophy had been ignored at Saint-Joseph. By the time he wrote *Les demoiselles*, he had concluded that he preferred the gods of the zodiac: "these friendly gods, indifferent and wise, rather than those who stubbornly hide themselves and pursue you in order to knock you up or tear out your liver."[27]

◆ ◆ ◆

The nineteenth-century poet Charles Leconte de Lisle had no substantial influence on Paul's fiction. Yet, Paul's very first publication was about de Lisle. Too insignificant to be listed on his curriculum vitae, it is a short dictionary entry, written at the request of Pierre Grimal for one of the dictionaries he was editing.[28] Paul assumes that he told Grimal about his appreciation of Leconte de Lisle's empathetic portrayal of animals and that Grimal made the request when he could not find an established scholar to write the entry. Grimal directed Paul's master's thesis about trained animals in Roman circuses. His wife was a fan of the circus. So they often talked about animals. Leconte de Lisle is a far more interesting figure than one might assume both from his almost complete neglect in English-speaking countries and from the fact that an editor of a French dictionary would assign him less than one page and encourage a student in his mid-twenties to write the entry.

Leconte de Lisle was a leader of the Parnassian movement in French poetry, a reaction against the emotionalism and excessive displays of the self in Romantic literature. Despite the official recognition symbolized by obtaining the chair of the deceased Victor Hugo at the French Academy, Leconte de Lisle was to some extent an outsider in France because of his childhood on the tropical island of Reunion in the Indian Ocean. In his writings he expounded a Buddhist-inspired philosophy despite his repulsion for institutionalized religions. The depth of his anguish about the impermanence of earthly life, however, shows that he missed the point of Buddhism. In touch with the scientific spirit of the times, especially Darwinism, he left the riddles of life as unsolvable puzzles in his poetry.[29]

Paul was also interested in the mid-1950s in Franz Marc's mystical paintings of animals. Paul sees similarities in the way the poet Leconte de Lisle and the painter Marc imagine a spiritual union between humans and animals. Creatures and humans suffer equally and without reason. To me, some of the most obvious similarities are in the poem "Midi" (The South), which parallels Marc's preference for depicting innocent animals in a state of dreamy, contemplative rest. The scene is described for readers who are disillusioned with human life, people who are no longer concerned about either forgiving or condemning. It is high noon. The South of France. The sun is radiant. White oxen lie on the grass and slowly dribble on their thick dewlaps. To a person who wants to forget the world of human strife, nature may be indifferent. But allowing one's self to be immersed in the numbness of the scene should provide pleasure. "The sun will speak to you in a sublime language. Absorb yourself infinitely in its unrelenting ray, and slowly return to the lowly and despicable cities with your soul seven times soaked in the divine void."[30]

Perhaps the painting by Marc that best illustrates the spirit of Leconte de Lisle's pessimistic poems is the 1913 cubist painting, *Fate of the Animals*. It depicts animals that are fearful and tense. The painter may have been more of a mystic than the poet and is less naturalistic. Could anyone in the years leading up to World War I create a more spiritual and joyful painting than Franz Marc's playful yellow cow? Both the poet and the painter were trying to understand how the world might appear to animals.

◆ ◆ ◆

Ignoring philosophical digressions about deception in personal encounters that might have accompanied the story, this is the plot of a comedy Paul aspired to write in the early 1970s. Upon arriving in Paris from the provinces, a beautiful woman meets a shady character at a sidewalk café. He longs to become a pimp. This looks like the perfect occasion to begin his career. She is apparently as naive as the stereotype of small-town people. He tries all the tactics he knows to seduce her, without success.

The woman casually remarks that she came to Paris in the first place to become a prostitute. She confides that she does not really know how to attract men. It's not that easy after all to attract customers who are safe, clean, discreet and wealthy. She asks him to demonstrate how it's done. He's so skilful that he actually picks up a man. This is not enough to become a proper whore. It takes trendy clothing, nice jewellery and a good car. To acquire the tools of the trade, he's the one who is turned into a hustler. In the meantime she gains so much weight she cannot work and lives off the money he makes as a gigolo.

◆ ◆ ◆

In the mid-1970s Paul was toying with another lesson on transitoriness. He wanted to write a novel using the newest vocabulary, ordinary slang and technical jargon. The topic was never specified other than saying it would be about inconsequential recent events. The point was to create a literary equivalent to Jean Tinguely's self-destroying mechanical sculptures. Machines that do nothing of practical value; a novel that does not communicate. The more quickly time would turn the story into an incomprehensible fossil, the better. Paul may not have read Tinguely, but these remarks from 1959 epitomize the spirit which appeals to him:

> Everything moves. Immobility does not exist. Don't let yourself be ruled by antiquated notions of time. Forget hours, minutes, seconds. Don't resist metamorphosis. . . . Be free, live! Stop "painting" time. Stop building cathedrals and pyramids destined to become ruins. Breathe deeply. Live in the present: live in time…for a wonderful and absolute reality.[31]

◆ ◆ ◆

Paul spent his entire academic career as a professor of French language and literature at the University of Toronto. At the time he was appointed in 1962, this was the largest department of French studies in North America. While he was unusually productive as a researcher, his academic publications are primarily about the semiotics of the performing arts, especially the circus; the history of semiotics; and non-verbal communication. The only literary genre which has attracted him as a theorist for any extended period of time has been the most disreputable, quite foreign to French literature, the limerick.

The influence of structuralism is clearly evident in his publications on limericks in which he looks for their unconscious deep structure. His claim that limericks about sex are really about cooking, and vice versa, requires far-fetched leaps of logic that no analyst can establish who remains close to the surface level of meaning in a text. He takes a limerick about a spinster who wears underclothes of metal and *seriously* argues that at an unconscious level this is a limerick about the difference between home-cooked and commercially canned food.[32]

♦   ♦   ♦

Outside the classroom Paul avoids discussions of literary theory. Even in class he tends to examine and critique the theories of others in a pluralistic manner rather than concentrating on his own opinions. Throughout his novels there are succinct statements about his appreciation of silence. Concerning the creative process about all one gleans from his publications are obscure aphorisms and humorous enigmas:

> The little reflexive state of being is born quickly—one may let it come or chase it away—it is rarely caused by alcohol or food— more often by fasting, rain, the vibrations of the train, sometimes by coffee—it forces you to quickly scribble notes on the margins of newspapers or on the backs of envelopes—the only problem is to make it last—to push back the printed text in the margins, to keep it there, and to let come whatever appears in its place—one may wonder if there is a passive little reflexive state—but it is only a superior form of sleeping—only the active little reflexive state con- stitutes an object that can be described—its greatest enemies are music and conversation—the calls of nature do not interrupt it—a neutral or benevolent presence may be favourable as long as it is silent and odourless. . . .[33]

♦   ♦   ♦

In 1980 at the request of an independent campus newspaper published in Toronto, Paul wrote an opinion piece about teaching a course on surrealism. The article advertised a week-long series of cultural events at Victoria College, which was open to the public. The events were somewhat less successful in 1980 than in previous years. But in titling the article "True Surrealists Will Avoid University of Toronto This Week" Paul was under- mining his own success. At least this was how it appeared to the Head of the French Department, who helped finance the series:

> I am not a surrealist but I feel close enough to many of the basic stances they took—during a period which was not different from ours—that I cannot fully accept the view that the surrealist move- ment survives only in commercials and textbooks. This is why I

undertook a few years ago the risky venture of teaching a course on surrealism. This sounds—and is—a contradictory endeavour. To submit to (non-existent) bell curves, tests on *Nadja* or Marcel Duchamp is indeed for me a Procrustean experience. But the alternative is not to teach surrealism at all and, as a consequence, to reduce the probability for today's students of coming across these texts which are one of the most lucid and generous responses to the deadly challenges of our time. A critical and daring call to what are man's best trump cards in the survival game: rebellious imagination and irrepressible resistance to dogmatic domestication; far from being a cult, surrealism is the antidote to any cult. . . .

One should not forget that these thousands of pages, pamphlets, posters and poems were written by enthusiastic young men and women in their twenties and that they remain so far, after sixty years of wars and collective madness, the most stimulating, challenging and refreshingly optimistic stances of our century.[34]

Strip-tease de Madame Bovary

Although a little fine-tuning remained, Paul believed he had finished his second novel in The Hague on January 15, 1973. He still wanted to select an epigraph for each letter in this novel of letters, but otherwise he thought the work was complete. The original title, *Jeux de lettres*, was supposed to inspire readers to look for words that are pronounced the same way but have different meanings. A whole series of provocative titles could be constructed with "Jeux," or "je" as well as "lettres" or "l'être": Letter Games (*Jeux de lettres*), Games of Being (*Jeux de l'être*), The I of Letters (*Je de lettres*), and The I of Being (*Je de l'être*).

One potential publisher suggested that readers might not remember a title such as *Jeux de lettres* or they might not get the implied message. Rarely at a loss for words, Paul immediately suggested an alternative, *Lettres à Madame Bovary*, a title the publisher liked. Later, Paul slightly modified the title and the novel became *Strip-tease de Madame Bovary*. The reference to Emma Bovary might be interpreted as intentionally guiding readers toward mistaken expectations or as a secret reference to a famous statement by Flaubert: "Madame Bovary, c'est moi."

Such explanations are not supposed to be for public consumption. Paul prefers that symbols be left in their "combinatory potential."

◆　◆　◆

All the epigraphs in *Strip-tease de Madame Bovary* come from the novel itself. The quotation heading the first chapter is repeated in the last letter. The one for the second chapter can be found in the next-to-the last letter. And so on.

◆　◆　◆

The reason a novel composed of letters exchanged between friends appeals to Paul is because it's likely to confuse readers. They have to work to make sense of information, which is not presented in a manner strangers can easily comprehend. Friends already know much about each other; basic information is old news that no longer needs to be reported. Information is conveyed piecemeal. The spontaneity of the writing also adds to the confusion.

In *Strip-tease de Madame Bovary* the writer and addressee of the letters are secretly competing with each other. They are part of a group trying to convince the elderly to travel to odd locations. The elderly are not aware that a game is being played at their expense. The older the traveller and the further the destination from Paris, the more points the contestants win.

The author admits in the seventeenth letter: "I tried many times to write you a totally incomprehensible letter, a wall of words and images against which you would beat your brains...but I could too easily imagine the detours your intelligence would have taken, subtle, inventive.[35]

Strip-tease de Madame Bovary is a false epistolary novel. The author of the letters is never certain that the addressee receives any of them. She does not reply despite scattered amorous and sexual messages. "Chère, comme j'envie votre silence!" the author writes in letter nine.[36] The letters become progressively shorter as the writer ages and loses his memory. Paul considered titling the book *Strip-tease à l'os* (Stripped to the Bone). Presumably the novel should consist of twenty-six letters because that corresponds to the number of letters in the alphabet. But one letter is missing. Little calls attention to its absence. It is letter fifteen. The identical sign can signify the letter "O," the fifteenth in the alphabet, the full moon and zero. The resemblance calls attention to the polysemic and conflicting nature of all symbols. Readers might infer that the missing letter would illuminate some of the confusions in the text. Towards the end of his life the author of the letters suggests that he may have actually written more letters than the number that form the book.

As Paul pointed out once in a conversation, even the word "letter" can represent a symbol for a sound used in speech and a written message addressed to a person. He compared this to the dissimilar meanings of "bar"—a coffee bar and a chocolate bar are different concepts.

◆ ◆ ◆

There are references in *Strip-tease* to the Chinese tomb sculptures at the Royal Ontario Museum. From 1970 to 1998 our apartment at 131 Bloor Street West was a half block away. On display were two stone gateways and stone sculptures of a pair of resting camels, two men, a small altar and an empty round tomb. Originally, the sculptures stood along the "spirit way," which led to the tomb of a Ming general, Tsu Ta-shou, who died in 1654. The Royal Ontario Museum does not possess the entire set of sculptures for this tomb. Absent are two lions, two tigers, two horses, and some small animals. Since the general died in a transitional era of China's history when the strict rules for funerary sculptures were being relaxed, he received camels and lions which earlier would have been reserved for the emperor and his family.

Given the focus of Paul's novel on the slow death of the character named Alice, it is consistent that he looks at these commemorative sculptures, from a distant time and culture, and notices the way the present transforms the past even in commemorating it. In the 1970s at the Royal Ontario Museum the tomb and all the sculptures were displayed outdoors. Intuitively, Paul perceived that something was inaccurate about the display. But other than noting the contrast between the ferocity of the lions and the serenity of the camels he did not know precisely what was historically incorrect.

The museum added to the display of the empty tomb two Tibetan-style guardian lions—just because they were Chinese—which had formerly stood in front of Prince Su's palace in Beijing. Tibetan-style lions became popular at the Qing court in the early years after the founding of the dynasty. But General Tsu Ta-shou is supposed to have been a fierce defender of the Ming dynasty against the Manchus. The display was inconsistent with his sense of patriotism and his allegiance to the Ming court. At least both the lions and the general's tomb were from the same province in China.[37] In fact it was me rather than Paul who was irritated at the curators for allowing children to climb all over these antique statues, as if they were animals on a merry-go-round. The guardian lions are now displayed outdoors at a different location; the other statues have been moved inside.

◆ ◆ ◆

At the 1974 music festival in Royan, Paul appreciated Sylvano Bussotti's experimental music, theatricality and frankness about his homosexuality so much that he impulsively dedicated *Strip-tease de Madame Bovary* to him. This is certainly a departure from the North American custom of dedicating books to spouses, lovers, parents, friends, anyone with whom a writer has a relationship or some deep-felt affinity. The composer and the novelist are unacquainted; they did not speak at Royan. There is no direct link between the composer and the novel's contents. This account of Bussotti's lecture yields some clues about the ideas Paul found so appealing:

> [Bussotti's] musical workshop sessions, "Catalogo Ragionato" and "Il Trionfo della grand' Eugenia" (in homage to Franz Salieri, the brilliant originator of the famous Paris transvestite revue) offered fascinating glimpses of his private world. With typical meticulousness he listed and commented on all of his own musical—and personal—idiosyncrasies, superstitions and symbols with a mixture of outrageous Cageian humour and utter seriousness. . . . His ability to observe himself, to follow the endless investigation of his own being, to explore every aspect of his own ego makes him one of today's most exemplary artists, all the more since he avoids any hint of narcissism by proceeding one step further and making himself the objective substance of his music. In this sense Bussotti is perhaps the only true humanist in today's musical avant-garde. The listener cannot fail to be impressed when he calmly explains his beliefs: that for him there is no borderline between the serious and the futile, between art and the artificial, between light and serious music, between essence and appearance.[38]

◆ ◆ ◆

A prominent character in *Strip-tease* is Lady Pamela, the drag name of one of Paul's university colleagues, who married in mid-life. Paul disapproved so intensely of what he saw as a hypocritical marriage that he wrote this sneering portrait.

The storyteller arrives at the home of Lady Pamela and discovers that she has surrounded herself with mirrors which are placed in all sorts of odd angles. Lady Pamela is distraught. She has just discovered a wrinkle in the right cheek of her ass. Another visiting acquaintance reassures her. Wrinkles don't matter: look for a lover who has bad eyesight. There are many attractive people who cannot see well. The storyteller, however, offers a different solution, one which Lady Pamela tries every day: "I told him that by bending, his knees on his stomach, his rear in the air, his skin would be stretched and his right ass would again become smooth."[39]

◆ ◆ ◆

Mr. Lamousse is an allusion to Earl Moss, a professor of piano at the Royal Conservatory of Music in Toronto. Miss Moss, as I nicknamed him, had a tendency to became angry with people for the most trivial reasons. We never understood why Earl Moss became angry at us. We took over his apartment in the Colonnade on Bloor Street when he moved to another floor of the building. Paul speculates that the broken relationship stemmed from the inability of our neighbours to distinguish between me and Moss playing the piano. They told Moss it was a surprise to learn that he had moved since they could still hear him playing the piano.

In the novel Lamousse becomes angry at Lady Pamela, not because her taste in music is the latest vulgarity, but because Pamela gives Lamousse bouquets of even-numbered flowers.

◆ ◆ ◆

The character Gilmour is a reference to David Gilmour, one of Paul's students in the late 1960s. He became a widely read novelist and a celebrity of sorts as the host of the weekly television program *Gilmour on the Arts*, which was aired by the Canadian Broadcasting Corporation. In *Strip-tease* Gilmour sends a postcard from Charleville in the Ardennes—the birthplace of Rimbaud—as a sign he has finally understood that the author will not provide him a way to attain wisdom.[40] Except for the address, the postcard is blank on both sides. "The Ardennes inspire wisdom" is the epigraph of the letter in which this incident is reported. This is not a fictitious incident. The actual postcard, published by the Rimbaud Museum in Charleville, was mailed by Gilmour on June 26, 1972. The back is indeed blank. On the front is a picture of Rimbaud as a boy in 1866 and his signature from 1870.

As an undergraduate, Gilmour (sometimes under the influence of drugs) used to "harass" Paul by asking questions outside of class. Not just questions such as why don't you quit teaching and write poetry (which he seems to have asked), but complex queries about philosophy and literary theory. Gilmour had already decided to be a novelist. Paul was both fascinated and irritated by the challenge. Since the conversations were in French, Gilmour was at a disadvantage linguistically. The reasoning behind Paul's refusal to provide formulaic answers is provided in part by

Wilhelm Reich's *Listen, Little Man!*, which he sees as a good summary of his philosophy of teaching. The Little Man on the street

> ...must learn to know reality which alone can counteract his disastrous craving for authority. . . . You dare not think that you ever might experience your self differently: free instead of cowed; open instead of tactical; loving openly instead of like a thief in the night. You despise yourself, Little Man. You say: "Who am I to have an opinion of my own, to determine my own life and to declare the world to be mine?" You are right: Who are you to make a claim to your life?[41]

The character Serrault in Gilmour's novel *Sparrow Nights* is modelled on Paul. In the Author's Note Gilmour thanks Paul and two other professors at Victoria College for teaching him in the late sixties and then again in the late nineties when he was middle-aged. In 1999 Gilmour read a manuscript version of *The Pleasures of Time*. I met him crossing Bloor Street near Spadina a couple of months before *Sparrow Nights* appeared in print. He said I would think he was a prick for stealing from it. Gilmour offered me some advice on revising my book that might sound superficial but was quite profound. He pointed out that although some entries had effective opening sentences, they were unfortunately buried in the middle of the second or third paragraph. It took me six weeks to make the alterations.

◆　◆　◆

On Sunday afternoons in the spring of 1978 Paul and I went sightseeing in provincial towns near Paris: Rambouillet, a city known for its forest and its castle that is the summer residence of the French President; and to distant Parisian suburbs, such as Saint-Germain-en-Laye, site of a fascinating archeological museum. On the last Sunday in April we visited the suburb of Sceaux where Paul studied at the Lycée Lakanal in 1954 and 1955. Sceaux is an affluent district whose large public park appears to shelter residents from the encroaching urban sprawl. *Strip-tease de Madame Bovary* begins with a detailed, tongue-in-cheek description of the house at 8 rue du Lycée in Sceaux:

> The architect was a great destroyer of partitions and he must have soon had the idea of changing the narrow economy of little bourgeois rooms into this free interior space opened on both sides by two large bay windows that allowed the garden to stretch right through

the house, shaping and colouring its airy atmosphere, expanding it with extra light, a wide path of greenery and sunlight.[42]

Viewed from the street, the building is unremarkable, the kind of early-twentieth-century house that too many middle-class families built in the suburbs of Paris. I was surprised the house existed. I had assumed it was fiction. And in a way it is incorrect to say that 8 rue du Lycée is the house in *Strip-tease*, although the family of the architect Jacques Depussé whose experiences are creatively recounted in the novel did reside there. Jacques Depussé and Jean de Mailly were the architects who designed the Tour Nobel at La Défense in Paris. Built in 1966, it was one of the first sky-scrapers at La Défense and was considered at the time of its construction as "une 'adaptation' à l'esprit français des gratte-ciel américains."[43] In the novel only a few of the exterior features of the Depussé home have been preserved, most obviously the garden and the sound of passing trains. However, the garden is less impressive than in the novel, the trains quieter.

Paul has not seen the house for a couple of decades. Little on the exterior has changed, but the view from the property has been ruined by new high-rise apartments in the valley behind it. Further down the street is a house designed by the Art Nouveau architect Hector Guimard, better remembered for his entrances to the Paris subway. The famous château in the park was destroyed during the Revolution.

I do not know why Paul decided to visit Sceaux. Perhaps it has something to do with the fact that he has begun "collecting sentences" again for another novel. He tentatively calls the novel *Hapax*, a term referring to words appearing only once in all of the surviving ancient Greek literature.

A few days ago we saw the Carolyn Carlson ballet at the Théâtre de l'Opéra. Afterwards, while having dinner nearby, Paul talked about his collection of sentences. The novel opens like this: "I live in a circular fortress above which flies a white flag. Sometimes I piss out the window. It's not vulgar. It's a geometrical pleasure."

◆ ◆ ◆

About twenty years later, in 1998, Paul and I are sitting in a Swiss Chalet restaurant on Bloor Street in Toronto. While eating our usual chicken with barbeque sauce and french fries, Paul starts to talk about his creative writing. He broaches the topic because of my desire to finish *The Pleasures of Time* as soon as possible. Of course, I am without paper and pencil. But writing down his comments would have bothered him and been counterproductive.

He is irritated by my misrepresenting the Depussé house in Sceaux. At the time of our only visit there I either ignored or did not understand his literary intentions. Expecting the description to be realistic is an obvious error. The book is not a sociological portrait of the Depussé family, although Jacques' wife is the model for Alice (her real name), one of his sons for Boum-Boum, his daughter Marie for Algane, and Jacques himself is "the architect." Descriptions in the novel incorporate Jacques Depussé's own words; however, this can be oratory which is a self-serving misperception. For example, the openness of the dwelling to the outside environment might be pleasant to experience in a public space but not in a private home. On the surface the family seems ideal. At a deeper level it is quite dysfunctional.

Citing one address and family suggests incorrectly that there is a single key to the novel. "In fact," Paul said, "there are several keys or perhaps too many." The sources are varied: Flaubert, Breton, fictitious details, as well as the Depussés' own experiences and remarks. He says I need to read Flaubert's *Sentimental Education* and learn the difference between *style indirect* and *style indirect libre*. One hint that the author of *Strip-tease* distances himself from realism is the detailed account of an object which could not possibly stand upright.

At the Swiss Chalet Paul cites André Breton's first manifesto of surrealism. Breton made fun of the formulas of realist fiction: "As a cleansing anecdote...M. Paul Valéry recently suggested that an anthology be compiled in which the largest possible number of opening passages from novels be offered; the resulting insanity, he predicted, would be a source of considerable edification. The most famous authors would be included."[44] Paul would not have read the manifesto at the time he wrote *Strip-tease*, but in trying to reconstruct his intellectual biography one always has to remember that he is the product of a highly elitist educational system. If in the 1950s he had not read the whole canon of French literature, it is likely that his fellow students or teachers had read everything and talked about it.

◆ ◆ ◆

Paul was part of a small circle of bright students at the Lyceé Lakanal: the future professors of French literature, Pierre Pachet and Marie Depussé; the future educator Claude Vivien; the historian Jean-Claude Allain; the future academic inspector Christian Tessier; and the Corsican, Francis Chiarelli, who lost touch with Paul. Except for Allain and Tessier, they formed a group they called the Opossums. Outsiders were relegated to the role of Inopossums. The nickname for Paul was Le Bouisc, a meaningless abbreviation for Bouissac that sounds Greek. Paul remembers his friends "living in [their] private world, like delayed adolescents a little bit." Pierre Pachet's recollections are more philosophical:

> Bouissac had then something childlike in his unexpected happiness (at the same time more adult than me): in this way he invented for our little group of friends a sort of secret vocabulary which I have forgotten except for the word "stralyse," by which he labelled the house of Marie, a house welcoming for us other students.
>
> As a sample of [Paul's] writing, I only have the dedication which he inscribed in a copy of the French translation of the diary of Kafka, which he gave me (in 1955? 56?), and where he wrote the phrase of Saint-Exupéry: "Nous avons goûté, aux heures de miracle, une certaine qualité des relations humaines: là est pour nous la vérité." This book of Kafka has always remained with me, and reading it has guided me. Bouissac chose it for me with taste.[45]

◆ ◆ ◆

Paul does not believe he can talk sensibly about Marie Depussé's autobiographical books *Est-ce qu'on meurt de ça?* (Do People Die from It?) and *Dieu gît dans les détails* (God Lies in the Details). The tone of these stories is too familiar to Paul. The mood of these self-absorbed stories, which seem to lead to whatever is depressing in any situation, was her chronic mood when he was socializing with her in the mid-1950s. He refers to Marie Depussé as a kind of female equivalent of Samuel Beckett, a writer she knew quite well. In *Strip-tease* the code name for the character based on Marie is Algane, derived from the Greek word for pain.

> For me it is such a test to read Marie's books. I can hear the intonations of her voice and see her facial expressions many years ago. Reading *Est-ce-qu'on meurt de ça?* is like taking a few steps backwards. When you understand it so well, you have the feeling that you are writing it yourself and at the same time that you just do not want to have anything to do with it.
>
> She has all this enthusiasm for people, from time to time, and a certain kind of irony. But there is always this contemptuousness for other people. You do nothing, if you are in this frame of mind. It is a sort of whirlwind that you just cannot get out of. You simply have to take off and never touch this frame of mind again.[46]

Paul is not aware of having seen any building Jacques Depussé designed, although he could not have failed to notice his tower at La Défense. Paul remembers Depussé speaking eloquently about the profession of architecture while making aesthetic compromises for financial reasons. His wife is remembered as provocative and blunt-speaking. Paul had a good relationship with her, although the difference between his poverty as a university student and the wealth of the Depussés created tensions, at least in Paul's mind. Mrs. Depussé was obsessed with death and was misled about the seriousness of the cancer which eventually took her life. The maiden name of Mrs. Depussé, Paul believes, sounds appropriately like the French word for worry.

In explaining that the conflicts within the Depussé family are problems caused by affluence, Paul invents an imaginary dispute. Owning three cars but having a two-car garage, the family members argue endlessly about whose car is going to be protected from the weather. The Depussé home in Sceaux is, in Paul's opinion, a house where a person does not feel comfortable anywhere. Whether this is from the layout of the rooms, the furniture or the tension within the household he cannot say. "There was always a feeling of imbalance." Although their garden was gorgeous, it was not possible to relax because of the passing trains. "It was very typical of the Depussé system." In the novel Paul writes: "It was the house; intolerable; a moving centre of gravity that haunted all of the rooms without being able to settle in any of them."[47]

Paul appreciates the minimalist literary style of *Est-ce qu'on meurt de ça?*. It is a style he identifies with, although readers of his novels might be led to believe otherwise. Twenty-seven years after the publication of his first novel he criticizes its style. "The style may not be the best of myself." Hyper-sophisticated prose was meant to be a parody of the literary efforts of students translating ancient Latin texts. "Sometimes I have used the same type of syntax—just for play or aesthetic purposes—to make things sound as if they were already long past and translated from a dead language. That's the type of effect I was working for."[48]

◆　◆　◆

A letter Christian Tessier wrote in 1958 from his home in the historic town of Issoudun in Indre province is a good indication of the intellectual conversations at the school when the students were in a serious mood. Tessier would have been twenty-two or twenty-three when he wrote:

I don't know where these words will reach you because you are no longer an "Haumesserian." I thought I would see you in Issoudun the 2nd or 3rd and that's why I left a note at the spinster's home, whose sect seems vivacious, although it is an atmosphere that is too confining. It almost sapped the rest of my energy when I passed by her place before my departure, counting on finding you there and not knowing yet your change of address—is it rue de Seine?

Issoudun is more Issoudun than ever. That is why I will probably stay here until the Competition [for entrance to the École Normale Supérieure]. Just read *Essai sur l'esprit d'orthodoxie* by Jean Grenier in which Communism and Catholicism are happily united, like tyrannies which all sound minds must get rid of. With a disconcerting ease—and a little facile although deliberately—Grenier, every few pages, shows the harmful effects of these ideas on people like Jacques Maritain and Marcel Prenant. In the end not much is left.

If your steps take you to Issoudun on April 30, you will see the ballet of the maternal society [Tessier's mother was a ballet teacher]—the complete *Peer Gynt*. I saw the piece at the Théâtre National Populaire—may all subsidies go only to plays of this level.

Eventually, read *Mythologies* by R. Barthes, which [our classmate] Maurel lent me—another person who has submitted to the martyrdom of Issoudun. The petite bourgeoisie is defined there as a world where relations are uniquely those between parents and colleagues, which I think is correct.

I've made another "abstract" painting although I am distancing myself more and more from abstractionism—M. de Gallard [?] and Altman alone are worth all the stellar galleries. I cannot convince myself that there are any intellectual risks in abstractionism and I see, for example in Kandinsky, the facility that one finds in many of the recent poems by Aragon, and which is due to the possession of too much technique—a danger that Hugo already complained about, speaking of his own poetry—Do you know Hugo said: "I am a man who thinks about something else."

Would you like to join a group visit [*un phalanstère*], this summer, in Provence, isolated, with an Armenian painter—I must have spoken about him to you—it is now something which is almost certain, and which I find more and more appealing.

One day you must come to Tours because I would like to introduce you to a sculptor that I must also have told you about.

Obviously I have spoken about everything and said nothing.

I am toying with some photographs and I cannot convince myself to agree with either Chestov or Kierkegaard, if it were not for the rehearsal, but I certainly have not understood them—and I have not understood anything in a summary by Fondane (a very condensed sketch of the kind [our teacher] Brun does) has not helped me progress. Unless they mean the same selfishness I have shown in cutting myself off for the moment from ["mother"] Popoff and her adventurers.

This letter will perhaps find you one day or another—"Paris stupide" [stupid Paris or stupid bet, perhaps a reference to Pascal's wager that God exists].

I don't ask that I be reassured but I don't want Régine Olsen. Read *The Question* [by the Communist journalist Henri Alleg] and other books about Algeria that were published by Editions de Minuit, and remember [Lorca's] *Mariana Pineda*.

A tout hasard.

At the beginning of the chapter "The Pleasures of Time" I'm observing the passing crowds while sitting at a sidewalk café, this quintessentially Parisian institution, as though it were the most natural place in the world to relax. For students who have benefited from government loans and grants throughout college or whose tuition was paid by their parents, it is hard to imagine the financial difficulties that challenged earlier generations of students. Paul felt comfortable in the 1950s if he had one hundred francs ($20) in his pocket. He never had the money to sit at any of the sidewalk cafés in the Latin Quarter, although the district was not gentrified yet and many cafés were cheaper than the Flore. Only after working in Canada was he able to patronize sidewalk cafés. The adventurers at "mother" Popoff's were students, artists and marginal people. Introducing Paul to these people was for Tessier a way of expressing his friendship. Paul was at the time rather conservative. Popoff ran a sort of greasy spoon restaurant near the Sorbonne. Poor students bought food, such as a couple of eggs, and took it to her obscure and dingy restaurant where she cooked it for them.

◆　◆　◆

On December 8, 1971, Jérôme Lindon wrote to report on the sales of *Les demoiselles*. He calculated that its sales then totalled 351 copies and estimated that the eventual outcome of the books already in stores would be another 200 to 300 sales. He explained that these figures might appear disappointing, but that they were far from insignificant. Lindon recalled that during his first meeting with Paul he had estimated a probable sales figure of only 200 copies. "This was not a fantasy. Many first books by young writers do not exceed this number. The fact of probably tripling this number, seems to me, a good omen for the prospects of your second book, which I impatiently await."

On January 10, 1972, Lindon invited Paul to participate in a publication related to Tony Duvert's *La lecture introuvable*, which he thought might turn out to be a sort of periodical. Paul drafted a polite response showing interest in the project, but he assumes it was never mailed. In fact, he thought Duvert's books were primitive and uninteresting. (Duvert refers to his own novel *Journal d'un innocent* as pornography: "This is a porno-graphic book I'm writing, all it needs is cock."[49]) As Paul remembers, Lindon justified his rejection of *Strip-tease* by saying that the structure of the book was too deliberate and methodical, not enough was left to chance. Lindon also implied that the content was too inhibited. The meaning of these remarks became more apparent to Paul when he was informed by Dalmas that Duvert had become the main influence at Minuit. Lindon was looking for some new wave to promote in hopes that it would become the equal of the Nouveau Roman. In principle, Lindon was not willing to explain in detail to authors the reasons why manuscripts were rejected for publication.[50] Returning Paul's manuscript on February 2, 1973, his vague explanation was that: "Your *Lettres à Madame Bovary* are evidence of a very polished, masterly work, which corresponds truthfully to your proposal. But it is precisely this proposal which is too foreign to me to convince me that I am the editor who is right for this book."

Lindon seems to have rejected a number of second novels from writers whose first books he appreciated. In Paul's case *Les demoiselles* had not sold well, no surprise given its publication in such an odd format. The surprise is that Lindon ever agreed to such a non-commercial venture in the first place. More importantly, Paul was unwilling to participate in the kind of socializing with pseudo-intellectuals and journalists that is required to successfully launch and sustain a literary career. He thought the public role of the author was nothing but torture. He did not want to make small talk at parties, write flattering reviews of books he disliked or pretend to speak the truth on television about every conceivable topic. In a 1994 interview Lindon was asked if the popularity of the social sciences had not deterred writers from pursuing literary careers, as they would have done in other eras. Although Lindon rejected the idea, it does make sense in Paul's case.

André Dalmas handed *Strip-tease* on to Georges Lambrichs, who was the director of a collection at Gallimard. Lambrichs had previously published Paul's short text "Descriptions des petits états rélexifs" in his diminutive journal *Les Cahiers du Chemin*. Although Lambrichs recommended publishing *Strip-tease*, his decision was vetoed at the upper levels of the company. Dalmas suggested some other options, but they also did not turn out to be productive. In addition, James Sacré was enthused about the text and came up with several projects for publication, none of which came to anything. In the end Paul decided not to pursue these leads any further and "let the manuscript sleep in (his) files."

Personal Interviews

It is difficult to step out of the role of lover and formally interview Paul. The interviewer-interviewee relationship seems awkward, distant and judgmental. Questioning him about the circus is easy. That is a topic he clearly enjoys talking about at length. But ask him questions about his creative writing and he becomes evasive and mildly hostile. Despite moments of irritation, he was certainly more indulgent with me than he probably would have been with anyone else in 1994 and 1995 when I recorded these interviews. Paul managed to postpone the first interview for three or four days, until the last minute before he left St. John's to return to Toronto.

Riggins: At least my recollection of what you have said over the years about your own creative writing has been the jokes and game-like features that connect your philosophical observations. Normally, you do not talk about the philosophical content or implications of your stories. Readers of *Les demoiselles* have to discover on their own that the two major characters are actually young male transvestites disguised as elderly women. Instead of resolving the confusion of gender and age at the end of the story, the narrator starts to retell the story again. In *Strip-tease de Madame Bovary* a group of Parisians play a game that is bound to be confusing to readers. Another game-like device in *Strip-tease* is in the fifth letter, a key letter, which is full of secret references to the number five in other works: fifth chapter, fifth reverie, fifth symphony, etc. What are you trying to say when you use such methods as a way of structuring narratives?

Bouissac: I don't like people who claim that they say important things, who are pompous. So whatever I have to say, I prefer to say it in a playful and apparently nonserious manner. That's all. I have always been interested in the Zen way of dealing with important things: short, implicit and indirect. Leave spaces for readers to fill in. You don't have to explain everything. Life is full of inconsistencies and ambiguities.

Riggins: You must have had a superficial understanding of Zen when you were younger. This is a topic you never mention.

Bouissac: I did a lot of reading when I was a teenager! From the ages of 12, 13, 14…[Paul counts from 12 to 41, an action I interpret as a way of shortening the interview. But one acquaintance interpreted Paul's counting as saying he's still a teenager.]

Riggins: The term the "New Novel," in reference to the aesthetics of writers such as Alain Robbe-Grillet and Nathalie Sarraute, first appeared in the spring of 1957. In the autumn of the same year the New Novel had its first popular success when Michel Butor won the Prix Renaudot for *La modification*. This was the experimental literature of your college years. Among the writers of the so-called New Novel, who did you most admire?

Bouissac: When I wrote *Les demoiselles*, I had never read any New Novels. I had not read Robbe-Grillet. People I knew probably did talk about the New Novel, however. When I started reading Robbe-Grillet and other people, I realized I had written a New Novel of sorts. I never spent much time reading modern, contemporary novels. After all, I seriously read Flaubert and Balzac only when I had to teach them at the University of Toronto. Not everything they wrote, of course, but much of it I read for the first time, although I had read most of their marginal works. My reading was never this type of mainstream literature. I read a lot of odd things, but not what you would expect people to read.

Riggins: What kind of odd things?

Bouissac: Odd things like books on Christian theology, Indian mysticism, linguistics, philosophy. All sorts of things.

Riggins: But you must have read about surrealism.

Bouissac: Not at all. I discovered surrealism when I decided to teach it. I never heard of surrealism in my school years.

Riggins: At least you read about surrealism as an undergraduate student.

Bouissac: No. I never heard of surrealism as a university student.

Riggins: Why do you dislike psychological novels?

Bouissac: I don't dislike psychological novels.

Riggins: Well, you often complain about psychological films.

Bouissac: Because it is heavy. It's always the same thing. It has nothing to do with life. It is sort of stereotyped. But I like psychological novels, what you call analytical novels in French. There are a few novels which I like very much.

Riggins: Such as?

Bouissac: *La Princesse de Clèves* by Marie-Madeleine de Lafayette, seventeenth century; *Dominique* by Eugène Fromentin in the nineteenth century; Benjamin Constant's *Adolphe*. I had to read that when I taught it.

Riggins: When you write, there are certain themes, certain ideas that you are consciously trying to convey.

Bouissac: It's not intention. Things just come. I'm chewing my tea. [Paul chews for several seconds a green tea leaf from China, another action that I interpret as a way of avoiding questions.]

Riggins: Nonetheless, everything was not unconscious. You were consciously saying something.

Bouissac: Well, it's not for me to say. I don't like people who write something and then spend the rest of their time explaining it. You say what you want to say and then let other people do whatever they want with it.

After I had studied for years toward my degrees in French literature and Classics at the Sorbonne, Mlle. Haumesser once said: "You are lucky to get a job in Canada. You have read nothing." She was endlessly talking about these beautiful novels she had read in her youth, novels from the beginning of the century, against which I had a lot of prejudices. They were these stupid psychological novels by Paul Bourget, things like that. And I had, because of my intellectual background, coming from the *khâgne* at the Lycée Lakanal in Sceaux [preparatory classes for the highly competitive entrance examination to the École Normale Supérieure in the rue d'Ulm], I had the utmost contempt for this literature. This was for me both too old and not old enough. It was the sort of embodiment of the bourgeois concept of art. And so, when she was always saying "Have you read that?" I would say "No." I would say "Maybe some day."

We could never talk about literature because at the time what I was reading for my courses were very early Latin and Greek novels, that is the first texts which are considered novel-type stories. She had never heard about that. And so I wouldn't even bother to talk about it, just listen politely and ironically to her literary enthusiasms.

◆　◆　◆

I still want to know how much Paul owes to surrealism. But I would not dare begin an interview with such a difficult question. I remind Paul that—as I recall—he had earlier not opposed my referring to him as a "novelist who identifies with surrealism." My next statement is about a conversation between him and the German curator Jörn Merkert, which occurred at a sidewalk café at Saint-German-des-Prés in the summer of 1976. In fact, I had misunderstood or poorly remembered the conversation. Claiming that Americans' childish optimism prevents us from understanding surrealism, Paul had told two stories about experiencing the strangeness associated with a broadly defined concept of surrealism. In the first story he was looking at events which he observed at the Place de la Concorde as if they were happening many years earlier. The second story was about the emptiness of Parisian cafés late at night.

Bouissac: First of all, I would say that in the summer of 1976 I had a very, I don't know how to characterize it, a general feeling about surrealism, but no technical knowledge because I never formally studied surrealist texts. They were not the texts which were very much alive at the time, in the 60s and 70s, when I started going to book stores in Paris and trying to buy what was appealing and exciting, something which was alive. I would have bought at the time any book just published by René Char[51], for instance, or any new book by Michaud, Ponge, Guillevic or a new book by Lévi-Strauss. The type of thing, if you were intellectually alive, that you were on the lookout for.

Now at this time for me surrealism had a historical significance. It was something which was not alive to me, except Jacques Prévert whom I read passionately with Jean-Gérard Nay as a teenager. But we were reading *Paroles* as poetic revelations, not as surrealist statements. It seemed as if surrealism were two generations old. At the same time it was too close for me to have been exposed to it in the high school system or the university system. So my knowledge, my actual knowledge, of surrealist texts was practically nil. I certainly knew there was a manifesto of surrealism. I certainly had not read it. But at the same time surrealism had already permeated the culture. Through exhibitions, it was present in my cultural environment. And it was marked by a coefficient of value.

Riggins: What do you mean by a "coefficient of value?"

Bouissac: Things which I would look at positively, if only because they were marked by a sign of marginality, subversion, cultural rebellion and so on. I never felt mainstream. There was this sort of general attractiveness or rebellious cultural movement in surrealism. A lot had touched me through discussions and conversations with friends. Certainly the ideas I had at the time, in the 70s, were far from being documented, if you see what I mean.

Now something which I had experienced, and still experience in the trivial aspects of everyday life in an urban setting, is the way it provides a lot of interesting artistic experiences. I don't know how to characterize it. Experiences which I later learned were what the surrealists were calling "the marvellous." For instance, the story of the Place de la Concorde is a memory I have of a German friend, Hans Daniels, who had studied in Paris. Whenever he came back to visit me, we started to drink cognac the moment he set his foot on the platform of the Gare du Nord. I think it was a day when we were sitting in front of the Tuileries looking at the Place de la Concorde thinking that what we were seeing were two-hundred-year-old postcards. This was a sort of transformation, transfiguration, looking at things from a distance. If you start looking at things this way, everything seems odd. He was much more surrealist in a way than he became after he married, became a politician and eventually Mayor of Bonn. All this aspect of him was completely erased, put to sleep. And also there was a part of German Romanticism or Modernism in these experiences.

I remember that the story of the café with all the chairs was not something Jörn said. I think it was something I was telling him that dated from this period. Hans Daniels loved to be in these cafés when they started piling up chairs, as if you were the last survivor at the end of the world. The café, which was the centre of social life, was suddenly going dead. There was some surrealism in the general aesthetic sense of these chairs being piled up late at night. I don't find in that anything interesting or extraordinary now.

Riggins: I agree that this is minor. It was not my point. I simply wanted you to clarify your position with respect to surrealism. It was accidental and unplanned that I began by mentioning something that is a very minor statement I recorded in my diary. Only a few months ago you did not mind being labelled a "novelist who identifies with surrealism."

Bouissac: I never did identify with surrealism. It is after the mid-1970s that I proposed this course at the University of Toronto. But I proposed to teach the course not because I knew a lot about surrealism. I knew just enough to teach it. All that I know about surrealism is something I learned in this course.

Riggins: But this is inconsistent with what you said or at least implied to me earlier.

Bouissac: Probably that is why I have interested students, because I was discovering things as I was teaching them.

Riggins: Why is there this hostility to being labelled "surrealist" which, I thought, did not bother you earlier?

Bouissac: If I have to identify with something, I would rather identify with surrealism than with whatever else you can imagine.

Riggins: In addition to the marginality and subversion, what else is appealing to you in surrealism?

Bouissac: I don't know. My attitude toward surrealism is very ambiguous. Very often when I teach the course…[The conversation is interrupted by an outburst of complaints that Paul makes about being interviewed and about the triviality of my concerns. Then he proceeds from the point where he had left off.]…I tell them that when I read Breton, at one moment I think he is the greatest genius and the next minute I come across something that makes me so furious I feel like throwing the book in the garbage.

Riggins: Can you give an example?

Bouissac: No. Nevertheless, I think that these people have addressed the most important questions of modern times, at least for Western people. Very often I point out that surrealism has very little relevance in countries like India which have not been conditioned by centuries of Cartesianism. I feel very uncomfortable speaking about these sorts of topics. The best thing is that you come across a student who has taken this course and see what he or she has to say about what I taught. What is this rat-a-tat-tat?

[Paul is referring to the noise of my typing. I was interviewing Paul over the telephone, writing down his statements on the computer while he spoke, as I have done on other occasions. He could have anticipated before the interview began that I would do this.]

Riggins: You know that I don't treat everything you say as sacred. [I was thinking of the way I often reject his advice.] But I can't remember precisely what you say, if I don't record it or immediately write it down. [Paul agreed, but in a nice way called me a "scavenger."]

Bouissac: Invent anything you want. It really does not matter.

Notes

[1] André Dalmas, "Les demoiselles, de Paul Bouissac," *Le Monde*, January 8, 1971, 12. See also Etienne Lalou, "La spéléologie aux enfers," *L'Express*, December 28, 1970, 54, and Daniel Jourlait, *The French Review*, April 1972, 898-899.

[2] James Sacré in a personal letter to Paul Bouissac: "Indeed it is without doubt the idea of having to put on paper how much pleasure I took in reading *Les demoiselles*, which paralyzed me! A kind of elegance, this book, just a bit too much, a worldly mocking mannerism in the first part, which revolves around a sort of emptiness or almost around something (what secret?) rather than nothing—a sort of chain of little reflexive states of being...I would have thought first of maidens who curiously step out of Robbe-Grillet's *Last Year at Marienbad* (but isn't it Châteauroux?). These descriptions of the little states of being reflect what I have just discovered, show me that the maidens often step into kinds of tropisms, not fleetingly, but full of self-corrections, like those of Sarraute; in contrast clearly broken, like minerals, eventually in despair due to the force of the transparent emptiness before this improbable adventure on the ocean where they encounter the Géraldine of Jean Cayrol, if not the Alice of the Englishman with a similar sounding name." Sacré refers to Paul's article, "Descriptions des petits états réflexifs," *Les cahiers du chemin*, Vol. 2, 1968, 110-116.

[3] Paul Bouissac, *Les demoiselles*, Paris: Les Editions de Minuit, 1970, 115.

[4] Jacques Hillairet, *Evocation du vieux Paris. Vol. 1*, Paris: Les Editions de Minuit, 1952, 37.

[5] Paul Bouissac, interviewed by Stephen Riggins, September 20, 1994.

[6] Bouissac, *Les demoiselles*, 171.

[7] Except for one poster depicting Rimbaud, which was given to a friend, Paul's collection of posters from the May Rebellion was donated in 1997 to the library of Victoria College in Toronto. See Vasco Gasquet, *Les 500 affiches de mai 68*, Paris: Balland, 1978, 140, 204.

[8] Michel Serres with Bruno Latour, *Conversations on Science, Culture and Time*, translated by R. Lapidus, Ann Arbor: University of Michigan Press, 1995, 4.

[9] Bouissac, 48.

[10] *Hippias Major* and *Hippias Minor*, in *Plato Early Socratic Dialogues*, translated by Robin Waterfield, London: Penguin, 1987, 229-293.

[11] Michele Ammouche-Kremers and Henk Hillenaar, eds., *Jeunes auteurs de Minuit*, Amsterdam, 1994, 1.

[12] Antoine de Gaudemar, "Jérôme Lindon, cinquante ans de combat littéraire," *Libération*, April 13, 2001; Alan Riding, "Jérôme Lindon, Publisher of Prizewinners, Dies at 75," *The New York Times*, April 16, 2001.

[13] Emile Henriot, "Le nouveau roman, *La jalousie* d'Alain Robbe-Grillet et *Tropismes* de Nathalie Sarraute," *Le Monde*, May 22, 1957; see also "Entretien avec Jérôme Lindon Directeur des Éditions de Minuit," in Ammouche-Kremers and Hillenaar, 12.

[14] Arthur Babcock, *The New Novel in France: Theory and Practice of the Nouveau*

Roman, New York: Twayne, 1997, 4-5.

[15] Stephen Harold Riggins, "Fieldwork in the Living Room: An Autoethnographic Essay," in Stephen Harold Riggins, ed., *The Socialness of Things: Essays on the Socio-semiotics of Objects*, Berlin: Mouton de Gruyter, 1994, 101-147.

[16] Bouissac, 117.

[17] Umberto Eco, *A Theory of Semiotics*, Bloomington: Indiana University Press, 1976, 7.

[18] Bouissac, 25-26.

[19] D.A. Miller, *The Novel and the Police*, Berkeley: University of California Press, 1988.

[20] Bouissac, 32.

[21] Bouissac, 33.

[22] Ibid.

[23] Edmund White, *Le Flâneur: A Stroll Through the Paradoxes of Paris*, New York: Bloomsbury, 2001, 166.

[24] Anon., *Distribution solennelle des prix*, Institution Saint-Joseph de Périgueux. Périgueux: Imprimerie Périgourdine, 1952.

[25] Paul Bouissac, *Berg*, manuscript in the possession of Stephen Riggins, 28.

[26] Paul Bouissac, letter to Léon Bouillon, in Georges Rocal et Léon Bouillon, *Jean Sigala (1884-1954): Mémorial*, Angoulême: Editions Coquemard, 1954, 81-82.

[27] Bouissac, *Les demoiselles*, 43.

[28] Paul Bouissac, "Leconte de Lisle," *Dictionnaire des biographies, Vol. II*, Pierre Grimal ed., Paris: Presses Universitaires de France, 1958, 872-873.

[29] Robert T. Denommé, *Leconte de Lisle*, New York: Twayne Publishers, 1973.

[30] As translated by Robert T. Denommé.

[31] Jean Tinguely quoted in Pontus Hulten, *Jean Tinguely: A Magic Stronger Than Death*, New York: Abbeville Press, 1987, 57.

[32] Paul Bouissac, "Decoding Limericks: A Structuralist Approach," *Semiotica*, Vol. 19, Numbers 1 & 2, 1977, 1-12.

[33] Paul Bouissac, "Descriptions des petits états réflexifs," *Les cahiers du chemin*, January 1968, Vol. 2 (Paris: Gallimard), 111.

[34] Paul Bouissac, "True Surrealists Will Avoid U of T This Week," *The Newspaper*, February 6, 1980, 4; see also "Semiotics and Surrealism," *Semiotica*, Vol. 25, Nos. 1/2, 1979, 45-58.

[35] Paul Bouissac, *Strip-tease de Madame Bovary*, manuscript in the possession of Stephen Riggins, 82.

[36] Bouissac, *Strip-tease de Madame Bovary*, 52.

[37] Jeannie Parker, "In Search of the Su Wang Fu," *Rotunda*, 25(1), 1992, 14-20; Barry Till, "A Chinese General's Tomb," *Rotunda*, 14(1), 1981, 6-11.

[38] Henry-Louis de la Grange, "Royan," *Music and Musicians*, Vol. 22, August 1974, 39.

[39] Paul Bouissac, *Strip-tease de Madame Bovary*, fourth letter, 23.

[40] Paul Bouissac, *Strip-tease de Madame Bovary*, 71.

[41] Wilhelm Reich, *Listen, Little Man!*, New York: Octagon Books, 1971, 9, 14.

[42] Paul Bouissac, *Strip-tease de Madame Bovary*, 1.

[43] Hervé Martin, *Guide de l'architecture moderne à Paris 1900-1990*, Paris: Editions Alternatives, 1986, 277.

[44] André Breton, *Manifestoes of Surrealism*, translated by Richard Seaver and Helen Lane, Ann Arbor, MI: University of Michigan Press, 1974, 6.

[45] Pierre Pachet, e-mail message to Stephen Riggins, March 14, 2000.

[46] Paul Bouissac, interviewed by Stephen Riggins, April 10, 1997.

[47] Paul Bouissac, *Strip-tease de Madame Bovary*, 2.

[48] Paul Bouissac, interviewed by Stephen Riggins, April 1997.

[49] Tony Duvert, *Journal d'un innocent*, Paris: Les Editions de Minuit, 1976, 75.

[50] Lindon, in Ammouche-Kremers and Henk Hillenaar, 8.

[51] Paul Bouissac, review of James Lawlor's *René Char, the Myth and the Poem*, *University of Toronto Quarterly*, XLVIII (4), 1979, 429-431.

Stephen Riggins, Paris, 1974, beside his portrait
by Ron Bowen.
Photographer: Paul Bouissac

Jörn Merkert, 1976.
Photographer: Hans Hartung. Copyright
Fondation Hans Hartung et Anna-Eva Bergman.

Leida Poesiat, Paul Bouissac and Stephen Riggins, Toronto, early 1980s.

The Pleasures
of Time

The concierge at our Paris apartment tells the mail carrier to deposit our mail in the "Boite Sacré," the holy box. The previous tenant was the poet James Sacré. Twenty-nine Boulevard Edgard-Quinet is a new apartment house opposite the Montparnasse Tower, Europe's highest office building. A neighbourhood historian informs us that number 29 was once the site of a popular brothel. But the building is gone and the address has no aura of history now. The fifty-ninth-storey tower outside our windows is actually attractive, but it's another adventurous high rise too close to the historic heart of Paris. This is the second time we have lived in Paris next to a malicious solution for modernization.

But our view is undeniably Parisian. A huge French flag flies above the square between the train station and the high rise. The Eiffel Tower is in the distance. We see groups of soldiers passing on their way back and forth to military bases, travellers struggling through blustery rainstorms. We catch glimpses of Jean-Paul Sartre sitting in the interior garden of our building and Simone de Beauvoir in the elevator when she comes to visit him. Sartre sits on a cement bench in the garden with that "fixed smile of universal kindness on his lips," which de Beauvoir describes in *Adieux: A Farewell to Sartre*.[1] The smile is the result of a slight facial paralysis. Sartre moved here to rent an apartment with a spare bedroom for the aide who spends the night when he needs assistance. In this building, he complains to de Beauvoir, he cannot work.

◆ ◆ ◆

Our late-night routine at Parisian cafés is to read American and French newspapers while watching the passing crowds. Especially on warm summer nights when the weather is perfect, I'm reassured about the goodness of humanity by the orderliness of these people who sensibly enjoy the amusements of urbane life, which is mostly conversation. I pay more attention to the dreamers than to the worthies. Being Canadian or American (depending on the mood), I happily cannot identify most of the local celebrities. There are, of course, a few coyotes in the crowd that even a myopic foreigner can spot. Those I choose to ignore despite my training as a sociologist.

An unworldly skateboarder, still an exotic sight in Paris, comes rolling down Boulevard Saint-Germain. Immersed in his art, he gracefully weaves in and out of the chaotic traffic, indifferent to the fear or irritation he arouses in drivers. He cautiously skates along with the lines of traffic. Then, more demonically, he begins to taunt the drivers head on, skating in circles around them as they attempt to inch forward. He slows up beside some drivers; recklessly races to catch up with others. Coming and going in every direction—before, behind, alongside. The young man wears street clothes, traces of face paint and a flamboyant hat. Customers at the Café de Flore are so impressed that they stand and cheer. The skateboarder disappears out of sight without either panhandling or fishing for compliments.

The Café de Flore—the café of the goddess of flowers—is still fashionable, but rarely a meeting place for intellectuals as it was in Sartre's heyday. The habitués do include the fashion designer Karl Lagerfeld and the journalist and semiotician Roland Barthes. The Deux Magots, which Paul and I frequent less often, has a pun on the label of its tea bags. Above a drawing of two Chinese wise men ("magots" in French) is a pun which must be read in English to make sense: 240.

In other words: two for tea.

◆ ◆ ◆

The cafés tolerate some unique characters who entertain for money. One bamboozles us with cheap notions of insanity. Her most surprising feature is her shoulder-length hair, a style kept alive in popular memory by the heroines of old Hollywood films. While playing a miniature accordion, she sings incoherent bits of melodies abruptly broken by imitations of chickens, cats and cuckoos.

The specialty of an old geezer who dons a sailor's cap is scaring women with a rubber rat. He holds the rat in his palm, thrusts it in their faces as they walk by and lets it fall the length of its tail. To the delight of people sitting at the cafés, he sometimes manages to elicit a scream. If an outraged boyfriend steals the rat, the sailor resumes the show by threatening to vomit on the feet of pedestrians.

♦   ♦   ♦

Six weeks ago, around midnight on June 17, I was walking home from Saint-Germain-des-Prés. I recognized a vaguely familiar face. The man was balding; dressed in drab, oversized clothing; "musclé comme une fraise." But, as I soon learn, he has that rare cultural sophistication I value so much. I knew that he had been seated for the past few nights at different sidewalk cafés. The intensity with which he appraised the characters in the passing social comedy made him conspicuous to anyone who was assessing the café patrons. We passed each other on the sidewalk, hesitated, turned around.

"Bon soir," he begins.

"Do you speak English?" I answer.

Not being obliged to speak French is a relief. We continue together down Boulevard Saint-Germain. Jörn is a curator at a gallery in West Berlin. He is in Paris for several months doing research on the Spanish-born sculptor Julio González. González was a friend of Picasso. A pioneer in the use of iron as a sculptural medium, he taught Picasso the techniques for working in iron.

I am walking home to 50 rue des Francs-Bourgeois (the Street of the Free Middle Class) without bothering to explain where we are headed. Jörn seems to like the unspoken message: if you come along, it's appreci-ated; if you choose to go your own way, it's still a fine night. Few gay couples in the 1970s believe in monogamy. I have just failed in seducing Lars' Costa Rican boyfriend. I am not enthused about putting myself on the line a second time.

"You know my being here with you is not the same as you being here with me," he says at the end of some happy moments.

◆ ◆ ◆

A few minutes after I introduce Paul and Jörn at the Café de Flore on June 22, Allan Bloom passes. He invites himself to join us. Bloom is a respected political philosopher teaching at the University of Toronto and a translator of Plato and Rousseau. He will later write the widely read critique of American education, *The Closing of the American Mind*, and serve as the inspiration for the central character in Saul Bellow's novel *Ravelstein*.[2] Certainly there is nothing delicate about Bloom. He is outspoken, combative, a darling of young conservatives. He characterizes himself, smoking a foul-smelling cigar, as a man who resembles a used car salesman from Miami. "I love pollution. I hate health food. I support Nixon."

In my eyes, Bloom's stature rises when I learn he is a native of Indiana. Although he talks about students in Indianapolis high schools giving the Nazi salute in the 1930s, he also jokes about the state's confusing geography. South Bend is in the north, a visiting Englishman complained. North Vernon is in the south. And French Lick wasn't at all what I thought it would be!

Bloom and Jörn soon fall into a zealous debate about Communism. Since Jörn lives in West Berlin, it is natural for Bloom to ask about his impressions of the German Democratic Republic. Although I agree with Jörn's opinions for the most part, he is no match for Bloom. Jörn tends to emphasize the constructive features of Communism. Bloom is so vehemently opposed to every idea the curator proposes that it is a pointless debate from the outset. The curator seems to have, though, a sincere desire to influence other people's opinions. Under the spell of Paul's charisma, I rarely have that urge anymore.

Two other topics that Jörn introduces are more memorable. The first is the circumstances surrounding the suicide of Jan Potocki, the author of an obscure collection of supernatural stories titled *The Saragossa Manuscript*.[3] Potocki, who lived from 1761 to 1815, was a Polish count, archeologist, linguist, politician and traveller. Since there are many tales and legends surrounding Potocki's death, I imagine Jörn's account is another myth. There was a staircase decorated with an elaborate banister in the count's home. One of the decorative elements on the banister was a metal ball. Every day as he passed, Potocki would file away a bit of the metal. When the ball had been reduced to the size of a bullet, he put it in a gun and shot himself.

Jörn tells a story about attending a party of avant-garde artists in Berlin. He had expected the party would be fun. It turned out to be quite dull until he found himself talking with a woman about angels. Have you ever seen an angel? Is it a good omen to see one? What would you do, if you encountered an angel? She fancied that a mortal's greatest achievement would be to keep an angel without it turning into a devil. They agreed not to contact each other until they had found an answer to this puzzle. Three years later the curator still has not heard from her.

Paul recounts some of his circus experiences. He explains to Jörn his vision of artistically renewing the circus—without violating its traditions—by creating a spectacle in which the circus meets the avant-garde. Circus performers would collaborate as equals with artists.

The next day Bloom says that someone silly enough to talk about angels is contemptible!

◆　◆　◆

"Nobody could be more queer than Allan Bloom," one of our friends in Toronto once said. Yet he came to be considered the most famous student of the conservative political philosopher Leo Strauss. How Bloom reconciled his public and private lives remains a mystery to us.[4] Bloom may have disliked multiculturalism, the blues and jazz, but he certainly appreciated the physical beauty of Black and Asian men. One would have thought that his own sex life, if nothing else, would have made him prize multiculturalism. In Bellow's novel, Ravelstein is larger than life, but practically everything he says and does seems remarkably true to life. We knew Bloom when he was "living in exile," to quote Bellows, and before he had written *the* book. I don't remember his Toronto apartment or his clothes being the epitome of good taste, which they seem to be in the novel. Probably I was blinded by my generation's taste. But at the Café de Flore Bloom did comment on his sports coat: "Someone told me tonight my sports coat looks like a bathrobe, a bathrobe for a dwarf. What do you think?"

We first met Bloom at a party in Toronto. The date may have been 1970. What I recall from that occasion is the way I was shocked by his bragging about the beauty of the male prostitutes he bought in Paris. "If you're going to be criminal in a little way, you might as well be criminal in a big way." Although I had tolerant attitudes about prostitution, I thought buying the services of prostitutes was an admission of personal failure. Bloom was certainly not a classic beauty. "People have said before that they couldn't hear anyone else when Bloom was around. But I've never heard anyone say they couldn't see anyone else."

I am not able to make sense of Bloom's idealization of homosexuality before the Gay Liberation Movement. Repression, he claims, made sex more erotic, mystical and significant. Unfortunately, repression has been replaced by "...a crippled *eros* that can no longer take wing and does not contain within it the longing for eternity and the divination of one's relatedness to being."[5]

Hogwash. How could a middle-aged academic, a political philosopher who apparently reads little about the sociology of intimate relationships, have the audacity to think that he is in a position to fathom the emotional experiences of his students?

◆ ◆ ◆

June 24, 1976, at the Café de Flore, Jörn suggests to Paul that they collaborate to create his avant-garde circus. The Berlin Festival is generously subsidized. The administrators have apparently run out of inspiration for annual themes. Jörn proposes that the circus become the theme for the 1978 festival. The avant-garde circus would be the highlight.

The curator has no money, absolutely no circus experience of his own, and little, if any, influence on the upper-level administrators at the Festival. We assume his motivation in making this proposal is to establish for himself a more conspicuous reputation in Berlin by organizing a major exhibition on the theme of the circus in art. In a letter to Paul, Jörn characterizes the project as "crazy-wonderful-utopic-realistic ideas" (January 31, 1977). Three-quarters fantasy, one-quarter plausible. Creating a circus with someone else's lavish budget is certainly an exciting prospect for Paul. But this project is such a long shot I am amazed he wants to take on the challenge. Even Jörn fears it might be as insubstantial as a soap bubble.

Later in the evening the conversation turns to surrealism. As we walk through a narrow side street where a café is beginning to close, Jörn says that he enjoys seeing the surreal image of chairs being treated as animate objects on par with people—customers finishing their last glass while chairs are being set upside-down on top of tables. Paul says he believes it is impossible for Americans (who tend to be so optimistic and straightforward) to really understand surrealism. He recounts a feeling similar to Jörn's: sitting in the Tuileries Gardens and trying to imagine that the park, the pedestrians, the Louvre—everything in sight—is merely a picture of a scene that occurred centuries ago.

The name of the gardens comes from the French word for roof tiles (tuiles). A factory making them was once located nearby. Only a callow tourist could stand in the heart of Paris, surrounded by such artistic reminders of glorious and tragic events, without meditating on human vanity and the irrevocable passage of time.

◆　◆　◆

If any orator could turn a pumpkin into a coach or water into wine, it would be Paul. His character in public tends to be a façade of playful irreverence, socially subversive humour which some people find too caustic. He especially likes to make jokes at the expense of those who take themselves seriously. Rather than repeating popular jokes he makes up puns. To quote a couple of recent examples: "wineocerous" and "catter-pillow." With the French accent he has never lost, he likes to mimic stereo-types the British have fabricated, pretending to be the absurdly French detective of Agatha Christie novels.

Paul and his school friend, Jean-Gérard Nay, lampoon pseudo-intel-lectuals who use words inappropriately. "Robin is an ambidextrous per-sonal name. Ambidextrous—like the snails."

◆　◆　◆

Paul playfully mystifies people, sabotages their taken-for-granted definitions of social situations. Responding to a waiter in a restaurant with nonsense answers is an example. Asked if he wants chocolate or cinnamon in his cappuccino, Paul replies "Italian vinaigrette with a bit of mayonnaise."

> The waiters think that they have not understood. They are not sure if I am serious or not. This is the type of nonsensical elements that you introduce in everyday life. It's something I learned at university and from the circus band conductor Dimitri Maximov. You have to be careful about the way you do it. Some people will just think that you are crazy. They do not have a sense that you can play with these types of things, with stereotyped formulas of everyday interaction. Maximov was very surrealistic or Dadaist in a sort of natural way by introducing this dimension of absurdity. He was also putting his finger in his mouth to make the popping noise of a bottle being uncorked. Then he looked very surprised as if he was thinking "who is opening a bottle."

◆　◆　◆

The street entertainers in front of the Café Apollinaire at Saint-Germain-des-Prés are a depressing spectacle in the summer heat. An unattractive thin man pretends to eat matches and razor blades. Hiding behind a mask, an accordion player performs vulgar tunes from the early 1900s. The woman who plays folk music on a hurdy-gurdy is drunk and sings that Jesus had a cock the size of a matchstick and that her grandfather with utmost French elegance spread his vomit on his bread because he did not want to waste anything.

◆ ◆ ◆

At the Café Apollinaire Paul once gave me this humorous epitaph which he wrote for himself:

Ci-git du néant Paul
    B   c
     ouissa
   j   nt
[Here lies Paul Bouissac enjoying nothingness]

◆ ◆ ◆

Almost as soon as the auditorium at the Cité Universitaire darkens for a screening of Ron Bowen's film *Peinture et Fugue en Sol Majeur* a wave of giggling breaks out. Quite a feat for an abstract animated film. Every musical climax forecasts an equally dramatic change in images. The whole thing is too predictable. Still, the reaction of the university crowd to this unintended humour hasn't dampened the spirits of the small group that gathers later in Ron's studio. Ron is good-natured about the teasing. In fact, he agrees with the public. If he is given the opportunity of making another film, he confesses, it will be better.

Ron is a small-town boy from Florida, in his mid-20s, tall, thin, blond; he's slightly uneasy with people. He devotes more time to painting than to filmmaking. Earlier he preferred abstracts. Now he is turning more and more to hyperrealism. Paul and I are his favourite Capricorns.

◆ ◆ ◆

When Paul asks that he paint a portrait of me, Ron takes several photographs to serve as yardsticks in my absence. The expressive features immobile; the settings: the interior of his apartment in the Cité Universitaire, a nearby sidewalk café, and a public park. "I picked up the photos yesterday," he writes, "and they turned out so well that I'll have difficulty deciding which pose to use. I'll probably end up using a close-up of the head in the park. The details in the face and glasses are very subtle and intricate. The dark browns in the tousled hair and the coat combined with the sumptuous greens in the background make for a very romantic effect. The face is stark and pale. This portrait should really give me a chance to let loose some of my long suppressed romantic tendencies."

A trial sketch, which in my opinion does not quite resemble me, may reflect such "long suppressed" feelings. The finished portrait is too realistic for that, although I do not mean to be critical. Initially, Ron had suggested a portrait which would not be demanding technically, perhaps only my head and a bare interior wall with sunlight streaming through an unseen window. If I had been given the opportunity of viewing the photographs before the portrait had been started, I might have chosen a second option, a close-up of my face with the sidewalk café in the background. Finally, Ron chose a third pose. I am sitting in the park, but seen from a distance rather than up close. He has ignored my suggestion that he should be more symbolic than representational, although the amount of space occupied by the landscape is consistent with my desire of avoiding excessive egotism.

Ron paints with the kind of intuitive taste characteristic of the best folk art. In the completed portrait he seems to have been concerned solely with my outward appearance, as though he were engaged in an exercise of testing his skill in realistically rendering the exterior of an object. No doubt he refers in the letter to the intricacies of the glasses, face and tousled hair because they were going to be a technical challenge for him. Ron did not know me well enough to make a revealing statement about my character, but it was also not his goal.

Dressed in a knee-length, brown winter coat, I sit alone on a bench in Montsouris Park, impassive and expressionless. My facial expression is actually less severe in the painting than in the photograph. The mist-shrouded park conveys a sense of enigma. The effect is due to light rain and fog rather than the artist's intentions. The discrepancy between the deep green of the grass and my winter clothing is caused by the warm winters in Paris. Seeing my entire body from a few feet away diminishes the chance that a viewer will establish a feeling of intimacy with me. I look straight ahead, not daydreaming, not profoundly lost in thought—simply existing. Leaning against the back of the bench, I sit relaxed and restful but at one end of the bench rather than in the middle. I seem incomplete in my solitude because I appear to be waiting for someone. But this, too, was unplanned. Ron had been resting on the other end of the bench before he got up to take the photographs. At least outwardly I am disengaged from all of the expectant emotions of waiting, whether positive or negative.

◆ ◆ ◆

A valentine from Paul, written in his imperfect English on a card decorated with dried flowers:

> Having learnt how it is like to be or not to be with my Toad. Having grown up more or less through the weeds of fatal unreason and knowing well how it is like to be wrong and to be right alone, I bless these days of walking through the snow, of shared joy and limited pain. Like these flowers which nature would wither, through wilful art and precious industry let us keep them a-smile in the garden of clear reason under the thousand suns of mutual love.

◆ ◆ ◆

"Your tulips have already opened," I complained the day after Paul bought them. "The petals will probably fall off tonight. That's too much to pay for a bunch of tulips that will only last two days."

"The tulips opened because they were awed by your presence," Paul replied. "Oh…no…they are all yawning."

◆ ◆ ◆

"At the moment in painting I'm working on too many different things at once. I seem to have a habit of getting myself in that situation. I can't pin myself down yet to one direction or style," Ron Bowen wrote us in 1974. Over the next two years he was taken captive by realism. Later, he no longer talked about abstract animated films. In Paris it was difficult to get access to filmmaking equipment. Besides, award-winning experimental films by Norman McLaren gave him a distaste for abstraction. Not only did Ron believe McLaren's work was more advanced than the ideas he hoped to realize, it also left him cold. He had not anticipated that he would react so negatively.

Then Ron switched to drawing: "For my own work I'm concentrating on drawing in coloured pencil for a while in order to increase my productivity. I was getting frustrated with the slow rate at which my painting progressed. The pencil goes much faster and I feel the spontaneity flowing in my veins again. At the moment I'm using the technique to get some portrait commissions out of the way."

He now lives in an old bakery in the working-class suburb of Gentilly. Commercial equipment decorates the apartment: bread racks, a marble-topped counter, neon lighting and a sign that reads "boulangerie patisserie confiserie." There is even a large display window, if he decides to exhibit his work for the benefit of pedestrians.

◆　◆　◆

I connive to accompany Ron when he goes to pose as a model for the Alabama-born artist Nall. Fred Nall Hollis is illustrating Lewis Carroll's *Alice in Wonderland* and *Through the Looking Glass*. His is a perverted reading, but one that in his opinion represents the suppressed content of the original. Nall's drawings suggest those of Dali or Beardsley: the same attraction to decadence, the same shock effect of vulgar, obscene caricatures. In Nall's case the shock effect is heightened by a trademark he uses— portraying humans as decaying antique dolls.

To get more variety in the faces of the caricatures, he asks his friends to pose as models. Nall's initial idea is to have Ron pose for the walrus, but he changes his mind when he realizes that this wholesome, all-American boy looks more like a carpenter. Since Ron is painting the interior of his new studio, Nall draws the blisters, cuts and flecks of white paint that dot his hands. Ron surfaces in other drawings by Nall, notably in his decadent version of Da Vinci's *The Last Supper* in which Jesus and the twelve disciples are antique dolls. Because I am not really acquainted with this man who cultivates decadence, perhaps it is best to let the portrait Ron drew of his friend speak for itself. Naked from the waist up, his chest covered by strings of beads, Nall looks at his reflection in a hand-held mirror.

Several months later when I am looking through unmagnified slides of Ron's art, I realize that my perception of this portrait is mistaken. Ron writes to correct my impression: "It was not my intention to show cool, contained self-admiration (not that I see Nall as *altogether* unlike that).... He is not looking at himself in the hand-held mirror, but at the viewer, as if to seduce him or her."

◆　◆　◆

Even though I know the drawing will not be flattering, I am so vain that I want to be a model for one of the characters in Nall's illustrations of Lewis Carroll. I convince Paul to pose as well. We serve as models for the lion and the unicorn in *Through the Looking Glass*. The lion and the unicorn fight, for no particular reason, over the king's crown. Some people give them brown bread or white bread; others give them plum cake before drumming them out of town. Nall draws realistic likenesses of our faces, although our expressions are theatrical and we have the bodies of stuffed dolls. Paul looks at me accusingly out of the corner of his eyes, his arms folded across his chest, while the king holds an empty dessert plate in my direction. With a conceited expression as though I am proud of my horn, I stare into empty space. Paul's mane resembles long chest hairs that stick above his collar. My horn is a *dragée* container, a paper cone which holds the candy made of sugar-coated almonds that is given to the participants at infant baptisms. The model for the king, who sits between us and is seen from the back, is Nall's friend. The king's crown is a lid from a cooking pot that reflects the viewer.[6]

♦   ♦   ♦

Nall has sent us a comic drawing that mocks our relationship. Paul thinks it is insulting. I do not find it objectionable, although the joke is at my expense. Paul is an old lion, who stands in the background on the kind of stool trainers use in circuses. The lion's mane is ill-kept; one eye open, the other half-shut. I am in the foreground, a young, bright-eyed pony with a striped horn, trotting so close to the viewer that only my head and upper back are visible. On my bridle and on the corners of my glasses are stars. I trot around the ring attached to a leash that Paul holds in his mouth.

I am thinking to myself: "I have arrived! I refuse to be less than you. I am the unicorn—with a horn!"

Through his spectacles, Paul observes my movements with some skepticism: "Give him the chance, inspiration, and perhaps he will amount to something!"

♦   ♦   ♦

Jörn invites us to a Saturday afternoon potluck dinner given by the sculptor François Baschet in his atelier on rue Jean de Beauvais. Among the dozen or so guests is an assistant to the minimalist composer Terry Riley, three or four South American women whose identity I never learn, Baschet's assistant, and a somewhat vulgar, middle-aged Texan, Dr. Gilbert Bleau.

The situation lends itself to questioning Paul about his work in the circus. Paul rises to the occasion, airing some of his plans for his experimental circus. To our surprise, Bleau says that he is in the process of writing a biography of Barbette, a transvestite music-hall star and trapeze performer who had a legendary status in the 1920s. Barbette was photographed by Man Ray and praised by Cocteau. Paul remembers seeing some drawings of Barbette's act by the Vesque sisters which Bleau had not unearthed. Paul also proposes recreating Barbette's trapeze act at the Berlin Festival. He asks Baschet if he would like to design musical sculptures for a clown act. Baschet is politely noncommittal but agrees to discuss the project at a later date.

The lunch ends in singing, camaraderie of the sort I thought had vanished long ago. The Texan attempts one of those mindlessly repetitive songs from Boy Scout camp, "Found a Peanut," and oddly enough, the French version of the Canadian national anthem. The South Americans sing folk songs with semi-professional skill. Baschet contributes a humorous drinking song, "Au Bon Vieux Temps du Roi Louis XVI." It is a song full of sexual jokes about an overweight baron who courts the Vicomtesse de Morlelart (or the Vicomtesse who Bites the Lard) at the home of the Baronne de Belognon (the Baronne of the Beautiful Ass). To cite one verse:

> Il profite de la pavane
> Pour lui glisser d'un air narquois
> Non vous n'êtes pas la première femme
> Dont j'ai pu constater l'émoi-tâtez les moi

[He took advantage of the dance/to tell her mockingly/No you are not the first woman/ Whom I have aroused—feel mine.] The humour stems from the similar-sounding words for arousal "[constater] l'émoi" and "[tatez] les moi" or "[feel] them," with "them" implicitly referring to the private parts of the male speaker.

◆　◆　◆

In the afternoon Jörn and I leisurely walk through the Luxembourg Gardens, down dusty paths between ordered trees, past the circular pond where boys sail miniature boats. He wants to show me the original merry-go-round of white elephants, scarlet lions, stags and horses, which as long ago as 1906 inspired Rilke to write a poem about childhood. As the riders pass on the merry-go-round, the poet observes:

> ...a little profile, scarcely yet begun.—
> And now and then a smile, for us intended,
> blissfully happy, dazzlingly expended....[7]

Although I am unusually talkative, Jörn compares my behaviour to the founding of a Roman city. The first step was to draw a circle for the site of the ramparts that would protect the inhabitants from invasions. It is not that I surround myself with a wall as a barrier to communication, Jörn says, but I remain inside my imaginary circle and do not invite people to step inside.

◆ ◆ ◆

The street cleaners in Paris still sweep with round brooms like the hearth brooms witches are supposed to have mounted for their nocturnal flights in the Middle Ages. Until a couple of years ago they were a bundle of stiff foot-long twigs. Their coarseness made them look handmade, whatever their origin.

Now the brooms have been modernized in an oddly illogical manner: the same old-fashioned round form that certainly looks inefficient, with new synthetic materials. Real twigs replaced by dark red plastic imitations.

The discarded carpets and old rags that are used to direct water along gutters at the edge of streets have attracted the eye of a photographer. There are enough subtle colours in these dirty scraps that he's produced a whole series of beautiful postcards.

◆ ◆ ◆

It is a beautiful thing to bring people together, Baschet says, at his Saturday potluck dinner. The rule in the open-door studio he considers his theatre is that no one is allowed to criticize others. He believes there is already too much hostility and competitiveness among artists. Those who attend are expected to show the best of themselves.

An inventor describes some of the bizarre animated machines he has made for a film and an ingenious idea for a fly trap. Unfortunately, I cannot describe them because his French is too difficult to follow. The topic of Paul's experimental circus arises again. Baschet comments that simplicity and innocence are two of the most appealing features of the circus. He hopes this venture will not destroy them. Baschet agrees to take part as long as he is enjoying himself and the circus does not become too intellectual.

Opening a battered plastic bag hanging on the door, Baschet removes a dozen miniature models of chairs. He complains about "the system" which obliges artists, if they want to make money, to specialize in one medium or one style. Baschet longs to design commercial furniture, but finds his path impeded by a system of people promoting protegés and colleagues who share their aesthetic vision.

It is not that the Baschet brothers are rejected by critics. They are ignored. Critics rarely write more than twenty lines of text about their shows because they do not know what to say, Baschet claims. Their work is regarded as sculptures by musicians. It's nothing but musical instruments to sculptors. Nobody takes it seriously. The brothers hope to nurture the musical potential of their sculptures but find musicians so offensive as human beings. François compares musicians and artists to café au lait. Sculptors are the coffee—happy, sex-oriented and unintellectual. Musicians and poets are the milk—chronically unhappy people who turn to music and poetry as an escape from life. Musicians don't realize that happiness is like a muscle. It can be cultivated and enriched.

◆ ◆ ◆

By the early 1960s François and Bernard Baschet had built about thirty "structures sonores" or sound sculptures. They had another one hundred in mind. Journalists used this kind of figurative language to describe them: flowers—metallic plants with blossoms of tropical dimensions; hollyhocks and blindweeds constructed from metal sheets; also windmills, flocks of birds in flight, zithers, outdoor barbecue cookers and xylophones of crystal rods.[8]

The sounds are compared to oriental chimes, bells in Buddhist temples that are rung by the breeze, Romantic organ harmonies, booming vibrations, resonant whoops, sepulchral hoots and savage barks.

◆ ◆ ◆

François Baschet enthusiastically relates the politics of their sculptures to the democratization of art. He strongly identifies with the working class because he associated with manual labourers and farmers during the Second World War. Sleeping outdoors with them and sharing their hardships taught him how they live and think. The Baschet brothers are also dependent on craftspeople to complete their sculptures. Since they cannot travel with heavy materials, they have to be accepted by the employees in local factories despite being "foreigners" in terms of class.

In contrast to the elitism of so much modern art, François claims that their work is resolutely modern and accessible to the public. Their sound sculptures are practically the only musical instruments which are played today that are not antique. Performing modern music on instruments designed in the eighteenth century, he insists, is like travelling in a horse cart.

Just before electronic music became popular the Baschet brothers enjoyed a brief period of notoriety, but not the kind of success they wanted. Eerie sounds associated with science fiction films could be produced on their instruments. As eerie music specialists they even appeared on popular television programs such as the Ed Sullivan Show. Prestigious museums, however, were unresponsive. They turned to building water fountains and educating young people.

François is interested in helping street kids and the pupils in technical schools by establishing competitions to design and build musical fountains. The goal is to encourage young people, who have low self-esteem, to take pride in their own creativity and the objects they make with their own hands. Because the sculptures are often constructed out of pieces of old machines, it is expected that they will be learning some elementary principles of physics and mechanics and perhaps how to repair machinery. "The fountains have to be beautiful," Baschet says. "I'm very fussy about elegance and discipline. No caricatures. No Walt Disney. If the builders choose images, they should be flowers or something from nature. Nothing vulgar." In educating children the Baschet brothers go a step beyond Karl Orff because of the non-conventional sounds their instruments make. In fostering the creativity of those excluded from the fine arts they go a step beyond John Cage, who believes everyone is a unique musician but does not put the principle into practice in a way that would change society.

François is the first to admit that art is not a cure for racism, xenophobia, classism or intolerance. But he has faith in a few basic principles for reaching out to people who relate only to lowbrow culture. He is convinced that in a half-century there will be festivals of popular creativity that are derived from his ideas. Passing on this knowledge matters to him. He does not want to die with all his secrets.

◆ ◆ ◆

When Paul was a boy, he liked to improvise dances to music broadcast on the radio. Despite being a university professor he still dances, if he's in a buoyant mood or trying to cure my sullenness. He prefers overly descriptive program music such as "The Flight of the Bumblebee on Bald Mountain." He dances to Mozart's "Turkish Rondo" and Dame Myra Hess playing "Jesu Joy of Man's Desiring." His repertoire includes "The Fire Goose" and "The Flederelephant." Even the delicate timbres, thuds and rattles of John Cage's prepared piano can inspire his fancy footwork.

Here is a typical dance. Paul is waltzing with his sports coat. He holds the coat in front of his chest as though it were a dance partner. At first, his face is expressionless. Then he begins to show dissatisfaction with his partner. Dissatisfaction gives way to ridicule. The waltz soon mutates into a game of peek-a-boo with the coat serving as a screen. Each time he peers above the collar he repeats the same expression of surprise. When he looks out from under the sleeves, his feelings evolve through the whole gamut of emotions.

"You could make money with me," he says, "if I was properly managed."

♦ ♦ ♦

Upon his return from a prisoner-of-war camp in Nüremberg, Antoine Bouissac did not appreciate his son's little silly ballets. Frivolous parodies were outlawed—too feminine, Antoine believed. But unless Paul's gestures have changed over the years, there would not have been a hint of effeminacy. Paul is robust like a bear. He conveys the impression of a mischievous bear taught to hop and pirouette by a circus clown. The macho father's intolerance was voiced in the context of the economic crisis that followed the Second World War. At times the family experienced real hardships.

♦ ♦ ♦

In a narrow street of the Latin Quarter a trained goat climbs a ladder. With no accompaniment other than the unchanging rhythms of a single drummer, the show has an almost medieval simplicity. The goat is decorated with a flower on one horn. It climbs hesitantly up to a small platform, naturally prolonging the suspense.

♦ ♦ ♦

Paul suggests that I compose a piece for piano using the gait of performing animals as the rhythm. He hopes I won't stumble like Stravinsky. In 1941 the Master was commissioned by the Barnum and Bailey Circus to write music for an elephant act. He should have politely declined. His "Circus Polka," choreographed by George Balanchine for "fifty elephants and fifty beautiful girls," received 425 performances. The most compassionate report comes from a music critic who whines that elephants respond "instantly to waltz tunes and soft, dreamy music, even to some military numbers of a particular circusy tempo. The involved music of Stravinsky's

'Elephant Ballet' was both confusing and frightening to them. It robbed them of their feeling of security and confidence in the world about them...."[9]

Paul's criticism of Stravinsky is not entirely different. Stravinsky never bothered to observe how elephants walk. The composer simplistically assumed that animals which are heavy must walk in a plodding manner. But elephants are graceful and lithe despite their dimensions.

How much respect Stravinsky showed for the traditions of the American circus, rather than the elephants, is a question that can't be answered. The public's disapproval is enlightening. But the commission came from a commercial circus. If American circus owners had conceived of their work as an art, the word "circus" would not have come to mean noisy and rowdy behaviour.

◆   ◆   ◆

July 3rd—the night before the American Bicentennial. I am sitting at an outdoor café opposite the Renaissance City Hall in La Rochelle, trying to think of questions to ask the uniquely American institution John Cage. Cage's playfulness, showmanship and eloquence—qualities generally sparse in avant-garde circles—have nourished more journalists than the pronouncements of any other modern composer. I want to consult him to see if it would be feasible to write a Ph.D. thesis on the diffusion of chance and indeterminant techniques of composition.

The interview takes place beside a hotel swimming pool, an ideal aural environment for Cage, maddening for anyone trying to record the conversation. Competing for attention is the noise of fighting sparrows, a couple of bathers, passing hotel guests and employees speaking three languages, a maid sweeping with a vacuum cleaner and an airplane overhead. All of this reverberates in a corridor behind us. Cage finds the sounds "rich and pleasurable."

For many years Cage has been urging music lovers to accept two heresies. The first is to enjoy environmental sounds in spite of their random, unstructured occurrence: "More than music, I like the sounds that we can hear when we don't make music. When we just listen. We can do that at any time. That's what I try to do." The second heresy is his use of intentionless, chance methods of composition (tossing coins, following tables of random numbers or imperfections on a page of blank paper) as well as indeterminate techniques of performance (allowing musicians to choose the order of the pages in a score). In Cage's language, chance is likely to result in a fixed piece of music that sounds much the same regardless of who plays it while an indeterminate piece of music will be barely recognizable when played by different performers. Both systems of ordering sounds make his music as meaningful—or as meaningless—as nature itself. "If we don't specify something, we have access to more possibilities. . . . I have always wanted my music to be in some sense—if it could be—a discovery. My father was an inventor. I don't think I want to be like my father but I have that characteristic he had. He gave it to me." Among his father's inventions was a submarine built just before World War I that set a record for the amount of time it could stay under water.

Cage speculates that the radical step he took of abolishing structure in his pieces and adopting chance techniques of composing would not have been possible without a close relationship with musicians like David Tudor, Earle Brown, Christian Wolff and Morton Feldman, as well as poets and painters who tended to be more open-minded than musicians:

Cage: The ideas about chance operations and absence of structure, or what I call process in music, were really established not by myself alone but in close conjunction with other musicians. . . .

Riggins: You didn't write indeterminate pieces before that?

Cage: I did, but the radical steps were taken in a spirit of togetherness and of a group working together. It was very radical to move from the notion of structure to the notion of process. It was difficult to do it. You can see, both in *Sixteen Dances* and in *Concerto for Piano and Orchestra*, and even in the *Music of Changes*, remnants of structure remaining.

The silent piece (*4'33"*), for instance, even though I had thought of it before, I didn't have the courage to actually do it. It was paintings by Rauschenberg, which corresponded with it, that gave me that courage, that determination.

Audiences should not be given music that is instantly appealing, Cage maintains. "To treat people as though they need to be pampered is already a mistake that moves them in the wrong direction." While he chastises music lovers and journalists for their ignorance and antipathy, just as often he laughs. In the interview he recalls an incident that happened a long time ago during his 1954 trip to European festivals of contemporary music:

I had written the speech called "45' for a Speaker" and I delivered it for the first time in London. I wrote it in the course of that tour. It was given in front of a very small audience. I think it was the Institute of Contemporary Arts, which is now a larger organization.

While I spoke, David Tudor played the *34'46.776" For A Pianist*. The audience made almost as much noise as we did. (Laughter.) And I got quite cross. It was my first trip to England.

The gratifying recognition Cage eventually received from classical musicians surprised him. He had not anticipated that so many concert societies would agree that a Buddhist-inspired and unimposing rebel was worth the fees he was charging to support his aging parents:

I made over a ten-year period, as you probably know, a study of Virgil Thomson's music and wrote a book, analyzed every piece. It was through Thomson's help that I obtained a Guggenheim fellow-ship, a grant from the National Institute of Arts and Letters in the late 40s. Before that, and even after that, I never had any money from music. It wasn't until 1958, and if you subtract twelve, I was practically fifty years old. Since that time through the rather large body of my work and also the necessity that arose for me to be the support of my mother and father, I learned of necessity how to be successful. (Laughter.) Now I'm more successful than I'd like to be. I go underground, like Duchamp, in order to do my work.

Before the rehearsal yesterday of his piece *Atlas Eclipticalis*, Cage lectured the musicians of the Residentie Orchestra of The Hague. Few of them seem to have understood the message, though. Because it was a hot day and *Atlas Eclipticalis* lasts over two hours without an intermission, the musicians were allowed to drink on stage and to leave briefly. The freedom of movement gave them ample opportunity to show the audience their contempt for the music. Today Cage says that if he could have closed his eyes, the sounds would have been beautiful, but since he had to watch, he found the concert a painful experience. Talking to me, he counsels:

Each person should act from his own centre and try not to impose upon the centre of someone else. In bringing sounds into existence we should also try not to impose ourselves on the sounds or to make the sounds funny or to make them powerful or anything like that. Don't push the sounds. Let them fly from their own nests. I was very pleased with that expression [which he had used in talking to the Residentie Orchestra]. I still am. (Laughter.) But then it didn't reach everybody.

I think that if you look closely at the relation of architecture to the performance of music, you see that many people are listening to music in situations in which they can walk around rather than being seated in rows. What we had last night was a curious situation in which the orchestra was invited to move around and the public was not really in a situation that permitted their walking around as freely as the orchestra.

Someone once told Cage that musicians would have to change their ways of thinking before playing pieces such as *Cheap Imitation*. It was unrealistic to expect this from an eighty-six-member orchestra. "We are not just eighty-six people," he replied. "There are billions of us and if we don't change our minds soon we are going to ruin the planet."

♦ ♦ ♦

"I would like to be a unicorn. I would rest my horn on your shoulder," Paul said to me.

♦ ♦ ♦

Paul, wearing an orange-coloured T-shirt: "You look like a mustached geranium in your blue pants and red shirt. Me, I'm the pumpkin. We could make a garden!"

♦ ♦ ♦

On our arrival at Grand Ry, a village near the border of Morvan and Nievre, where we spend the weekend with Jörn and three of his friends, we find the wife of Jean-Claude sunbathing and reading Mickey Mouse comic books. Other artless pleasures that weekend include leisurely outdoor lunches, flying kites, hiking, pickling cucumbers and massacring a plague of wasps. During one of our rambles we visit a "réparateur d'oiseaux chanteurs et automates" who shows off a motley collection of music boxes and a violin-playing toy monkey dressed in an eighteenth-century costume. Except for weekends, Jörn is staying alone in Grand Ry in order to work more efficiently on his study of González. Our hosts' farmhouse dates to 1559. The date's carved on the back wall.

I give Jörn a tedious letter I wrote about the events of the past month since we parted. Spontaneously, he reciprocates with a copy of a letter he wrote to a friend. The section about Paul and me is titled "Paul and Stephen or the circus and the cat or experiences with angels. . . . Are they really angels? or life completely different and as dreamed, imagined, wished for, hoped for." Jörn wonders if he will finally learn to enjoy cats, since Paul claims that I have a feline personality.

Grand Ry is about to draw its last breath. On weekends the population may swell to a mere fifty people. So few people live here that the place has no restaurant, not even a real grocery, but there is a general store of sorts serving alcoholic beverages. I am thinking how picturesque the store is— even though painfully bare—until one of Jörn's friends mentions that the proprietor's wife is remembered as a young woman who dated older men so she could steal their wallets. Even now in old age she tries to cheat her regular customers of a paltry ten or twenty centimes.

On Sunday afternoon we catch the Paris train in Autun because Jörn wants to show us the remarkable Romanesque sculptures from the Church of Saint-Lazare. One of the most famous shows a standing angel reaching across a bed to awaken the three wise men.

Paul casually suggests to Nall the next week that if he draws a portrait of Jörn, we will be happy to buy it. Both to our delight and regret, because we cannot afford it, Nall takes Paul's remark seriously.

Jörn wrote that one day in Grand Ry he was depressed because he was alone, we had left for Canada and no mail arrived. After drinking a full bottle of wine he fell asleep. At first he thought he was dreaming when he was unexpectedly woken by Nall, who had come to spend a few days. During his visit, Nall made several open-air watercolours of sunsets and old buildings, a portrait of Jörn as the rabbit in *Alice in Wonderland* and the portrait of Jörn, which we were supposed to buy. In this personal portrait Jörn is given the body of a stuffed doll. His fingers are about to be burned by the cigarette he has smoked to the end. His other hand clenches an arm of the chair in which he is seated. A slight smile crosses his face. Behind him is a paper box holding books, including one about González, and a large leafy plant. The suggestive posture of a frog that decorates an ash tray reminds Jörn of himself. Hanging from the ceiling is a sticky paper flycatcher that trapped a fly and some feathers.

◆ ◆ ◆

The ballet music from *Faust* inspires Paul to poke fun at Gounod's excessive sweetness and grotesque theatricality. He opens his eyes wide and smiles, threatening to show off his deft footwork. But a mood of restraint takes over. He "dances" with only two fingers on the table. Then he creates a "puppet ballet" by sticking his big toe in and out of a hole in his sock.

◆ ◆ ◆

Paul's delight in imitating animals: the awakening squirrel—stretches his neck, looks in all directions, brushes his moustache with the side of his hand. The enraged elephant—wrapping his "trunk" (his arm) around me when I ask him to do something he does not want to do. The rabbit—soap bubbles on his wiggling foot in the bathtub.

His most frequent imitation is the little mouse who speaks in a high falsetto voice and is fond of Nikita Mandryka's cartoon of a horrible rat performing an old song: "On...dit que j'ai de belles gambêêtttes..." ("They...say that I have beautiful legggs..."). The little mouse says he loves me and is happy. Cuddly and defenceless, his life is complicated by a bossy tomcat named Manitou.

◆　◆　◆

Le Mange Tout, located at 30 rue Lacépède, the far edge of the Latin Quarter, is the hub of our daily life. It's owned by one of Paul's cousins. Jean-Paul Bouissac does more than anyone else to simplify our existence. He collects our mail, lends money, stores our property, occasionally gives us leftovers, sells wine at reduced prices, and once even found an apartment for us. He is an enthusiastic anglophile, like Paul. After training in fashion, Jean-Paul worked for a few years in London. He says that when taxes on clothing and luxury goods soared, he was obliged to return to Paris. Unemployment led to opening the restaurant. He was never trained as a cook.

It should not be a surprise that the restaurant's decor was planned first, the food second. The decoration is completely modern. No antiques. No candles. No beamed ceiling. None of the domestic animals that enliven some French restaurants. Spotlights shine on white walls that are plain except for a poster of a single red apple and two small reproductions of paintings by Maurice Sarthou, who has eaten at Le Mange Tout. There are about a dozen dark blue tables, a bright blue and orange rug, flower boxes in the window, and a vine coiled around a column. Animated by the fashionable customers Jean-Paul likes to attract, the restaurant has visual warmth despite its austerity.

Managing Le Mange Tout so conscientiously wrecks Jean-Paul's personal life. When it opened, he did all the work himself and lived in a tiny room in the basement. Now that he can afford a cook as well as an apartment, he still does most of the preparation of the food. Although the restaurant is a success, it's too small to be really profitable. It was financed in part by a seasoned old chap whose most significant gift to his friends is his effort to educate them—with a conservative bias. He once entrusted us with this truth, "I've never met an intelligent man who could not speak French."

Le Mange Tout does not specialize in any particular cuisine. On the menu are dishes such as "canard à la Salers" (duck cooked in a mountain herb and brandy sauce), "boeuf aux olives" (beef with olives), and "la poule à la sarriette" (chicken with savoury). Jean-Paul has invented some dishes of his own, purées that are a blend of fruits and vegetables—carrots and pears, for example.

The restaurant needs a more alluring name. Paul failed to convince Jean-Paul to call it Le Cru et le Cuit (*The Raw and the Cooked*) after the book by Claude Lévi-Strauss. Le Mange Tout could be translated as The Romano Bean or The Eat Everything. Apparently, the French does not have the vulgar connotations that the English seems to have. Jean-Paul chose Le Mange Tout because he thought it would make it easy to recall the address, a block from Place Monge.

◆ ◆ ◆

The retired Director of the Zurich and Basle zoos, Heini Hediger, looks with sympathy for signs of mental sophistication in animals and questions the unique status humans grant themselves. He is convinced that an earlier generation of psychologists went too far in conceptualizing animals as mere machines. Out of a concern for ecological truth, he was one of the first zoo directors to take birds such as oxpeckers out of the aviary and allow them to live free with adult rhinoceros on whose backs they like to perch. The Basle Zoo under his direction was the first zoo to successfully breed the Indian rhinoceros. Because of the interest Paul and Hediger share in the behaviour of animals, Hediger gives us a personal tour of the Zurich Zoological Gardens. Along the way he explains some of the ideas in his book *Psychology and Behaviour of Animals in Zoos and Circuses*, ideas that underlie his meticulous observations of animals in captivity.[10]

Hediger says that the fantastic way parasites are able to hop from one host to another convinced him the evolution of species must not be governed solely by chance. The proof he gives is the life cycle of a flat parasitic worm called the liver fluke (Dicrocoelium dentricum). Although understanding how this host-parasite system functions is easy, it is difficult to imagine how something so complex could emerge in the first place. Adult liver flukes live in the intestines of sheep. But during earlier stages of their lives they colonize two other hosts and modify their behaviour to suit their own needs. The life cycle begins when the microscopic eggs of liver flukes are expelled in sheep manure. The eggs are accidentally ingested by snails as they move across pastures eating sheep feces. Inside the snails the eggs hatch into larvae, but this foreign substance causes the snails to cough. They cough up the larvae, wrapped in slime which ants like to eat. Inside the ants some of the larvae move to the intestines; others to the brain making the ants crazy. Normally, ants would avoid dangerous locations such as the tips of blades of grass, but in their crazed state they are no longer prudent. The ants, along with the larvae, are eaten by grazing sheep. Inside the sheep the larvae turn into adult liver flukes.

◆　◆　◆

The question of what topic to choose for a doctoral thesis surfaced in 1957 while Paul was completing his master's thesis and working as a tutor for the three sons of Pierre Grimal, a professor of Latin at the Sorbonne. Grimal is well-known as an editor of important reference books on Roman civilization and classical mythology, as well as being the author of books on Roman gardens and the antique theatre. As a student in Classics with a strong interest in philosophy, it occurred to Paul that it was worth studying the conceptual transformations brought about in the works of ancient Greek philosophers by the succession of translations they underwent. Many Greek philosophical texts were first translated into Arabic, then in the Middle Ages from Arabic into Latin, and came to the West through these Latin translations. (Paul eventually wrote a Ph.D. thesis about a totally unrelated topic, methodologies for notating gestures, which was published as *La mesure des gestes*.)

When Paul proposed studying these translations with the people who could advise him, they recommended that he learn classical Arabic and then Syriac. The earliest translations were into this particular Semitic language. Paul began classes in Arabic, working at the same time under the supervision of Grimal on his M.A. thesis about trained animal exhibitions in ancient Rome. Paul passed the first-year examination in Arabic and started the second year, but then his studies were interrupted when he was drafted into the air force at the age of twenty-five, the limit of postponements allowed students.

Paul was a sort of Catholic leftist, essentially apolitical but leaning toward what was called "social Catholicism." While he had vaguely heard about Morocco from family conversations with a retired cousin who had been a forestry administrator there, he was not sympathetic to the colonial repression which was then the focus of French politics. So he seized the opportunity to view the country from a totally different angle when the chance came his way after his first year of Arabic.

With the intention of enticing them into cooperation programs, the Moroccan government wanted young French professionals not tainted by the colonial experience to get acquainted with Moroccan cultures and institutions. Shortly after Morocco became independent from France in 1956 and the legitimate king, Muhammad V, was returned to power, a Catholic student association in collaboration with a Benedictine community in the Middle Atlas mountains sponsored a group visit. Under the supervision of two priests, approximately twenty students participated in the trip. They went to Rabat, the capital, where they were official guests of the government. King Muhammed V granted them an audience in the palace. The archbishop of Rabat and several high civil servants and political leaders spoke with them. They visited the leader of the opposition, Mehdi Ben Barka, and spent time in the city of Fez. According to Paul:

I made friends very quickly with some Moroccan students. I could not yet speak Arabic, but I could write simple sentences. They sort of adopted me and called me Sidi Hassan [Master Hassan]. I bought a jellaba and a tarboosh, which is a grey hat similar to a long fez. I was naturally suntanned. They took me to the great, ancient university of the Islamic world called the Karaouine. Non-Moslems were not supposed to go inside. I saw thousands of old manuscripts there, some of them kept in big jars. I was told that nobody had ever examined them. I was very excited by seeing these manuscripts because I wanted to do this study of translations.

We went to Azrou in the mountains and spent some time there in seminars and discussions. We took a trip to the furthest south I have ever been in Africa, which is Ksar-es-Souk [presently called Er-Rachidia]. On the way we slept at the blue spring of Meski, outside, under the palm trees. I have a great memory of the windstorm that night which blew down a palm tree. I even wrote a poem about it which is in *Les demoiselles*.[11] After that I was so enthused I asked what the conditions were to become a Moroccan citizen. But this was the year when the Algerian War started. It put an end to all of my plans. Several classmates from Périgueux died there. Tragedy became a part of my generation.[12]

♦ ♦ ♦

I did not want to stand on the shoulders of giants. Anyway, there were no giants in the sociology of music other than Theodor W. Adorno, whose politics and pessimism are suspect. Classical music did not interest any of the founding fathers of sociology other than Max Weber whose one tome on music, to be uncharitable, is a volume-long footnote about the history of rationality. So my method for finding an original topic for a Ph.D. thesis was to rummage through journals that had no connection to music. This led me to the diffusion of innovations. The classic study concerns the decision of farmers in Iowa to plant hybrid corn. The remoteness of the topic was the quality that most appealed to me.

From the beginning of my quest I knew that many sociologists who investigate the diffusion of innovations are applied researchers motivated by a desire to accelerate the acceptance of new inventions. It is rather easy in such cases to define what is new and to determine exactly when an individual adopts a product. Ideas are more subtle, because the line between the old and the new is so ambiguous, especially in the arts. There is no obvious line of progression. Dozens of precursors can be found for practically any artistic movement. Two British composers interest me in particular, Elizabeth Lutyens and Cornelius Cardew. Lutyens is the first British composer to be seriously influenced by Arnold Schönberg; Cardew is the first to follow John Cage.

In London I consulted nine composers, the traditional and the experimental, to test my ideas. When I inquire about the differences between innovators and early adopters, most of them reply that intuitively the distinction seems to be valid for contemporary music. But they disagree about what constitutes a true innovation and who should be considered an innovator. Their irreconcilable views about the fundamentals of my project convince me to abandon it and to grope for another topic. Geoffrey Bush was a scholar and composer who championed British music. His compositions are characterized by an appreciation for uncomplicated communication with audiences. In his interview with me he was remarkably indifferent to fashion and innovation.

> I admire Elizabeth Lutyens. I think she is a person of integrity who knew what she had to write and she wrote that way. That's what I think a composer should do. The fact that she was ignored ten years ago is as irrelevant as is the fact that she is in the public limelight now. She is a person of integrity. That's much more important than being an innovator.
>
> A real innovator in this country is Michael Tippett. I think he is a completely original mind. Original, not in any technical sense,

but a man who thinks everything out for himself, whose style has undergone the most enormous changes. He is forever changing. Some of it is the most fiendishly difficult music. He is very difficult to pigeonhole; a very strange and original mind.

Cornelius Cardew seemed to me, with due respect, an imitation Cage. Now he has renounced all this and become a henchman for Chairman Mao. If that's the way he feels, good luck to him. Who am I to crab what everybody else does? Who is the first person here to imitate Mendelssohn? Who was the first person to imitate Handel? Who either knows or cares!

In one very difficult piece Tippett attempts to convey the ecstasy of eternity, which is quite a subject! He has a complex mind like a jungle. Sometimes you get absolutely overgrown with all the junk there; but when you come out into a grove, it is marvellous. After the two lovers in *Midsummer Marriage* meet again, they sing and for about ten minutes there is real joy in Tippett's music. It bounds along. I find it very difficult to think of any twentieth-century music that is full of ecstasy. That is something so rare in contemporary music. Tippett is the sort of man I would regard as a real innovator. (July 11, 1974)

How can music progress in any real sense when the most old-fashioned of composers can be viewed as contributing something "new" to music?

Nikolaus Pevsner, one of England's best architectural historians and the author of erudite guides to the architecture of every county in the nation, claims that conservatism is a recurring but not a permanent characteristic of the visual arts in England. "If England seems so far incapable of leadership in twentieth-century painting, the extreme contrast between the spirit of the age and English qualities is responsible. Art in her leaders is violent today; it breaks up more than it yet reassembles. . . . England dislikes and distrusts revolutions. That is a forte in political development, but a weakness in art."[13] Pevsner's claim is not made dogmatically. He readily admits in *The Englishness of English Art* that there are a few notable exceptions, most obviously the sculptor Henry Moore.

I ask if Pevsner's statement applies to music. On this they seem to agree. English composers are obliged to work within the constraints imposed by the public's intellectual laziness and cautious moderation. But none of my interviewees is helpful in getting my research off the ground. They imply that musical organizations do not play a determining role in the public's rejection of the experimental. Public taste is the cause; musical organizations, like music itself, the result. But what, then, is responsible for public taste? Artistic conservatism becomes a trait of English character that defies rational explanation.

Francis Routh, whose compositions have been described as Stravinskian neoclassicism with English characteristics, was one of the founders in 1964 of the Redcliffe Concerts of British Music. His opinions on the role of institutions in shaping public taste are typical of other interviewees.

> There is a great force of conservatism in this country which just doesn't want to know about artists and intellectuals. When I suggested [to you] that William Glock [head of music at the British Broadcasting Corporation] had done a great deal of harm, along with a great deal of good, what I meant was that he failed to take into account the nature of the people he was dealing with. Otherwise, one simply breeds reaction. That's exactly what has happened. I think the harm that William Glock has done is that he has bred great hostility to his ideas by not taking into account the nature of the English character.
>
> I think in a way Elizabeth Lutyens has done the same. I'm not saying she would have had greater success if she had watered down her ideas. Maybe she wasn't entitled to success. I don't know. What I know of her music suggests to me a sort of crusader rather than a composer. She was blazing a trail. She wasn't creating music.
>
> Do you know the song "O Saison, O Chateaux?" That's one of her highlights. In my opinion a composer is not a crusader. You have to, as it were, take these influences and filter them through your creative mind and use what you wish to and reject the rest. That's exactly what Stravinsky did. I think it is perhaps what Lutyens hasn't done. (July 8, 1974)

♦ ♦ ♦

I would not have dared ask the English composer Brian Ferneyhough for an interview if I had known anything about him. But Paul gives me few options. During the 1974 music festival in Royan, Paul insists that I not let the opportunity of collecting information for my thesis slip away. Ferneyhough is my pick only because he is one of the few invited composers who is a native speaker of English. I know absolutely nothing about his music beyond the information printed in the program. Ferneyhough's frankness in disclosing embarrassing information makes this the most emotionally compelling of all of my interviews with English composers. At the end I ask him why he is so cooperative. "You had enough interest to ask," he says. "People usually don't. I am a person who likes—I am being quite honest now—who likes the confirmation of being asked [for interviews] because I am always insecure enough to need that.... I am a person who will never succeed in things like interviews or press conferences because I always place myself so much publicly in question."

Ferneyhough thinks my understanding of innovators is simplistic. Composers who synthesize popular trends may be professionally isolated as well, for instance Jean Barraqué. Even Marcel Duchamp despite associating with fellow artists was "isolated in his head." Ferneyhough studied with Lennox Berkeley at the Royal Academy in London, but he insists that all teacher and student managed during composition lessons was to play Bach duets on the piano. Berkeley examined his compositions only once and then did not catch his intentions. It begins to dawn on me that the teacher-student relationship, which seems so simple and direct, is more complicated than I had anticipated. An educator's legacy to the next generation may be oblique, open to multiple interpretations, or of no consequence.

Ferneyhough begins to talk about the Birmingham School of Music, calling it a dreadful factory for the mass production of bad school teachers.

I was of course very militant in those days and as a composer I was laughed out of court by all and sundry as I had been at school.

At the age of 16 I had a dramatic experience. There was an old record of part of Varèse's *Octandre*. You perhaps know the piece. Magnificent work. This was the first dissonant composition I ever heard in my life and I have never forgotten it. I listened to this record for three solid days until it was worn out. I sat in school during the dinner breaks and every time no one else was there I played this record obsessively. It was only about seven minutes of music. It wasn't even the whole piece. It was an old history of music collection. And I just sat and listened to this fantastic piece of music. I didn't understand a damned thing about it. I only knew that this was it. This was music.

For days and days I sat at the piano and played the most vile dissonances that I could possibly find. I'd play and play, hours and hours, the same chords until I had worked these ghastly diatonic chords out of my head.... This time my career was decisively influenced I think in a very definite direction....

Following this is a discussion of Ferneyhough's complex relationship with two teachers, Ton de Leeuw and Goffredo Petrassi. Although he is willing to talk about these experiences in detail, this information, is not flattering, particularly for someone who at the time is himself teaching music. With Klaus Huber, Ferneyhough managed to establish a relationship that was much more constructive.

Ferneyhough: I met Klaus Huber at the Gaudeamus Foundation in '68, the first year I was there. He struck me then in a curious way as a very gentle and very saintly man. At the time we had a misunderstanding. My music, for completely irrelevant reasons, seemed to him to have a great deal in common with his own. This has been the source of fruitful misunderstandings ever since.

Riggins: What did Huber think you had in common?

Ferneyhough: We had a certain very tight structuralism in small movements which were connected together. . . .

I came from Schönberg-Webern mixtures. I developed the most incredibly one-sided complex technique at this stage of composition. There was a megalomaniac length of pieces and intricate developments. One or two motives, I suppose, would be ultimately derivable from the aesthetics of Boulez, although at that stage I didn't really know much about his compositional techniques. I had seen the scores, looked at them totally unintellectually, and thought this was nice. I tried something similar.

Klaus Huber's music has gone in the direction of a sort of aesthetic mysticism. He wants to say things about time, about the human experience in the face of eternity. The personality as it's given in a moment, for instance in relation to the horrors of war in his piece *...inwendig voller Figur...*, based on a Dürer woodcut which sort of prefigures atomic war. His violin concerto, *Tempora*, is a piece based upon growth out of nothing. It's a mystic principle of sound. Stones are rubbed and banged together. This is gradually extended into long notes and into Gregorian chant at the end. A great score.

He thought at this time that I had the same spiritual attitudes. But I don't. I am totally irreligious. I am a person who is perhaps obsessed with a certain dry pedanticism which contrasts with the wilder side and the megalomaniac side. It is by juxtaposing these two extremes that for me any form of creative activity is possible. . . .

...I try to write music which is totally hermetically closed within its self, a closed universe within which a person may discard his earlier personality, his earlier preconceptions and absorb these totally illogical sets of presuppositions which I present to him. It's like a labyrinth. It works on so many different levels. One can choose in which direction he moves within this labyrinth of possibilities.

Riggins: From what you say none of your teachers had an influence upon your compositions?

Ferneyhough: Yes. Klaus Huber has had an effect upon my compositions in that he was the first person who ever encouraged me to keep on composing at a very late date indeed.

Riggins: But did Huber direct your interests in any way or were they already formed?

Ferneyhough: He directed my interests in no way whatsoever. I was a terrible pupil because I always copied out my pages in neat script before I took them to him. So I couldn't possibly alter anything as a consequence of what he said. Every week I would go with some nice new pages. He would say: "Ah…yes…well…yes. Yes. Explain me that. Explain me that. How does that go? Yes. Yes." And then we talked about something totally different. It was very stimulating. What could he say? He couldn't say: "Well, that doesn't work. That doesn't work." If he did, I would say: "It's too late. It's there now." (March 26, 1974)

◆　◆　◆

Paul improvises a new ballet which ends by tossing a newspaper in my lap. It's called "Home Delivery!"

◆　◆　◆

On a rainy Sunday afternoon Paul and I go to the Tate Gallery in London to what we conclude is an over-publicized exhibition of modern British art. A sidewalk near the Tate Gallery is peppered with manhole covers. Paul imagines that the manhole covers and the bit of surrounding concrete are historic paintings—the concrete with a few squiggles, Rococo; a cover whose decoration has been worn away by pedestrians, Impressionist. Just before it starts to rain again we sit in Green Park where Paul, alluding to my hobby of collecting Queen Victoria memorabilia, says I had "brainwashed" him into having a nightmare last night that he was cooking for Queen Victoria. Some of the magnificent trees in the park are dying, marked for future destruction with an X, unorthodoxly interpreted by Paul as a multiplication sign. At the edge of Hyde Park we walk past a group of Sunday painters and souvenir vendors. The "Tateless Gallery," he says.

On the way home Paul expresses what I am thinking. It was a depressing day, but it would have been much worse alone.

◆ ◆ ◆

"You look like a little cow that can't find any passing trains to watch," Paul says one night in a gay bar, noticing how impatient I look.

◆ ◆ ◆

A flashback to 1972. Paul and I are in Europe making plans for a year-long visit to the Netherlands which will allow us to spend weekends and holidays in Paris. One of Paul's friends, an art historian, has a weekend retreat on a hill overlooking the village of Hausen im Tal in Baden-Württemberg. With only a little imagination, Jürgen's centuries-old house might be seen as an ideal setting for a low budget vampire film. The medieval castle on the property has fallen into ruins, now nothing more than a few collapsed walls. Originally the home of the estate's gamekeeper, Jürgen's house sits in isolation near a precipice. Inside are a rare antique tile stove and symbols of violent excess—perhaps as many as two dozen mounted deer antlers. At night, the darkness would alarm the faint-hearted. From the windows hardly any reminder of civilization is visible except for a distant string of lights. They illuminate a miniature golf course. The art historian resents this frivolous intrusion into his lofty isolation.

Past residents had more serious preoccupations when they were surveying the scenery. It was in this hideout that the philosopher Martin Heidegger sought refuge at the end of the Second World War, anticipating that any day the Allied troops would drive up the winding road to arrest him for his Nazi sympathies.

◆ ◆ ◆

A message from Paul, written while he is travelling by himself establishing contacts for his Circus of the Century at the Berlin Festival:

> I love you so much, my toad, and I feel so close to you, even at a distance, like now, that to write to you is a painful experience. It makes the separation more concrete, more objective. That is precisely what I deny by having you always present to my mind, by emitting little "ploops" when I return home as if you were here. To be away from you like this is always a test for my inner balance. I feel as stupid and incomplete as half an apple. Truly it makes me

cry to experience the distance of a letter and I have to stop. Your toad, Paul. (August 15, 1977)

In the homespun baby talk that Paul and I use, like all happy lovers, "ploop" means: hello, goodbye, thank you, no thanks, come here, hey, look at this and, don't act so foolish. Among the indispensable possessions which I transported to Toronto when I moved there in 1969 was my pet guinea pig, named after the muppet character Miss Piggy. Guinea pigs have a whole repertory of sounds but the most endearing is the little squeal that sounds like a whistling tea kettle. How do they learn so easily to recognize the sound of the refrigerator door opening? Because their squeal is so difficult to imitate, the parody Paul and I make evolved into an easily vocalized "ploop."

◆ ◆ ◆

A fragment from a letter written at Burg Wartenstein, near Vienna, where Paul is attending an anthropological conference:

There is nothing which I wish more now—so intensely—than you being here because it is beautiful, quiet, luxurious. You would fit so well in this castle. I can almost see you, where you would like to sit for reading, or run, or the people you would like to talk to. (August 28, 1977)

◆ ◆ ◆

At home, seated at the dinner table, the irrepressible little mouse dances with one of his "belles gambêêtttes" and one arm, then bobbing his head, to Tchaikovsky's *1812 Overture*.

◆ ◆ ◆

The juggler Christian Marin worries that Paul might be a lawyer when they meet for the first time. Dressed in a suit and tie, Paul has travelled to Rheims to meet Christian and finds him practising in a gymnasium. But Christian is pleased when he learns the purpose of Paul's visit, the first time a circus impresario has gone out of his way to recruit him. Toly Dedessus le Moutier, one of a team of foot jugglers called the Castors, had suggested to Paul that Christian might be ideal for The Circus of the

Century. Christian has artistic aspirations. In the ring he uses the more exotic name Chris Christiansen. Paul already had some impression of Christian because we had seen him juggle at Annie Fratellini's circus. Christian and Paul chat so long that evening, a night of summer thunderstorms, that Paul misses his train back to Paris.

Alexandre Bouglione and Christian Marin perform as a team on the sidewalk at Saint-Germain-des-Prés.[14] Bouglione does a simpler version of an act he presented at the Cirque de Paris. Dressed in tights decorated like a Ballets-Russes costume for Nijinsky, Bouglione balances on a free-standing ladder to an excerpt from Stravinsky's ballet *The Rite of Spring*. Christian says that as a juggler working on the sidewalk in good weather he can earn 500 francs a day. Many nights, though, he has no place to sleep other than in his van.

Christian avoids the security of a stable personal life. In that sense, he embodies the romantic ideal of an itinerant circus performer. He invites Paul and me to dinner at a neighbourhood restaurant, paying with 190 one-franc coins collected through an afternoon of juggling. The method of payment is a bit outside the norm for the classy environment. It amuses the waiter.

◆　◆　◆

Although Christian knew better than anyone that his juggling act was not perfect, he was reasonably satisfied until Alexandre Bouglione called him a "whore." Christian was shocked that Bouglione would be critical just because he often smiled to the public. Bouglione then told him about Jean Genet's essay "The Tightrope Walker," which has had an impact on Christian's concept of his act. If a reader substitutes "ball" or "club" for the word "high wire" in Genet's essay, many of his ideas will be applicable to juggling, even though few jugglers are going to flirt with death.

Genet takes, at best, a minor art form and through poetry endows it with heroic stature. The tightrope walker enacts dreams which will cause others to dream. In the circus ring where dust can be transformed into flecks of gold he is a privileged being because of the delicate self-discipline the constraints of the wire impose. The public frightened by danger looks away. The tightrope walker is not accorded the respect he deserves. Genet recommends that the tightrope walker dress in the daytime like a dirty hobo in order to elevate his status during his evening performance. His costume should be chaste but provocative, the makeup outrageous, to call attention to the fact that sane people would not do this for a living. "Don't dance for us but for yourself," Genet writes. "We came to the Circus not to see a whore but a solitary lover pursuing his image that flees and vanishes.... It is this solitude that will fascinate us."[15]

◆ ◆ ◆

Out of the darkness a whimsically dressed young man emerges, walking along Boulevard Saint-Germain with a cello, a chair, a trunk and miniature cages filled with white rats. He is dressed in a red braided jacket that resembles a second-hand band uniform; on his back is a huge cone-shaped tail, a sort of cornucopia straightened at the end. He exaggerates his eccentricity by stooping and tilting his head to one side. He and his female partner attach a rope between a tree and a picturesque antique street light. Even before he announces the show a crowd forms, puzzled by his costume and the white rats, whose cages look like miniature circus wagons. Balancing on a free-standing ladder, he introduces himself.

He calls himself Monsieur Branlotin, Prince of Crimea. Perhaps in English he might call himself something like Mr. Beatoffsky, since his name is derived from the slang word for masturbation. He aggressively banters the public, "Close up that gap. There's a draft!" To discourage onlookers from giving small change he says, "The rats don't like yellow coins…except for ten franc coins of course." To people who drift away without paying during the show he shouts, "Say goodbye when you leave!"

This little sidewalk show consists of acts that technically speaking are simple, but they are presented with a sense of the theatrical which even the best circuses rarely attain. It is not, of course, that easy to balance on a free-standing ladder; however, a real acrobat would be able to perform such feats, which Monsieur Branlotin cannot do, as cross over the ladder or stand on his/her hands on the top rung.

The first act, "Zoé the Sidewalk Spider," consists of a female dancer using her arms as another set of legs. Then "three brothers of Crimea" (that is three rats) perform animal acts normally associated with large animals. On a tabletop they jump from stool to stool, leap over objects, even jump through a miniature flaming hoop. They crawl along a sus-pended rope. If they hesitate or go in the wrong direction Monsieur Branlotin has a tiny whip to discipline them. One "brother" climbs a small ladder Monsieur Branlotin balances on a knife held between his teeth. Another pulls a cart by a collar around its neck.

The common lion act in which a trainer puts his head in the animal's mouth is reversed. "La princesse Kéké, la plus tendre, la plus amoureuse va recevoir le baiser de son père, le grand Branlotin." Mr. Branlotin thrusts the rat's head in his mouth and walks around the circle of spectators.

And then there is the stunt which I won't watch. "Et maintenant, public, on va passer enfin aux choses sérieuses avec Trestac, l'acrobate, le dernier acrobate qui nous reste. Découvrez-vous pour le saut de la mort. C'est bien des rats. C'est pas du caoutchouc." After asking the public to remove their hats in honour of the rat, Branlotin throws it high up into the air and catches it as it falls.

Zoé dances again—this time gesturing like a bird to a cello accompaniment played by Monsieur Branlotin. He requests a woman to come forward from the audience in order to make her a "Princess of Crimea." To achieve such honour she has to remove his boots so the finale can begin. Bare-footed, he balances on the tightrope. The young tree quivers: "Circus performers and trees cannot thrive at the same time. You have to choose. It's a crucial time for ecologists!" Balancing on one foot on the rope, he plays the cello while Zoé twirls a flaming baton.

◆ ◆ ◆

At a sidewalk café not far from the Montparnasse Tower, Paul, I and Christian Marin have taken shelter behind the glass that protects diners from the spring rain. The lunchtime crowd is starting to wander back to work. Paul and Christian are captivated by the kind of shop talk only circus fans and performers understand.

Being unemployed this winter (1977), Christian has had time to learn two new circus acts. One is the Washington trapeze; the second, an act which does not have a technical name as far as I know, consists of walking up and down a free-standing ladder while balancing a sword on a knife held in the mouth. Tomorrow Christian is leaving with a new circus which Alexandre Bouglione and the Pauwels family are establishing. Christian will be one of the stars of the new show. He says Bouglione calls him "my only performer" because everyone else in the show is related to the Bougliones.

The risks are real. One minute Christian emphasizes the humane decency of Alexandre Bouglione and Pepette Pauwels; the next minute he threatens to desert if the venture turns out badly. Christian is going to drive out of Paris tomorrow with only 100 francs, approximately twenty dollars, not enough to pay for gasoline if Bouglione does not lend him some money. (At least Christian's bank account is not empty.) Christian has not signed a contract with Bouglione, whom he considers a friend. Money should not interfere with friendship, he says.

The next day Paul seems depressed. At first, he says it is due to the wind and rain. Later, he confesses that it is because he wishes he could leave with the circus and experience once more the excitement of touring around France with a troupe of acrobats, clowns and trained animals.

◆ ◆ ◆

Christian is back in a week. He angrily tells us the management did not live up to his principles. The weather was nasty and the show opened in a recklessly competitive situation, a festival where Bouglione and Pauwels had to compete with other circuses. Christian found himself treated more like an employee than a friend. He abruptly left, as he had threatened. Bouglione himself soon returns to the sidewalk, a sure sign that the circus folded shortly after losing its star.

Luckily, Christian has found another job. He juggles and presents a Washington Trapeze act at the Cirque Aligre, the new circus of Monsieur Branlotin and Bartabas. Christian was already acquainted with Branlotin and his friends and appreciates what they are doing with circus traditions, although he finds it odd. "Plus la bohême que le cirque," he complains.

Christian chose this itinerant life. For that reason his experiences are somewhat different from those of many of the offspring of old circus families. The more common pattern is for a circus career to be imposed on children. Even in adult life they often have no choice but to stifle their individuality for the sake of the family which works as a team under the authority of an elder. Christian does not suffer from the sadness and ambivalence that arises from such family repression.

◆ ◆ ◆

Only after six false starts—a halting, zigzagging, meandering, skipping trail—do I finally decide to write a musical counterpart to Harrison and Cynthia Whites' *Canvases and Careers*. Over a period of about a year I have written six proposals, excluding my interviews with British composers, for a thesis on four different topics. All are about some aspect of musical innovation: the diffusion of chance and indeterminate techniques of composing, which would have dealt in particular with the influence of John Cage on modern music; a comparison of the career patterns of three experimental composers (Ives, Varèse and Cage) with the careers of three of their traditional contemporaries; the reception in England and France of the music of four innovative composers (Wagner, Schönberg, Cage and Stockhausen); the conservatism of British music between 1880 and 1939. In the opinion of my formal adviser all of the proposals are unacceptably superficial. I have continued seeing him because I feel other professors take their role as adviser too casually and that if I worked with them I would discover midway through my research that it was impossible to finish. No one at the University of Toronto is an authority on the sociology of classical music or the fine arts, specialties which are poorly defined in the profession.

Writing an institutional history of nineteenth-century French music might seem to be an obvious topic. My adviser mentioned *Canvases and Careers* the first time we talked. It was probably the only book in the field he had ever read. My resistance for such a long time was due to my poor knowledge of French and my low opinion of nineteenth-century French music, which is shared by most classical musicians. "Music suited for evening dress," Berlioz complained, "soothing, slightly dramatic in tone, but simple and colourless, with no unusual harmonies, unwonted rhythms, strange forms or unexpected effects. . . ."[16]

◆　◆　◆

Perhaps 150 people, including the high wire artist Philippe Petit, gather to watch Christian perform at his customary spot beside Les Deux Magots. I was naively apprehensive when I used to worry about the safety of Petit in the summer of 1970 as he crept across a tightrope between two trees along Saint-Germain, maybe twelve feet above the ground. He later walked between the two towers of Notre Dame Cathedral and between the twin skyscrapers of the former World Trade Center. Petit compliments Christian for juggling four ping pong balls with his mouth. Christian reacts by thinking to himself that praise for one trick means the rest are unsatisfactory. Christian brashly addresses Petit as *tu*. The celebrity responds with the more distant *vous*.

I have not said enough about Christian's asceticism. He criticizes shows which cater to spectators but are not physically difficult. His preference for the apparently effortless and the understated, shows decontaminated of vulgarity and gaudiness, entangles him with the meddling rascals who own circuses. He would rather risk a row or as a last resort work alone on the street than compromise.

Christian refrains from speaking to sidewalk spectators, generally saying nothing more than "à votre bon coeur" at the end of his act. He has the urge to jest with spectators like Monsieur Branlotin, but it makes him feel awkward. At the conclusion of his show, he aristocratically waits for spectators to come to him. As soon as the first one has stepped forward Christian begins to circulate through the crowd with his hat.

Here is an outline of Christian's juggling act as you might have seen it in circuses and nightclubs circa 1977. On Parisian sidewalks the show was similar but the amount of time devoted to some of the tricks would have differed. The third component (due to wind) and numbers six and seven (due to the constraints of time) were not normally performed outdoors.

(1) Juggling with three, then five balls, using a succession of different movements. (35 seconds)

(2) The juggler balances on his head on top of a pedestal while simultaneously circling rings which are suspended from his ankles and juggling three balls in his hands in this upside-down position. (30 seconds)

(3) Juggling with four ping pong balls using the mouth to propel and catch them. (60 seconds)

(4) Standing on his feet, the juggler throws a soccer ball into the air with one foot and catches it on the nape of his neck, then he allows the ball to run along his spine and the back of his legs while moving into a handstand position. He stops the ball on the sole of one of his feet while balancing on his right hand, holding his left hand vertically against his body. (40 seconds)

(5) Juggling with four clubs, then varied movements with three clubs. (120 seconds)

(6) Eight rings are made to gyrate around his arms and one leg, while he stands on the other leg, and balances a rotating ball on the tip of a rod held in his mouth. (35 seconds)

(7) Starting in a vertical position with a soccer ball between his legs, the juggler propels the ball into the air by making a somersault and then catches the ball on a stick held in his mouth. (5 seconds)

♦ ♦ ♦

Historians believe that Place Saint-Germain-des-Prés is the spot where Camulogenus, chieftain of the tribe of the Parisii, assembled his troops in 52 BC to defend Paris against Caesar's lieutenant Labienus. The appearance of the square today dates mostly from the nineteenth century, but the original church was begun in the middle of the sixth century. Having defeated the Visigoths in Spain, King Childebert I brought back from Saragosa, as war booty, the tunic of Saint Vincent. The Bishop of Paris, Germain, convinced the king to construct a basilica to house the relic in the fields outside the walls of Paris. Thus the name Saint Germain of the Fields. The basilica was consecrated on December 23, 558, and is supposed to have been a remarkable building decorated with mosaics and a gold-leaf roof. A monastery and vast properties were attached to the basilica. The site became a popular location for short pilgrimages from Paris. The basilica served as the necropolis for Merovingian kings. However, the basilica was destroyed in the ninth century by Norman invaders. The church was rebuilt between the years 990 and 1014. The bell tower which dominates the square today is the oldest surviving tower in Paris, although the steeple is nineteenth century.

Throughout the Middle Ages buildings continued to be erected on the grounds of the monastery. One of these, the Chapel of the Virgin was a "Gothic jewel" that resembled Saint-Chapelle, according to the Paris historian Jacques Hillairet. The basilica itself was enlarged. The church today is basically Romanesque in design but the choir is Gothic. At the height of the monastery's intellectual influence its population may have reached 10,000. The library possessed an estimated 50,000 books and 7,000 manuscripts. However, the monastery was closed during the Revolution, one of many measures taken to restrict the power of the Catholic Church. In 1793 the refectory began to serve as a storehouse for gun powder, the Chapel of the Virgin a storehouse for charcoal and the basilica a refinery for saltpetre. On August 19, 1794, the gun powder exploded. The explosion and the resulting fire left the complex in ruins. Eight years of water from the refinery weakened the foundations of the basilica and portions of the building, notably the two bell towers, had to be demolished in the early nineteenth century. Vestiges of the Chapel of the Virgin are exhibited at the Musée de Cluny.

◆　　◆　　◆

It had never occurred to me that completing a Ph.D. thesis would require so much determination. Of the winter of 1977 I have hardly any unique memories except watching the snow fall one lovely night on the Champs-Elysées and the Musée de Cluny, remnants of the Roman baths in Paris. If the work required nothing more than reading in the French Archives or the National Library from 9 o'clock until 5 o'clock, I would enjoy it. Gathering scattered information about the social history of nineteenth-century French music is a pleasure. I am often discovering basic facts most graduate students in music would already know. But I also have to devote the evening to writing, if there is any hope of finishing in time. When I embarked on this trial, I had read only three books in French in my entire life, one being the children's edition of Paul's *Le cirque est mon royaume*. Paul claims to be playing the role of the "grumping rod" for my thesis, which he christened "Scores and Scorns." I feel I have a right to expect that my spirit will haunt the Palais-Royal on cloudy, grey afternoons. Nearly every afternoon I take a break at about 3 o'clock and stroll through the garden to join the old ladies who feed the pigeons and sparrows.

◆　◆　◆

Paul: "You have hair like a grasshopper, ears like an earthworm, ladybug eyelashes, a butterfly mustache, a spider nose and caterpillar eyes."

◆　◆　◆

As Paul's novel *Les demoiselles* draws to a close, the main protagonists find themselves on a boat travelling to Tangier. One evening as a way to kill time they decide that each person will tell a story. Through a lottery that consists of choosing among toothpicks of different lengths, the ship captain is selected as the first speaker. This is the story he tells.

In primordial times the gods and giants enjoyed playing handball:

...naturally the gods always won. They penalized the giants each time they lost. The giants settled without complaining because they were good-hearted souls. One day after the giant Tilbury missed the ball, the gods asked him to create the world. He took an old ball, that was no longer used, and carefully rounded it by turning it in the palms of his hands; then he planted trees and, last, created animals and people. The gods congratulated him and decided from then on to play only with this ball, because they were greatly amused to see people running with frightened expressions each time they twirled it in space. . . .

One day while the gods and the giants rested from a stormy match, it happened that Tilbury, who had grown fond of his work, thought of taking a close look at his creatures, and raised the earth to his big face, blew on the clouds that surrounded it and noticed, with surprise, that the people appeared distressed and frightened. He immediately felt great sadness and decided to let them participate in the general jubilation, but as he had no way of talking to them, he decided to communicate his joy by sharing a good laugh with them. And Tilbury, right next to the earth, began to laugh, to laugh, to laugh, until he was out of breath. The gods and the other giants circled around him, wondering what could be the reason for his happiness. And when he explained it to them, they all moved closer to him out of curiosity. But everyone burst out laughing, ridiculing him, because the tremors of the giant's laughter had only increased the misery of the people: the surface of the globe was completely cracked, dented, torn apart. Those people who had not perished in the earthquake were crying, holding onto each other, seized by violent fear. This spectacle deeply moved the heart of the good giant; he started to cry out of compassion and his tears of love streamed down on the earth. But the mockery of the gods and the other giants increased when they saw what a catastrophe the pity of their creator was for the people. Those who had not perished under the weight of boulders or in gaping cracks were now carried away and drowned in the flood of his tears. The beautiful jewel of the gods had become a shapeless ball bristling with points that hurt their hands, all wet, with big spots that made it sticky and slippery, without speaking of the rotten odour that started to be released. Everyone made fun of Tilbury without tact and did not cease making all kinds of sarcastic remarks, and even the female giants, who spent their time plucking the geese that the goddesses roasted, came closer, drying their big hands on their aprons. They added to the mocking remarks of their husbands. The wife of Tilbury was the most impertinent of all. The good giant became mad at himself, ashamed, in despair at the thought that they would continue to say he was unintelligent and awkward. In a gesture of despair, he threw the earth so far into space that it disappeared from the eyes of everyone and no one ever saw it again.[17]

Paul distances himself from the moral of this story by having the captain state it in a manner that tends to undermine its authenticity and credibility. According to the captain, he heard the story from a grandfather who enjoyed travelling. The captain seems to know nothing else about its origins. The grandfather always concluded the story by saying: "That's why, even if you are a giant or a god, never look for ways to save humanity."[18]

◆ ◆ ◆

The serious and the satirical can be confused so easily in *Les demoiselles* that Paul's personal values are difficult to decipher. Paul claims that the captain's story illustrates his personal philosophy. His actual behaviour, however, tends to be the opposite, at least from my experience. Paul always attempts to assist friends and acquaintances even if they oppose his ideas or show little appreciation, which is frequently the case. Examples include his excessive concern about my welfare ("The things I have to read," he reacted. "You never think it's excessive at the time!"); his commitment to exhibiting untested artists at Victoria College; and his offer to introduce Ron Bowen to some famous Parisians so that he could establish a reputation more quickly by painting their portraits. (Never a social climber, Ron declined the offer.)

Paul tried to help Christian Marin by introducing him to Alain Ohrel, a childhood friend who at the time was "Secrétaire Général des Hauts-de-Seine," a high-level administrator in the French bureaucracy. Paul thought that if Ohrel met Christian, he would be willing to hire him to entertain people at official functions. One of Ohrel's brothers-in-law is a daredevil who flies hang-gliders. So Ohrel could talk about the circus with some understanding, despite its distance from his own life.

◆ ◆ ◆

Paul gave copies of his books to Christian including one with the dedication: "Pour Chris Christiansen qui a de toute éternité sa place dans le Panthéon du cirque."

◆ ◆ ◆

Among the handful of people who offered advice on my thesis, Howard Brotz was not the most active, but he did play a key role during the painful and endless stage of writing proposals. Brotz was an authority on Jewish culture whose best-known book is probably *The Black Jews of Harlem*. Despite having only a layman's knowledge of classical music, Brotz made me realize that I did not know enough about any of my topics to draft a proper research proposal. He suggested that at first I forget altogether about proposals and concentrate on writing a conventional history of the musical enterprises during whatever era interests me. I should not worry about whether my ideas will be considered history or sociology. There is no reason why I must have a well-articulated theory to test before I begin the research. A theoretical framework will gradually emerge in the process of writing.

My study of sociology has been plagued by people who insist that sociology should be modelled after the natural sciences. If you cannot measure a phenomenon, your knowledge is meagre, they claim. Brotz, in contrast, was an advocate of informal ethnography and historical research, probably because of his training at the University of Chicago in the 1950s. In the ethnographic tradition emphasized at Chicago, researchers were supposed to obtain information by interacting with ordinary people in everyday situations. Brotz's advice to ethnographers was as simple as "just go and talk to people." Ethnography requires tact and patience rather than methodological rigour. Informants gradually disclose information that is personal and potentially discrediting. Their insights—with all their ambiguities and contradictions—cannot be conveyed in a brief interview with a total stranger, certainly not through a multiple-choice questionnaire. Chicago School ethnographers had to be flexible intellectually, to be willing to change the theme of their research in mid-stream depending upon the level of cooperation from informants.

Howard Brotz's obituary contains a statement about his character which, I think, parallels the advice he gave students: "[His] second characteristic was his remarkable ability to reformulate and reconceptualize the research all the while maintaining that he had not veered from its original course. It was his absolute unpredictability, along with his talent and aptitude for tying together seemingly unrelated strands of the study, which made the work both enjoyable and, at times, frustrating."[19]

♦ ♦ ♦

Almost every night after working until 11:00 o'clock Paul and I go to a neighbourhood bar. In Toronto it's often a piano lounge on the fifty-second-storey of a nearby skyscraper that has one of the best panoramic views in town. Sitting there quietly beside a couple of large semi-tropical plants, I was thinking to myself that I was aging. Paul could not have realized this.

At that precise moment he said, "Among these plants you look like a beauty painted by *le douanier* Rousseau."

♦ ♦ ♦

Sunday there is another crisis over my thesis. It has been a cold and rainy spring in Toronto. Worse yet, the libraries have started treating their patrons in an offhand manner by closing on Sunday. Studying in social isolation is intolerable. I am upset because I had planned to type a final version of one chapter but kept stumbling across awkward sentences. This thesis has wrecked my social life. There would be no reason to record any of these sad experiences, if Paul had not compensated by doing animal imitations all day long. As he said, "you could open a zoo with me!"

First, Paul is a "rock and roll fish." He lies on the floor on his stomach; feet together, slightly raised; his arms in the same position; and rocks forwards and backwards. He imitates the improbable "canard à sonnette" (the rattleduck). Paul waddles like a duck, holds his arms away from his body the way birds cool themselves, grasping in his mouth a key chain. I watch a "flying mermaid," a "nose-eating fish," and a whole series of nameless animals that Paul invents clutching in his mouth a folded newspaper to represent weird beaks and noses. Finally, a purring cat crawls across the floor to rub his head on my leg.

Despite all this, I continue to look so despondent that Paul claims I resemble a "frying catfish."

◆ ◆ ◆

Paul has left for six weeks in Europe while I remain in Toronto in order to work on my thesis. Referring to my benign attempts to cook stuffed tomatoes, he scribbles from Paris:

> My dearest Toad. It is not fun to travel without you. The closest I can feel to you is to do scrupulously what you asked me to do for your dissertation.
>
> I returned last night from Périgueux after three days of over-feeding and lonely walks in the city....
>
> I went to Saint Germain but Christian does not seem to be around this year. No Branlotin either.... I am trying to write down my paper! (at the Bureau d'accueil des professeurs d'universités étrangères). And I do not have the nice feeling of knowing that my toad is having his tea at La Chope and that I am going to see you in a moment. I will never go away for so long. I miss you so much. I am crossing the days one after the other as when I was in the army. There are 21 left.... I cannot wait until I am back home with my toad and his famous "tomates farcies." Lots of kisses, cuddlies, petites souris, ballets, belly dancing. Ploop! Ploop! I love you.

◆ ◆ ◆

Paul's "centre of gravity" at the University of Toronto is not the French department but Victoria College where he was first hired. Victoria College is a sedate institution. Its administrators are not shy about celebrating their ties with the English-Canadian establishment. By the time Paul retires, his career at Victoria will have spanned thirty-seven years. His presence there is an anomaly unless one sees employing him as an example of the English love of the eccentric. He says that because he never felt protected by any of the cliques at Victoria he "had to be on his toes all the time and work harder than other professors." He believes some of the staff showed subtle disdain for him until he received a Guggenheim Fellowship.

The person who is responsible for Paul coming to Canada is Alan Ross, who recommended that he be hired at Victoria College. Ross had an unusual background for a university French instructor. He excelled at golf, bridge and rifle marksmanship, and had a distinguished military career in World War II which included serving with Canadian military intelligence. Ross was also a skilled amateur pianist who liked to play both classical music and jazz for friends. His academic specialty was seventeenth-and eighteenth-century French literature, but he was known primarily as an entertaining teacher, translator and university administrator. In an interview with a campus newspaper Ross stated that in Paris he had been impressed by Paul skipping lunch in order to save money to buy books.

In 1960 Ross was staying in the apartment of Mlle. Marie-Louise Haumesser, 76 rue des Saint-Pères in the seventh arrondissement, where Paul had lived earlier. The rent was just beyond what Paul could manage and he had moved to a less expensive residence. Haumesser and her dinner guests appreciated Paul's circus stories and so he often returned for dinners. Ross described in a 1975 campus newspaper story how he

> …met this young guy in the French Army [actually the Air Force] who had lived at Mlle. Haumesser's a few years earlier when he was a student at the Sorbonne. He used to drop by for lunch or dinner from time to time. I got talking to him and I was really impressed with his scholarship. He'd passed his École Normale Superieure written exams but had missed one question on the orals. Damn hard exams, too. . . .
>
> The guy had a sense of humour. That's something you have trouble finding in French academics. They seem to get mouldy or something after awhile. The same may be true of *all* academics, I suppose. But Bouissac had a sense of humour. . . .[20]

Admittedly, there may be some unfairness in contrasting two Victoria faculty members, Paul Bouissac and Northrop Frye, but the differences are enlightening. Unlike so many literary specialists, Paul considers Frye a pompous monster of conventionality and conceit for allowing the New Academic Building, where he had his office, to be named after him. Frye also willingly posed for a bronze bust and at least three paintings, which were displayed on campus during his lifetime. This is in marked contrast to Paul's "anarchistic dealings with authorities" and his low opinion of all self-appointed elites, whether social or intellectual. Several other members of the staff at Victoria felt that the attention accorded Frye was excessive. The philosopher Francis Sparshott wrote on the cover of one of his books of poems that for years his office was directly underneath Frye's office but that nothing trickled down.

What to buy as a birthday gift for one of Victoria College's most esteemed retired women professors? After some deliberation, Paul purchases Chinese fans: "After all, they say her conversations are all hot air."

◆　◆　◆

Doug Martin wears some utterly worthless jewellery reflecting the taste of a cosmopolitan magpie. On a chain around his neck hangs an animal bone he found in Wales. A clear, spherical button he found in Switzerland is pinned on his T-shirt. It is fastened with a gold-coloured safety pin he picked up on a London sidewalk. On his jacket is a small mosaic pin left in his Toronto apartment by the previous tenants. Except for white shoes, he is dressed entirely in blue. Dark blue corduroy jeans, a dark blue T-shirt with a tiny insignia, a blue denim jacket. His T-shirt is too short and exposes his navel.

Doug is subletting Ron Bowen's studio this spring while Ron visits his family in Florida. Doug has just arrived from Bern where he lived in a commune. He talks about his experiences in Switzerland: the personality conflicts, the beauty of the countryside, the opening of an exhibition by H.R. Giger.

As a part of his service to Victoria College Paul has volunteered to help organize art exhibitions. Rather than hanging pictures in a conventional gallery-like setting, he uses the hallways of classroom buildings in order to reach those students who would not go out of their way to see an exhibition. Paul likes to discover the artists himself, the younger and more obscure the better. One of his discoveries is Doug Martin, whom he first met at an outdoor exhibition in front of Toronto city hall. Martin's style might be described as magic realism. In our Toronto apartment we have a double self-portrait of Doug, on one side of the canvas leaving for Europe, on the other side returning. He floats, standing unsupported in the sky. The trip has transformed him. He returns dishevelled, encircled by sea gulls, yet liberated and happy.

Paul succeeded in convincing Victoria College to commission from Doug a portrait of Canada's star literary scholar, Northrop Frye. Few other art lovers at Victoria would have advocated taking risks with a portraitist who had barely graduated from the Ontario College of Art. The picture is a floating image of Frye, who without the support of a chair sits in the sky above a desert landscape. In reference to the Beatles' song "Lucy in the Sky with Diamonds," the painting has come to be nicknamed "Frye in the Sky."

Doug wanted to avoid duplicating predictable formulas and conventional settings. From a practical point of view, posing Frye in a chair would have resulted in an image, he believed, that was too static. So Doug photographed Frye sitting outdoors on the steps of one of the Victorian relics on campus. Then back in the studio he transcended the old building. Doug was already making paintings that in some vague way might be considered spiritual: ethereal, floating images, which he compares to the dreams of surrealists; and Madonna-like pictures of his sister. The portrait of Frye combines both of these qualities. Doug relates it to the hippie ethos of the early 1970s rather than to Northrop Frye's scholarship. This imposing seated figure might suggest a medieval icon, a religious figure from the Renaissance or an antique god. The background was prompted in part by Doug's inexperience as a painter. While the desert landscape and sunset are dramatic and moody, they were relatively easy to paint in the form of sterile silhouettes. "I wanted to give the portrait a twist. I guess inadvertently I gave it some symbolism. But I don't know that I thought too far into the symbolism."[21]

♦ ♦ ♦

Outwardly, we seem unrelated: the cheerful, spirited Frenchman; and the American who looks as though he took Saint-Saëns' alleged remark about performing music to heart—"Surtout pas d'émotion." But some strangers mistake us for brothers and our birthdays are one day apart (January 16 and 17). Since Paul is twelve years older than me, we share the same astrological signs in both the Chinese and Western systems. Paul contrasts our dispositions by saying that he puts "sugar on my vinegar" and "honey on my thorny remarks to make them palatable." He actually appreciates the fact that I so often shoot down his ideas. It discourages self-centredness. Paul is the oldest child in his family; I am an only child. We both come from working-class backgrounds. The gist of our differences is that Paul is superficially outgoing but on a more private level withdrawn. If it is possible for me to correctly understand my own self, I would say that I am the opposite.

♦ ♦ ♦

Leo Delibe's "Passepied Number Six" from the collection *Six Dances in the Old Style* is a romanticized, nostalgic version of eighteenth-century music. You would expect Paul to prefer something more modern, but it was a piece he liked in the limited repertoire of Marie-Louise Haumesser.

Another jewel, whose title he has forgotten, was a piece of salon music by Benjamin Godard. Mlle Haumesser appreciated the kind of music that was popular in middle-class parlours at the turn of the century. She had somehow managed to inherit the piano of the statesman and soldier Maréchal Louis Hubert Lyautey, a key figure in pacifying and governing colonial Morocco who was noted for his tolerance and humanism. Despite Paul's judgment of Mlle. Haumesser as "ethnocentric and the epitome of the stupid French bourgeoisie," they had a warm relationship. In a book about lions which she presented to Paul, she labelled herself his "Old Parisian 'mother.'"

◆ ◆ ◆

Both Paul's mother, Marguerite, and his aunt, Raymonde, learned to play the piano well enough to perform for guests: Chopin's easier pieces; sentimental songs by Renaldo Hahn; waltzes by Strauss; and Paul's favourite, Albert Ketelbey's circus-like "In a Persian Market." They briefly gave him lessons when he was eight or nine years old. His mother did not have any patience; his aunt was a better teacher. He says he improvised at home for hours on end and that he once knew how to read music.

Partly in reaction to my disdain, he stopped improvising. He was making up variations on his own melodies, one melody in each hand, normally without a chordal accompaniment. Either the sustaining pedal was held too long, blurring the notes, and the soft pedal held so briefly that it had little effect or he used both pedals at once as a security blanket. Entire pieces were played mezzo-forte.

◆ ◆ ◆

Marshall McLuhan is not an authority on surrealism, but he is an appropriate speaker on the topic. His ideas about irrationality and non-linear thinking parallel those of the Surrealists and Dadaists. Paul managed to convince McLuhan to give a lecture at Victoria's Surrealist Day, an annual series of lectures, exhibits, films, demonstrations of automatic writing and collective art. The Surrealist Day was Paul's idea. It grew out of an interdisciplinary course which was also his initiative.[22]

McLuhan believes that highly rational thinking requires literacy. It began to be undermined in the 1950s when television became the public's preferred form of mass communication. Television and the face-to-face contact of oral cultures convey information in a similar manner. They reveal the subtleties of emotional expression that are poorly recorded in writing. This discourages critical reflection about the intellectual content of messages. Unlike a book—a relatively permanent object that can be consumed at a reader's own pace—television programs instantly disappear. For that reason they are more easily misperceived. McLuhan incorporates the technique of collage into academic discourse, thus creating a mosaic of incoherent statements. His disparate juxtapositions of unrelated ideas suggest widely diverse meanings to different readers.

On the same panel with McLuhan are two committed surrealist artists, Ludwig Zeller and his wife Susana Wald. Zeller and Wald are Chilean immigrants to Canada whom Paul met after their daughter enrolled in his surrealism course. They make enigmatic visual puzzles in the form of collages fabricated out of antique prints. For them, surrealism is a deadly serious matter. Paul deliberately places the artists and McLuhan on the same panel, anticipating that their opposing views may result in a lively discussion.

Overbearing and superficial, McLuhan lectures his audience, claiming surrealism has no legitimate claim to depict the truth about life. Generalizing too easily and too crudely, he seems to think that surrealism is merely a reflection of technological inventions and he questions its seriousness. In the process of formulating these ideas, he makes some minor historical errors.

Zeller and Wald are so outraged that they publicly declare they can no longer share the stage with McLuhan. They move to seats in the auditorium because they want to confront him face to face. Zeller, talking passionately in Spanish which his wife calmly translates into English, says that while McLuhan may be a famous intellectual, he is ignorant about surrealism.

Paul fears that things will soon go haywire. It occurs to him to ask someone in the audience to calm the atmosphere by playing the piano. The pianist is one of the few eccentrics on campus. Although conventionally dressed at the conference, he attracted attention a few days earlier in the music school where he appeared with one foot wrapped in a plastic bag, carried a ribbon in his mouth, and conversed with himself, interspersing British and French accents. While McLuhan is speaking, Paul has the pianist start playing unannounced. Although a mediocre musician, the pianist has the nerve to drown out someone of the stature of Marshall McLuhan. The panel ends unexpectedly when Paul has the lights turned off and begins to project a film by Buñuel.

That evening Paul gives a party at our apartment for some of the people involved in the day's activities. The Zellers and the McLuhans sit three or four feet apart politely ignoring each other.

◆ ◆ ◆

Every phase of my thesis *Institutional Change in Nineteenth-century French Music* was an ordeal, whether it was the sorcerer's insatiable demand for proposals or the two months of typing my voodooism. Only once in the last fifteen months did I see my adviser and that was to hand him a penultimate copy of the manuscript. "My strategy is to have as little to do with this thesis as possible," he's rumoured to have said at one point.

Both in Paris and in Toronto I was afflicted with classic symptoms of stress. Tackling an overly ambitious topic in a foreign language and compensating for an undistinguished graduate career was partly to blame. The thesis required hundreds of aspirins and thousands of cups of tea. I endured intense headaches, on two occasions lasting for a full week, which aspirin and tea could not cure. The slightest movement in the library would cause the back of my head to throb, but I could swim forty lengths in the university's competition-size pool without pain. As soon as I began dressing to go back to the library, the headaches returned.

In Toronto the thesis was finished in the spacious glass-walled reading room on the second floor of the Robarts Library. I enjoy working at "Fort Book" because of the inspiration of so many ambitious students. The library, however, looks as if the architects were preoccupied with planning defenses against protesting flower children.

Attending concerts and films was difficult because of the jealousy I felt towards other people's achievements—toward anyone's achievements. Books on topics unrelated to my work vexed me because I felt oppressed by too much information. I sought refuge in sleep. Never before had I experienced the desire of emptying my mind of all thought—just vegetating in the sunshine. I relinquished much of my social life. There were pains in my lower back which I finally realized were not the result of exercise, as I had thought at first, but from leaning forward at the typewriter.

◆ ◆ ◆

I find the defense of my thesis (January 17, 1980) annoying because no one is sufficiently informed about my topic to ask provocative questions. Most Ph.D. candidates must feel this way. For one brief period, we, the real experts, swagger because the information is at our fingertips. My ambition had been an evaluating committee composed solely of authorities on nineteenth-century French music—for a degree in sociology, let's not forget. My ideal external examiner would have been Jacques Barzun, the biographer of Berlioz. Instead, there is one musicologist, specializing in another country and another era, as well as six conventional sociologists. I am relaxed, though, because I know scheduling it is a sure sign there is a high probability of acceptance. Paul worried more than I did and got diarrhoea. He did not tell me he was going to the old Victorian house where the examination was held. I was surprised to see him sneaking along the corridor—between trips to the bathroom—as I sat in the hallway awaiting the committee's verdict.

Harrison White prefaces his comments on my thesis by writing: "I congratulate Mr. Riggins on his scholarship, assiduity and sensitivity in carrying through this ambitious study. I recommend that it be accepted, substantially as is. May I make my comments in the form of suggestions for where to go from here, towards possible future publication?" The socializing after the defense unearths a little Hoosier humour. Aware of my interest in southern Indiana history, White jokes that I appear to be a typical Hoosier. He imagines we are emotionally reserved but sentimental about the landscape of our state. Consequently, he thinks someone should undertake a special study of Indiana painters. "Residents of Indiana," he remarks, "tend to be so fond of the landscape of their state that if you dropped a Hoosier from an airplane, he would be able to say whether or not he had landed in Indiana. No one else would see the difference."

♦ ♦ ♦

From Harrison White's letter of recommendation, written on the stationary of Harvard University:

…In sum, I am testifying that Dr. Riggins would be a very valuable person to have as part of a research team. That can be extrapolated in many directions: for example, I would be very pleased to encounter a Riggins as an expert librarian or archivist to help me in some research. His very strengths in these directions make me less sure that he would be either very happy or successful in more mainline sociological research situations. The extreme care he took in censoring his claims inhibited his theoretical scope as a sociologist in his thesis, and I should say that would hold true in other situations from having listened to his ripostes during the oral exam. I should make it clear that it is not a matter of his being too diffident to assert his ideas; Riggins has quite enough strength of presence and stubbornness to put forward and support his ideas. . . .

♦ ♦ ♦

John Cage sits on a wooden bench in a lobby at the music school of the University of Toronto. He leans slightly forward in an accommodating manner, legs crossed at his knees, arms folded in his lap. He looks fragile and vulnerable, as though he has not dealt with journalists for years, but we both suffer from colds. Only once during our conversation (January 31, 1982) is there a hint of his wide, open-mouthed laugh. He seems to have aged considerably since I last saw him six years ago.

Cage's praise for Toronto is effusive. Claiming that he has visited a half-dozen times, he compliments the city's cosmopolitan character and its musical life. He even declares that he and the choreographer Merce Cunningham find more commitment to the fine arts in Toronto than in New York. It is Toronto that has the guts to give the first complete realization on stage of his piece *Roaratorio*. The concert will be in celebration of his seventieth birthday. The date of the concert is auspicious, the birthday of James Joyce. If this were not enough, the concert is supposed to be a tribute to Toronto's own Marshall McLuhan.

Cage complains to me about the abuse he received from the musicians of the New York Philharmonic, although this happened a long time ago:

> Leonard Bernstein gave my *Atlas Eclipticalis* seven-and-a-half minutes of rehearsal. And then the orchestra smashed the contact microphones each day and I had to replace them. Then, unashamed, they said "come back in ten years and we'll treat you better." It was fifteen years ago. They probably would treat me better now, but not much.
>
> I know now that if an orchestra rehearses a work seriously and for a sufficient length of time that the musicians, in spite of themselves, will become interested in the work just as the composer was. But they [the musicians of the New York Philharmonic] don't have enough time to become interested.

On the program of one concert in Toronto was the *Freeman Etudes*, pieces so difficult that they are rebellious even in the hands of virtuoso performers. Because such demands seem to contradict his earlier opinion that everyone is by nature a musician, irrespective of his or her level of skill, I ask him to justify the piece. He answers by relating the music to politics:

> I have the feeling that at this particular time everyone is surrounded with a sense of the impossibility of accomplishing what must be done if the environment and if society are going to continue. Even

Buckminster Fuller has recently written a book called *Critical Path* in which his optimism gives way to warning. The example of someone doing the impossible seems to me to be relevant to the world's situation in which we find ourselves. And that's why I made the *Etudes Australes* and the *Freeman Etudes*. If we can see someone doing what can't be done, then we, too, in our lives may do what can't be done instead of giving up.

The origin of *Roaratorio* was a suggestion made in the 1960s by Marshall McLuhan that Cage write music using the ten thunderclaps from Joyce's *Finnegans Wake*. The thunderclaps are 100-letter cryptograms that resemble sound poems. McLuhan thought they were obscure references to the thundering consequences of technological changes in society.[23] *Roaratorio* is a circus-like happening of sounds: environmental noise recorded in Ireland, portions of the novel read aloud by Cage, and live Irish folk music. I asked Cage what he finds inspirational in McLuhan's writings:

McLuhan's function was, it seems to me, that of a revelatory critic of the time. Many of his ideas corroborated what one experiences in an exploratory sense in making art and music. Other of his ideas, besides being corroborative, were revealing of possibilities he hadn't thought of. If you ask me to give you instances, I am not sure that I can, but I was able to feel stimulated by his work, particularly the very short piece that was printed in a magazine called *Location*.[24]

Cage seems unperturbed about the passing of the intoxicating spirit of musical innovation that characterized the 1960s:

I don't have the feeling that the times are conservative. I think there's both a great deal of interesting music being written and there's a lively interest among performers and listeners in it. I think if we are going to have any pessimism it is not in the field of art but in the field of politics and the treatment of the environment, the treatment of the world as a whole as I suggested earlier. There we are certainly lacking things, but art seems to me to be getting along fairly well. I have new ideas and I still have a good deal of energy. I receive more invitations to do things both from myself and from outside myself.

To anyone young and interested in the arts during the 1960s, the name John Cage has a special aura—he epitomizes the whole avant-garde movement. Even among us, however, his musical revolution has not progressed very far. We still seem to prefer the early pieces such as the *Sonatas and Interludes* in which he has neither abandoned intentionality nor discovered abundance, anarchy and the three-ring circus. The fact that so few listeners want to talk about their emotional reactions to the later works is to me a sign that Cage's ideas have failed musically. Cage can assert his individuality by abandoning choice in arranging sounds, but once that extreme position is taken in American music whoever else wants to use sounds in a Zen manner "to quiet the mind" is likely to be defined as an imitation John Cage.

My generation still seems to enjoy Cage's ideas more than the music. We're like one of his friends who reportedly shouted as she left in the midst of a purposely nonsensical Zen lecture: "John, I dearly love you, but I can't bear another minute."

◆ ◆ ◆

Incongruities. When Jörn visited Toronto, the incongruity he most appreciated was the trails of smoke rising from the roofs of ultramodern skyscrapers as if it was smoke from the crude fireplaces of another century. Michel Foucault appreciated the butch men with tight-fitting T-shirts that read "Our Lady of the Sorrows Swim Team."

◆ ◆ ◆

"You're like a little worm," Paul grumbles, " who lives in a pear and sticks his head out to say 'don't do that, don't do that, don't do that.' And then he crawls back in and goes to sleep."

◆ ◆ ◆

For me, it was the architect and painter Khoa Pham who first made sense out of hyperrealism. We were introduced at a dinner in Paris by our mutual friend Ron Bowen. Khoa judges realism from the vantage point of an artist who prefers abstract art but has never ceased making realistic drawings and paintings, especially as favours for friends. The passages I most appreciate in the tribute to Bowen, which Khoa and I co-authored in 1987, are the moments when the student is autobiographical.

A casual viewer presented with abstract and realist paintings by Ron Bowen would probably believe that they were the work of different artists. Yet there is a continuity between the two styles. The debt to abstraction in

Bowen's realist art is evident in the restricted symbolism and in the way objective reality is treated as abstract shapes and colours arranged in harmonious compositions. In his portraits Bowen gives equal importance to the figure and to the background. This interest in intricate patterns and objects, a preoccupation perhaps acquired during his training as a commercial artist, serves to accentuate the flatness of the picture plane, a primary issue in modernist art. From a distance these details are certainly recognizable objects, but up close they become configurations of non-representational hard-edge shapes, not unlike the controlled splatters of his abstract paintings. Sometimes backgrounds and accessories are more animated and detailed than faces. The carnival organ in his portrait of the cook Paul Bocuse is an example. The colourful organ is brightly lit while Bocuse's face is in the shadows. In other portraits Bowen's taste for complex patterns is shown by details such as palm fronds, shadows cast by foliage, Venetian blinds and intricate female clothing, all of which accentuate the abstract qualities of his compositions.

His concern for abstract principles in his realist work is also evident in the manner in which he frames his images. Bowen acknowledges that his awareness of composition in realist paintings developed only after painting abstracts. Judging from the collage of a piece of cloth, a chewing gum wrapper, an envelope and a leaf, composition was not emphasized in his commercial art courses, because the objects in the collage causally overlap each other. Bowen's realist paintings are classical in terms of composition. Pyramid compositions are used to structure individual and group portraits; centralized arrangements are used for still lifes; and strong geometric figures, such as rectangular fields, structure landscapes. Trees lose their distinctive characteristics and are stylized to the point of simply being rounded shapes. Foliage is regularized like textile patterns.

The continuity between abstraction and realism can also be seen in his adjustment of colours. He does not adhere to all the hues in the photographic studies that serve as the basis for the realistic works. The tonal relationship between the different parts of a painting is continually adjusted until Bowen achieves a preconceived balance, the canvas becomes a unified surface of colours. In the portraits he dresses and poses subjects as though they were only patterns of colours. Not surprisingly he often turns a work in progress upside down or looks at it reflected in a mirror to verify its balance as a two-dimensional composition. Even in his paintings from the 1980s, he does not abandon associating colour and musical harmonies. Sometimes a combination of colours in an environment strikes his fancy and is the initial motivation for a painting. This is particularly true for his Florida sunsets.

The early stages of both styles reveal painterly qualities. In the abstracts he first allowed the paint to splatter, drip and run, and in the realist works the brush strokes are loose and evident. But then as the paintings near completion, all the looseness is glazed over, defined and narrowed down to a final hard-edge image. "The aim is to achieve a certain luminosity and intensity of colour (or visual music) that is simply not there in the initial loose stage. Other painters may well achieve this in a one-stage, spontaneous and loose painting. I can't."

Most of the landscapes reveal the presence of humanity, but curiously most are devoid of figures. Fields are ploughed, wheat fields are ready for harvest, docks reach out into the lake, but the only human presence is the viewer. Nature becomes patterns of colours devoid of animate life. In the best of his landscapes, as in the paintings of the dock and the porch of his parents' home in Florida, this emptiness acquires a mysterious and suspended quality—a still, contemplative atmosphere.

♦ ♦ ♦

At the Institution Saint-Joseph, the private Catholic high school which Paul attended in Périgueux, he choreographed (if the word is not too pretentious) a humorous mini ballet for an annual fundraiser. Its title was "Le Ballet O'Cédar," a pun on the name of a popular brand of broom (in French, Balais Océdar). He and his adolescent male classmates danced as they saw fit, scantily attired in colourful crepe paper. His friend Jean-Gérard Nay, fellow choreographer who played bouncy music on the piano, remembers that throughout the performance one nun kept cautioning another: "Don't look, sister! Don't look!"

Paul knew little about ballet or any form of dance. He had seen Marguerite Frapin's small ballet school at the municipal theatre in Périgueux. The wife of a medical doctor, Frapin created in 1947 the "Cercle d'Initiation Artistique." In the Institution Saint-Joseph, the old municipal theatre, and Périgueux's Casino de Paris she and her students gave performances of music and dance. Singers from the Bordeaux Opera were sometimes invited. Madame Frapin danced in such ballets as "Les Noces de Jeannette" and "Pic et Pan," which evoked the life of the circus and the legend of St. Nicolas. Paul was especially excited by a piece called "Romanesca." Clown acts were the other inspiration. Paul would not have known much about clowning either, but the effect of "Le Ballet O'Cédar" was comic and suggestive of clowning.

♦ ♦ ♦

The title of this book, *The Pleasures of Time*, comes from one of Paul's idols. The keys to happiness are in our own hands Michel de Montaigne declared in the late 1500s, writing from his castle in southern France. The joy that can be found in the simple pleasures of everyday life, Montaigne believed, can be increased through reflection and the rationing of pleasure. Not only should we thoughtfully relive past experiences we should also give ourselves something to look forward to in the future.

> To enjoy life requires some husbandry. I enjoy it twice as much as others, since he measure of our joy depends on the greater or lesser degree of our attachment to it. Above all now, when I see my span so short, I want to give it more ballast; I want to arrest the swiftness of its passing by the swiftness of my capture, compensating for the speed with which it drains away by the intensity of my enjoyment.[25]

For someone as susceptible to nostalgia as I am, it is easy to relive the past. My dream is to live in a flea market. Postponing pleasures for the future, however, continues to annoy me.

If some readers interpret my preference for the anecdotal and the ephemeral as an emphasis on the superficial, I would defend myself by saying that it has been done because of my awareness that for all of us chaos is never far away.

◆ ◆ ◆

Through a Catholic priest who was an old friend of his grandfather, Théophile Frêne, Paul was first made aware of Arabic languages. His grandfather and L'abbé Rouet had been classmates in primary school and the two boys remained life-long friends. Father Rouet was the priest called to Périgueux to baptize Paul, Frêne's first grandchild. "One of the Frêne family fixtures," Paul calls him.

During summer vacations, when Paul and Jean-Gérard Nay spent time sight-seeing by train and bicycle, Paul got to know Father Rouet better.[26] The cyclists travelled by train to Châteauroux, the home of Paul's Aunt, Raymonde Frêne. (Alternatively, they went to the city of Richelieu, where Nay's grandmother lived. This is why Richelieu appears in *Les demoiselles*.) These trips could be lengthy. From Châteauroux, they went to Bourges or Valençay or Loches. Several times they spent a few days at Father Rouet's parish home in the village of Sainte-Thorette near Bourges. Father Rouet had been a professor in a Catholic college, but he was not inspiring—in Paul's eyes—"just a sort of ordinary parish priest who was more like a retiree." He obviously had a little affair with his maid, Paul confides. Paul no longer remembers the exact circumstances, but at some point he received all of Father Rouet's books in Arabic. His aunt may have asked the priest for them since she spent time at his parish caring for him when he was elderly.

In a letter from the early 1950s, dated July 26, Jean-Gérard writes Paul: "I'm going to send a note to Father Rouet. I hope that we will see him again to savour there the 'great enlightenment of the Middle Ages' and to be 'free like the fields of wheat.'"

◆　◆　◆

It may be bad sociology to imagine that people who inhabit a geographical region share a similar character. But this statement about the typical Périgordin, which concludes Ian Scargill's book on southwestern France, is nevertheless a fitting description of Paul: "The Périgordin is a complex personality, sociable but independent, superstitious but full of good sense, welcoming but distrustful of authority. He is an individualist, respecting freedom, yet easily feels concern for others, and in elections he expresses his outlook with a tendency to vote left—but not far left— of centre."[27]

Geographically, Périgord resembles southern Indiana. Both areas are covered with low forested hills. Agriculture is more important than industry for the local economies. In popular poetry Indiana is remembered for family farms and village life: frost on the pumpkins, fodder in the shocks and Little Orphan Annie frightened by ghost stories. Until recently many farmers in Périgord lived in poverty. However, Périgord was also a land of squires. Within the upper class, family rivalries were expressed in building beautiful castles, country mansions and town houses. To outsiders the symbols of the province are elitist: gourmet food, truffles, pâté de foie gras, medieval and renaissance castles. Although Hoosiers have not yet experienced their first golden age, Périgordins have enjoyed three—as well as centuries of decline and instability.

The first golden age in Périgord was the Upper Paleolithic era, circa 30,000 BC, which has left some of the world's most famous cave art. The village of Les Eyzies, the "capital of prehistory," and the cave of Lascaux, the "Sistine Chapel of prehistory," are both located in Périgord. The second golden age is the Roman occupation from 56 BC to the 3rd century AD Périgueux, which the Romans called Vesunna, has been the province's administrative and commercial centre ever since the conquest. Remnants of Roman buildings are still visible, including the ruins of an amphitheatre, a temple and city walls. The third golden age is the eleventh and twelfth centuries. Périgord is one of the French provinces with the most castles and fortified churches from the early Middle Ages. Of its approximately one thousand churches, half of them are at least partly Romanesque.

There is, though, a sinister aspect to much of this architectural heritage. A patina of age cannot hide the fact that some of the design features of these buildings are a reflection of the greed and cruelty of both locals and foreigners. Alamans invaded Périgord in the third century AD; Vandals and Goths in the fifth century; Arabs from Spain in the eighth; and Vikings, who set Périgueux on fire, in the ninth. Rivalries between four local barons created havoc in the Middle Ages. During the Hundred Years War (1345 to 1453), Périgord was the scene of brutal fighting when the partition of France by English and French monarchs cut through the province. Catholics waged war against Cathars in the twelfth century. During the Wars of Religion between Protestants and Catholics in the sixteenth century Périgueux was again partly destroyed. There were also violent rebellions by the poor in the 1590s and in the 1630s.

One of the strangest aspects of Paul's character is how little interest he shows in any of this local history except for the prehistoric art. Considering that his first university degree is in Classics, his derision for people who cultivate history is even more odd. Paul knows Périgord quite well. The visits since his early twenties have been brief, though. He says it is not that he dislikes Périgord, but other places came to interest him more. To Paul as a youth, his home province would have been associated with the past rather than the future. His perception would have resembled the perceptions of many provincial residents throughout the country. But Périgord's economic decline, which had begun in the 1870s, would have strengthened this kind of attitude. The railroads disadvantaged Périgord because of the increased competition they fostered. Disease destroyed the vineyards. Coal which might have fuelled industries was scarce.

French citizens from middle-class and working-class families tend to be ambivalent about the artistic symbols of an elite which for centuries has used the fine arts for political ends. Paul explains when I put him on the spot:

> I was interested in Périgord as a youngster. Some of the professors we had in high school, and particularly the famous Léon Bouillon, fed us stories about the history behind the castles. We were taken to all these places. We went from church to church. It is true that there is a saturation of signs from the past in Périgord. Often I have compared the province to a time capsule because all the layers of habitation from the previous centuries have left something. You

cannot travel more than two or three miles in the countryside without finding remnants from either the remote or the recent past.

My criticism is that these things remain for very haphazard reasons. The buildings which are the most famous are signs of oppression and tyranny. I have reacted against worshipping the Middle Ages, which was a part of my high school education. The Middle Ages were wonderful because they were supposed to be a Christian society. I have come to see this as cultural conditioning and brainwashing. The prestige of ruins was also a part of Romanticism. We were invited to admire elements of architecture, the beauty of past styles, which is actually as false as admiring unpainted Greek temples and statues. We know the Greeks painted them in violent colours like Hindu temples. What we were taught is a falsification of the past. This was also true of the prehistoric caves, where local guides told all sorts of stupid stories that had no factual basis whatsoever. Some of the castles were supposed to be haunted. Some places had paranormal phenomena. The inhabitants of one convent were supposed to have been possessed by the devil.

Now everything is sanitized, lit—"son et lumière." What a tourist gets out of these places, which have been cleaned up, is a mishmash of different historical eras and conditioning devices. Tourism is a machine for spreading ignorance. What were these beautiful medieval castles? They were bunkers for gangsters. There were four families in Périgord operating like organized crime syndicates preying on the population and fighting each other.

Périgord was a remote country, remote from the central power in Paris. It remained backward. It was very dark before electricity. I had friends who lived in castles in the country. You have no idea how wild and remote these places were in the 1950s. My great-grandparents lived next to a river. They had a fabric mill. When my grandfather went to primary school, he had to cross a little woods. Wolves still lurked in the woods. My grandfather hit his clogs together to scare them away. Noise is always good protection. He had to be especially cautious in the winter. Périgord was one of the last areas in France to lose its wolves. People were still telling stories about wolves when I was a youngster.

To see this transformed into a Disneyland is just irritating to me. Périgord has become a big tourist machine. Of course, to a great extent all these signs of history have been constructed by the culture of our own time. People see a reconstructed farmhouse with beautiful furniture. This luxury is nonsense. My disdain for the past is consistent with my eighteenth century ideology of progress and enlightenment. I cannot really worship an obscure convent which was the stronghold of an abbot or a lord.

You force me to speak. So I improvise. You will not take silence for an answer. I have to produce something. On the other hand, you will hear me on another day saying how incredibly interesting it is to be born in a place on the earth which has all these layers of history dating back 40,000 years.

◆ ◆ ◆

Paul refers to the petty squabbles which his family breeds as "that swamp!" Neither of us thinks that most of them are significant enough to explain to other people.

◆ ◆ ◆

The bourée "L'aïo de Rotso," which Canteloube arranged for his famous collection of folk songs, is a humorous story told in the Langue d'Oc dialect: do not drink pure water from the well, my little one. It will kill you. Drink a swig of wine. It will do you good! Paul remembers his grandmother, Lucie (Lacroix) Bouissac, singing this song at home when he was a boy. A different note is sounded in a story Paul tells about his grandmother's frugality. Her husband had bought a ten-volume dictionary, which had been delivered to his office. When he brought the first two books home, he endured such an outburst of reproach from his wife that he did not dare let her see the other ones. They stayed hidden in his office.

The books were not a secret from Paul, though, who consulted them when he was doing his homework. One Sunday morning, while the grandfather was helping Paul, some information needed to be checked that could only be found in the last volumes of the dictionary. Realizing this, Paul commented without thinking: "Oh, it's not here. It's in one of the other books in your office."

"What other books? You didn't tell me you bought more books!" his grandmother angrily protested.

◆ ◆ ◆

Having met Paul's family only once many years ago I tend to misperceive their social class by applying simplistic American labels. "Working class" and "lowbrow" capture the spirit in some ways but not the inconsistencies, such as a rather high level of culture. This was, after all, France. In adulthood Paul belittles his family's artistic taste, but still thinks it has "some credibility." He lists objects in the houses of his grandparents as evidence: a set of ivory Mah Jong tiles stored in an elaborately carved wooden box embellished with dragons, a bronze Chinese dragon, Algerian handicrafts, antique French furniture dating from the early and the mid-nineteenth century. One of the family friends was a female artist; another was a professional entertainer. There was contact with the outside world. In the family photo album Paul's aunt, who had pizzazz, could be seen riding a camel in Algeria.

I infer from his story about her husband secretly buying an expensive ten-volume dictionary that Paul's paternal grandmother was anti-intellectual. He corrects me to say that her concern was financial, although he never saw her read anything other than newspapers. Lucie Bouissac was the person who motivated him to be an achiever at school. As a boy, every Sunday morning he went to mass at the Catholic high school, which had a chapel, riding by bicycle from the castle (Castel Fadèze) to the other side of town. In the schoolyard after the mass a priest distributed students' marks, classified and ranked, for the week and the month. After Paul had his slip of paper, he went to his grandparents for breakfast. If he was first in the class, she gave him the equivalent of maybe $5.00. For second, $2.50. For third, $1.00. This was his allowance.

Grandmother had simple ideas about things, but she was the one in the family who supported me the most. She was more nurturing than the other women in the family. She was very authoritarian. You could not object to what she had decided. She was very pious in late age. Every day before dinner she went to her room for prayers. But she also told jokes.

I was not alienated in the context of the family. In a way it was a very supportive milieu. The main meal was lunch. I was coming every day from the college on bicycle. The conversations at lunch included talking about what we were doing during our morning school work. We children rehearsed our school lessons on the way to school with our grandfather.

Also, there was the fact that I was often sick from childhood diseases between ages five or six and twelve. During the war we did not have the right food to eat. Mother was overly protective, being alone while her husband was in a prisoner-of-war camp. Conditions of life in the castle were not particularly comfortable. It was drafty and cold. When my father returned home from Germany, he invested time to make sure that I would not turn out like he did. He did not pressure me to play football. The family invested a lot in the education of the children, but the grandparents did this more effectively than the parents.

Mother kept in contact with many family members; my father was less interested in cultivating his family. I grew up surrounded by four grandparents, an aunt and two sisters. It was a type of family that has become the exception in France today. Jean-Gérard Nay and I started to participate in a culture of rebellion, maybe at age 17. We made fun of family wisdom. I emancipated myself from this very saturated family universe in which I grew up. At the same time Jean-Gérard and I were very much involved in Catholic organizations. We were lucky to be brought up by priests who were fairly intellectual and certainly not fanatical.[28]

Between the ages of fifteen and twenty-five it took great effort, Paul says, to emancipate himself from the Catholic Church and from the family out-look on life. On the application for high-school students to visit England that Paul completed as a teenager was a list of questions about personal traits: sportive, intellectual, etc. It was Paul's father who would not allow him to check the category "intellectual." Nonetheless, Paul's father was the first person to teach him Latin. He reminds me that he is the third generation in his father's family to study the Classics.

◆　◆　◆

It puzzled me that neither Paul nor I had heard of a French sculptor so significant that a museum is devoted to his work. While exploring all the landmarks of Montparnasse, guidebook in hand, I passed the Bourdelle Museum. Mammoth sculpted heads extend above the brick wall sur-rounding the courtyard.

A few days later when we visited the museum, Paul noticed a detail from a statue called "La France," which Emile Bourdelle made in the mid-1920s. France is depicted allegorically as a young, eternally vigilant woman with a spear. She has raised one of her hands above her eyes, perhaps shading them from the bright sun in order to peer into the distance. Beside her a snake is coiled around a post. It rests its head on the top as if it were sunbathing. It appears to be mischievous, almost smiling. What the snake is supposed to symbolize is a mystery. And why does La France ignore it? Perhaps it is some obscure reference to Greek mythology. But in this patriotic, serious statue the snake seems to be an out-of-place bit of comedy.

Ever since that afternoon at the museum Paul wants to "do the Bourdelle snake" when he and I are alone in the apartment elevator—to rest his chin on my shoulder.

Notes

[1] Simone de Beauvoir, *Adieux: A Farewell to Sartre*, Harmondsworth: Penguin, 1985, 49.

[2] Allan Bloom, *The Closing of the American Mind*, New York: Simon and Schuster, 1987.

[3] Jan Potocki, *The Saragossa Manuscript*, Trans. Roger Caillois, New York: Orion Press, 1960. Jean Potocki, *Manuscript trouvé à Saragosse*, Ed. René Radrizzani, Paris: José Corti, 1990.

[4] See Robert Fulford, "Saul Bellow, Allan Bloom and Abe Ravelstein," *Globe and Mail*, November 2, 1999 and Mark Greif, "Bloom in Love," *The American Prospect*, Vol. 11, No. 14, June 5, 2000.

[5] Bloom, 122.

[6] Nall, *Nall-Alice*, Nice: Presses de l'imprimerie Toscane, 1996, n.p. The drawings of Ron Bowen, Jörn Merkert, Paul and me, which are dated 1979, were actually completed in 1976 according to my recollection.

[7] Rainer Maria Rilke, "The Merry-go-round," *Prose and Poetry*, New York: Continuum, 1984, 186.

[8] Sourien Melikian, "The Baschet Brothers: The Sounds of Sculpture," *Art News*, Vol. 72, October 1973, 70-71; Anon., "New Ways to Make Noise," *Time*, August 10, 1962, 39.

[9] Eric Walter White, *Stravinsky: The Composer and his Works*, Berkeley: University of California Press, 1979, 414.

[10] Heini Hediger, *Psychology and Behaviour of Animals in Zoos and Circuses*, New York: Dover, 1970.

[11] Paul Bouissac, *Les demoiselles*, Paris: Les Editions de Minuit, 1970, 167-168. While Paul was travelling in Morocco, he was reading Roger Stéphane's *Après le mort de dieu*. Paul scribbled in his copy of the book notes from the lecture he heard by the Imam of Fez.

[12] Paul Bouissac interviewed by Stephen Riggins, February 20, 1994.

[13] Nikolaus Pevsner, *The Englishness of English Art*, Harmondsworth: Penguin Books, 1956, 193-194.

[14] Christian Marin and Alexandre Bouglione are photographed in Claude Jaquin's book *Paris la fête*, Paris: Guy Authier, 1977. See photographs numbers 42 and 43 as well as pages 112-114.

[15] Jean Genet, "The Funambulist," *Evergreen Review*, April-May, 1964, 32, 48; "Le Funambule," *L'atelier d'Alberto Giacometti*, Décines: Editions L'arbalète, 1958, 175-204.

[16] Hector Berlioz, *Memoirs*, New York: Dover, 1960, 96.

[17] Paul Bouissac, *Les demoiselles*, Paris: Les Editions de Minuit, 1970, 162-166.

[18] Bouissac, 166.

[19] Anon., "Howard Brotz, 1922-1993," *The Jewish Journal of Sociology*, XXXVI(I), June 1994, 39.

[20] Anon. "The Circus has Caught M. Bouissac," *Vic Report*, 3(2), March 1975, 2.

[21] Douglas Martin's painting of Northrop Frye is reproduced in John Robert Colombo's *Canadian Literary Landmarks*, Willowdale, ON: Hounslow Press, 1984, 192.

22 During his tenure at the University of Toronto Paul created three new courses at Victoria College. One was an interdisciplinary course on Surrealism (VIC 312Y). The second was Introduction to Semiotics and Communication (VIC 120Y). The third was about Romanticism, but given Paul's other academic commitments this course did not remain long in the calendar.

23 See Eric McLuhan, *The Role of Thunder in Finnegans Wake*, Toronto: University of Toronto Press, 1997, xiii.

24 Marshall McLuhan, "The Agenbite of Outwit," *Location* 1(1), Spring 1963, 41-44.

25 Michel de Montaigne, *The Essays of Michel de Montaigne*, London: Penguin, 1991, 1263.

26 Jean-Gérard Nay is the author of a novel, *Le dilemme de pelikan* (Paris: Editions L'Harmattan, 1997), and a study of management practices in Japan, *Manager au Japon, un Itinéraire* (Paris: Editions L'Harmattan, 1994). He is a brother of the journalist Catherine Nay.

27 Ian Scargill, *The Dordogne Region of France*, Newton Abbot: David and Charles, 1974, 220.

28 Paul Bouissac interviewed by Stephen Riggins, January 29, 2000.

Employees of the Martin County Tribune, circa 1908, Loogootee, Indiana. Reba Chandler is seated at the far right.
Photographer: Alonzo Spears

Main Street, Shoals, circa 1900.
Photographer: Willis Landis

Weathered and vandalized stop signs, Loogootee, mid-1980s.
Photographer: S.H. Riggins

Interlude:
Indiana Fugue

Standardized, imperative, the stop sign is everywhere you go, always the same: an octagonal, red face; "STOP" in white letters; a narrow white border just inside the edge. Additional information, if any, is written on a plate beneath. A stop sign is an even-handed guide, rational and benign, aimed at the common good. Drivers usually obey, but it depends on what they know about intersections and whether they think anyone is watching.

In the town of Loogootee in the mid-1980s stop signs rarely adhered to the letter of the law. Vandals, weather and bureaucratic negligence conspired to produce concrete poetry on every street corner. Red they were, but in a surprising variety of non-conforming shades: grayish pinks, pastel reds, reddish oranges, brownish reds, violet browns and all the hues between. The most common background colours were pink and yellow, but some signs were frankly yellow, others unabashedly pink. Time faded red into pink, flaked it off in patches, and revealed the true yellow underneath. The paint remained longer where brush strokes were heavy.

A clerk at city hall told me these traffic signs were bought second-hand. Their recycled state had prolonged their life span way beyond the norm. There were signs with flat and signs with raised surfaces; signs that had messages printed directly on the face. One had "state highway" in relief on the face even though it was posted on a side street. Some signs still had their original coat of paint. Others had been repainted by hand without the original paint being stripped away. It did not seem to trouble city officials if they selected the wrong shade of red or a type of paint which had little resistance to the weather.

◆ ◆ ◆

I'm sitting beside Paul at a highway truck stop outside Washington, Indiana, waiting for a Greyhound bus. The bus no longer stops at Loogootee, fifteen miles east. We sit on the trunk of my parents' dusty Chevrolet in a gravel parking lot. I'm sporting tan hiking boots, black 501 Levi jeans (the model with the button fly), a dark blue T-shirt. And I'm chewing jaw breaker bubble gum. Behind us is a bulky, red vending machine for Coca-Cola, and to the side a white cylindrical gas storage tank. The farmland in the distance is covered with maturing wheat and bales of hay. Black horses are grazing. On the hood of the pickup truck he drives through the parking lot, a young man has mounted the rebellious sign "Tasmanian Devil." The restaurant window advertises: "Super Special Summer Salad Bar. All U Can Eat." A nighthawk flies back and forth under the outdoor lights eating insects which it detects through the reflected sound waves of its call. Paul's spelling for the name of my home-town: L-hoho-g-hoho-t-hehe. I experience the contentment of twilight animated by Paul's humour. He spurts: "If this bird detects your button fly with its radar, we're in trouble."

◆ ◆ ◆

I like to think of myself as an amateur Hoosier historian. Many of my significant others are people of earlier generations with whom I can have only virtual relationships. That does not make them less important. I am an only child. I spent a considerable amount of time with adults when I was growing up. They made the past alive for me. My identity and values were inadvertently molded by their deeds and their tales. My Indiana is not the whole state but the picturesque southern third. It begins near the town of Martinsville, about thirty miles south of Indianapolis, and extends to the Ohio River. Is my fugue the tale of an escape? A theme of infinite variations, like a nostalgic music of the heart? A tale of wandering away and meandering back to my point of departure? In a drawer of my office desk in St. John's is an antique butter knife from home. I keep it to open my most treasured letters. The knife is not efficient, but it's decorated with art nouveau daisies and curving lines. It belonged to my substitute grandmother—actually, to the couple whose house she and her husband inherited.

◆　◆　◆

A stop sign at the corner of Pine Street and Ackerman Drive is a bold, manly red. It is the achievement of a city worker who selected an improper dark shade of red in a shiny finish with a depth like water, and had a fondness for thick and sensuous lettering with sloppy borders. After someone tried to fold the sign up as if it were a paper boat, city workers unfurled it. But they never bothered to touch it up with new paint. The fold marks have left wide crevices that expose the bare metal underneath.

◆　◆　◆

One of my favourite roads for bicycling is a gravel road east of Loogootee that many years ago was the bed of a train track. Part of the route is situated on the gentle sloping side of McGonagle's Rock, a low ridge. On the east side of the road are small, geometrically ordered fields of corn, crossed by a tree-lined stream. On the west side, grazing cows watch the odd passerby and turtles sunbathe on a fallen log in a pond. I usually follow this road as far as the bridge over Boggs Creek. The creek forms a pool of water here, at the base of a worn sandstone bluff. The shaky iron bridge that passes over the creek is scary. Its floor of wooden planks looks too flimsy to support even a thin bicycle rider.

At this spot the gravel road meets a highway. The bluff must have been prettier before the highway and a second bridge were blasted through it. Although I have been told the pool used to be a popular fishing hole, I am not able to learn its name. We all know the pool by an informal name not printed on any map. Even local historians cannot help when I ask for information. Maybe the pool has no proper name because there are so many places like this in southern Indiana.

I'm told that an African-American man was riding a train. For some reason "they" were after him. To escape capture he jumped from the train and fell into the fishing hole. His body was never found because the pool is a bottomless pit. The storyteller says that the man got away. Where reality becomes folklore in this tale is impossible to tell. The whole thing may be a fisherman's tall tale. However, this story seems to be responsible for the name that everyone knows but never writes. This scenic pool, good for catching catfish and associated with boyhood fun, they call "Nigger Hole."

A few people still fish here, although in an age of artificial lakes, municipal swimming pools and television, the pool no longer means much to fishers. There are still occasions when people need to refer to the Nigger Hole Bridge. A politically correct name has yet to emerge. One white family—with humour—simply refers to it as *"that* bridge."

◆ ◆ ◆

On August 23, 1862, an African-American man named Pleasant Hart went to the Martin County courthouse to record his "freedom papers," proof that he had never been a slave. The affidavit reads:

> State of North Carolina, Granville County.
> David I. Young, a freeholder of the county and state aforesaid, maketh oath—that he has known Pleasant Hart, a free man of colour about twenty years, that the said Pleasant Hart has during that period been [known?] as a freeman; that his mother is a free woman, and that his wife is also reputed to be free, that they have been in the uninterrupted enjoyment of their rights, both civil and political, ever since his first acquaintance with them.
> The said Pleasant Hart is probably rather upward of thirty years old, five feet ten inches high, and a tolerable good-looking coloured man. His wife is a bright mulatto woman, and appears to be about twenty years old.
> Signed on September 20, 1838[1]

I have heard of Pleas Hart, as he was informally called, only because I came across a reference to him while searching through old newspapers. In a 1927 newspaper column Hart is cited as an example of the violence African-Americans feared because they were surrounded in southern Indiana by a population that included many Confederate sympathizers. Hart was "cruelly murdered" in Martin County by members of a subversive organization called the Knights of the Golden Circle. The perpetrators were never punished, although their identity was known. The journalist condemned the murderers, but excused other residents by saying that they were "too much bowed down by their own sorrows [from the Civil

War], and too much in fear of the traitors at the head of the Golden Circle to give [Pleasant Hart's] murder more than a passing thought."[2]

A vague date of death is given on Hart's tombstone, "October 1863." Also inscribed is his age—"about 55." The only symbol of loss and mourning is a hand whose index finger points upward, and the message "gone home."

Mr. Pleasant H. Hart was buried in Pleasant Valley Cemetery.

♦ ♦ ♦

If stories told in the family are correct, it was the impact of slavery on poor Whites which led to my maternal ancestors moving to Indiana in the 1820s. The Ledgerwoods are Scotch. Their journey to the Midwest was by way of Northern Ireland and then Virginia, where they were living by the mid-eighteenth century. Samuel Ledgerwood moved to Knox County, Tennessee, probably in the first decade of the nineteenth century. Married in 1808, he served briefly in the War of 1812 and then sued the American government in 1815 for withholding part of his salary.

My mother was told as a child that Samuel died before he had obtained legal ownership of his land in Tennessee. His widow, Sarah, who was left with four young children, married Isaac Hembree in 1818, a native of Dublin, Ireland, and seven years her junior. Isaac Hembree (1797-1860) was supposed to have been good to the children, but as my mother tactfully put it, he was "not ambitious." The oldest son, James (1809-1848), while still a teenager, had to work as a farmhand to support his mother and her children. James worked for a large landowner. He lost his job in the late 1820s when the owner of the farm began buying slaves. James is supposed to have convinced the family to move to the untamed wilderness of the Indiana frontier. The family travelled by wagon, bringing along a couple of cows. The trip took about a year, which included a winter in Kentucky. The younger children, including my great-grandfather Nathaniel who was about twelve years old, walked most of the way.

♦ ♦ ♦

The corner of Church and First Streets, a four-way stop, is the brightest corner in town. The background colour for all four signs is a canary yellow with random spots of pink. The signs seem to say STOP with a frisson of hipness, mindless of the fact that drivers are only seconds away from eternity. Pink and yellow, the colours of a Florida art deco hotel, are quite out of place in the Midwest farm belt.

◆ ◆ ◆

Along the trails in the Martin State Forest are public signs informing visitors about the surrounding environment. One sign defines a wolf tree, a white oak. These are trees, located in an open area or pasture, that grow quickly, wolfing up space when other trees are not competitors. The short trunks and wide crowns of wolf trees make them of little value for timber production. The sign explains that although these trees have character and the public enjoys them, "too many characters" would spoil the forest.

◆ ◆ ◆

John Anthony (1802-1886), "Loogootee's man who tried to fly," was one of countless obscure men in nineteenth-century America who made experiments in human flight. No discussion of his irrepressible urge to fly, to soar aloft on summer zephyrs, can escape the realm of myth. Only a few trifles from his storehouse of knowledge have come down to us. In his early life Anthony was a shoemaker; later, he farmed. In the 1840s he was fined for selling spirits without a license. But he also gave away a small plot of land from his farm to serve as the site for a one-room school. Whoever noted Anthony's passing in the Martin County Death Records of January 5, 1886, kindly listed his occupation as "worked at flying machines."

Anthony's last public experiment was supposed to take place at a fair in Loogootee in September 1881. The *Martin County Herald* of September 1 includes these brief advertisements:

> The overshadowing attraction [at the fair] will be John Anthony's flying machine. He will fly beyond doubt.

> A continual stream of people could be seen last Sunday visiting Uncle John Anthony's artificial bird.

> There is big talk at Washington [Indiana] to attend the fair to see Uncle Anthony flap his wings, and fly over the trees. We will be there; won't you?

A local historian has concluded that Anthony disappointed the fair-goers and didn't show. A few days earlier he had injured himself attempting a trial run from the roof of his barn. Anthony's crusade to conquer the skies made him the butt of crude jokes.

While Anthony was recovering from the crash, it is said that a halfwit wanted to know what caused the failure. When the injured man explained that he did not know, as he used his wings exactly like the buzzards, the person meekly inquired, "Did you spread your tail?"[3]

Once the possibility of human flight had become a reality, the tone of the stories changed to admiration. Until the middle of the twentieth century people believed they had seen something special in John Anthony and continued talking about him. This first story is from the 1920s; the second from the 1950s.

Wm. H. Batchelor lived a near neighbour [to Anthony] and he says the machine was mounted on four wheels, the modern ones mounted on two; and that it had a platform where Anthony was to sit during flights, and had wings at each side and a tail, similar in principle like the Spirit of Saint Louis, which was used by Lindbergh in his ocean flight. No motive power was provided by Anthony other than such manipulation as he could make himself.[4]

I was about ten years of age at the time and we schoolchildren had a lot of fun with Mr. Anthony's "Buzzard," as we loved to call his machine, which was constructed of heavy cotton material. We worked hard helping him get it started down the incline, which he built for that purpose, and it was great riding on the track. The efforts were not entirely in vain, for we got a great thrill helping him to make it fly. Although very young at the time I remember distinctly that it flapped its wings four times before crashing. I often heard Mr. Anthony say "Some day people will be flying through the air like birds."[5]

Coda No. 1. What motivated John Anthony? What values does this man represent? Personal ambition and a willingness to stand up to public ridicule on the positive side, I suppose, or foolishness and quixotic eccentricity on the negative. He certainly had strength of character: he made at least two public attempts to sail the skies and promised a third effort when he was almost eighty years old. On the other hand, Anthony seems to have lacked even rudimentary scientific knowledge: he could be viewed as simply irrational rather than laudably ambitious.

Coda No. 2. If I'm right that Anthony lies in an unmarked grave in St. John's Cemetery in Loogootee, no soaring buzzard, dove or even chicken decorates his grave. No photographs survive. Paul thought of a solution to compensate for this gap in the historical record: drop a porcelain statue of a man and make a model of the broken pieces.

◆ ◆ ◆

Labor Day is supposed to be hot and sultry—an ideal day to eat watermelon and play baseball for the last time before school begins. But it's overcast and cool. I borrow a bicycle from one of my cousins and ride through Loogootee and some of the surrounding countryside, past level fields of wheat and corn.

I am looking for displays of lawn ornaments, the public art of the American heartland. I pass Virgin Marys and pink flamingoes. Antique bathtubs are sometimes turned on end and half buried to make a grotto for Virgin Marys. What could Virgin Marys possibly be doing with pink flamingoes?

Perhaps the answer is that neither is edible? People don't eat pink flamingoes and no one had sex with the Virgin Mary? According to the Newfoundland anthropologist George Park, the Virgin Mary is sometimes depicted with snakes at her feet, good triumphing over evil. Maybe flamingoes eat small snakes as well as little fishes?

Both Virgin Marys and pink flamingoes seem so unreal. Flamingoes because their bodies are out of proportion to their spindly legs.

◆ ◆ ◆

Vandals have nearly obliterated a stop sign on High Street with white paint. This produces the optical effect of reversing the foreground and background colours. It now looks as though a few messy lines of red have been strewn randomly across a white surface. In black spray paint that makes soft edges, they awkwardly scribbled STOP on top of the original machine-made letters in relief. The black on the letter S had run. The oval of the P is unfinished. Its vertical line, broad and stubby, merges with the O. A yellow fleck or two, ghosts of the sign's undercoat, are visible above the lettering and along the raised border. Above the T is the suggestion of a circle and an interrupted line, both spray-painted in a medium grey. Like the outline of an obscured crescent moon, two grey arcs bisect the T. The actual message is mundane—and barely legible—the number 81, a mark from the class of 1981, whose members were obviously inexperienced in the use of spray paint. But the defaced sign has a meditative quality. Understated sensuality exists in harmony with nervous energy.

◆　◆　◆

Mobile homes are common in the American Midwest in contrast to Europe where the less affluent are more likely to live in apartment buildings. The sight of so many mobile homes in Indiana suggests to Paul that they deserve sociological study. He wonders what type of people live in such homes. How are they regarded by their neighbours who reside in permanent dwellings? What is the folklore of mobile homes? How do the constraints of space affect interior decoration? In Paul's opinion, the term "mobile home" is an oxymoron. Referring to this contradiction, he suggests "Still Wheels" as the title for a paper. His French accent is so strong that for several weeks I think he has given me the mysterious title "Steel Wheels."

◆　◆　◆

The artist Bill Whorrall is collecting the folklore and historic photographs of southern Indiana, playing the role I would like to have claimed had I not emigrated. Despite being an outsider, Bill has become the best source for humorous anecdotes because of his research. Here is a story another so-called outsider gave him concerning the odd customs of local residents.

One Saturday night the storyteller noticed a car parked for a long time beside a country road not far from his house. He went out to investigate and found two elderly men—dressed to a T—sitting in the car. They were behaving themselves while drinking whiskey. They said that they got dressed up like this every Saturday night to go drinking.

"Where are you going tonight?" the storyteller asked.

"We're already there!" they replied.

◆　◆　◆

Prior to another grimy encounter with hooligans there was a yellow and pink sign at the corner of North Oak and Clark streets. They veiled STOP with exuberant, arm-length arcs of black spray paint in contrast to the tight gestures of an earlier painter touching up the red. Rust has claimed flakes of white from the raised border and lettering. Rust has also drained the colour along the centre line where two rivets hold the sign to its metal pole. Although it has suffered at the hands of vandals, the result is warm and lyrical. As a work of abstract art, this sign is sombre and haunting. The colours seem elegiac, as though alluding to the grief following the failure of a romance.

◆ ◆ ◆

In my family we tend to have pale skin. But like most of those who arrived on this continent in the eighteenth century, we have in our ancestry some Native Americans. My Native great-great-grandmother from South Carolina, Mary Golighty, probably died in the mid-1800s.

The pioneer cemetery is now just a clearing in the woods. The site of a Native camp is the best place to see wild flowers in bloom.

◆ ◆ ◆

In the late 1930s Maie Clements Perley arrived in Bloomington with her husband, who had just been hired to teach at Indiana University. Mrs. Perley was certainly not an ideal observer of Midwestern customs. She was hopelessly snobbish. She may also have been rather blind to male beauty. She complained about shirtless men in hot weather. But Mrs. Perley managed to get her observations published in 1940 in a book titled *Without My Gloves*. One of the first sights she noticed was the men loitering downtown. The two-or three-storey brick buildings surrounding the square have not changed much, although several, including the Beaux Arts courthouse, have been elegantly restored. "The courthouse steps were littered with men of all ages. They sat huddled and slovenly, minus coats and unshaven, looking spineless and aimless except for their continual spitting which was accomplished with ear splitting regularity. The scene was as benighted and moronic as a chamber of horrors."[6] And Mrs. Perley didn't even get inside the courthouse john.

William gives me examples of the way silence can be both liberating and oppressive. He is old enough to remember cruising in Indiana in the early 1950s. Born in 1925, "smack dab in the middle of the Jazz Age," his mother won second prize in a Charleston contest while she was carrying him. He is a gardener, Sufi, aspiring poet and ex-hotel desk clerk, who knows the Bloomington square better than the Perleys did.

He cruised public places: parks, libraries, bus and train stations, hotels, movie theatres and roadside toilets. To the next generation none of these are unexpected places to look for public sex. The surprise is that one of the most popular locations in the Midwest used to be county courthouses and city halls. It's such an odd juxtaposition of deviance and hyper conformity in the same place. In addition to Bloomington, the list of Indiana cities where William had sex in courthouse washrooms includes: Martinsville, Columbus, Greensburg, Kokomo, Anderson, Muncie, Lafayette, Madison,

Greenfield, Nashville, Frankfort and Franklin. From his travels in Ohio and Kentucky, he could see that the same activities were taking place there. The exception was Illinois. However, William attributes this to the size of county seats in the state rather than to any difference in people's attitudes.

Basically, William agrees with Mrs. Perley. But the professor's wife failed to notice that there were actually two groups of loiters around the Bloomington square, the "stonies" on one side (limestone workers, farmers, manual labourers) and the "gown people" (university students and employees) on the other. Both classes of men were using the toilet for recreation. The most exotic detail from William's experience is the way the spittoons in the stalls served as mirrors to spy on men out of hand out of sight. He grumbles that on rainy days the straight men loitered in the toilet vestibule. They were not queer bashers, although he figures they must have known what was happening. They did not cause any problems other than accidentally disrupting the action.

The toilet has been converted into an office. If one looks closely at the exterior window sills on the ground floor, it can be seen that the edges of one window have not eroded as much as the others. Before the remodelling, this was the exterior doorway to the restroom. Indiana courthouses are typically buildings erected after the Civil War in beautiful Greek and Roman Revival styles. The washrooms were a public convenience, usually located on the ground floor or in the basement, and had an exterior entrance. Offices were on the second floor. Men's and women's washrooms were far apart, often on opposite sides of the building. "What would you say," William asks,

> was the thinking behind the architects and builders when they built these places? Do you think any of them ever thought about sex? Surely the upright citizens of the state must have known it was happening and never talked about it. It was just like the gay sex clubs in Victorian Britain. Everybody knew about it, but you just didn't talk about it. It was a different mindset. I don't believe the male sex drive has changed that much over the centuries. I think there is just more self-examination now.

From his experience, the best courthouse action, which drew gay men from all over the Midwest, was in Columbus, Indiana.

> It was a four seater. And there were more than four glory holes because some of them had high ones and low ones. Cruising was

tolerated for years and years, open twenty-four hours.... Word got around. Much more writing back then on the walls. Oh Lord! Every wall in the one in Columbus was completely covered with writing. I don't remember the authorities ever whitewashing them out. If anything, it would be the gay men who would erase the old messages and write new ones. Always dates, seldom times, not too much on telephone numbers. Mostly one-liners: "My doctor says I have a rare blood condition and every day I need a cup of jism. Can you help?"

Several courthouses had their half-senile custodians. I had a nodding acquaintance with the custodian in Columbus. We never said a word. As far as I remember, I was never chased out of any of these courthouse johns by anybody, although I stayed there for hours. In Martinsville (and I went there more often than anywhere else) there were regulars who were there for hours and every day of the week. But that's all pretty much past. Not nearly as exciting to me now....

There's a certain type looking for a man, or thinks he is, that does not want another homosexual. In some of those more or less public places, you thought, "Oh, boy. I'll get a straight man." Of course, I've changed my attitude, realizing that there is no such thing as getting a straight man. "Trade" we called it back then. You didn't have to pay them, but they didn't do anything. Why in the world I found that exciting I don't know. If I found them interested in me, it turned me off.[7]

♦ ♦ ♦

On a warm summer evening I'm doing Tai Chi outdoors, exercising at the athletic grounds at the western edge of town. The most prominent feature of the landscape is the wide sky. Tai Chi does not distract me from appreciating the fleeting spectacle overhead—an exhilarating display of colours projected onto the ragged remnants of scattered showers. There is even a double rainbow. And every summer evening the colours fade into a darkness enlivened by meandering fireflies.

Since the prairie turns to hills on the opposite side of town, it seems as though the athletic grounds are the beginning of the fabled Midwestern prairie which extends from here to Illinois and beyond. I savour this same view of the sky that my substitute grandparents enjoyed from their yard two blocks away. Cultivated farmland still begins in the next field and reaches to the horizon to end in groves of trees. In the far distance: fields of green corn, a couple of red barns and silos, a grain elevator, train tracks that lead westward. As I exercise outdoors, and friendly games of baseball, basketball and tennis are played, life in this small town seems so wholesome and sane.

But not everyone at the athletic grounds enjoys the virtues of village life. To some, this is Dullsville. The athletic grounds are also a place where teenagers congregate in cars during their nocturnal cruising about town. They drive in a circle that stretches from a laundromat, to a car wash, to the school—places at different ends of town where they find the space to park and talk without interference from adults. One evening while I was exercising a teenage boy shouted at me out his car window, "Hey, you look stupid," and drove away. I chose to disregard his remark. The next night he was bolder, got out of his car, and shouted, "Hey, you look stupid. That's faggot karate!"

I was surprised that he felt so strong about this. He had no idea who I was or even what I was doing. I considered shouting back: "Nobody gives a fuck what you think!" But it seemed best to ignore him. There is a time and place for discussing differences of opinion. The athletic grounds on a warm summer evening is not the place. Why is this boy so concerned about policing the public sphere, I wondered, keeping men in line whose conduct does not quite fit his uninformed standards of masculinity? Ridiculing Tai Chi is also an expression of religious intolerance and racism since it is Taoist and Chinese in origin.

As gays and lesbians, we have had to fight for our rightful place in public life. We have no intention of reverting to the silence and hypocrisy of the past or giving in to the hazing of those who know nothing about justice. Too many lives have been ruined for too many years. Despite holding such opinions, I thought it was best on this occasion to take precautions to avoid future incidents. I moved to the far side of the track to exercise. No one is going to shout for a quarter of a mile. I began to leave the track before dark, taking a path which avoided teenagers.

What the little redneck did not realize is that he was shouting "faggot" in one of the places where I was belittled as a child. When the captains of baseball teams in primary school selected members for their teams, they made their choices according to perceived athletic ability, beginning, of course, with the best players. I was inevitably humiliated by this experience since I was either the last or next-to-the-last player chosen. I vied for position with a boy stigmatized by extreme poverty because his parents lived in a shack beside the town garbage dump. (He subsequently became a minister.) Once during lunch hour when we were supposed to be playing baseball, I and a couple of castaways collected butterflies in the outfield.

Later in class the teacher, with good intentions, publicly complimented us for being entomologists. However, I found the praise embarrassing. It just called attention to what I understood to be a sign of deviance.

It is not just boys insecure about their masculinity who are homophobic. Not long ago I sat through a sermon in which the minister referred to a grandmother who continually sent money to a grandson in California, "an alcoholic who led a homosexual lifestyle"—as though there is only one gay lifestyle. I am sure some grandparents squirmed in their seats when they heard this, or like me, blocked it out and silently conformed. The minister, the most talented organizational leader in the church's history, certainly did not consider himself a bigoted and oppressive person. More compelling than vision are the bonds of convention.

◆　◆　◆

The two sensations I like to use as cues to recall happy childhood memories are the experiences of twilight on idyllic summer evenings and eating Concord grapes. Both remind me of Reba and Guy Chandler, who were my substitute grandparents. All of my biological grandparents died before I was born. While I used to see the Chandlers in all the seasons of the year, I remember with the most pleasure the visits on summer evenings. To the glow of citronella candles to ward off the mosquitos, we sat outdoors in their yard at the corner of Brooks and Vincennes streets in Loogootee. The talk was of town scandals, local history, national politics and nature. Reba and Guy grew Concord grapes in their backyard, not more than half a dozen vines, but they tasted better than those of my deceased grandmother whose grape arbour still lingered.

It is hard to imagine someone being alive in the 1980s whose father was born as long ago as 1836. However, this is the year Reba says her father Charles Francis Brown was born in Ohio. He worked as a newspaper printer and editor in several Indiana cities, she says. Reba (1888-1983), the youngest of three children, was born while the family lived in Martinsville. Sadly, her father was far from ideal. When his youngest daughter was a child, he walked out on his wife, leaving her a single parent. The "widow," to use Reba's euphemism, returned to her hometown, lived with a disabled brother and supported the family as best she could as a dressmaker. Reba remembers making paper dolls from illustrations in her mother's old copies of popular fashion magazines such as *The Designer* and *The Delineator*. What Reba did not talk about were her mother's financial hardships which made the daughter an ardent opponent of divorce. Reba followed in the footsteps of her older brother, working as a journalist for the *Martin County Tribune* in Loogootee until her marriage in 1912 to the veterinarian Guy Chandler.

To describe Reba it might suffice to say that people used to tell her she looked like Eleanor Roosevelt. Reba had mixed feelings about the comparison. Not only was Mrs. Roosevelt better known for her intelligence, Reba and Guy rarely made a kind remark about Franklin D. Roosevelt's left-wing politics.

◆　◆　◆

Reba enjoys making denigrating jokes about her appearance. "I wonder if I should go to the wedding? Maybe they'll want to hide me in the broom closet."

◆　◆　◆

"I don't know who planted the dandelions in my yard but they sure did a good job!"

◆　◆　◆

"Scat my cats!" Reba says. "I didn't know it was going to rain."

◆　◆　◆

She remembered the political debates which were hotly contested on the school playground in 1896. The most contentious issue in the Presidential campaign the year she began her formal education was whether the standard for paper money would be gold or silver. As the child of a family supporting the gold standard, she proudly wore a gold cap to school one day but got into a fight with a little girl supporting the opposition. Teachers took them to the principal, a man whose height frightened her.

"I thought he was going to chop my head off level with my ankles," she joked to me.

Instead, the principal suggested that little girls stay out of politics.

◆　◆　◆

"A cat couldn't sneeze in this town without everyone knowing it."

◆ ◆ ◆

From one of Reba's letters: "Loogootee is just as gay and festive as ever and so modern. The woman who has been operating the…eatery has left town with some woman's husband—so we are keeping up with the world."

◆ ◆ ◆

"Am glad you like your work," she wrote me in Toronto, "but don't forget that you are a Yankee Doodle Dandy."

◆ ◆ ◆

Reba and Guy's lifestyle was established long before the advent of the consumer society in America. They obviously believed that respectable people were supposed to live frugally, avoid debt and save money for the uncertainties of the future. I do not think it is outlandish to compare their lifestyle of abstinence to the American Natives who lived so lightly on the land. The Chandlers made few changes to the house given them by an invalid they had cared for. It retained the same casual, old-fashioned decor. They did not even remove the picture on glass of the Grand Canyon, a tourist souvenir, that the invalid had hung in the front window. Reba kept a diary, mostly about weather conditions, which she discarded at the end of every year. Much of her creativity was devoted to the solution of crossword puzzles. What use are finished crossword puzzles? The Chandlers did not save letters and personal memorabilia other than two photograph albums from their early years and the last surviving letter from Reba's grandfather, written in 1850 when he was on his way to the California Gold Rush. No professional photographer made their portrait as a couple. Despite Guy's training in veterinary medicine, they preferred the wild birds that visited their yard rather than domestic pets.

One of Reba's jokes contains more than a kernel of truth about their frugality: "All the shops are blossoming out in Christmas colours even before we have our Thanksgiving turkey; so really we ought to just keep it until next month."

◆ ◆ ◆

"I'm not the person who put the snow on the sidewalk. I'm not going to be the one who takes it away."

♦   ♦   ♦

A few years before the First World War, Loogootee was disturbed by a mysterious window peeper known as the "woman in black." It was commonly assumed that this person was a male transvestite—no one could imagine a woman being a voyeur. The appearances ceased without his or her identity ever being discovered. Reba was then a teenager and living with her mother at the edge of town. She and her closest girlfriend, Emma Norris, walked home together nearly every night from the newspaper office where they worked. One pitch-black night they became so frightened that they asked a man they had accidentally encountered to accompany them. He walked them halfway home, but decided to turn back before reaching the little tree-shaded bridge the girls dreaded the most. Trying to hide his own fear, he told them they were surely so near their destinations that they no longer needed him. The girls were so amused by his fear that they laughed the rest of the way home and for the moment forgot the woman in black.

One day Reba and I labelled the pictures in her oldest photograph album, "Ye Book of Good Times," to quote the title. The album contains amateur photographs, grainy and a bit out of focus, of her circle of friends dressed in their Sunday best circa 1910. In most pictures her friends stage comic scenes. The most inventive tableau shows four young women holding a rug in front of themselves to give the impression they are wearing one dress. The women appear to be as tall as Amazons and to have oddly articulated legs. Behind the rug, they are standing on chairs. Their boyfriends lie on their backs on the ground, their feet sticking out horizontally underneath the rug.

Three other photographs in Reba's album show Emma Norris standing alone in the middle of a dirt road flapping her arms as though trying to fly, several couples sitting on a haystack clutching their hats with the identical gesture and two couples solemnly posing for a fake wedding ceremony. A framed copy of this last scene hung in the Chandlers' dining room.

♦   ♦   ♦

"We all had a nice Christmas. No ice, no snow, no mistletoe."

♦   ♦   ♦

"My life has been such a prosaic one it could be condensed into a short paragraph." From the letters she wrote to me in the last years of her life, this is the paragraph which I think is the best illustration:

> You know about April showers? Well they have turned into downpours and my basement is a sea of soft mud. We had a terrific storm last Sunday night and a near one today. Such celestial fireworks we seldom see. I pulled my chair up to the back door this afternoon and watched the long, forked lightning play over the sky and it was scary. I have a great deal of respect for scientists but they can't put on a show like that or do anything to stop it. The astronauts were lucky to get home but their usefulness has benefited any of us very little. Great accomplishments yes, but little value to humanity. Who am I to question that?—but a cat may look at a king.

♦ ♦ ♦

Having been a tomboy, Reba never learned to sew well. Nor did she learn to cook with more than average skill. "I guess I'd rather play with the dirt outdoors than indoors" is the way she sums up her approach to housecleaning.

♦ ♦ ♦

She refers to green salads as "the leavin's of the garden."

♦ ♦ ♦

"We have had a beautiful wet day, damp around the edges and pouring down in the middle."

♦ ♦ ♦

After her second marriage to a Mr. Hinshaw, Reba's grandmother moved to Lawrence County, Indiana, near the village of Spring Mill. The corn they raised on their farm was ground at a picturesque limestone gristmill built in 1817 and 1818. The village subsequently became a ghost town. But in 1927 it began to be restored as a living-history museum and became the key attraction of a state park. Surrounded by dense forests, Spring Mill village is now the place that gives visitors the most romantic notion of what it was like to have been a nineteenth-century pioneer in southern Indiana.

In the last years of her life, Reba's mother, Martha (Dilley) Brown (1846-1930), gradually lost her eyesight. The family assumed it was caused by the necessity of sewing at night to the weak light of coal oil lamps in order to support her children. They thought it was a kindness not to tell her about the restoration of Spring Mill. They feared she would want to visit and the sad experience of not being able to see the log and stone buildings would be more painful than the thought that the village had just vanished from the map, like so many others.

◆ ◆ ◆

About a visitor who was slow to leave the house: "You could have played checkers on his coattails as he went out the door."

◆ ◆ ◆

Years after his presidency, Franklin D. Roosevelt remains one of the devils of American history to the Chandlers. Reba is reading Elliott Roosevelt's book *An Untold Story: The Roosevelts of Hyde Park* that reveals many of the intimate secrets of his parents' marriage. "I don't know why any son would want to write a book like this about his parents," she said, "but I guess that's the Roosevelt in him."

◆ ◆ ◆

Reba never learned to drive a car, and as a backseat driver, she likes to interpret road signs literally. With the kind of mock naiveté of someone seeing a "do not pass" sign for the first time she says: "Now, how do they expect us to get there if we can't pass?"

◆ ◆ ◆

She used to quote George Bernard Shaw on flowers: "I like children, too, but I don't cut their heads off and stick them in water."

◆ ◆ ◆

The yard on the south side of their home was an ideal place to watch the passing clouds, the setting sun and the stars. The vegetable garden had become a lawn by the time of my adolescence. Their house sat at the edge of town. The yard backed onto unfenced farmland. Less than two blocks away were wild roses, Osage orange trees, trumpet vines and a brook of clear water. Street lights were dim and far apart. Even the century-old maples in their front yard did not obstruct our view of the western sky. Guy could locate and name the most visible constellations. I remember looking for them on warm summer evenings with a feeling of security as though they were imperfections in the living-room wallpaper.

Clouds meant more to Reba and Guy than to anyone else I knew. One afternoon I was sitting in their yard, fluffy cumulus clouds drifted by, and we tried to recognize shapes in them. Guy was less devout than his wife. "Some day I'll ride by on one of these clouds and wave down to you," he whispered.

"And I'll wave right back!" she quickly said reassuringly.

Now that Reba has reached such an advanced age and I am so frequently away from home, there is always the fear when we part that we will not see each other again. She kisses me when I leave and repeats each time the same words. "I'll try to be here when you come back."

♦　♦　♦

I suspect that her best jokes were borrowed from newspaper or radio personalities. However, she remembered them, unlike the rest of us. Maybe someone such as Will Rogers said them first, but they became hers. She was wittier in person. She had a way of laughing at her own words, making them sound funnier than they might look on paper. My selections of her quotations probably makes her appear more Buddhist than she was in reality. Reba represents, to me, village life at its best—and most limited.

I have called Reba and Guy Chandler my surrogate grandparents. It might be more accurate to say that I had a surrogate grandmother but no grandfather. Not only did Guy lack Reba's wit, he was also less patient with children. He was in frail health and had to rest every afternoon. According to one story, he had lost some of the flexibility in his hands, because of the amount of time they were immersed in water while he inspected meat at the Chicago stockyards. The window blinds in their home were drawn because bright sunlight hurt his eyes. He insisted on drinking water without ice.

I learned about Guy's radical politics from other people many years after his death. No one else among my parents' relatives and friends had such faith in self-reliance and unrestrained capitalism. Guy was an opponent of labour unions despite his experiences at the Chicago stockyards. Even now I cannot make sense of the Chandlers' voluntary poverty. Self-denial seemed to be taken to an unhealthy extreme. Their voluntary poverty, more than any other characteristic, invalidated—in my eyes as a child—their conservative and moralistic political convictions. "Frugality means to have little desire for material goods, but worldly people use frugality as a cover for stinginess," the sixteenth-century Chinese philosopher Huanchu Daoren wrote.[8] I am still confused about which term, stinginess or thrift, is the proper label for the Chandlers' lifestyle. This sombre side of their lives might be ignored, if the politics of bigotry and hatred were not too important to casually overlook.

In the 1920s Guy Chandler was a zealous leader of the Ku Klux Klan. As there were few visible minorities to target in Indiana, the hostility of the Klan was directed mostly against Catholics. Loogootee has a large Irish Catholic population surrounded by Protestant farmers. On horseback, and unmasked, Guy led the Ku Klux Klan parade through the streets of Loogootee in April 1924, attracting one of the largest crowds in the town's history. Six Deputy United States Marshals from Indianapolis, who were in plain clothing, accompanied the march, as well as county and city police, eighty special police and forty Deputy Sheriffs. City officials tried without success to block the rally by passing ordinances against demonstrations, but after negotiating with members of the Klan the ordinances were withdrawn.

The local newspaper's editorializing about the Klan parade was motivated primarily by the publisher's awareness of his economic interests. To take sides in such a polarized conflict was risky. The editor sidestepped the real issues, praising the town in awkward, exaggerated language associated with advertising and crude civic promotion. According to "old citizens," the Klan parade was the "greatest occasion ever experienced by the city of Loogootee, as a host, in point of numbers of strangers visiting it." Estimates of the crowd that day vary from 4,000 to 18,000. Guy Chandler's farm, about a mile southwest of town, was selected as the "official rendezvous." The weather is supposed to have been "auspicious for a big gathering" although a small shower of rain fell in the afternoon. In addition to the thousands of visitors arriving by automobile early Saturday, a special train with four "well filled coaches" arrived at six o'clock from Vincennes. In the early evening an airplane "ascended from this point and encircled the city until quite a late hour and entertained the crowd with the dropping of bombs which, when exploded, formed American flags to which were attached balloons that kept them floating in the air for some time and for long distances." The airplane was decorated with lights that formed the outline of a cross.

At eight o'clock between 250 and 400 masked and uniformed marchers formed in line to walk from the Chandler farm to the centre of town. At the front and rear were "hundreds of automobiles." Street lights were turned off just before the parade started to discourage the marchers, but this only made the event more impressive. The march followed streets that had been chosen in advance to lessen the likelihood of violent confrontations. At issue, in particular, was whether the marchers would dare to walk past St. John's Catholic Church. At the conclusion of the march, people returned to the Chandler farm for a program of speeches and initiation ceremonies. Three fiery crosses were burned, one in honour of each group of initiates (men, women and children). One marriage was also celebrated during the Saturday evening ceremonies with the husband and wife dressed in Klan regalia. The *Indianapolis News* won a Pulitzer prize that year for its editorializing against the Klan. The *Martin County Tribune* concluded:

> It must be conceded that those who came as visitors and those who live here as citizens, proved themselves to be well poised people of sound discretion and excellent judgment and richly deserving the applaudits and good will of all concerned for the part each played in preserving law, order and peace upon a very unusual occasion.[9]

In the months following the rally many of Loogootee's residents boycotted Guy Chandler's veterinary business. Later, he could save face by claiming that horses had been his livelihood and that the automobile put an end to his business. This is at least partly true. The Chandlers moved briefly to Denver and in 1927 to Chicago, where Guy worked at the stockyards until his early retirement in 1938.

◆　◆　◆

Reba used to tell a story about a friendship she formed with a Jewish woman in Chicago. "Before I came to America," the woman would say, "I never thought I would like a gentile woman as much as I like you."

I don't know what this story meant to Reba. I can't remember if her husband was in hearing range when she told it. She obviously cared deeply about him. She was grief-stricken when he passed away, but insisted on staying alone the night after the funeral so she could begin to adjust to living by herself. Guy passed away in his sleep. The night before he died Reba went to church as always since her husband had not seemed ill. She returned home to find him asleep in bed. She always regretted that she had not stayed home to spend the last night with him.

◆ ◆ ◆

Speaking in the early 1970s: "The only place you find morality these days is in the dictionary."

◆ ◆ ◆

On North Street a stop sign has a rust streak the full length of its surface, passing through the letter T as if a bicyclist has run over it with sandpaper tires. The S on a pink sign on First Street has been turned into an 8. The centre of the O is plugged. The upper-right corner of the T inflated. Lodged above the O are two wads of chewing gum, and below the message deep rusty scratches. The staple of graffiti artists everywhere, "fuck," is spray-painted across another rusting sign with the freedom of a handwritten script that dims the message of restraint required by social order.

One sign is fading into obscurity, relinquishing both its red and white, as though it is beginning to fret about forcing actions on the public. "Those who assert themselves are not illustrious," the *Tao Te Ching* teaches.

◆ ◆ ◆

The epitaphs on local tombstones may not be original, but they record the heartfelt sentiments which people wanted to preserve in stone. Dying when Indiana was still the frontier, Jesse Moris's siltstone tablet tombstone is one of the few surviving monuments in the Green Cemetery, located atop a low hill surrounded by forests and farmland. Unlike those pioneers commemorated with common fieldstone and little engraving, Morris received an imposing monument decorated with a large, six-pointed star circle and smaller, half-star circles on each shoulder. Carved in graceful letters, as sharp now as the day they were made, is this inscription: "In memory of Jesse Moris who departed this life Nov. 29, 1845...age .. 38 .. years...No kindred si or soft parenthal tear suthed my pale form or grieved my mornful bier...with strangers was my dying trust reposed...by strangers hands my dying eyes was closed...by strangers was my humble grave adorned by strangers honerd by strangers mornd." The carver had to squeeze "tear" into the space between two lines of the text.

◆ ◆ ◆

It is not just rain and lichens that have taken a toll on these tombstones. The Victorian sentiments they record seem so naive today that some epitaphs have become inappropriate jokes, though they remind visitors of the most tragic experiences. Harry Crook was an infant who died on September 2, 1873, age one year and twenty-four days. His humble tombstone in Dover Hill Cemetery is adorned with a carving of a single rose and a lamb. "Sweet Harry unto earth a little while was given," the epitaph reads. "He plumed his wings for flight and soared away to Heaven."

The cooper Henry J. Hyman has left a sentinel marker which allows me to make friends with his ghost. No one ever mentions him or the family. His tombstone in Loogootee's Goodwill Cemetery consists of two limestone barrels sitting on end atop a low limestone platform. A small barrel (eighteen inches long and forty-two inches in circumference) sits on the lid of a larger barrel (thirty inches long and fifty-seven inches around). On the upper barrel is a shallow indentation, a hole signifying that it is a container for liquids. It would matter to a cooper whether the sides of the barrels are straight or bulging. So it is worth noting that these have a slight bulge. On the head of the upper barrel is a limestone adze, a tool for smoothing timber. In square, robust lettering on the pitch of the barrel, the most prominent area of display, is this inscription: "Henry J. Hyman. December 3, 1819-July 1, 1898." In smaller, italicized lettering are the more personal messages. Between the upper chime and booge hoops: "A cooper by trade." Between the two lower hoops: "The sun is the source of all animal and vegetable life."

Hyman's epitaph is subtle, but it is a declaration of agnosticism as strong as he could have made it without causing offense. I like to believe it was Hyman's occupation which inspired a spiritual philosophy that is unusual for this region. A barrel is a useful object because it is empty. In Taoist philosophy an appropriate symbol of human life is an empty, drifting boat. But any empty thing—barrels as well as valleys in the landscape— hold "wonderful, glorious and splendid pure emptiness" (Han Shan, circa 730 AD)[10] Emptiness, at the heart of everything and everyone, is not a source of despair and nihilism. It represents tranquillity, serenity and stillness—all comforting experiences.

Notes

[1] Martin County Courthouse, Shoals, Indiana, *Miscellaneous Records*, Vol. Two, 7.

[2] Carlos McCarty, "Miscellaneous Records," *Martin County Tribune*, March 10, 1927, 8.

[3] Harry Q. Holt, *History of Martin County, Indiana, Volume II, with Partial Autobiography of the Author*, Oxford, IN: Richard Cross Printers, 1966.

[4] *Martin County Tribune*, June 23, 1927.

[5] As quoted in the *Loogootee Tribune*, November 29, 1951.

[6] Maie Clements Perley, *Without My Gloves*, Philadelphia: Dorrance and Company, 1940, 167.

[7] Quotations from a personal interview conducted by Stephen Riggins in 1994.

[8] Huanchu Daoren, *Back to Beginnings: Reflections on the Tao*, Thomas Cleary (trans.), Boston: Shambhala, 1990, 64.

[9] "Had Big Crowd—With Thousands of Visitors Law, Order and Peace Observed and Protected in Loogootee," *Martin County Tribune*, May 1, 1924.

[10] J.P. Seaton and Dennis Maloney (eds.), *A Drifting Boat: Chinese Zen Poetry*, Fredonia, NY: White Pine Press, 1994, 33.

Location of Théophile Frêne's hardware store, Châteauroux, early 1980s.
Photographer: S.H. Riggins

Chris Christiansen juggling, St.-Germain-des-Prés, Paris, mid-1970s.
Photographer: S.H. Riggins

The Search for the Unexpected

In May of 1980 a performance art critic for the *Village Voice*, Sally Banes, accompanied Paul Bouissac to a performance of the Ringling Brothers, Barnum and Bailey Circus at Madison Square Gardens. Paul was in New York giving a course on his circus research at New York University. The information overload and the poor taste exhibited at three-ring circuses had made Banes "dizzy" as a young girl. She had appreciated neither the technical skills of the performers nor the poignant, liberating qualities of a migratory lifestyle. Paul ennobled the circus at the expense of the theatre. Banes did not seem to mind.

> Circus is difficult to watch, and it is also very complicated, very precise. It's not like the theatre, where the information is highly redundant. Here there are maybe 40 acts, only a few minutes long each, and within each act there are six or seven events. That's a lot of information to process.[1]

Paul is never condescending toward circus artists, although he does not begin his study by inquiring about their intentions as performers. Some may be puzzled by his comments, but his research flatters the circus as an institution. Circus acts are ephemeral. Most performers are grateful for the attention they receive, especially when it comes from an academic who ascribes an heroic status to them. In attributing esoteric and eternal messages to the circus, he elevates it to the level of the fine arts and to a central position among mass media. He reminds his readers that the circus may be criticized for its lack of innovation, but the same criticism is frequently made of poetry.

Except for *Circus and Culture*, which appeared in 1976, Paul's writings on the circus are scattered in obscure journals. He has, though, mulled over the possibility of publishing another collection of circus essays in a volume titled *L'Opéra des yeux* [The Opera of the Eyes]. This chapter is an effort to summarize his circus research for lay readers. I'll try to avoid making anyone cross-eyed. His academic writings unrelated to the circus will be ignored for the most part. Also, many of his circus articles are easy to comprehend and do not need an introduction. The result may make his achievements look thinner than they are in fact. I concentrate on key articles about methodology and theory. Theoretical issues are usually the motivation of his writing in the first place. But I begin with why and how he became a semiotician.

♦   ♦   ♦

Unlike the Russian scholar Mikhail Bakhtin who theorized about the carnival on the basis of literary examples,[2] and whose ideas have been borrowed uncritically by so many people, Paul approaches the circus as a participant observer trained in the social sciences. The European one-ring circus has inspired countless painters and writers, but Paul emphasizes how much their ideas differ from the real institution. He speculates that there are five common themes about the circus in the fine arts, all of which tend to be more mythical than ethnographic: ambivalence about nomadism, a poetics of the body, the idealization of risk, the sublime in art and the sad clown.[3]

In his conversations and publications Paul mentions three people, with whom he had personal connections, who exemplify the unsystematic outlook he wanted to avoid. One of the most influential philosophy teachers at the Catholic high school Paul attended was a priest who had been a leader of the anti-Nazi opposition in Périgueux. In the literature on the French Resistance Father Jean Sigala is appropriately called a "red curé." After having been a prisoner of war for a brief time in Germany he returned to his old teaching position. Sigala "made no secret of his hostility to the Armistice and his wish to continue the fight by any means."[4] He was repeatedly reprimanded by the Vichy authorities. The organization Sigala helped launch, "Combat," is of such importance locally that it is publicly commemorated with a plaque honouring its members at the entrance of the school where he taught, the Institution Saint-Joseph. Sigala fostered a strong empirical orientation in his students. In many respects this may be ideal, but taken to an extreme it can hamper the development of theoretical models. It discourages speculation.

Despite his antipathy for history, the circus drawings and diary of Marthe and Juliette Vesque interested Paul because many of their sketches record the whole sequence of routines that constituted an act. Normally, all that has been preserved from the circus past are such inconsequential things as a few images of daring highlights, some tawdry costumes and the basic plots of comic dialogues. The Vesques' collection at the Museum of Traditional and Popular Arts in Paris is so complete that it includes a letter from the sisters' mother, which may recount the very first time her daughters saw a circus, and the last drawing Juliette made on her deathbed. Paul's editing and publication of their work in microfilm form made their sketches accessible to a large public for the first time.[5]

He calls the Vesque sisters "ethnographes sauvages" because they worked with an ethnographer's concern for accuracy but without a theory defining what was important. In a rather undiscriminating manner they attempted to document everything, even itemizing the clothes drying out-side performers' homes and listing their addresses according to type of residence. Although the sisters sought to publish their work, nothing come of their aspirations. They may have been reluctant to choose among the drawings and the diary entries because any selection, even one by the artists themselves, would have excluded some of the information that they gathered so meticulously. Also, preparing the manuscript for publication would have forced them to neglect the living circus for an annoyingly long time.[6] Working within the context of the academic specialty called semiotics is, for Paul, one way of avoiding the eclecticism of Father Sigala and the Vesque sisters.

Semiotics is the study of signs or, as some would say, the science of signs. It is a subdiscipline within the wider field of communication studies. The focus is on the way messages are communicated and understood through the use of written, oral, gestural or artifactual signs—anything which can stand for something else. The communicators can be humans, animals or machines. Exactly how communication takes place through the coding and decoding of signs (along with the inherent miscommunication) is a topic other social scientists examine. But because of the diversity of messages and communicators which semioticians study, it is possible that they are better situated to develop a unified conceptual framework for these activities. Some people think that semiotics has been most successful when applied to literature and related fields such as mass media. In many respects Paul is at heart a literary scholar. He has simply applied semiotics to the somewhat atypical field of live public performances.

In a speech given in 1996 he argues that semiotic analyses have a liberating effect for students. In the right hands semiotics can help to promote a civil society. A kind of anthropology at home, semiotics is not tainted by an association with colonialism, like anthropology proper, or vulgar Marxism as is true for sociology. "Semiotics' reliance on the concepts and terminology of modern telecommunication technology and information theory, as well as the linkages it developed with evolutionary biology, have...endow[ed] its approach with a universalism which makes its models somewhat immune to the danger of being exploited by various forms of localism, tribalism and fundamentalism."[7]

♦ ♦ ♦

One of the most important lessons Paul learned from the anthropologist Claude Lévi-Strauss was to reject a cautious approach to theory construction and to be "boldly speculative." Paul had initially thought, because of Father Sigala, that a proper theoretical model required a lifetime of research. Lévi-Strauss convinced him that no one could ever acquire enough information to build such perfect models and that it is possible to develop theories with limited amounts of information. Lévi-Strauss thus served as the model of a scholar searching for the unexpected and the surprising. This is not the same lesson other students may have learned from an intellectual who became the most quoted anthropologist in the world in the 1970s.[8] They may have been more impressed by his denigration of philosophy, his meticulous scholarship or his austere writing style. Unlike Lévi-Strauss, Paul has been throughout his career as immersed in "field work" as in theorizing. In that sense perhaps he never forgot some of Sigala's lessons, despite agreeing with Lévi-Strauss about the desirability of being a politically disengaged intellectual.

Paul's first contact with Lévi-Strauss occurred during the academic year 1961-62 when he audited one of his seminars at the École des Hautes Etudes en Sciences Sociales. These were the most productive years of Lévi-Strauss' career and the most exciting time to have studied with him. He had published *Structural Anthropology* in 1958 and would publish *The Savage Mind* in 1962. When Paul was young, he had a contradictory character, "both bold and shy." Because of his success in the elitist competitions of the French educational system, Paul felt confident to approach someone of Lévi-Strauss' stature to ask permission to audit a seminar despite not having formally studied anthropology. Understandably, he was somewhat marginal in Lévi-Strauss' seminar because of his atypical background and interests.

We can only speculate about why someone of the anthropologist's stature accepted Paul as an auditor. Other students must have made similar requests. However, Lévi-Strauss was himself an autodidact in anthropology[9] and may have appreciated that quality in the young student. It is uncharacteristic of Paul to seek out the advice of older men and to maintain long-term relationships with them. Firmin Bouglione and Lévi-Strauss are exceptions. Students who attended Lévi-Strauss' lectures or heard his spontaneous reactions to questions may have been privileged because the anthropologist liked to test ideas in semi-public venues. Paul tells a story about a seminar he attended in which Lévi-Strauss beautifully analyzed a myth about a constellation of stars and then the next week redid the analysis because he had learned in the meantime that the constellation looked different in the southern hemisphere. In his study of Lévi-Strauss, David Pace describes how,

> Once the secondary literature is thoroughly assimilated, [Lévi-Strauss] begins to try out his own ideas in his seminars, an arena in which he can explore blind alleys and yet protect himself from premature exposure of his thoughts through a strict prohibition on the use of tape recorders by his students. Only at the end of his careful and painstaking process is he prepared to share his ideas with the public through the medium of scholarly monographs and articles.
>
> …The world of a Breton or a Malraux, a Sartre or a Camus has vanished. How many previous leaders of French intellectual life could have said with Lévi-Strauss, "I have no social life. I have no friends. I pass half my time in my laboratory, and the rest in my office." For better or worse the direct face-to-face encounter with peers, the development of cliques, the search for followers, the review, the café—all these have disappeared from the process of intellectual activity or have been sublimated within an academic structure in which they have taken on a completely different meaning. The philosophe has been replaced by the academic.[10]

The term structuralist is sometimes used to describe literary theorists and social scientists who are strongly influenced by linguistics.[11] More precisely, structuralism is a kind of linguistic determinism in which it is assumed that the meaning of words or signs does not lie in what they refer to but in the way they relate to each other as a system of meaning. A structuralist is looking for the general rules underlying the most basic units in a message that demonstrate how the human mind orders experiences. It is assumed that the system creates the uniquenesses of the messages rather than the reverse. For many researchers, structuralism is an aid in defamiliarizing the commonsensical. It spurs one to look for the commonality in practices which at first glance would seem to be unrelated. If it were not for the technical language which sabotages the humour, Paul's structuralist article about why circus horses have feathers would be quite funny. In general he does not think it is productive to look for origins of customs in the ancient myths of other cultures. Thus, he hypothesizes that the winged horse Pegasus, which occasionally makes an appearance in advertisements and popular entertainments, has nothing to do with why horses wear coloured feathers on their heads. Then he observes that chorus girls in vaudeville and burlesque also tend to be decorated with colourful feathers and wonders, from a male perspective, what women might have in common with horses.[12]

Structuralism tends to be ahistorical and antihumanist. Lévi-Strauss' structural anthropology is the origin of Paul's tactic of reducing the complexity of circus texts to two opposing categories of thought. The binary oppositions readers encounter most frequently in his circus research include nature and culture; human and animal; society and individual; otherness and assimilation; dominance and submission.

Structuralism is probably one source, among others, of Paul's proclivity for assuming that the conscious self is little more than a reflection of social or biological forces. This is reflected in his appreciation of the Gaia hypothesis that life and the environment form a single self-regulatory organism and in the "new animism" which undermines the distinction between humans and animals.[13] More significantly, because he has written often about the topic, this tenet of structuralism is reflected in his appreciation of the concept of meme: ideas which replicate themselves by parasitizing the human mind. If memes are parasite signs, they are relevant to semiotics.[14] An example of how Paul applies this idea to popular entertainment can be found in one of his best essays, which is about the way spectacles with horses provided a blueprint for the treatment of the bicycle when it was first introduced in the circus.[15]

In the 1970s Paul continued to attend Lévi-Strauss' seminars whenever we were in Paris. They met privately maybe once or twice a year, although their relationship tended to be more professional than personal, consistent with David Pace's remark that the anthropologist did not really cultivate followers. Lévi-Strauss once tried to enlist Paul's help in importing North American squirrels for his country home in France. In Paul's words, Lévi-Strauss was "unfailingly supportive of all of [his] research endeavours." His letters of recommendation certainly carried a lot of weight in advancing Paul's career.

◆　◆　◆

The endorsement Lévi-Strauss obligingly wrote for *Circus and Culture* when Indiana University Press requested a blurb for the cover:

> The circus is the living depository of some of the most ancient arts of civilization. Through it, people continue to communicate with animals and with some of the higher powers lying within the normal aptitudes of the species, which, for this reason, is endowed in our eyes with supernatural prestige. We are lucky that Professor Bouissac, who himself is a man of the circus, has at the same time the intellectual capacity and the literary talent necessary to elaborate a theory which has always been lacking and which this book presents in a particularly brilliant manner.

The dedication Paul wrote in the fly-leaf of the copy of *Circus and Culture* which he presented to Lévi-Strauss:

> To Claude Lévi-Strauss whose precise, concrete and constant encouragements have helped bring this first stage to its conclusion. I hope that this work which he kindly agreed to inscribe with his own words will sensitize a larger number of people to the threatened treasures of the circus and thus increase its chances of survival. With respect and gratitude.

◆　◆　◆

Paul received a B.A. from the University of Paris in 1955, specializing in French literature and Classics. His M.A., also from the University of Paris, was awarded in 1958 and included a thesis on wild animal training in the Roman Empire. If he remembers correctly, he did not hear of semiotics until 1963. This was a year after his ghost-written autobiography of the circus director Firmin Bouglione had appeared in print and a year after he had been appointed a sessional lecturer in French at the University of Toronto's Victoria College.

In December 1963 Paul asked Lévi-Strauss if he would supervise his Ph.D. thesis. By then affiliated with the prestigious Collège de France, Lévi-Strauss was no longer at a university which would allow him to direct a thesis. He advised Paul to see Algirdas Julien Greimas at the École des Hautes Etudes. Lévi-Strauss obviously thought that Greimas' approach to structuralism was very promising. The anthropologist had managed to secure a small room for Greimas at the Collège de France which resembled a closet more than a real office. The seminar itself was given once a week in a modest library. Space was so cramped that late-comers had to perch on the window ledges.[16]

March 31, 1964 is the date of Paul's first letter to Greimas. Professor Greimas was enthusiastic about Paul's plans for a thesis and told him that one of the topics of great interest in semiotics was gestures. Within a few weeks Greimas formally agreed to be the director of Paul's thesis, eventually titled *La mesure des gestes* [Taking the Measure of Gestures]. As organizer of a conference on narratology at Urbino in the summer of 1969, Greimas invited Paul to give a paper on narrative structures in circus acts. The day after the presentation on September 7 Paul was having an espresso in the café near the conference centre and was introduced to Thomas Sebeok by the American-Israeli literary theorist Benjamin Hrushovski. Sebeok told Paul how much he liked his presentation, and asked if he would like to come to Indiana University to speak about a similar topic. He also invited him to submit the lecture for publication. This marked Paul's first involvement with North American semiotics. It was an auspicious beginning because Sebeok was for decades the key organizational figure in semiotics in the United States. There is an odd quality about Paul's career—someone who has such disdain for establishment figures is nonetheless surrounded by them.

Anticipating that Paul's work might constitute a breakthrough in the study of gestures, Greimas added one of his conference presentations to a special issue of *Pratiques et langages gestuels*. At the time no perceptible animosity had surfaced between Greimas and Sebeok. Both were participating in the constructive first phase of the semiotic movement, launched officially in Paris in 1966 under the leadership of the Slavic scholar Roman Jakobson and the linguist Emile Benveniste.

What I was considering as the most exciting and valuable approach to ethnology was then structuralism. Since I was sent to Greimas by Lévi-Strauss, Greimas was a part of this aura. Indeed his seminar was extremely interesting. The attendance was international. People who had just arrived in Paris to complete their doctoral studies like Julia Kristeva and Tzvetan Todorov were regular participants. Others included Christian Metz, Jean Cohen and Jean-Claude Coquet, who were to become the main exponents of what started in the late 1980s to be called the School of Paris. At the time Greimas was very open to discussions. He considered his first book a mere tentative proposal and welcomed critical discussions.[17]

In the summer of 1970 when Greimas saw the final draft of Paul's Ph.D. thesis, he was either angry or disappointed that his student had produced an empirically-oriented work making only minimal use of his models and theory. However, the other members of the jury, Jean Cuisenier, Director of the Museum of Traditional and Popular Arts in Paris, and Bernard Pottier, a professor of linguistics at the Sorbonne, appreciated Paul's work. During the oral presentation of the thesis they defended him against Greimas's criticisms.

Despite some lingering tension, Paul attended Greimas' seminars in the 1970s far more regularly than those of Lévi-Strauss. He had quite a few friends there. He used to say it was the most interesting seminar in Paris, not necessarily because of what Greimas was saying, but because of the international crowd he attracted. On a regular basis there were maybe fifty people, sometimes closer to eighty. Greimas himself was contributing only minimally to the seminars. He usually gave only three or four lectures a year.[18] Progressively, the antagonism between Greimas and Sebeok intensified. Greimas identified Paul with Sebeok and became less friendly. Nonetheless, Greimas was part of the initial group of scholars Paul invited to the first International Summer Institute for Semiotic and Structural Studies in 1980.

...Greimas said that he might send someone to tell North America about the latest developments in his school. At this point he was really acting as a sort of master and he was contemptuous of what he called "American semiotics," which he believed did not exist or at least existed only in name.

...The group which had been at the beginning very open in terms of discussion and membership started becoming very restricted, at least in my view. The group moved toward a sort of dogmatism when Greimas started to call his theory the "standard theory of semiotics." At this point they referred to what they did as "sémiotique" as opposed to what Barthes was doing, which he was calling "sémiologie." Greimas had been a friend of Barthes and showed impatience toward his success in the media. Barthes was more charismatic. He had more media savvy and he was writing things which were more "dans le vent," if I can say that.[19]

Sociologists or anthropologists who have an interest in understanding the conventional ways stories are told, for example as an aid in discovering the bias of journalists, may find the early work of Greimas quite stimulating. The later work seems unnecessarily technical and esoteric even to someone with a tolerance for academic jargon. However, Paul does not share my opinion. He considers the later developments in Greimasian semiotics a natural outgrowth of what came before. He continues to regard Greimas' contribution as historically important and far from being exhausted. Among the semioticians of the second half of the twentieth century Greimas is the only one who produced a system and a method. Following Greimas, a student knows how to undertake research. But that does not mean that his theories stand.

For Greimas, the criterion of science is consistency. It is not empiricity. It is fundamentally an idealist approach in the philosophical sense. His system is built on what he called "axioms," primary truths that the mind intuits. In a way there is a sort of Cartesian reliance on the intuition of the individual researcher in the pursuit of truth. It is very different from the approach based on the consensus of a community derived from empirical evidence.

Abandoning Greimas' ideas is partly social in Paul's case, a consequence of his emigration to Canada, and his perception of the incestuous qualities of the Greimasians. In the 1970s Paul became increasingly aware of the implication for the social sciences of evolutionary theory. His identification with the philosophy and methodology of the natural sciences also turned him away from the Greimasians.

I moved toward an evolutionary semiotics in the sense of a perspective which is diametrically opposed to idealism. Because the problem—it may not actually be a problem—a characteristic of the Greimas approach is that narrative structure is an a priori form of understanding. You cannot make sense of anything except through a narrative structure. In as much as evolutionary theory has meaning, it is because it is under the dependence of a priori structures. For

Greimas, evolutionary theory is a discourse. Like he says, if it is a meaningful discourse, it is because it complies with elementary narrative structure. You cannot have meaning without that.

There was a misunderstanding between historians and Greimas. For Greimas, history is not the discovery of fact. It is a discourse which makes sense in as much as it implements these basic mental structures. These are abstract and philosophical choices which it is difficult to refute. If you accept the premises, everything is a discourse. When people criticized Greimas and his followers, the latter went as far as replying "we are not interested in criticisms from outside. We are only interested in criticisms from within the system." So how do you nevertheless do research and believe that you are doing something reasonably scientific?

Although the political upheaval of May 1968 in France had repercussions on the way some French scholars conceptualized popular culture, becoming more sensitive to the potentially subversive aspects of everyday life, it had no real impact on Paul.[20] He was in Canada during the demonstrations but did return to Paris for the summer when police were still visible on the streets. By the 1980s he had become less interested in contemporary French scholarship. He often complained about the linguistic parochialism of Francophone academics. In fact, Paul was never a conventional structuralist. The influence of both Lévi-Strauss and Greimas on his writings became less tangible after the publication of *Circus and Culture*.

◆ ◆ ◆

Semiotics is a qualitative type of research which seeks to uncover hidden meanings in texts, which are defined as "assemblages of signs."[21] Generally, semioticians look at texts for the abstract principles that create coherence. For example, Paul refers to circus acts as texts. The term is not useless jargon. It implies there are common features among the conventions of face-to-face interaction, film and television, public performances and print media. The meaning of any message is assumed to be subtle and fluid. A message acquires meaning by its relationship to other signs and by the social context in which it occurs. The reader, listener or viewer is not free to project any sort of meaning into its content. There are preferred interpretations which are commonly known and which are bound to influence perception. This is why Paul examines speech, gestures, objects, costumes and music in circus acts in such minute detail and as objectively as possible.

The social and political messages conveyed from the circus ring are the focus of his research, not the personal lives of performers or the management of circuses.[22] These are certainly legitimate topics of anthropological and historical study in Paul's view. He is not above gossiping about them. But from a practical and ethical point of view this kind of research is difficult. It intrudes too much into the privacy of people's lives. For instance, how can one frankly discuss in print the repression parents exert on their children in order to make a living out of them as partners in a circus act? Guaranteeing anonymity for informants is nearly impossible due to the small number of performers in any one specialty. Also, Paul anticipates that performers would tell researchers what they want to hear rather than the truth as they see it. The circus is infamous, after all, for the liberties which it takes with the truth.

The radical questioning of truth and of speculation about the ideal ethical relationship between researcher and subject, preoccupations of anthropology in the 1980s and 90s, had little impact on his work. They are mentioned in his writings, for instance in his unflattering assessment of academic rivalry:"...a deep moral crisis when it turns out that human agents are...objectified as 'others' and ultimately construed as mere tokens in some academic power game based on social predation."[23] But turning the spotlight on messages conveyed in public spared Paul the moral agonizing over ethics which social scientists who study people's private lives cannot escape.

Typical of most researchers in semiotics, Paul never surveys spectators or circus fans in order to gather information about their interpretations of shows. He does note spectators' level of enthusiasm for acts or performers, but that is all. His justification is that spectators are not able to articulate in a sophisticated manner what an act means to them and exactly how this meaning was conveyed symbolically. Thus he tends to treat the audience as an undifferentiated mass. Age, class and gender differences are usually ignored despite his awareness that they do matter.

Paul wrote about the circus for nearly three decades before producing an account of his research methods. A researcher who never laughs, he claims, is in a privileged position to understand humour.[24] Although extreme, this is a good way of describing the scientific procedure of establishing an outsider's account of a performance. Paul prefers to talk about writing a "verbal copy" of a performance rather than a description. The latter term is burdened by social scientists' simplistic notions of objectivity and the emphasis of literary writers on being entertaining and inventive. This heritage tends to undermine the goal of producing a systematic account which is so comprehensive that it would enable others to re-enact the performance. The problem of how to represent performances in verbal texts is not solved by turning to film in order to capture the richness of lived experience. Film simply postpones the process of turning reality into words. Unobtrusively making notes while viewing the show or speaking into a tape recorder are Paul's normal procedures. In both cases the act is viewed repeatedly to verify his initial impressions.

He cites two of his papers as examples of his best efforts in producing verbal copies. One is an investigation of two acts—George Carl's comic masterpiece of feigned incompetence and the aerialists Johnny, Mario and Betty Zoppe who fake an accident. This paper is published in my book *Beyond Goffman*. The second essay, published in the journal *Semiotica* in a special issue on the circus which Paul edited, is about different types of trained horse acts that were presented in 1985 at the Knie Circus.[25] I would add his account of a high wire act by the Burger sisters, who were performing in Blackpool in 1978, and his extemporaneous account of Henri Dantès' lion act in the first chapter of this volume.[26] The brevity of the list is partly a consequence of the fact that some of Paul's best essays are not detailed descriptions of individual acts. They are either structuralist explanations or they deal with the evolution of a particular type of circus act.

◆ ◆ ◆

Rather than beginning with absolutely no preconceived ideas about a circus act, Paul advocates bearing in mind some model of communication. His own is based on Paul Grice's research on the tacit principles of conversations and on his own reflections about the differences between good and bad performances.[27] Paul calls these five principles the golden rules of performance. (1) *Accountability*. An implicit contract is established between performer and audience in the advertising for an act and the live presentation by the master of ceremonies. This creates expectations about the type of performance and the pleasure which spectators can anticipate. Performers must attempt to meet these expectations, if they want to to be appreciated. (2) *Effectiveness*. Information needs to be conveyed to the audience in a manner that is both orderly and rhetorical. Obstacles to effective communication such as obscurity, unnecessary repetition and ambiguity ought to be avoided. (3) *Relevance*. Information is more effective if performers stress its relevance to members of the audience. (4) *Timing*. Performers need to keep in mind audience norms with respect to time, for example, the speed with which information is typically conveyed, normal reaction times and the anticipated length of performances. (5) *Propriety*. This requires showing respect for the audience's notions of public etiquette.

Sensitivity to these principles of communication should make it easier for researchers to imaginatively put themselves in the roles of performers and to describe the act.[28] Paul has no trouble finding virtuoso performers who meet these criteria. Nearly every act he analyses in his writings exemplifies these golden rules.

◆ ◆ ◆

One of the exciting aspects of Paul's essays is his application to the circus of ideas other scholars developed when trying to explain written myths and folktales. The research he published in *Circus and Culture* is engaging evidence of Greimas' claim that narrative structures transcend types of messages and even cultures. Two decades after the appearance of his book it still seems the best introduction to his research despite the greater subtlety of his more recent work. He was angered by the extensive copy editing Indiana University Press inflicted on the manuscript because it diluted some of the idiosyncrasies of his writing style. Yet, it undoubtedly made the volume more accessible to the uninitiated.

Performances are seen as acts of communication consisting of static and dynamic components. The static components are the deep, underlying structures of acts, which remain the same regardless of performer. They are generally below the level of consciousness for both performer and spectator. The ease with which circus acts are understood by audiences in different countries is proof that static components do exist. (The exception is clowning which tends to be more culturally specific.) The dynamic components are the features which change from one performer to another or from one act to the next. Since journalists, historians and ordinary spectators are more attentive to the dynamic features, it was more innovative in the 1970s to explore the unchanging elements.

To those unacquainted with abstract models about the universal features of culture it would not be self-evident that stories told live in the ring might be ordered into sequences similar to the stages of written stories. Using an acrobatic act as an example, because it is so simple, Paul theorized (following Greimas) that circus acts consist of five chronological stages: (1) *Identification of the hero*. The acrobat is introduced by the master of ceremonies and the information printed in the program. (2) *Qualifying test*. This is a relatively easy feat which confirms the acrobat's basic competence. (3) *Main test*. The most difficult display of the acrobat's skills. (4) *Glorifying test*. Physically, this should not be the most difficult movement of the routine but it looks challenging and it is presented in a dramatic manner by a drum roll and the master of ceremonies asking for silence from the audience. (5) *Conclusion*. The public recognizes the performer's claim to heroic status by applause.

Even more abstractly an act can be reduced to only three narrative stages: (1) *Presentation of a situation*, such as standing upright. (2) *Introduction of a disrupting factor*, for example a moving trapeze forty feet off the ground. (3) *Control of the disruption*, as when the acrobat manoeuvres the trapeze and demonstrates the theme of human survival through biological superiority. Both models are supposed to be a first step in scrutinizing the unique features of an act and how they are utilized to tell a story. There are, of course, many dramatic ways of claiming heroic status as well as displaying courage.

The binary opposition nature versus culture, for example, is used in a fascinating way to explain the underlying differences between classic zoos and circuses. The classic zoo appeared in the nineteenth century but it was still common in the mid-twentieth century. Classic zoos presented single animals or pairs of animals in individual cages, overlooking a species' normal territorial and mating requirements. Although ethical advances have resulted in larger cages accommodating the male/female ratio that occurs in the wild, species are still rigidly separated from each other and from people by bars, moats and unbreakable glass. In zoos animals are rarely humanized. The pet names of animals, known to the staff, are not usually posted for visitors to see. Employing clear-cut categories—as in myths—zoos accentuate the differences among species and how radically humans differ from animals. In contrast, visitors to circuses observe animals performing feats associated in everyday life with other species. Animals are humanized through clothing, personal names and gestures. Presentations also include metaphorical elements, as if a tiger were a trainer's mistress or as gentle as a lamb. Employing ambiguous, overlapping categories—as in rites—circuses depict the basic similarity among all the highly evolved species including animals and humans.

> ...If it is true that myths and rites are the result of two complementary *mouvements de pensée*—one organizing the experience in a network of discontinuous categories, the other attempting to compensate for the inadequacy of the system with respect to the actual experience of everyday life—the zoo can be legitimately viewed as a visual mythical discourse and the circus as its complementary rite, at least in some aspects of the treatment of the animals it displays.[29]

◆ ◆ ◆

Having described the universals of performances, there seemed to be few reasons to dwell on the topic. Since the mid-1970s Paul has turned his attention almost exclusively to the nuances of individual acts. The most interesting studies, regardless of the decade in which they were published, typically contain some far-fetched idea which may puzzle readers to such an extent that they question his seriousness. In one example, Paul proposes that clowns defile the sacred notion that people are profoundly different from animals.

This scenario involves a tramp clown and a white-faced clown. The first is conceptualized by Paul as an exaggerated symbol of nature: ugly, dressed in a vulgar fashion, masculine, facial makeup that emphasizes natural protuberances, large mouth, dishevelled hair and behaving in a way that shows either misunderstanding or disrespect for conventional rules. The latter is an exaggerated symbol of culture: elegantly dressed, somewhat androgynous, artificially white face, thin lips, asymmetrical eyebrows, hair hidden by a hat and an enforcer of conventional rules. The male tramp clown is dressed as an outrageously vulgar woman. He pushes a baby carriage into the ring. At first he behaves like a conventional mother or nanny. Loud shrieks come from the carriage. The clown runs from the ring, returning with a gigantic bottle of milk. The bottle is quickly emptied. The child starts crying again. At this moment the audience discovers that the carriage does not contain a human infant but a live piglet wrapped in clothes. The white-faced clown enters. From this point the story can have a variety of endings. Sometimes "the child" continues to urinate copiously on the clowns, at other times on a member of the audience.

The substitution in the act exposes the underlying similarity between human infants and animals, a fact society tries hard to deny through pronatalist ideologies celebrating parenthood. It is difficult, expensive and time-consuming to raise children. If human populations are to increase, there must be a mystique which exalts parenthood. Confusing a beast for an infant—especially one which is the very essence of animality—undermines the parenthood mystique. Although the pig is a domesticated mammal raised for food, it is on the borderline of the pet category. Unlike most farm animals, it is nearly as hairless as a human. Its expressive face is easily humanized in caricatures. Until the start of factory farming, pigs were traditionally fed leftovers from the kitchen table. Through this kind of critique, the widely circulated postcard showing Prince Charles, his wife Diana and a pig—which has been substituted for their first-born son—acquires a new meaning that is broader than just anti-monarchist sentiment.

♦ ♦ ♦

In 1973 Paul was awarded a Guggenheim Fellowship for a research project on clown performances. We lived in Paris from November 1973 to August 1974. The research required occasional visits to England. For Paul, grants are in part rewards; in part, contracts. He preferred to look at the Guggenheim as a reward because he thought that an obsession with meeting the terms of a contract might stifle creativity. In his opinion it is important that the dynamics of research not be so impeded by expectations that the scholar is prevented from making unanticipated discoveries. Too much planning is likely to kill research.

The proposal was to compile a systematic record of clown acts, including dialogue, gestures and clothing. Given the amount of work this was supposed to entail, the first stage was devoted to a single clown. Paul's preference was the Frenchman Charlie Cairoli, whom he called "one of the greatest clowns of our time." Cairoli had performed for more than thirty seasons at the Blackpool Tower Circus in England, a stationary circus which obliged Cairoli to invent new acts every year. He had a workshop where he created objects for his show, such as a toilet seat strung as a harp. These humorous objects reminded Paul of the jokes of the nineteenth-century clown Joseph Grimaldi, the "Michelangelo of buffoonery." In the ring Cairoli reminded some spectators of a middle-aged Charlie Chaplin: classic black vest, bowler hat, tiny round nose, a good-natured but crafty personality.

Although it is not mentioned in the proposal, Paul was convinced that at a deep level there were similarities between the radical social critique of Herbert Marcuse and the themes of this naive comedian. This may be one reason why the working-class spectators of Blackpool were so enthusiastic about Cairoli. Paul observed one of the clown's acts in 1978 which presented variations on the employer-employee relationship. Paul's paper titled "The Syntax and Semantics of Chaos" illustrates a point he makes elsewhere: there is always an underlying order in the staged chaos of the circus. The act opens with the circus hands and the master of ceremonies carrying a table into the ring on which a bucket of white paint and a chair is sitting. One of the employees awkwardly removes the chair overturning the bucket of paint. The master of ceremonies pretends this is a real accident. Three clowns, including Cairoli, then enter the ring dressed as construction workers. They appear to be on their way home from work. They carry with them a bucket and a tray for plastering which is covered with lather.

The master of ceremonies asks Cairoli to clean up the mess, "for old time's sake," although it is past the hours of work. A series of gags ensues which always ends with someone being covered with paint or lather. Eventually, the master of ceremonies returns. Disgusted with the mess, he orders a circus hand to clean it up. He says to the clowns: "You see, that was simple. Five seconds! The job is done and the man is clean! Look at yourself!" The three clowns gang up on the circus hand and coat him with paint and lather.

All the sequences of the act are constructed in a similar manner. An assailant, using a liquid or semi-liquid, is intentionally aggressive toward an unsuspecting target. Every character is in turn aggressor and victim. A climax is created by the performers establishing temporary alliances. Paul summarizes the spectacle in the form of a table that lists the components of each phase of the act: the aggressor, the aggressive action, the person who is targeted, the part of the body which is targeted, the substance used and the object which contains this substance. The conclusion spectators derive from this act, Paul assumes, is that if you are a worker, it does not matter how good you are: you always suffer. In pre-Thatcherite Britain the working class knew the proletariat was always punished. The act presented two models of worker, some unionized, some playing the game of the bosses: in the end everyone gets wet.

◆ ◆ ◆

Paul has taken a consistent, some would say mistaken, stance towards academic institutions. In these debates his rhetoric is wonderful. Its emotional intensity suggests autobiographical motivation. What grates on the nerves of some people is the extent to which he idealizes marginal institutions and vilifies the mainstream. Semiotics "has subsisted for a long time in the interstices and cracks of mainstream institutions, being sometimes tolerated, sometimes ignored, nevertheless relentlessly working toward the hybridization of knowledge under the nose, so to speak, of the self-confident 'apparatchiks' of mainstream disciplines."[30] He compares semioticians' search for intellectual validity in the works of founding fathers as "totemism." The big names of modern semiotics are dismissed as "grand barons."[31] Most discrediting of all is his belief that intellectual continuity—the ideal for many—may be an indication of failure: "Would it not be possible to entertain the idea that semioticians form a sort of medieval rear guard, intellectually fascinated and paralyzed by a model (the sign) and cultivating an outdated *doxa* in the form of a terribly repetitive history?"[32]

Semioticians who want to mine the past for insights useful in contemporary research are ostracized. Since many semioticians have been trained in literature and philosophy, an attachment to the past is not surprising. For Paul, this is disciplinary nostalgia, a dead end, and he does not hesitate to use comedy to ridicule pretensions. Looking backwards distracts semioticians from engaging with contemporary science. "My motivation…is not a philosophical commitment to semiotics, but a commitment to science."[33] So he claims that it is essential for semioticians to have an understanding of how the brain and the body function. In coding and decoding signs, human and animal communication cannot be free of biological constraints. In light of his own humanistic and literary education, fidelity to scientific methods would seem, at some level, to be counterproductive because it does not utilize what he can do best.

The theme of the first editorial Paul wrote for his newspaper *The Semiotic Review of Books* (SRB), "The lesson of Durkheim," was the way the Durkheimians provided the ideal model for collaborative research. This group of scholars, named after one of the founding figures in sociology, Emile Durkheim, was most active between 1890 and the outbreak of the First World War. Assuming no one could be a professional sociologist by reading only sociology, they ransacked all the social sciences for whatever might be relevant to their emerging discipline.

Beginning in 1990, Paul edited *SRB* for over a decade before passing it on to Gary Genosko. The review continues but with more emphasis on cultural studies and less input from natural scientists. At the start it was published in the form of an inexpensive newspaper to save money. Then in 1996, when Paul created the Cyber Semiotic Institute, it became available on the Internet. The cyber institute was later incorporated into a wider Internet site called the Open Semiotics Resource Centre, which offers free publications, advertisements of future conferences, advanced non-credit courses, bibliographies and the archives of *SRB*. Paul's editing of a one-volume encyclopedia of semiotics, published by Oxford University Press, is another example of this collaborative approach.[34] Paul sees semiotics as a "global workshop." When he assumed the editorship of the *Canadian Journal of Semiotics* in 1981, he renamed it *Recherches Sémiotiques / Semiotic Inquiry (RS/SI)*, hired a professional designer (Helen Mah of Dragon's Eye Press) to redo the journal physically and sought a more international group of contributors.

Paul gave his colleagues at Victoria College the impression that they were on the cutting edge of research. In 1973 he founded the Toronto Semiotic Circle, an informal group of professors who were interested in linguistics, communication, animal behaviour and literary theory. The members met six or eight times a year for lectures. The Circle also published thirty monographs. "From the outset, the Circle was not a divisive organization but a congenial group whose founding members were mature scholars. Their philosophical convictions were somewhat tempered by a small dose of skepticism and their genuine interest was the interdisciplinary circulation of ideas rather than the promotion of a particular doctrine."[35] The page-long history of the circle which Paul wrote downplays his key role in the organization. It was his brainchild and it lapsed once he devoted his full-time attention to other concerns.

Paul was also a tireless organizer of over thirty conferences and four month-long International Summer Institutes for Semiotic and Structural Studies (ISISSS). Only two of the conferences (on Foucault and Cocteau) might be seen as orthodox topics in French studies. He lured a procession of famous academics to Toronto including philosophers Michel Foucault and Jacques Derrida, semiotician and novelist Umberto Eco, anthropologist Mary Douglas, feminists Luce Irigaray and Theresa de Lauretis, psychologists Jerome Brunner, Karl Pribram and Howard Gardner, philosopher of language John Searle, literary theorist Paul Ricoeur, mathematician René Thom, social critic Ivan Illich and novelist Percy Walker. More often than not the stars of ISISSS and the conferences were people whose research Paul did not particularly admire. He thought they would "make a good poster," attracting participants to more substantial lectures by middle-rank academics. In terms of advancing his own career locally this organizational work was not the most effective strategy because it was not obvious that Paul was the ringmaster of these events. He invited colleagues to be co-organizers or collaborators, but chose people who would "not interfere with his plans."

His outstanding contribution to Victoria College was the four month-long International Summer Institutes for Semiotic and Structural Studies in 1980, 1982, 1984 and 1987. The organizational structure of ISISSS was also his idea. The justification was that the economic crunch that began in the mid-1970s made it difficult to invite high-profile speakers to the University of Toronto. As much as possible the institutes were organized to be self-financing, relying on one-time grants and money from participants. There were 150 to 180 registered full-time participants at each ISISSS but many more people attended a few lectures or one of the weekend conferences. The goal was to create a "synergy of resources," centred alternatively at the University of Toronto and various American universities during the other years. Another reason for ISISSS was that semiotics was coming of age and many in the field agreed that summer institutes comparable to those in linguistics would bring together specialists from a variety of domains and provide advanced teaching for students and colleagues from all over the map. A kernel of collaborators for ISISSS existed in Toronto through the Toronto Semiotic Circle. Paul benefited from the help of supportive and resourceful multi-disciplinary committees. The choice of invitees was normally a result of long discussions. Sometimes some committee members insisted that certain temperamental scholars not be invited because they would make his task nearly impossible.[36]

> I often joked that I had to handle elephants and prima donnas. Indeed, we dealt with big egos which required constant attention as do stars and dangerous animals in a circus program. They had to be properly fed—paid. We had sometimes to reduce the chances of contact between two or more elephants because of potential clashes. They had to be handled with kid gloves.
>
> My personal enjoyment in dealing with all the problems and difficulties was that I experienced them in the light of my previous circus experience. I metaphorized the selection of a program as if it were a circus program in which you have to balance various specialties. The whole venture was set up in an environment of risks because its success depended entirely on how many people from outside the University of Toronto our program would attract. The institutes were in a sense nomadic since there was no permanent institutional structure. Rather it was like pitching our tents in the no-man's land of the academic disciplinary landscape. There were a lot of practical problems of securing contacts with high-profile professors who would provide a high degree of visibility in the same manner as a circus program must have some highlights that are featured on a poster.
>
> Like a circus, there was no institutional burden to carry except repeating the performance with a different program. ISISSS was always characterized by a certain amount of precariousness and required a lot of snap decisions and improvisations with the imperative that the show must go on.[37]

In Toronto all courses proposed for the ISISSS had to be cleared by the School of Graduate Studies and carried half a credit, although most participants were simply auditors, many full-time professors. Course credit required a minimum of twenty-four hours of contact with students, both formal lectures and seminars. Since each month-long institute consisted of between fifteen and twenty courses, the timetable was dense. It had to be strictly observed. A class could not start late and end late. It was necessary to assert an authoritarian management which was out of character with Paul's commitment to creative freedom and anarchistic thinking. That's why he always tried to orchestrate an institutional environment that furthered the creation of a sort of "counter institute." He secured classrooms for practically anyone who wanted to conduct critical discussions or alternative approaches within the texture of the institute itself. Rebellious ideas were given space and an audience. An impression of the atmosphere at the counter institutes is conveyed in a review of the first ISISSS in 1980:

> Perhaps the most remarkable feature of the month's activities was the lively, even passionate, argument and discussion that continued through all our waking hours. Those of us who lived in the dormitory accommodation would often sit up into the small hours, debating the nature, future and direction of semiotics. Sometimes we pontificated, sometimes lapsed into irreverence or irrelevance; but nobody was willing to waste any of that precious time. . . . Activities hardly seemed to stop at all. . . . The evening lectures gave all interested visiting scholars the opportunity of flexing their intellectual muscles before a sympathetic audience.[38]

◆　◆　◆

Paul is a critic of psychologists' efforts to teach abstract concepts such as colour, shape and numbers to animals. He thinks these experiments are marred by the kind of wishful thinking that resembles pet owners projecting feelings and reasoning onto their animals. "What does a question mean to a parrot?" is the seemingly flippant way he criticizes I.M. Pepperberg's efforts to communicate with an African Grey Parrot named Alex.

No one doubts that animals can recognize perceptual differences and similarities. If they had not mastered these skills, they would have vanished long ago. But what do recognizable differences mean to parrots when they involve animals that are neither prey, predator or mate? Paul theorizes that among humans the meaning of questioning varies depending on the social context in which it occurs. A question may be a request for an exchange of information between people of equal status, for instance a driver asking the location of a street. A question may be an indication of social inequality, as when an answer is demanded from someone of lower status. Questioning is also an aspect of teaching, when the student realizes that the teacher already knows the answer. Unless parrots are able to imagine models of communication, he claims, true symmetrical interspecies communication cannot take place.

In Paul's opinion, psychologists who try to teach human-like communicational competence to animals and to conduct dialogues with them are guilty of fantasizing that all minds can communicate and that communication is always good. This is "the benign side of the human drive toward the mastering of other forms of life. It should not be forgotten that from horses and elephants to dolphins, dogs, pigeons and micro-organisms, *Homo sapiens sapiens* has consistently used the mastery of inter-species communication for warfare."[39] Evolutionary competition between species—what Paul terms the semiotic arms race—often favours non-communication because it keeps competitors from discovering food supplies and vulnerabilities. Hiding information from other species can be a useful evolutionary strategy. Perhaps elephants were better off before humans discovered that they can communicate over long distances via low-frequency sounds which are beyond the range of human hearing. Our eavesdropping on elephant communication makes it simpler to fully domesticate the species. Now that it is easier to breed them in captivity it may no longer be necessary for large herds to survive in the wild. The genetic variety of elephants may be reduced by the human selection of desirable traits.

Although Paul has demonstrated a life-long interest in the scientific literature on animal behaviour, whether in captivity or in the wild, he shows more enthusiasm for reading about animals than seeing them in the wild. He is oddly insensitive to popular Romanticism's emphasis on human emotional and spiritual responses to natural scenery. Nor does he seek the restorative powers of untamed wilderness. Writers in this vein, such as John Muir and Aldo Leopold, he never reads. Most professional people in Toronto have a cabin in Muskoka. This holds no appeal either. In our more than thirty years together we have visited countless zoos and circuses, but no national and provincial parks in North America, despite my having lived for three years in Alberta not too far from the Rocky Mountains. (Paul has, however, visited national parks in India.) Animal liberationists who campaign for an animal-free circus are anathema to him. Neither of us is a strict vegetarian, but we have reduced the amount of meat in our diet.

Readers trying to make sense out of Paul's audacious analyses of circus acts might like to know that this is his favourite compliment about his research: "I'm not sure I was convinced by what you said, but it made me think."

Notes

[1] Sally Banes, "Reading the Circus/And You Thought it was Just for Fun," *Village Voice*, May 26, 1980, 37.

[2] Mikhail Bakhtin, *Rabelais and His World*, Bloomington: Indiana University Press, 1984.

[3] Paul Bouissac, "The Circus as a Topos of European Literature and Art," in Earl Miner and Haga Toru, eds., *The Force of Vision, I. Proceedings of the XIIIth Congress of the International Comparative Literature Association*, Tokyo: University of Tokyo Press, 1995, 447-454.

[4] H. R. Kedward, *Resistance in Vichy France: A Study of Ideas and Motivation in the Southern Zone 1940-42*, Oxford: Oxford University Press, 1978, 26. See also Georges Rocal and Léon Bouillon, *Jean Sigala (1884-1954)*: *Mémorial*, Angoulême: Editions Coquemard, 1954.

[5] Paul Bouissac, "Un cas d'ethnographie sauvage: L'oeuvre de J. et M. Vesque," *Revue d'ethnologie française*, Vol. VII, No. 2, 1977, 111-120; Paul Bouissac, "L'Amour ethnographe," Préface to Marthe et Juliette Vesque, *Le Cirque en images: Archives d'ethnologie française*, Paris: Larose et Maisonneuve, 1978, 19-27; Marthe et Juliette Vesque, *Le cirque en France de la Belle Epoque à la fin de la deuxième guerre mondiale*, Tomes I et II, 18 cahiers d'études iconographiques, catalogue analytique, 722 documents iconographiques, Paul Bouissac, ed., Archives et Documents, Institut d'Ethnologie, micro-édition (Microfiche AOO 883 144).

[6] Lévi-Strauss wrote Paul to congratulate him on his research about the Vesques' drawings. His message is another sign of the formality and mutual respect which characterized their relationship: "I thank you for having sent me your two articles on the Vesque sisters. Reading them was a delight; you have rendered the most beautiful homage to these exceptional persons. I consider their botanical drawings to be masterpieces, and I await with even greater impatience, after having read your work, the publication of their drawings concerning the circus. Happy to know that you continue to pursue your beautiful work." (February 1976).

[7] Paul Bouissac, "Can Semiotics Progress?," *The American Journal of Semiotics*, Vols. 15 and 16, 2000, 12-13. This article was the Thomas A. Sebeok Fellowship Lecture for 1996.

[8] David Pace, *Claude Lévi-Strauss: The Bearer of Ashes*, Boston: Routledge & Kegan Paul, 1983, 7.

[9] Marcel Hénaff, *Claude Lévi-Strauss and the Making of Structural Anthropology*, Minneapolis: University of Minnesota Press, 1991, 18.

[10] Pace, 4.

[11] Hans Bertens, *Literary Theory: The Basics*, London: Routledge, 2001, 67.

[12] Paul Bouissac, "Why Circus Horses Have Feathers: The 'Truth' of Natural Objects," in Marc de Mey et al, eds., *International Workshop on the Cognitive Viewpoint*, Ghent: University of Ghent Press, 1977, 46-52.

[13] Paul Bouissac, "Gaia no kigoron o mezashite" (Toward a Semiotic Theory of Gaia), Interview with Masao Yamaguchi, Translation by Fumito Saito, *Herumesu*,

45, May 9, 1990, 42-52; Paul Bouissac, "Semiotics and the Gaia Hypothesis: Toward the Restructuring of Western Thought," *Philosophy and the Future of Humanity*, Vol. 1, No. 2, April 1991, 168-184; Paul Bouissac, "What is a Human? Ecological Semiotics and the New Animism," *Semiotica*, Vol. 77, No. 4, 1989, 57-77.

[14] Paul Bouissac, "Why do Memes Die?," in John Deely, ed., *Semiotics 1992*, Lanham, University Press of America, 1993, 183-191; Paul Bouissac, "Editorial: Memes Matter," *Semiotic Review of Books*, Vol. 5, No. 2, 1994, 1-2; Paul Bouissac, "On Signs, Memes, and MEMS: Toward Evolutionary Ecosemiotics," *Sign Systems Studies*, Vol. 29, No. 2, 2001, 624-646.

[15] Paul Bouissac, "Technological Innovations and Cultural Semiosis: The Ritualistic Appropriation of the Bicycle by the Circus," in Marlene Landsch, Heiko Karnowski and Ivan Bystrina, eds., *Kultur-Evolution: Fallstudien und Synthese*, Frankfurt am Main: Peter Lang, 1992, 169-197.

[16] Paul Bouissac, "Eclaircies de la parole," *Semiotica*, Vol. 112, Nos. 1/2, 1997, 49.

[17] Paul Bouissac interviewed by Stephen Riggins, February 12, 1999.

[18] Paul gave three presentations in Greimas' seminar: "Pour une expression mathématique des gestes" (December 19, 1967), "Structures poétiques vs. structures narratives" (January 31, 1974), "Les modalités dans le discours visuel" (February 1, 1978).

[19] Paul Bouissac interviewed by Stephen Riggins, March 7, 1999.

[20] Brian Rigby, *Popular Culture in Modern France: A Study of Cultural Discourse*, London: Routledge, 1991; Ben Highmore, *Everyday Life and Cultural Theory: An Introduction*, London: Routledge, 2002.

[21] Daniel Chandler, *Semiotics: The Basics*, New York: Routledge, 2002, 2.

[22] Paul Bouissac, "Introduction: The Circus—A Semiotic Spectroscopy," *Semiotica*, Vol. 85, Nos. 3/4, 1991, 189-199.

[23] Paul Bouissasc, "The Construction of Ignorance and the Evolution of Knowledge," *University of Toronto Quarterly*, Vol. 61, No. 4, Summer 1992, 462.

[24] Paul Bouissac, "From Joseph Grimaldi to Charlie Cairoli: A Semiotic Approach to Humour," in Antony Chapman and Hugh Foot, eds., *A Funny Thing, Humour: Proceedings of the International Conference on Humour and Laughter, Cardiff, Wales, July 14-16, 1976*, London: Pergamon Press, 1977, 115-118.

[25] Paul Bouissac, "Incidents, Accidents, Failures: The Representation of Negative Experience in Public Entertainment," in Stephen Harold Riggins, ed., *Beyond Goffman: Studies on Communication, Institution and Social Interaction*, Berlin: Mouton de Gruyter, 1990, 409-443; Paul Bouissac, "From Calculus to Language: The Case of Circus Equine Displays," *Semiotica*, Vol. 85, Nos. 3/4, 1991, 291-317.

[26] Paul Bouissac, "System Versus Process in the Understanding of Performances," in Ernest Hess-Lüttich, ed., *Multimedial Communication, Vol. II: Theatre Semiotics*. Tübingen: Gunter Narr Verlag, 1982, 63-74.

[27] H. Paul Grice, "Logic and Conversation," in Peter Cole and Jerry Morgan, eds., *Syntax and Semantics: Speech Acts*, New York: Academic Press, 1975, 41-58.

[28] Paul Bouissac, "The Semiotic Approach to Performing Arts: Theory and Method," in Roberta Kevelson, ed., *Hi-Fives: A Trip to Semiotics*, New York: Peter Lang, 1998, 41-54.

[29] Paul Bouissac, *Circus and Culture: A Semiotic Approach*, 121.

[30] Paul Bouissac, "Can Semiotics Progress," 16.

[31] Paul Bouissac, "L'institution de la sémiotique: stratégies et tactiques," *Semiotica*, Vol. 79, Nos. 3/4, 223.

[32] Paul Bouissac, "Praxis and Semiosis: The 'Golden Legend' Revisited," *Semiotica*, Vol. 79, Nos. 3/4, 301.

[33] Paul Bouissac, "The Potential Role of Semiotics for the Advancement of Knowledge," *Recherches Sémiotiques/Semiotic Inquiry (RS/SI)*, Vol. V, No. 4, 1985, 340.

[34] Paul Bouissac, Editor-in-chief and contributor, *Encyclopedia of Semiotics*, New York: Oxford University Press, 1998.

[35] Paul Bouissac, "Semiotics in Canada," in Thomas A. Sebeok and Jean Umiker-Sebeok, eds., *The Semiotic Sphere*, New York: Plenum Press, 1986, 83.

[36] In "An Encyclopedia of Semiotics: ISISSS '82 in Review," *Semiotica*, Vol. 45, Nos. 1/2, 1983, 104, Roger Joseph wrote: "Readers of this journal may be surprised to encounter Foucault, Pribram and Searle at an institute devoted to semiotic and structural studies. It is to the credit of Paul Bouissac, the director of ISISSS '82, and his capacious notion of the parameters of what is entailed in semiotic analysis, that the participants were given an opportunity to sample such a broad and illustrious group of scholars."

[37] Paul Bouissac interviewed by Stephen Riggins, September 19, 1999.

[38] Michael Herzfeld, "The Music of the Hemispheres: ISISSS '80 in Review," *Semiotica*, Vol. 34, Nos. 3/4, 1981, 221.

[39] Paul Bouissac, "Ecology of Semiotic Space: Competition, Exploitation and the Evolution of Arbitrary Signs," *The American Journal of Semiotics*, Vol. 10, Nos. 3-4, 1993, 159.

Stephen Riggins playing
the piano, St. John's
Newfoundland, 2003.
Photographer: Ho Tam

Rue Guy de la Brosse, Paris, 1974.
Photographer: S.H. Riggins

Michel Viala and Paul Bouissac, Paris, early 1970s.
Photographer: S.H. Riggins

Stolen Time

In the Toronto of 1969 no one would have thought of finding an authentic French structuralist at the Saint Charles Tavern. Dark, windowless and smoky, there was nothing romantic about the Saint Charles. An oval-shaped bar, long but narrow enough that patrons could dimly see the men facing them. In the rear were cheap tables. Located near a commercial intersection, Yonge Street two blocks north of College Street, the building had been erected in 1871 as a fire station. A dilapidated, wooden clock tower was all that remained of Engine House Number Three. That the tavern was as cozy as an oversized barn was not a surprise since the building dated from a time when fire stations housed horses. The Saint Charles had also served as a distribution centre for the hay and feed for horses at other fire stations. After the building was sold by the fire department because traffic on Yonge Street interfered with the operation of fire trucks, it had been transformed into a used car depot.

During my first two weeks in Toronto I lived a block from the Saint Charles at the College Street YMCA. All it took to find congenial company at the YMCA was to leave the door slightly ajar. But I quickly realized that I would have to summon up the courage to go to a bar, if I hoped to meet anyone other than travellers sweeping through town. The first time I stepped across the threshold of the Saint Charles I met no one. The second time someone vaguely interesting whom I never saw again. The third time I met Paul. It was late September 1969. I had been in Toronto for about one month. Paul was sitting at the bar of the Saint Charles Tavern and I moved to sit beside him. I started the conversation with the most banal first-liner, asking if he had a cigarette. Actually, neither of us smokes. We talked for a while. Then he whisked me off to the nearby lounge on the roof of the chic Sutton Place Hotel, which had live music and a dramatic view of downtown skyscrapers.

Paul had been described four years earlier in *Maclean's* magazine as "a short plump pedant of thirty-one, given to wearing sedate black suits and a black homburg. He has a soft Charles Boyer accent, a prim donnish chuckle and brown eyes that peer owlishly through horn-rimmed spectacles."[1] I would have made him sound more handsome than this. For me, he grew a mustache and updated his clothing. Before arriving in Toronto at age 23, I had already read Alfred Kinsey, D.H. Lawrence and various sociologists who specialized in "deviance." A staff member at Indiana University's Kinsey Institute of Sex Research had interviewed me during the pretest stage for one of their studies of gay men. I had fond memories from 1967 of the way gay men had appropriated the outdoor market on Elizabeth-Platz in Munich, Germany, not far from my university residence.

We began living together within a week of our first date. Paul needed roommates to share the expenses of his eight-room apartment at 110 Bedford Road, a Victorian brick house in the trendy Annex neighbourhood. The furniture in Paul's own rooms and in the common living room was second-hand discards from friends. Even the Salvation Army would have hesitated to put them up for sale: over-stuffed couches and chairs worn on the arms, a wooden dining table carved with the names of his dinner guests. At my suggestion we accommodated American draft dodgers resisting the Vietnam War.

Three months later we experienced an "eclipse." We quarrelled over my continued attachment to my lover in Indiana, named after a hero of the American Revolution. Paul found an apartment for me with some other men who lived across the street at 101 Bedford Road, and I moved there for two or three months. Nothing is left of these quarrels except for two of Paul's brief messages. This message is illustrated with a drawing of a rotund toad which has a tear in its eye:

Dear Toad. This is a little word of apology which I feel I owe you, in the lucidity of this morning. Please forgive me for having over-drank, having been sick, desperate without reason and having woken you up in the middle of the night. Storms are a part of nature and depressions belong to the universal landscape. A sorry and repenting Toad.

We had begun to see each other again but the occasions were still somewhat strained when Paul wrote:

Dear Stephen. I am curious (not yellow)[2] to hear Berlioz's *Requiem* tonight—because of a certain taste of mine for Requiems which is not entirely psychologically motivated; because its powerful structure and sound does not come through my speakers satisfactorily and it makes it difficult to get the most favourable aspect of it; and because it is conducted in memory of Charles Munch for whom I always had a great admiration. If you feel like trying the experience with me (2nd gallery) and if you happen to be free tonight—could you give me a ring (I mean a phone call) around 7:00 tonight. If not could I have the pleasure of escorting you on the 31st to the art gallery (see invitation attached). I suggest that we leave at home, locked in a safety box, Mrs. Pride and Mr. Resentment. (March 5, 1970)

♦ ♦ ♦

One night in June 1981 I wander off to Saint-Germain-des-Prés to watch the street performers. June has been exceptionally cold. But the night's fine weather attracts more people to the street. Otherwise, nothing is unusual. Romain Rolland once wrote that the French capital is a collection of small towns, which rarely mingle: musical Paris, scientific Paris, fashionable Paris, political Paris, working-class Paris, et cetera.[3] In retrospect, I see with some dismay that what I found that night is the Paris of tourists. Here is my impression—a stranger's—of what was before my eyes twenty years ago and has now vanished. It won't seem much of a loss. Gaze too closely at street performers (with some exceptions) and their sublimity starts to fizzle. They're best sampled amidst beautiful buildings, chats with friends, flirting and window shopping.

Battling for attention in front of the centuries-old stone church are an Egyptian father and son acrobatic team; two jugglers whose name might suggest the quality of their act, the Ball Boys; a reckless jazz band; an unruffled goat climbing a ladder (the same trainer I noted earlier but a different animal); and a rogue setting off Roman Candles in the midst of the crowd. Their flaming balls shoot as high as the church steeple creating panic when they threaten to shower us with sparks.

Cautioning that "nous ne sommes pas de vrais jongleurs," two blond acrobats play with fire in order to attract a crowd. From that perspective they triumph, although the lustre of their act is their tempting muscular bodies. The husky acrobat puffs up the significance of their exertions with the flippant rhetoric of a Monsieur Branlotin, without his inventiveness, light-heartedly announcing what turns out to be so simple the pretense is a gag. They break their very first promise—to strip completely as they disrobe. Underneath their formal suits are matching undershirts and shorts. The lighter acrobat has the dexterity to stand on his hands and build a support of wooden blocks. On one hand he balances atop his partner's head. In the next-to-last trick they transform themselves into stagehands by enticing two spectators to enact the balcony scene from *Romeo and Juliet*. This time it is effective because the actors enjoy being buffoons. The finale: more fireworks.

The vendors' products are worthy of a dull provincial fair: sliced coconuts and watermelons, commercial candy, sandwiches, cheap toys, bad art, scarfs, jewellery, puppets, Rubik's cubes, glow-in-the-dark neck-laces, tiny baby dolls that swim in water. Soaring above all this commotion are a couple of mechanical birds put into flight by two nimble Italian men, dressed in revealing, striped T-shirts, who flirt with the passing women. Birds so unpredictable, they sabotage their salesmanship.

◆ ◆ ◆

One of the lingering charms of Paris is the mentality of people who refuse to abide by stifling conventions. Shopkeepers joke with their customers, even if there is a queue. Arab and Black immigrants play music in the streets, eloquently amassing a circle of compatriots who might otherwise find little that reminds them of home. A solitary Breton bagpiper poignantly humanizes the barren square in front of the Montparnasse train station.

The most impersonal institution in the city is the subway, a site of petty strife that arises when people treat each other as obstacles thwarting their path. But both in the stations and the cars, musicians are common. Everyone blithely ignores the preachy signs: "Pour votre tranquillité spec-tacles et quêtes sont interdits dans les voitures. Ne les encouragez pas!"

A subway car becomes the stage for a puppet show called "Le petit prince." The plot is squeezed to the minimalist dimensions that can be sandwiched between three or four stations. Two men attach a beach towel, covered with stars, a rainbow and the message "Le petit prince," between vertical poles in the subway car. Passengers further along the car notice the puppeteers only when they begin to hear electronic music reminiscent of a sound track from a science fiction film. Thrust above the towel to open the show is a quivering pink rose. Soon the music becomes violently dramatic, more like a Wild West film. The rose vanishes and two villains take control. They, too, quickly expire, succeeded by the wee monarch who does not have to prove his heroic status except by his good looks. The prince dances to a song by the Beatles with what I believe is a fox. Despite the message of the song being discredited daily, it retains its utopian charm—"All You Need Is Love."

◆ ◆ ◆

How can I possibly get down on paper the torrent of words that pour from Christian Marin's mouth? My task would be easier if I knew something about the demands juggling makes on the body. Christian says he views his work in a "radically different way" than he did three years ago. He came to realize that he was not equally dexterous; one hand was too passive. So stunts that required a lot of speed were beyond his grasp. Also, he had developed a way of holding the upper part of his body which made his shoulder and chest muscles tense. To break that habit he spent hundreds of hours juggling on his knees. It was a depressing time. The quality of his juggling deteriorated so drastically in his eyes that he began to wonder if there was any point in continuing. Earning a living was especially difficult when he had to work in the old manner to support himself while trying to learn new techniques in practice sessions.

It is not necessary now to work on the street, but he thinks he may return in the autumn. He has toured parts of Africa (where people mistook him for a sorcerer) and earned enough money entertaining at a nightclub in Estoril, Portugal, to live for the immediate future. For the first time in ages he had a real boss in Estoril and nearly quit on opening night. He has also been touring France with a little circus, made by friends, called the Compagnie Foraine.

Christian has relinquished his teenage illusions of glory. He admits to himself, and to us, that his moment may never come. He has lost none of his superhuman desire to surpass his limitations nor his commitment to living on the margins of society. Perfection in the arts of the circus does not take one far in society. Most nights he still beds down in his hand-painted red and blue van. He does worry occasionally, and understandably, about what will become of him in the future.

French circuses have been smitten by "la poésie," according to Christian. He sees this as a result of circuses affiliating themselves with the "maisons de la culture," government-financed cultural centres which emerged in France in an effort to destroy the customary way the fine arts were used to exclude and denigrate the less privileged. Popular entertainments can help acclimatize the non-elite to France's twentieth-century cathedrals. Christian is not critical of the political goal. His complaint is that poetry does not help performers master physical skills. Directors of circus schools, who adore poetry, rarely educate students to the point that they can turn professional. Either their students end up on the street or in some other domain of show business.

◆ ◆ ◆

Rennes-les-Bains, in the département of Aude, is a sort of large-scale Grand Ry. The small-town spirit is evident when residents interrupt their conversations long enough to scan the strangers. Although it is a resort for convalescents seeking mineral-water cures, it has few of the facilities associated with such places. Tourists are likely to be rustic southerners. The town's location between two hills, however, is picturesque.

Undisciplined gardens are cultivated beside the path that runs along the stream to the camp grounds where the Compagnie Foraine has pitched its tent. Upon arriving, we are told that Christian has gone to "répéter dans la forêt." So typical. Later, we are startled to discover him putting on his "opera makeup," an unexpected extravagance of eyebrows which extend all the way back to his hairline and white powder around his eyes. It gives him a devilish air.

The tent for the Compagnie Foraine might seat two hundred and fifty spectators. The audience could not have exceeded sixty or seventy, very few considering that Rennes-les-Bains has little to offer except good weather. Christian's participation aside, the show is pathetic. The Compagnie Foraine needs him more than he needs it. But even for Christian, hampered by an uneven wooden floor which would not stay in place, this is not a happy moment. Christian's eighteenth-century costume: a white shirt with frills, vivid blue breeches decorated with a blue ribbon above the calf, white socks and shoes. The music is fragments from Stravinsky's neo-classical *Histoire du Soldat*. The props: four clubs, then three ping pong balls, and finally the essence, one soccer ball. It is an adaptation of his earlier act and concludes the show. Working quietly with a group as lowly as the Compagnie Foraine gives him the possibility of earning a living while being ignored by those who matter.

After the show he tells us about an original juggling act he is in the process of creating, five to seven minutes with a single soccer ball. The act is set in motion as a kind of confrontation/encounter between the ball and the performer. In the dark the ball is placed in the middle of the ring. Then illuminated by spotlights. Christian somersaults into the ring.

"A saint of the circus" is the way Paul describes Christian. He also says that a person has the chance to meet a restless, obstinate idealist like Christian only once or twice in a lifetime. This lofty opinion needs to be recorded because it is not at all certain that circus historians will ever take the slightest notice of Christian Marin. He's such a joy to the spiritless cashiers who dominate the business.

Christian is so possessed by his juggling that he boasts: "I have forgotten the world for the last three years."

◆ ◆ ◆

In Arabic "Abu," which can be abbreviated as Bu, means "the father of." Paul fancies that Bouissac might be translated as the father of Issac. This pattern of naming men in adulthood according to their first-born son, Paul discovered when he was learning Arabic, is evident in *A Thousand and One Nights* which has characters named Abu Isa, Abu Kir and so on. The Bouissacs are not an old Périgord family, but originally came from a region further south, Lodève in the département of Hérault. This is part of the region that was conquered by the Arabs in the eighth century. Although Paul's paternal grandfather frequently talked about family history, Paul knows little about ancestors who are more than a couple of generations older than himself. But in light of what he later learned of the history of Mediterranean civilizations, his name might indicate Arabic roots. A common sense knowledge of French history would lead one to think that in the Middle Ages the Bouissac family must have been part of the interesting southern French civilization in Languedoc which was the victim of brutal ethnic and religious persecution by northern Frenchmen. Paul protests to Quebecers who want to separate from the rest of Canada that he is not a French nationalist. Their ancestors persecuted his ancestors in the Middle Ages.

In Paul's opinion, both of his grandfathers tentatively rose above their working-class and peasant origins but failed to attain secure positions in a higher social class. Paul identifies more with his grandfathers than with his father. He likes to think he shares some of their personal values: their ideology of the self-made man, their belief in hard work and an intolerance for people who fail because of laziness. Paul's paternal grandfather,

Gabriel Bouissac (1880-1961), was the son of Alexandre Bouissac (1850-1932), who had worked as a "filateur-mécanicien" in the carding industry, preparing fibres for spinning into yarn. Local priests noticed Gabriel's intelligence. He was sent to study for the priesthood, eventually dropping out of the seminary, but not before obtaining his "baccalauréat," no small achievement for the nineteenth century. Along with some colleagues, Gabriel Bouissac established a wholesale grocery business in Périgueux in 1921, the Société Nadeau-Chéron-Bouissac. In 1931 the company became the Société Périgourdine d'Alimentation. In old age Gabriel Bouissac could still recite by heart the Greek and Latin poetry which he had learned in school.

Paul's maternal grandfather, Théophile Frêne (1871-1952), was a metal worker in Châteauroux. Although not as well-educated as Gabriel Bouissac, he was endowed with a strong personality and an entrepreneurial spirit. To a remarkable degree, he possessed what Paul calls "an intelligence of the hands." Frêne was sociable and fond of entertaining. He was a member of the last generation of Frenchmen who completed the Tour de France, the demanding apprenticeship which included extensive travelling in order to work with master craftsmen.[4] Frêne "could do anything with metal," Paul recalls. In the course of time Frêne became the owner of a hardware store in Châteauroux and opened the first company in town that installed central heating. Retiring about four years before the outbreak of World War II, Frêne had made the financial arrangements for a comfortable retirement but had not anticipated the war or the period of inflation that followed. Even though he owned four houses, his final years were difficult because government restrictions prevented the owners of property from increasing rent while property taxes and maintenance costs kept rising. As a boy, Paul disliked visiting this grandfather because he was woken up early in the morning to help with the welding in the workshop that Frêne had maintained on one of his properties. Paul's chore was to pull the cord that operated the bellows. Now, Paul believes, he would appreciate hearing Frêne talk about his early years, especially his experiences as an apprentice.

On several occasions Paul has mentioned how much he enjoys teaching Zola's novels, in particular *L'assommoir*. The vivid working-class slang that Zola's characters speak reminds Paul of his grandfather Frêne. Because of his social mobility Frêne was speaking in a different context than the characters of the novel, expressing himself indirectly by quoting the speech of others. But he knew exactly what it meant, undoubtedly having used these expressions as an apprentice.

"Don't fart higher than your ass" is the advice Paul recalls his father giving him. Paul felt it was necessary not only to ignore his father's advice, but to do the opposite. His parents were ashamed of his association with the circus when he began working for the Cirque Bouglione during his student days in Paris. They kept his work a secret from the neighbours. "We would have put you on a farm right away, if we had known you were going to do that," his mother complained. It was only after the publication of his book *Circus and Culture* that their attitude began to change.

◆　◆　◆

Théophile Frêne's weather vane: a bouquet of four tulips, one blossom and two leaves bending gracefully in each direction. Sticking out of the middle of the bouquet is a staff and direction markers bearing the first letter in French for each direction, N, S, E and O. Above the direction markers is a swallowtail flag and a crescent-shaped moon. A little man, who has raised a telescope to his eye, stands inside the crescent moon.

◆　◆　◆

Théophile Frêne apparently went to Le Havre, where relatives lived, to learn the profession of metal working. Approximately a year later, at the age of 17, he ran away and started to make the Tour de France. Frêne is supposed to have made the journey by foot, as was the custom. This is the story Paul was recently told by an elderly cousin. Frêne had an independent character, was hard-working and critical of people who did not seem to get ahead. The grandfather criticized his brother, an army officer, and even his own father, an overseer on a farm, for that reason.

While showing the cousin around the farm one day, Paul's great-grandfather remarked, "This is where I sit when I get tired."

"Even before you're tired," Paul's grandfather added.

From the stories, Théophile Frêne seems to have been difficult to get along with. He had been a "terror" among his playmates. He and his brother did not speak for years. However, the cousin did claim that Théophile's wife Marthe Pitard (1879-1947) could lead him around by the nose. Late in life the great-grandfather worked as a janitor at the art school in Châteauroux. At least on one occasion, he posed for a portrait.

◆　◆　◆

Walking along a main road near the train station in Périgueux, Paul could see as a child the warehouses of Antoine Lacroix, his great-uncle. Paul can still visualize the large black sign "Etablissement Lacroix." Antoine was a legend in the family. Charismatic and enterprising, he was a wholesale grocer who at one time owned (along with his second wife the Widow Surssat) the castle Château de Lalande, west of Périgueux in Annesse et Beaulieu. The twenty-room castle is now a hotel and restaurant. But the Lacroix family also felt a lot of resentment toward Antoine because he bequeathed all his money and property to his wife.

Uncle Antoine was what the French call a *notable*, someone known to everybody in town. Part of the family legend concerns Antoine's kindness and generosity. Paul's grandfather became a prisoner of war near the end of the First World War. (Just as his father was a prisoner during the Second.) Antoine Lacroix, who was too old to serve as a soldier, cared for his sister and her son, Paul's father. Other stories which are told in the family tend to show that Uncle Antoine had a common touch despite his exceptional wealth. He was always friendly with people of lower status. Once Paul's father pointed to a spot along the road where a *cantonnier* or a roadman used to live. A *cantonnier* was someone who lived at the side of the road and was supposed to maintain it. Uncle Antoine befriended the roadman and on occasion lunched with him on canned sardines from his warehouse.

Paul's grandmother worshipped her brother. Even today, Paul identifies with Antoine Lacroix, although he died in 1921. His grandmother displayed Antoine's painted portrait in a prominent place in her house. But after her death it was banished to the attic. Paul's mother had mixed feelings about Antoine. Many years later Paul retrieved the portrait, signed "Th. Le Bernet 1900," in order to hang it in our Toronto apartment. It is one of only two pictures of Paul's ancestors which he displays at home. (The other is Ron Bowen's drawing of his aunt Raymonde.) To pick a composer whose appearance resembles Antoine Lacroix, it would be the young Erik Satie: medium length beard and mustache, short hair, pince-nez, arched eyebrows, a youthful but mature face with a pensive expression. For me, the personal significance of these stories about Antoine Lacroix is that it took Paul decades to give me this information in a way that made it meaningful.

◆ ◆ ◆

As a juvenile prank, Paul was secretly introducing snails into his grandmother Bouissac's house. She would spot them slithering up the walls or along a mirror. How they got there was always a great mystery she never solved.

◆ ◆ ◆

The brutally short telegram: "Auntie died funeral Monday 2:00 o'clock affectionately Mother." Circumstances did not allow Paul to fly to France for the funeral of his aunt Raymonde Frêne (1900-1982).[5] He went a few weeks later to settle the estate. Raymonde bequeathed nothing to her sister or nieces, everything to Paul.

At my request, this anti-Proust who is so disinclined to revisit the past wrote a letter from Châteauroux, which is one of the few times he expressed in writing his opinions about his family:

It is both a moral and physical test. I found myself in charge of this house and its contents of three generations or so and under the pressure of my parents who hated my aunt for her decisions. I will spend tonight and tomorrow Sunday in Périgueux and I feel as usual sick at the thought of it. The house and its decor and furniture was much alive and personalized. My aunt had a relatively active social life and she had everything you can imagine for entertaining her friends and relatives. She was also religiously conserving whatever was connected with her parents, mostly as it was. It's still the house I knew when, as a few years old, I was coming for vacations with my parents and my sister. The memory revived by the mere sight and smell of the house consists mostly of the festive atmosphere when we arrived in it at lunchtime in summer with the smell of cantaloup waiting on the table set in front of the door-window opening on the garden. Smells also of fine food cooking in the kitchen and pastries that my aunt was cooking herself, and she was excellent at it. In fact whatever I can do now as far as cooking is concerned comes from her, mostly through observational learning when I was helping her. Now, once this homage paid to the past is over, I have to assess the situation and there is no way that we can save this or revive it. It is erased in fact, except in a few of my brain's neurons. Châteauroux is atrocious—small provincial town—conservative—nothing of what makes the pleasures and enjoyment of our lives. The house was well-kept but on the verge of needing major repair, a part of the top of the roof was blown away by the wind last week. I must have it fixed before leaving because it will rain in the attic if I leave it this way. This is why I have decided to sell the house. This means that the house must be emptied within a week! I love to dismember signs and symbols! to deconstruct the meaningful system of an 82-year-old life, while

respecting a few of my aunt's wishes such as having her grandparents' tomb restored in the cemetery.

On the other hand this house represents a style of life, an ethic,
a mountain of prejudices which inspires in me a great disgust. All
the limitations I experienced are there and I have to think of it
when I empty the drawers in the garbage bags (don't worry I save
for you old letters and photos). But it took me two days before I
could start. (April 10, 1982)

Elaborating on the feelings expressed in the letter, Paul said that when he
was dispersing the last worldly possessions accumulated by his grandparents and aunt, he "felt like an executioner." Most nights in
Châteauroux he stayed alone in the house. It was a frightening experience
that made him reflect on the fragility of the meaning of things.

♦ ♦ ♦

I had hoped to see New York City through Christian's eyes. But from the
town of St. Felix de Lodez Christian wrote to explain why he could not
take part in a conference at New York University on theories of performance.
Since the participants included both theorists and practitioners, Paul had
requested that the organizers invite Christian.

An incident prevents my coming to New York. I am sorry for you
because I do not like to break promises, but for the last two
weeks my left-right problems have begun again and I am physically
incapable of doing anything whatsoever. It is worse than before.
Thus I am now stopping all training for some time and I am going
to the seashore in order to rest and to think about nothing. I hope
that you do not mind, but above all I do not want to appear
ridiculous or to embarrass you in presenting an imperfect show....
(August 13, 1982)

From Perpignan, nearly a month later, Christian wrote about his torturously
slow progress toward achieving what he was created to do:

Now my training is making progress; however, I still cannot work.
I ran into several problems, but I believe things are going better.
The lower part of my body takes an ideal position, but whatever
moves around is not yet adjusted to this new position. As a consequence the juggling is displaced and that's why I cannot control

my juggling anymore. A few months ago everything went better because the lower part of my body did not move or barely moved, but the relaxation now changes this and my body must learn again…I discovered my weaknesses. I tried to correct them. Alas, the weaknesses were hiding an abyss. All of this is logical but I have to pay heavily for my mistakes. Alas!! I have no regrets what-soever. This experience has been invaluable. Socially, this is certainly a dead end, but I don't care.

Since March, I have not performed, but I have been able to relearn everything from scratch. I had a contract for Italy, Switzerland, Spain and Mexico with the Magic Circus but I gave all of that up.

I hope that everything is going well, affectionately. (September 8, 1982)

◆ ◆ ◆

A flashback to 1972. The windows in our kitchen and living room face a humble cobblestone courtyard embellished with a few potted plants. On the opposite side is an artist's vine-covered studio. In warm weather the courtyard is home to the concierge's two pet tortoises. Taking them out of the rain one day, she claims they are "chauds comme des lapins." "My little acrobats" and "my little 'bons hommes,'" Madame Antona calls them in a voice which still betrays her southern origins, although she must be the oldest concierge in Paris.

We have rented for ten months, November 1972 to August 1973, a small apartment in the Latin Quarter at 5 rue Guy de la Brosse. The apart-ment is conveniently located on this block-long street between Place Jussieu and the Jardin des Plantes. Our metal dining table is the sort that is supposed to be used outdoors in a garden or patio. The heater is awk-wardly located inside a closet. The metal shower resembles a filing cabinet missing its drawers. The kitchen is primitive. But the apartment is insulated well enough that we can rent a piano.

Unfortunately, at the end of our street is one of the architectural scandals of the decade, the Jussieu science faculty. Insensitive to the character of the district, it is a stridently modern glass and metal building with a sky-scraper in the centre. Bordering the building is a dry moat that seems to serve no purpose other than to hinder student protestors. A desolate plaza greets those entering the building. Students have made the centre messier—if perhaps more human—by plastering it with graffiti and posters. Even President Pompidou publicly admits that he wishes he had lowered the height of the tower. From the opposite side of the Seine, it mars the beauty of the Left Bank.

◆ ◆ ◆

The entrance to number 55 rue de Grenelle, where Paul and I are spending July and August 1983, is amazing. Unfortunately, the grandeur is only a façade. We walk through a door built into a four-storey, sculptured fountain erected between 1739 and 1746 by the "king's sculptor," Edme Bouchardon. It might be more appropriate to refer to this fountain, called the Four Seasons, as a public sculpture because it provides so little water for the public. Voltaire did not care for the Four Seasons and dismissed it by saying: "What kind of a fountain has only two taps...?" He did approve, however, of the way authorities in Paris in the mid-1700s were destroying "les monuments de la barbarie gothique" and ridiculous village fountains that "disfigured" the capital.

In the centre of the fountain is a seated woman, an allegorical representation of the city of Paris. At her feet are two reclining nudes, one male, one female. The muscular male represents the Seine; the female, the Marne. To the side are four bas reliefs, allegorical figures of the four seasons, each of which has wings to symbolize the rapid movement of time, and an image of the constellation that the sun passes through during that season.

The fountain was constructed with two doors, but I do not know if we are entering our building—an insignificant modern apartment house— through the door which once led to a monastery or the one which led to the reservoir where the water for the fountain was stored. Probably, it's the latter. The balcony of our apartment is attached to the top of the fountain, and is large enough for a small dining table. From here we have a picture-postcard view of the rooftops of the seventh arrondissement.

◆ ◆ ◆

Christian performs on Boulevard Saint-Germain with the woman who used to be Zoé the Sidewalk Spider in Monsieur Branlotin's act. (Branlotin's rats have contacted tuberculosis. He'll have to train a new batch.) Separated from her husband and having children to support, Zoé needs extra money.

It is Zoé's long, loose dress which dramatizes her *danse serpentine*, beguiling viewers who don't see the simplicity of her movements. From time to time she shouts gypsy-sounding gibberish. She is accompanied by a female drummer who bangs a monotonous rhythm. Unsmiling, the drummer looks as though she stepped out of a shabby production of *Mother Discourage*, according to Paul, and any minute is going to publicly announce a catastrophe.

Last week they considered transporting a mule to Paris for the drummer to ride while playing. That surely would attract a crowd, they thought. But, as Christian says, the mule turned out to be "très speciale." It was afraid of many things, including the van that was supposed to transport it. The mule was also unwilling to walk backwards. Since it could not turn around in the van, it had to either back in or back out.

Christian once talked about making a circus act with just a single soccer ball. That's the act he does now after drawing a crowd with gymnastic exercises. The ball rolls over his body, fingertips to fingertips, and from his head to the soles of his feet while he does a handstand. He bounces it on his head and shoulders. He somersaults with the ball between his feet, throwing it into the air. When it falls, he lets it rebound on his head. Unless there is an accident, he never touches the ball with his palms.

Christian believes the *amuseurs publics* and the *saltimbanques* have lost their glitter at Saint-Germain-des-Prés. There are just too many competitors, mostly mediocre, for any of them to make an impression. Christian alleges that his approach to juggling has much in common with modern dance. He met a couple of dancers and it's through them that he developed these ideas. Modern dance has status; performers are concerned about art— something almost unheard of in the circus—and they have good facilities. The circus in France continues to decline; another couple of bankruptcies occurred this spring. As a result, there are few places where Christian can work. The Knie Circus in Switzerland may be one of the best circuses in history, but no French equivalent exists. The alternative is, for the most part, small circuses which pay poorly and which Christian rightly criticizes as unartistic.

Christian claims he is happy. He has not succeeded in balancing runny blueberry jelly on an uneven croissant, but he does what he wants. If offered the opportunity of juggling in New York again, he would refuse. In his opinion his own juggling still lacks finesse, but it's better than a year ago. At least, he has "sorti de l'auberge." The Grand Magic Circus, which is really a theatre company despite its name, employed him for several months recently in one of its productions. He performed the segment of his old act in which he propels and catches ping pong balls with his mouth. Now he's considering this proposal: with an appropriate outfit, impersonate a hen juggling eggs with her oviduct.

◆ ◆ ◆

Not wanting to look vulgar, one street musician hauls her loudspeaker in an old-fashioned market basket made of cane. But the amplification so many musicians are now using seems counterproductive. Crowds listen more attentively when the softness of the music requires some effort on their part.

◆ ◆ ◆

A modern version of an old carnival attraction brightens Place Saint-Germain-des-Prés. It is a life-sized cut-out of Mitterrand and a headless guest sitting on a couch at the Elysée Palace. For a price, anyone can appear to be the president's guest.

◆ ◆ ◆

The most compelling topic of conversation at a dinner in the summer of 1983 with Michel Foucault and his lover Daniel Defert is AIDS. The media in France are reporting the panic which is occurring in the United States. At this point there are only a few diagnosed cases in Europe. Foucault comments that events in the United States are "bizarre and interesting," an indication he looks at remote events unfolding in other people's lives. As journalists tell us, it can take years for the symptoms of AIDS to surface. Every sexually active gay male who lives in North America or has visited there must wonder if a time bomb waits to explode inside his body. Most frightening of all is the ignorance about the biological structures that spread the disease.

Have we arrived at the end of an era of casual sex? many of us wonder. Shouldn't we have sex with as many men as possible since it may be our last chance? Caution answers in the negative, of course. One friend visiting Paris on vacation does frequent bars and steam baths, revelling in the melancholy thought that we were wrong when we thought we were witnessing the dawn of a new era. Instead, it is the twilight.

◆ ◆ ◆

An unsentimental, hurried visit to Châteauroux. No reminiscing on Paul's part. He made me scurry down the street where his aunt resided because he did not want to speak to the neighbours. But the woman who lives directly opposite Raymonde is standing in front of her door. There is no way to avoid her. She and Raymonde had a pact that if their shutters were closed at a certain hour in the morning, they would call each other. If no one answered, they would notify a family member. So it is this friend who first reported Raymonde's death. Because Raymonde had appeared to be improving earlier in the week, Paul's mother returned home to Périgueux.

Paul managed to sell the family home and to dispose of its contents, although not the shop at 42 rue Grande he now owns jointly with his mother. Even in the best of times it would be difficult to find a buyer for a building over two hundred years old that is constantly in need of repairs, despite the charm of its odd angles, rough edges and the patina of the immemorial. There is an irregularly shaped interior, narrow but long, and a ceiling of wooden beams. Its size surprises me. Paul's grandfather had his hardware store here. The family lived in the back and the upstairs, where Paul's mother was born. The most recent tenants have opened a creole café which sometimes gives concerts.

◆ ◆ ◆

Few cities in France conjure up the Middle Ages as beautifully as Carcassone. It retains the best fortifications in Europe, not just one but two city walls with fifty-two towers. During the day and early evening Carcassone is overrun by tourists. Around midnight its mystique is more evident. Tonight's troubadours play to entertain themselves rather than the wives of noblemen at a sycamore-shaded cafe. Either they're American or American-inspired. A young woman sings softly and strums a guitar. One friend accompanies her by improvising in a relaxed, jazzy style on a soprano recorder. Another companion toys with a harmonica.

Paul and I chatter about a gay friend who, I criticize, is chronically unhappy because he loiters around Marseille. If he were more adventurous, he would flee to Paris where he could have a better life. Paul says I don't understand what it means for southerners to settle in the North, where they still encounter discrimination although more subtle than before. Paul has a "gut sympathy" for people from the South. When he was young, he enjoyed reading about Cathar heretics. He has enough interest in the topic to buy another book about them on our trip, but I doubt that he will read it. He is not patient with any of the political movements advocating ethnic revival in southern France.

At about the same time, Paul and four of his classmates from Périgueux arrived in Paris. Paul was the only one able or willing to remain. One of his sisters also found the capital was too much for her. Paul avoided the prejudice southerners confront because he was "energetic" and fortunate to have been friends in school with boys whose families were from other parts of France, Alain Ohrel (Normandie) and Jean-Gérard Nay (Touraine). Another friend was Pierre Poumeyrol whose father was from the South but had been posted as an army officer in various regions of France. Through these friendships, Paul lost some of his native provincialism and mitigated his southern accent.

Paul was advised to set his sights on Paris by Father Léon Bouillon, who thought his promising teenage student was espousing offbeat ideas. A middle-aged teacher of the humanities, Bouillon had been appointed to lead the Boy Scouts at the Institution Saint-Joseph. He was better acquainted with pupils than would have been true for many of the priests. (Bouillon is also remembered by Jean-Gérard Nay for opening the eyes of his students to French poets such as Paul Valéry.)

During the summer of 1955, the period between Paul's first and second years of university, he was offered a position as a private tutor for two sons of a Périgueux family named R. Paul assumes Mme. R. asked the staff at the Institution St. Joseph to recommend a student and that he was their choice because he had been active in the Boy Scouts as a cub master. Paul consequently spent much of the summer at the family's small castle, "Le Paradou" (let's call it), located outside Périgueux a few miles from Montaigne's castle and tower. In the morning he was supposed to teach two of the sons and to supervise their homework, one after the other, because they were in different grades. In the afternoon he enjoyed the liberty of doing his own work, which was preparing for Latin and Greek examinations.

Mme. R. is remembered as easy-going, a touch extravagant, "exuberantly Catholic but on the liberal side." She was far more alive intellectually than the people in Paul's family. With her, there was the possibility of real conversations. Paul compares Mme. R.'s freedom of imagination with that of Maximov and Marie Depussé. Mme. R., a Corsican, may not have had the intelligence of Marie Depussé, but she could put some distance between herself and the bourgeois order of her surroundings. Mme. R.'s father was a high-profile ship tycoon, who had a mythical stature in the household. The rare occasions when the tycoon visited were big events.

Many aspects of the R. household were attractive to Paul. Although not large, Le Paradou was located in the midst of fields. Living there was a way of recuperating Castel Fadèze, this time being integrated into the social life of the residents of the main floor. Also the meals included absolutely first-class Périgordian specialties.

There were all these children in the household, more than the two which I tutored. Like kids in most affluent families, they didn't have any social complexes. It took a while for them to respect me. I was there in a position just above the servants but at the same time I had an obvious friendship with their mother who was treating me as an equal. I was privy to their inside jokes. When the guests were telling stories, supposedly funny stories that the children thought were not very good or when the children did not like the guests, they had a secret code that allowed them to pass judgment and communicate with each other unobtrusively. They would discreetly take their table knife and slowly lower the blade toward the table. This was a homophonic pun made with an object. The message was "lamentable" ("lame en table" or, literally, blade on the table, which obviously does not work in English).[6]

It was at Le Paradou that Paul learned to appreciate under-cooked meat. Mme. R. liked her meat hardly warm in fact. She was infamous for happily gobbling down raw fish, according to rumours. Supposedly, she ate live fish straight from the river whenever the opportunity arose.

Mme. R. was elegant, although somewhat plump, and wore the style of makeup expected of a woman who enjoyed an upper-class social life. Her intense religious concerns were also appealing to Paul at this stage in his life. She insisted that one of the priests occasionally come to say mass in the little chapel at the castle. Naturally, the priests in Périgueux tended to be complacent about her exuberance because of her wealth and generosity. However, Mme. R. was outraged once by the puritanical lessons a nun was teaching one of her sons in primary school. Mme. R. tried to kiss her son when he returned home. He ran away crying. Women who wear makeup are daughters of the devil, the nun had warned.

Whenever Paul teaches Stendhal's *The Red and the Black* he tends to imagine that the story is occurring at Le Paradou, the roles of the leading characters filled by family members. Paul's position there tempted Jean-Gérard Nay to make ironic allusions to the imagined parallels with the hero in the novel. Practically the only similarity, though, was the fact that the tutor was indeed the object of a certain amount of attention within the household. In the context of this "mad, crazy household" the husband of Mme. R. was fairly sedate and usually busy elsewhere.

Without assistance from his family, Paul had to find sponsors to help him reach Paris. In theory, students were required to attend a university in the region where they lived. But, of course, exceptions were always a possibility for those who knew the right people. One of the visitors to the R.s was a Mme. Poirier, who was so impressed by Paul that through her son, a philosophy professor at the Sorbonne, she helped to arrange for the offbeat intellectual to study at the Lycée Lakanal in Sceaux. (Paul later forfeited a five-year fellowship because it required that he go to school in Bordeaux.)

Paul reminded Mme. Poirier of Jean-Paul Sartre, whom she presumably knew when he was the same age. She was not alone in imagining this resemblance, which included a slight ocular dissymmetry. At college Paul was given the nickname "*bizut* Sartre," the freshman Sartre, I would guess for his existential outlook as much as his intelligence. Paul supposes that Mme. Poirier also valued his "surrealist turn of mind." Mme. Poirier is one of three women who gave Paul decisive help at turning points in his life. The other two are Mme. Grimal and Mlle. Haumesser. It was his skill in talking to older (sometimes unfashionable) people, a trait Jean-Gérard Nay says he envied, that resulted in the assistance. Paul never enjoyed the benefits of this kind of relationship with older, sophisticated gay men. He tended to feel more comfortable with heterosexual women. Looking back on his life, he once commented to me that he was "surprised by the social audacity of his youth."

◆　◆　◆

Christian: "I live in the clouds. I live in the unreal. I don't even care about fucking." He does, though, sleep with his arms around a pillow due to lack of physical affection, as he pointed out. Continuing to talk about how lucky he is to be totally absorbed by his work, he remarks: "I like working on the street. I wouldn't be happier working at the Lido. It's bizarre, isn't it?" He criticizes the way everything in the "pragmatic circus" has to follow the same norms, even to the extent of regulating the length of acts. This "logique du monde" is a kind of "aggression" against circus artists, in his view. Performing on the street allows him to live outside "le théâtre de marionnettes."

◆　◆　◆

An autobiographical quotation from a letter Christian wrote to the Ministry of Culture concerning the deplorable state of the circus in France:

> Other people speak for Circus Artists; they never express themselves publicly in words.
>
> Twenty-three years of stubborn and solitary training, seven of which were at the edge of Hell, of violent adventures, happy and unhappy, crossing the world from East to West, give me the power to know—finally—the secret possibilities of a soccer ball.

This ball, my mirror, allows me, rather forces me, to speak with resolute force.

◆　◆　◆

As the ghost writer of Firmin Bouglione's *Le cirque est mon royaume*, Paul wrote the following inscription in the copy of the book which he presented to his parents: "To the authors of the author's author."

◆　◆　◆

If it rained when Paul worked as a barker for the zoo of the Bouglione Circus, he sometimes took shelter under the elephant tent. On occasion he played chess with the animal trainer, Julio Hani, on a bale of straw. The trainer was an unusual circus man, intelligent and quiet. Hani and his British wife, a native of Blackpool, had hundreds of glass, china and ivory sculptures of elephants in their trailer. One irritating aspect of playing chess with Hani was that he was more interested in winning than in enjoying himself. He would pick off his opponent's pieces as quickly as possible, giving no time to plan strategies. To Paul, this was a cheap victory.

Hani was very soft with elephants. People claimed the elephants were doing less and less under his guidance because he was not tough enough. But, in Paul's view, Hani had good control over them. Paul tried to convince Hani that chess-playing elephants would make an entertaining act. An elephant, responding to a trainer's barely perceptible gestures, can be taught to move anything from one spot to another. But for this to be an amusing spectacle, it requires an audience that comprehends the rules of chess.

Hani suffered from a cardiac disease that eventually led to an odd but beautiful death. He was presenting a comedy act with a horse. Dressed as a cowboy, the trainer and the horse talk and make jokes. At one point in the act the horse and trainer lie down together. Hani covers himself with a blanket; the horse steals it; Hani takes it back, the horse steals it again. During his final performance Hani lay down beside the horse. The horse pulled the blanket off as planned, but then nothing happened. Hani had died of a heart attack.

◆　◆　◆

Christian (as best as I can remember an hour later): "For me sex is like washing my hands. It's purely hygienic. The moment it becomes emotional

I flee. Besides, who wants a lover who does nothing except practice juggling from sun-up to sundown. I've never had any lasting feelings of love
for anyone; in the few cases when it might have happened we weren't
mutually attracted. I'm a slave to my work. Life would be intolerable
otherwise."

Christian is supposed to leave in four days for the Edinburgh Festival
where he will perform in a production of *West Side Story*. Christian will be
one of the anonymous actors in the fight scenes. Typically, he is not certain
if he will go: something may intervene at the last minute. He has no idea
if he will fly or go by train. He does not know his salary because the terms
of the contract are confusing.

◆ ◆ ◆

In Lucerne, the backdrop for the Circus Knie is one of the tallest peaks in
the Alps. After the evening show on July 27, 1981, we sat with Ken Little,
his wife and with Pipo (Philippe Sosman), the white-faced clown, beside
a Volkswagen camper. It was a warm summer night. Faint light came from
a flickering candle on a table and from a campfire not far away tended by
Rolf Knie.

Ken Little is here gathering material for a Ph.D. thesis. A Canadian, he
has been given a part-time job as an assistant for the clowns; his wife is
paid for taking pictures of children riding ponies in the zoo. Ken has not
yet narrowed his research down to one topic. He's at the "vacuum cleaner"
stage of research (a stage I know all too well), sucking up every speck of
information he comes across, however trivial it may be. I also note a familiar
stubbornness and a foolish reluctance to accept the guidance of others,
including Paul's advice.

The most memorable theme of the conversation was Pipo's. He is
about thirty years old, finely featured, which is normal for a white-faced
clown. Pipo's interest in America seems to stop with the era of Fred
Astaire. He wants to recapture something as subtle and elusive as walking
the way clowns did forty years ago. The cloth used for costumes nowa-
days is too stiff and inflexible, preventing clowns from walking with the
freedom that was possible earlier. Although the decoration and embroidery
may vary, French clowns are limited to only one basic shape unless they
buy costumes abroad. The sole manufacturer of theatrical costumes is
reluctant for financial reasons to provide more variety.

Pipo admires his father, who bore the same name and was one of the
best white-faced clowns of his generation. He showed us a photograph of
his father in a clown suit decorated with half circles reminiscent of abstract

paintings by Robert Delaunay. Pipo was demonstrating both his father's taste and the artistic possibilities that have been lost in recent decades. Despite the admiration for his father and his desire to perpetuate clowning traditions, he does not seem paralysed by the past. Junior is very much his own person. If there are so few good circus clowns today, it is because, in Pipo's opinion, there are so few good circus managers. Jérome Medrano, manager of the circus where his father was employed, matched performers he thought would make ideal partners. Today most managers would not bother.

◆ ◆ ◆

When I first agreed to interview Michel Foucault in June 1982, I was rather nonchalant about the experience. But as the time for the interview approached, the task became more and more daunting. I decided to focus on Foucault's personal life because I felt there was a need for someone to gather biographical information which could be used in exploring the psychological and social origins of his ideas. It was one of the most personal interviews he ever gave although it is far from confessional. Since then the public has learned more about Foucault's private life than anyone needs to know. I did not want to debate Foucault (which would have been presumptuous anyway) because I felt that conventional history and sociology—whether purely academic or politically motivated—were more valuable than his far-ranging speculative thinking. The interview took place on the balcony of our apartment on Bloor Street overlooking the University of Toronto.

It's one thing to feel you're boring an average Joe. It's something altogether different to worry that you might be boring Michel Foucault, who'd rather be alone in the library than in a gay bar on Church Street, a fancy mid-town restaurant or a private supper for middle-aged academics. There are a number of brief passages about silence in Foucault's writings. I begin the interview asking about this topic because his appreciation of silence—so different than the perspective of some feminists—is consistent with the personality of a man who seems to be profoundly anti-social.

Stephen Riggins: One of the things that a reader can unexpectedly learn from your work is to appreciate silence.[7] You write about the freedom it makes possible, its multiple causes and meanings. For instance, you say in your last book that there is not one but many silences. Would it be correct to infer that there is a strongly autobiographical element in this?

Michel Foucault: I think that any child who has been educated in a Catholic milieu just before or during the Second World War had the experience that there were many different ways of speaking as well as many forms of silence. There were some kinds of silence which implied very sharp hostility and others which meant deep friendship, emotional admiration, even love. I remember very well that when I met the filmmaker Daniel Schmidt who visited me, I don't know for what purpose, we discovered after a few minutes that we really had nothing to say to each other. So we stayed together from about three o'clock in the afternoon to midnight. We drank, we smoked hash, we had dinner. And I don't think we spoke more than twenty minutes during those ten hours. From that moment a rather long friendship started. It was for me the first time that a friendship originated in strictly silent behaviour.

Maybe another feature of this appreciation of silence is related to the obligation of speaking. I lived as a child in a petit bourgeois, provincial milieu in France and the obligation of speaking, of making conversation with visitors, was for me something both very strange and very boring. I often wondered why people had to speak. Silence may be a much more interesting way of having a relationship with people.

Riggins: There is in North-American Indian culture a much greater appreciation of silence than in English-speaking societies and I suppose in French-speaking societies as well.

Foucault: Yes, you see, I think silence is one of those things that has unfortunately been dropped from our culture. We don't have a culture of silence; we don't have a culture of suicide either. The Japanese do, I think. Young Romans or young Greeks were taught to keep silent in very different ways according to the people with whom they were interacting. Silence was then a specific form of experiencing a relationship with others. This is something that I believe is really worthwhile cultivating. I'm in favour of developing silence as a cultural ethos.

Riggins: You seem to have a fascination with other cultures and not only from the past; for the first ten years of your career you lived in Sweden, West Germany and Poland. This would seem a very atypical career for a French academic. Can you explain why you left France and why, when you returned in about 1961, from what I have learned, you would have preferred to live in Japan?

Foucault: There is a snobbism about anti-chauvinism in France now. I hope what I say is not associated with those kinds of people. Maybe if I were an American or a Canadian I would suffer from some features of North American culture. Anyway, I have suffered and I still suffer from a lot of things in French social and cultural life. That was the reason why I left France in 1955. Incidentally, in 1966 and 1968 I also spent two years in Tunisia for purely personal reasons.

Riggins: Can you give some examples of the aspects of French society that you suffered from?

Foucault: Well, I think that, at the moment when I left France, freedom for personal life was very sharply restricted there. At this time Sweden was supposed to be a much freer country. And there I had the experience that a certain kind of freedom may have, not exactly the same effects, but as many restrictive effects as a directly restrictive society. That was an important experience for me. Then I had the opportunity of spending one year in Poland where, of course, the restrictions and oppressive power of the Communist party was really something quite different. In a rather short period of time I had the experience of an old traditional society, as France was in the late 1940s and early 1950s, and the new free society which was Sweden. I won't say I had the total experience of all the political possibilities but I had a sample of what the possibilities of Western societies were at that moment. That was a good experience.

Riggins: Hundreds of Americans went to Paris in the '20s and '30s for exactly the same reasons you left in the '50s.

Foucault: Yes. But now I don't think they come to Paris any longer for freedom. They come to have a taste of an old traditional culture. They came to France as painters went to Italy in the seventeenth century to see a dying civilization. Anyway, you see, we very often have the experience of much more freedom in foreign countries than in our own. As foreigners we can ignore all those implicit obligations which are not in the law but in the general way of behaving. Secondly, merely changing your obligations is felt or experienced as a kind of freedom.

Riggins: If you don't mind, let us return for a while to your early years in Paris. I understand that you worked as a psychologist at the Hôpital Ste. Anne in Paris.

Foucault: Yes. I worked there a little more than two years, I believe.

Riggins: And you have remarked that you identified more with the patients than the staff. Surely that's a very atypical experience for anyone who is a psychologist or psychiatrist. Why did you feel, partly from that experience, the necessity of radically questioning psychiatry when so many other people were content to try to refine the concepts which were already prevalent?

Foucault: Actually, I was not officially appointed. I was studying psychology in the Hôpital Ste. Anne. It was the early '50s. There was no clear professional status for psychologists in a mental hospital. So as a student in psychology (I studied first philosophy and then psychology) I had a very strange status there. The *chef de service* was very kind to me and let me do anything I wanted. But nobody worried about what I should be doing; I was free to do anything. I was actually in a position between the staff and the patients, and it wasn't my merit, it wasn't because I had a special attitude, it was the consequence of this ambiguity in my status which forced me to maintain a distance from the staff. I am sure it was not my personal merit because I felt all that at the time as a kind of malaise. It was only a few years later when I started writing a book on the history of psychiatry that this malaise, this personal experience, took the form of an historical criticism or a structural analysis.

Riggins: Was there anything unusual about the Hôpital Ste. Anne? Would it have given an employee a particularly negative impression of psychiatry?

Foucault: Oh no. It was as typical a large hospital as you could imagine and I must say it was better than most of the large hospitals in provincial towns that I visited afterwards. It was one of the best in Paris. No, it was not terrible. That was precisely the thing that was important. Maybe if I had been doing this kind of work in a small provincial hospital I would have believed its failures were the result of its location or its particular inadequacies.

Riggins: As you have just mentioned the French provinces, which is where you were born, in a sort of derogatory way, do you, nevertheless, have fond memories of growing up in Poitiers in the 1930s and '40s?

Foucault: Oh yes. My memories are rather, one could not exactly say strange, but what strikes me now when I try to recall those impressions is that nearly all the great emotional memories I have are related to the political situation. I remember very well that I experienced one of my first great frights when Chancellor Dollfuss was assassinated by the Nazis in, I think, 1934. It is something very far from us now. Very few people remember the murder of Dollfuss. I remember very well that I was really scared by that. I think it was my first strong fright about death. I also remember refugees from Spain arriving in Poitiers. I remember fighting in school with my classmates about the Ethiopian War. I think that boys and girls of this generation had their childhood formed by these great historical events. The menace of war was our background, our framework of exis-tence. Then the war arrived. Much more than the activities of family life, it was these events concerning the world which are the substance of our memory. I say "our" because I am nearly sure that most boys and girls in France at this moment had the same experience. Our private life was really threatened. Maybe that is the reason why I am fascinated by history and the relationship between personal experience and those events of which we are a part. I think that is the nucleus of my theoretical desires. [*Laughter.*]

Riggins: You remain fascinated by the period even though you don't write about it.

Foucault: Yes, sure.

Riggins: What was the origin of your decision to become a philosopher?

Foucault: You see, I don't think I ever had the project of becoming a philosopher. I had not known what to do with my life. And I think that is also something rather typical for people of my generation. We did not know when I was ten or eleven years old, whether we would be German or remain French. We did not know whether we would die or not in the bombing and so on. When I was sixteen or seventeen I knew only one thing: school life was an environment protected from exterior menaces, from politics. And I have always been fascinated by living protected in a scholarly environment, in an intellectual milieu. Knowledge is for me that which must function as a protection of individual existence and as a comprehension of the exterior world. I think that's it. Knowledge as a means of surviving by understanding.

Riggins: Could you tell me a bit about your studies in Paris? Is there anyone who had a special influence upon the work you do today or any professors you are grateful to for personal reasons?

Foucault: No, I was a pupil of Althusser, and at that time the main philosophical currents in France were Marxism, Hegelianism and phenomenology. I must say I have studied these but what gave me for the first time the desire of doing personal work was reading Nietzsche.

Riggins: An audience that is non-French is likely to have a very poor understanding of the aftermath of the May Rebellion of '68 and you have sometimes said that it resulted in people being more responsive to your work. Can you explain why?

Foucault: I think that before '68, at least in France, you had to be as a philosopher a Marxist, or a phenomenologist or a structuralist and I adhered to none of these dogmas. The second point is that at this time in France studying psychiatry or the history of medicine had no real status in the political field. Nobody was interested in that. The first thing that happened after '68 was that Marxism as a dogmatic framework declined and new political, new cultural interests concerning personal life appeared. That's why I think my work had nearly no echo, with the exception of a very small circle, before '68.

Riggins: Some of the works you refer to in the first volume of *The History of Sexuality*, such as the Victorian book *My Secret Life*, are filled with sexual fantasies. It is often impossible to distinguish between fact and fantasy. Would there be a value in your focusing explicitly upon sexual fantasies and creating an archaeology of them rather than one of sexuality?

Foucault: [*Laughter.*] No, I don't try to write an archaeology of sexual fantasies. I try to make an archaeology of discourse about sexuality which is really the relationship between what we do, what we are obliged to do, what we are allowed to do, what we are forbidden to do in the field of sexuality and what we are allowed, forbidden or obliged to say about our sexual behaviour. That's the point. It's not a problem of fantasy; it's a problem of verbalization.

Riggins: Could you explain how you arrived at the idea that the sexual repression that characterized eighteenth and nineteenth century Europe and North America, and which seemed so well-documented historically, was in fact ambiguous and that there were beneath it forces working in the opposite direction?

Foucault: Indeed, it is not a question of denying the existence of repression. It's one of showing that repression is always a part of a much more complex political strategy regarding sexuality. Things are not merely repressed. There is about sexuality a lot of defective regulations in which the negative effects of inhibition are counterbalanced by the positive effects of stimulation. The way in which sexuality in the nineteenth century was both repressed but also put to light, underlined [and] analyzed through techniques like psychology and psychiatry shows very well that it was not simply a question of repression. It was much more a change in the economics of sexual behaviour in our society.

Riggins: In your opinion what are some of the most striking examples which support your hypothesis?

Foucault: One of them is children's masturbation. Another is hysteria and all the fuss about hysterical women. These two examples show, of course, repression, prohibition, interdiction and so on. But the fact that the sexuality of children became a real problem for the parents, an issue, a source of anxiety, had a lot of effects upon the children and upon the parents. To take care of the sexuality of their children was not only a question of morality for the parents but also a question of pleasure.

Riggins: A pleasure in what sense?

Foucault: Sexual excitement and sexual satisfaction.

Riggins: For the parents themselves?

Foucault: Yes. Call it rape, if you like. There are texts which are very close to a systemization of rape. Rape by the parents of the sexual activity of their children. To intervene in this personal, secret activity, which masturbation was, does not represent something neutral for the parents. It is not only a matter of power, or authority, or ethics; it's also a pleasure. Don't you agree with that? Yes, there is enjoyment in intervening. The fact that masturbation was so strictly forbidden for children was naturally the cause of anxiety. It was also a reason for the intensification of this activity, for mutual masturbation and for the pleasure of secret communication between children about this theme. All this has given a certain shape to family life, to the relationship between children and parents and to the relations between children. All that has, as a result, not only repression but an intensification both of anxieties and of pleasures. I don't want to say that the pleasure of the parents was the same as that of the children or that there was no repression. I tried to find the roots of this absurd prohibition.

One of the reasons why this stupid interdiction of masturbation was maintained for such a long time was because of this pleasure and anxiety and all the emotional network around it. Everyone knows very well that it's impossible to prevent a child from masturbating. There is no scientific evidence that it harms anybody. One can be sure that it is at least [*Laughter*] the only pleasure that really harms nobody. Why has it been forbidden for such a long time then? To the best of my knowledge, you cannot find more than two or three references in all the Greco-Latin literature about masturbation. It was not relevant. It was supposed to be, in Greek and Latin civilization, an activity either for slaves or for satyrs. [*Laughter.*] It was not relevant to speak about it for free citizens.

Riggins: We live at a point in time when there is great uncertainty about the future. One sees apocalyptic visions of the future reflected widely in popular culture. Louis Malle's *My Dinner with André*, for example. Isn't it typical that in such a climate sex and reproduction come to be a preoccupation and thus writing a history of sexuality would be symptomatic of the time?

Foucault: No, I don't think I would agree with that. First, the preoccupation with the relationship between sexuality and reproduction seems to have been stronger, for instance, in the Greek and Roman societies and in the bourgeois society of the eighteenth and nineteenth centuries. No. What strikes me is the fact that now sexuality seems to be a question without direct relation with reproduction. It is your sexuality as your personal behaviour which is the problem.

Take homosexuality, for instance. I think that one of the reasons why homosexual behaviour was not an important issue in the eighteenth century was due to the view that if a man had children, what he did besides that had little importance. During the nineteenth century you begin to see that sexual behaviour was important for a definition of the individual self. And that is something new. It is very interesting to see that before the nineteenth century forbidden behaviour, even if it was very severely judged, was always considered to be an excess, a *libertinage*, as something too much. Homosexual behaviour was only considered to be a kind of excess of natural behaviour, an instinct that is difficult to keep within certain limits. From the nineteenth century on you see that behaviour like homosexuality came to be considered an abnormality. When I say that it was libertinage, I don't say that it was tolerated.

I think that the idea of characterizing individuals through their sexual behaviour or desire is not to be found, or very rarely, before the nineteenth century. "Tell me your desires, I'll tell you who you are." This question is typical of the nineteenth century.

Riggins: It would not seem any longer that sex could be called *the* secret of life. Has anything replaced it in this respect?

Foucault: Of course it is not *the* secret of life now, since people can show at least certain general forms of their sexual preferences without being plagued or condemned. But I think that people still consider, and are invited to consider, that sexual desire is able to reveal what is their deep identity. Sexuality is not *the* secret but it is still a symptom, a manifestation of what is the most secret in our individuality.

Riggins: The next question I would like to ask may at first seem odd and if it does I'll explain why I thought it was worth asking. Does beauty have special meaning for you?

Foucault: I think it does for everyone. [*Laughter.*] I am near-sighted but not blind to the point that it has no meaning for me. Why do you ask? I'm afraid I have given you proof that I am not insensitive to beauty.

Riggins: One of the things about you which is very impressive is the sort of monastical austerity in which you live. Your apartment in Paris is almost completely white; you also avoid all the *objets d'art* that decorate so many French homes. While in Toronto during the past month you have on several occasions worn clothes as simple as white pants, a white T-shirt and a black leather jacket. You suggested that perhaps the reason you like the colour white so much is that in Poitiers during the '30s and '40s it was impossible for the exterior of houses to be genuinely white. You are staying here in a house whose white walls are decorated with black cut-out sculptures and you remarked that you especially appreciated the straightforwardness and strength of pure black and white. There is also a noteworthy phrase in *The History of Sexuality*: "that austere monarchy of sex." You do not fit the image of the sophisticated Frenchman who makes an art out of living well. Also, you are the only French person I know who has told me he prefers American food.

Foucault: Yes. Sure. [*Laughter.*] A good club sandwich with a Coke. That's my pleasure. It's true. With ice cream. That's true.

Actually, I think I have real difficulty in experiencing pleasure. I think that pleasure is a very difficult behaviour. It's not as simple as that

[*Laughter*] to enjoy one's self. And I must say that's my dream. I would like and I hope I'll die of an overdose [*Laughter*] of pleasure of any kind. Because I think it's really difficult and I always have the feeling that I do not feel *the* pleasure, the complete total pleasure and, for me, it's related to death.

Riggins: Why would you say that?

Foucault: Because I think that the kind of pleasure I would consider as *the* real pleasure would be so deep, so intense, so overwhelming that I couldn't survive it. I would die. I'll give you a clearer and simpler example. Once I was struck by a car in the street. I was walking. And for maybe two seconds I had the impression that I was dying and it was really a very, very intense pleasure. The weather was wonderful. It was 7 o'clock during the summer. The sun was descending. The sky was very wonderful and blue and so on. It was, it still is now, one of my best memories. [*Laughter*.]

There is also the fact that some drugs are really important for me because they are the mediation to those incredibly intense joys that I am looking for and that I am not able to experience, to afford by myself. It's true that a glass of wine, of good wine, old and so on, may be enjoyable, but it's not for me. A pleasure must be something incredibly intense. But I think I am not the only one like that.

I'm not able to give myself and others those middle range pleasures that make up everyday life. Such pleasures are nothing for me and I am not able to organize my life in order to make a place for them. That's the reason why I'm not a social being, why I'm not really a cultural being, why I'm so boring in my everyday life. [*Laughter*.] It's a bore to live with me. [*Laughter*.]

Riggins: A frequently quoted remark of Romain Rolland is that the French Romantic writers were "visuels" for whom music was only a noise. Despite the remark being an obvious exaggeration, most recent scholarship tends to support it. Many references to paintings occur in some of your books but few to music. Are you also representative of this characteristic of French culture that Rolland called attention to?

Foucault: Yes, sure. Of course French culture gives no place to music, or nearly no place. But it's a fact that in my personal life music played a great role. The first friend I had when I was twenty was a musician. Then afterwards I had another friend who was a composer and who is dead now. Through him I know all the generation of Boulez. It has been a very important experience for me. First, because I had contact with the kind of art which was, for me, really enigmatic. I was not competent at all in this domain; I'm still not. But I felt beauty in something which was quite enigmatic for me. There are some pieces by Bach and Webern which I enjoy but what is, for me, real beauty is a "phrase musicale, un morceau de musique," that I cannot understand, something I cannot say anything about. I have the opinion, maybe it's quite arrogant or presumptuous, that I could say something about any of the most wonderful paintings in the world. For this reason they are not absolutely beautiful. Anyway, I have written something about Boulez. What has been for me the influence of living with a musician for several months. Why it was important even in my intellectual life.

Riggins: If I understand correctly, artists and writers responded to your work more positively at first than philosophers, sociologists or other academics.

Foucault: Yes, that's right.

Riggins: Is there a special kinship between your kind of philosophy and the arts in general?

Foucault: Well, I think I am not in a position to answer. You see, I hate to say it, but it's true that I am not a really good academic. For me intellectual work is related to what you could call aestheticism, meaning transforming yourself. I believe my problem is this strange relationship between knowledge, scholarship, theory and real history. I know very well, and I think I knew it from the moment when I was a child, that knowledge can do nothing for transforming the world. Maybe I am wrong. And I am sure I am wrong from a theoretical point of view for I know very well that knowledge has transformed the world.

But if I refer to my own personal experience I have the feeling knowledge can't do anything for us and that political power may destroy us. All the knowledge in the world can't do anything against that. All this is related not to what I think theoretically (I know that's wrong) but I speak from my personal experience. I know that knowledge can transform us, that truth is not only a way of deciphering the world (and maybe what we call truth doesn't decipher anything) but that if I know the truth I will be changed. And maybe I will be saved. Or maybe I'll die but I think that is the same anyway for me. [*Laughter.*]

You see, that's why I really work like a dog and I worked like a dog all my life. I am not interested in the academic status of what I am doing because my problem is my own transformation. That's the reason also why, when people say, "Well, you thought this a few years ago and now you say something else," my answer is, [*Laughter*] "Well, do you think I have worked like that all those years to say the same thing and not to be changed?" This transformation of one's self by one's own knowledge is, I think, something rather close to the aesthetic experience. Why should a painter work if he is not transformed by his own painting?

Riggins: Beyond the historical dimension is there an ethical concern implied in *The History of Sexuality*? Are you not in some ways telling us how to act?

Foucault: No. If you mean by ethics a code which would tell us how to act, then of course *The History of Sexuality* is not an ethics. But if by ethics you mean the relationship you have to yourself when you act, then I would say that it intends to be an ethics, or at least to show what could be an ethics of sexual behaviour. It would be one which would not be dominated by the problem of the deep truth of the reality of our sex life. The relationship that I think we need to have with ourselves when we have sex is an ethics of pleasure, of intensification of pleasure.

Riggins: Many people look at you as someone who is able to tell them the deep truth about the world and about themselves. How do you experience this responsibility? As an intellectual, do you feel responsible toward this function of seer, of shaper of mentalities?

Foucault: I am sure I am not able to provide these people with what they expect. [*Laughter.*] I never behave like a prophet. My books don't tell people what to do. And they often reproach me for not doing so (and maybe they are right) and at the same time they reproach me for behaving like a prophet. I have written a book about the history of psychiatry from the seventeenth century to the very beginning of the nineteenth. In this book I said nearly nothing about the contemporary situation but people still have read it as an anti-psychiatry position. Once, I was invited to Montreal to attend a symposium about psychiatry. At first I refused to go there since I am not a psychiatrist, even if I have some experience, a very short experience, as I told you earlier. But they assured me that they were inviting me only as a historian of psychiatry to give an introductory speech. Since I like Quebec I went. And I was really trapped because I was presented by the president as *the* representative in France of anti-psychiatry. Of course there were nice people there who had never read a line of what I had written and they were convinced that I was an anti-psychiatrist.

I have done nothing other than write the history of psychiatry to the beginning of the nineteenth century. Why should so many people, including psychiatrists, believe that I am an anti-psychiatrist? It's because they are not able to accept the real history of their institutions which is, of course, a sign of psychiatry being a pseudo-science. A real science is able to accept even the shameful, dirty stories of its beginning. [*Laughter.*]

So you see, there really is a call for prophetism. I think we have to get rid of that. People have to build their own ethics, taking as a point of departure the historical analysis, sociological analysis and so on, one can provide for them. I don't think that people who try to decipher the truth should have to provide ethical principles or practical advice at the same time, in the same book and the same analysis. All this prescriptive network has to be elaborated and transformed by people themselves.

Riggins: For a philosopher to have made the pages of *Time* magazine, as you did in November 1981, is an indication of a certain kind of popular status. How do you feel about that?

Foucault: When newsmen ask me for information about my work, I consider that I have to accept. You see, we are paid by society, by the taxpayers [*Laughter*] to work. And really I think that most of us try to do our work the best we can. I think it is quite normal that this work, as far as it is possible, is presented and made accessible to everybody. Naturally, a part of our work cannot be accessible to anybody because it is too difficult. The institution which I belong to in France (I don't belong to the university but to the Collège de France) obliges its members to make public lectures, open to anyone who wants to attend, in which we have to explain our work. We are both researchers and people who have to explain publicly our research. I think there is in this very old institution—it dates from the sixteenth century—something very interesting. The deep meaning is, I believe, very important. When a newsman comes and asks for information about my work, I try to provide it in the clearest way I can.

Anyway, my personal life is not at all interesting. If somebody thinks that my work cannot be understood without reference to such and such a part of my life, I accept to consider the question. [*Laughter.*] I am ready to answer if I agree. As far as my personal life is uninteresting, it is not worthwhile making a secret of it. [*Laughter.*] By the same token, it may not be worthwhile publicizing it.

◆　◆　◆

The living-room clown pretends the paper money in his hand is a patrolling fritillary. He tries to snare it with his free hand. The butterfly glides, dives, veers, gyrates—all but parachutes. It resists a friendly tickle. After glaring fumbles, Paul twists one of his ears and spits out water. The wheezing prey expires in the hands of the sour-faced lepidopterist. To Vladimir Nabokov, no doubt, this would be more proof that even sophisticated people rarely understand the mind of butterfly collectors. But then Nabokov did not see the ideological messages in the vaudeville acts of the Berlin Wintergarten.[8]

◆　◆　◆

Until Paul and I moved to The Hague I shared the prejudice of most people who have grown up in a hilly environment. I thought that flat, intensively cultivated farmland was bound to be dull. Despite their dissimilarities, the Dutch countryside eventually seemed as beautiful as the wooded hills of southern Indiana, accidentally preserved by the region's economic decline. The landscape of Holland makes one think that the residents know how to enjoy life. According to my Dutch teacher, the pride they take in their country is expressed in a beloved aphorism: "God created the world, but the Dutch created Holland."

Paul and I lived in Marlot, an affluent suburb of The Hague, from the autumn of 1972 until the summer of 1973. Our rented house, 490 Bezuidenhoutseweg, was a brick, semi-detached building, less opulent than some of its neighbours. Our second-floor apartment was a kind of time capsule packed with an eclectic mix of objects that ranged from the slightly obsolescent to the antiquated. The living room was furnished with tasselled, cloth lampshades; a worn, art nouveau carpet; a carved walnut-stained armoire; a television set that might have been only a few years old but seemed antique given the speed of electronic innovation. The armchairs and couch were somewhat uncomfortable, as might be expected in a rented apartment.

To a foreigner like myself The Hague did not seem particularly wel-coming, although its inhabitants politely struggle with less euphonious languages than their own. But Marlot retains many vestiges of its agricul-tural past. The local train station is situated in the midst of pastures. A five minute walk takes us to cultivated farmland and a wooded park.

My happiness in The Hague was tempered by the social isolation of our neighbourhood, which depressed me on lethargic afternoons, and the inconvenience of living in a suburban area without a car. Paul was not as annoyed by the isolation because of his research as a Fellow in Residence at the Netherlands Institute for Advanced Studies in Wassenaar, an institute which frees scholars from teaching for one year but not from the onslaughts of moody lovers. Paul and I spent as much time as possible in Paris; I read the *London Times* and listened to the BBC, turning Holland into an imaginary extension of Great Britain while I struggled to complete two overdue essays for graduate courses. It was in The Hague on November 20, 1972—Elizabeth Windsor's silver anniversary, I'm embarrassed to say—that I began the diary which is the basis for this book.

♦ ♦ ♦

The logic of the absurd fell on more fertile ground in Utrecht than in any other Dutch city, according to the painter Hendrik Poesiat. Utrecht in the 1930s was generally considered to be a *kunstloze stad*, a city without art. But if Poesiat had not moved to the vicinity of Utrecht as a young man, he thinks he would never have become a surrealist whose works might remind one of the Belgian artist Magritte. From 1931 until his emigration to Canada in 1956, Poesiat lived in the village of Woerden, outside Utrecht. One of his contemporaries, Johannes Moesman, is quoted as saying "we hated Utrecht but were practically unable to free ourselves from it."[9] The same has probably been said by Poesiat.

Utrecht had a bizarre, disquieting atmosphere—in contrast to the rest of Holland—which instinctively made its inhabitants receptive to magical and fantastic forms of realism. Poesiat comments in his unpublished memoirs:

On the surface Utrecht had a Victorian, bourgeoisie-like quiet but one sensed the existence of a secret underground life—a rotten disreputable secret that could not quite be pinpointed. The motionless, black-green waters of the canals, the rats, the age-old houses with their catacomb-like cellars, the centuries-old history of the city all created a weird, uncanny atmosphere.

Situated outside the densely populated area that connects Amsterdam and Rotterdam, Utrecht is somewhat isolated from the rest of Holland. Poesiat believes the social isolation of the city led to a high rate of psychological abnormalities. He talks about inhabitants who appear to be normal but whose minds seem to follow an illogical, sometimes unintentionally sinister train of thought. Utrecht is also predominantly Catholic. The mystical elements of Catholicism perhaps parallel the surrealists' fascination with the occult and the irrational.

Poesiat's career was sidetracked by the Great Depression, World War II and by the necessity of supporting a family. The earliest paintings which he displays at home were completed between the mid-1930s and the early 1940s. Then there is a gap of two to three decades in which he painted little other than some commissioned portraits. In the 1970s, he resumed his career at the point that he had abandoned it despite the passage of time. The paintings that were completed in the 1970s are the most interesting in his career although they're in a dated style. One no longer expects to find living representatives of his kind of surrealism.

Surrealist thought penetrated the artistic milieu of Utrecht a few years before Poesiat arrived. Near the end of World War I, Willem van Leusden, who was then making paintings influenced by the movement known as De Stijl, organized an informal drawing club as a means of reducing the cost of hiring live models. In the mid-1920s three younger men joined the group, Johannes Moesman, Willem Wagenaar, and Louis Wijmans, and the four became a nucleus for the diffusion of surrealist ideas from outside the country. Wagenaar is supposed to have been the driving force who inspired the group. His contagious enthusiasm and organizing abilities, perhaps more than his artistic talent, seem to have accounted for his influence. Wagenaar also opened a bookstore which became an outlet for surrealist publications. Poesiat received much of his formal education in art at the Vrije Akademie in Utrecht after dropping out of the School for the Graphic Arts in Amsterdam because the curriculum emphasized applied art. "The kingdom of the artist is not of this world," he explains.

To this descendant of French Protestant refugees who arrived in Holland in the mid-seventeenth century, the discovery of surrealism was liberating. "Intoxicated" is the word Poesiat uses to describe his mood when he first discovered Freud's books on the workings of the unconscious. By the mid-1930s surrealism had become an international movement that encompassed warring factions. It was the illusionist tradition of surrealism developed by Magritte and to a lesser extent by de Chirico that appealed most to him. Poesiat follows the logic of dreams and the unconscious in juxtaposing unlikely subject matter in his paintings, but the process of painting itself is not free and spontaneous. He appreciates the craftsmanship of sixteenth-and seventeenth-century art. This is one reason why he rejected a couple of fashionable surrealist techniques of creation, automatism and chance. The model of Magritte and de Chirico inspired in Poesiat a more mystical, complex imagery than was the case when he followed the models brewed by another contemporary movement, The New Objectivity. Poesiat's pre-surrealist portraits tend to be sombre and symbolically straightforward. Background details allude to the social instability of the time. Surrealism, on the other hand, let him avoid the banality that soon came to characterize The New Objectivity.

Poesiat's surrealist message may be eerie and elusive, but it is rarely distasteful. A typical painting from this phase of his career is *After the Last Train*, a warning of impending doom. The exterior of a turn-of-the-century Canadian train station is depicted realistically. Where the name of a city should be displayed on the façade is the message "ex nunc." The station seems to be located in the middle of a lake. The platform extends to the horizon, but waves of water submerge the track in mid-distance. Running along the platform is a naked woman who carries a signalling lantern for train conductors. There is no witness, however. Similar lanterns dangle from the limbs of a dead tree; others lie discarded on the platform. In the foreground, surrounded by water, is a statue of an ancient Greek philosopher. In one hand the philosopher holds a manuscript; the other points to a signalling lantern in a rectangular cavity in his chest. A storm threatens in the distance. Light comes from an unseen source and casts a purplish tint on the scene. Poesiat calls it a "sour colour." It is one detail of this painting that is purposely "vulgar."

Poesiat emphasizes the differences between his art and that of Magritte. Poesiat does not appreciate the absurd elements of Magritte's humour whose symbolism is dismissed as "cerebral and contrived." Poesiat's preoccupation in the second phase of his career with the mystery of death has few parallels in Magritte. While Poesiat refers to his mature style as "macabre Romanticism," Magritte was more classical in outlook. However, the two share a number of conventions: obscuring the boundary between the animate and the inanimate, merging physically incompatible features of a setting, inside and outside, day and night; inverting the natural size of objects.

Poesiat speaks eloquently and with obvious pleasure about his personal vision of surrealism, in the process revealing intimate feelings. Most paintings are in some way autobiographical. Several incorporate elements of unexplained violence. "Dreaming is the essence of life and gives it direction," Poesiat says. "It is awakened consciousness, not dreams, that is unreasonable."

Poesiat's vision is tempered by an emotional reticence in marked contrast to some of his old friends in Utrecht. The painting by Moesman entitled *Adieu* in which he exaggerates the sexual features of an embracing couple can be compared to Poesiat's version of the same theme, *The Unknown Constellation*. Poesiat desexualizes the embracing couple. They have become constellations of stars, whose shapes are accentuated by smoke, held aloft by a giant hand that reaches up out of a lake.

Poesiat's message is far from bleak, but it is not necessarily reassuring or redemptive. The painting called *The Empty Chair* depicts his mother-in-law and daughter. Both are stylized to such an extent that they represent any elderly woman or child of their generation. In the centre of the picture the child pulls a toy dog on wheels. She looks at an empty turn-of-the-century armchair. Objects from that era are a frequent element in Poesiat's paintings. Due to their age and solid construction they have come to represent tradition and propriety. Thus they seem to lend themselves to his intention of questioning appearances. In the background the grandmother, who has turned away from the viewer, walks through a landscape of gigantic skeletons. Tied to the chair is what might be a balloon, another insubstantial symbol of the spirit. But it could just as well be a hole in a wall through which hangs a rope—or perhaps an umbilical chord. Despite sentimental touches in this painting, the cuteness of the child and the toy dog, nothing holds out the promise of an eternal life comprehensible in human terms. "What I have to say, even if it is morbid, as it may often seem, is said as Schubert would have said it. He had a dark side in his character and music but it was never sadistic or cruel."

"I do not coat my paintings with pleasant feelings that can easily be digested," Poesiat explains, "I try to express an *unheimlich* feeling. The same mood is often felt by the viewer in his own life, but he does not want to face it. It is in him as well as in me. People don't want to look in the mirror. My art poses a threat because it comes from a region that is not under the control of the human will or the human consciousness."

◆　◆　◆

In their Toronto living room Hendrik and Leida Poesiat carefully exhibit the public dimension of their lives. Few objects recall the early days of their marriage when they used orange crates for furniture. Nothing recalls Hendrik's major occupation in Toronto, twenty-some years working as a decorator for Simpson's department store. He has carefully preserved copies of the political cartoons he drew in Holland but none are on display in the room. He worked as a cartoonist for regional newspapers in Woerden, Bodengraven and Alphen. The papers covered the political spectrum. Once a week he had to satirize a news story without offending a left-wing, centrist or right-wing readership.

The room highlights Poesiat's work in the traditional fine arts, although there is one picture of a mural made for a zoo in Holland and another of a theatrical costume he designed. (The Poesiats have been quite active in Toronto's Dutch theatre community.) No object visibly associates him with the surrealist movement, except for his paintings and a few books in the bookcase. Surrealism might be represented in the form of material artifacts by "found art" or objects used in some bizarre, alien manner. Instead, visitors find only pragmatic "make-dos" such as a wastepaper basket turned into a storage container for important papers. Just beside the front door is a watercolour of a Dutch farmhouse with a thatched roof. The picture helps to convey the status and ethnicity of the couple. While the farmhouse was drawn because it is picturesque, the couple inform visitors that the inhabitants of the house were members of the underground resistance to the Nazis. The picture thus unlocks a conversation about the Poesiats' own work in the underground resistance.

The living room might be construed as having a conventional and egalitarian flavour. The characteristic that conveys this impression is the way the room is saturated with small objects of sentimental value. Apparently expensive and inexpensive objects are clustered as though equally important, especially on a tabletop and in a knick-knack cabinet. A Chinese jade snake and miniature screen might be the most valuable objects on the table. But they are hard to notice when displayed among greeting cards, dried flowers, an inexpensive commemorative spoon from Amsterdam, a pendant that reproduces the famous painting van Gogh made in Arles near the end of his life, *Cafe Terrace, Evening*, and a porcelain Buddha whose bald head has been profanely decorated with a yarn cover, originally made for a jar of jelly and which looks like a woman's old-fashioned bonnet.

Poesiat's personal appearance is consistent with the bohemian role of the artist. His thin, upturned mustache and beret make one think of Salvador Dali. However, the flavour of the Poesiats' living room could be seen as serving a disidentifying function in the sense that surrealist values are not represented. The room contradicts expectations of an unconventional lifestyle. No migrant bohemian could accumulate such a density of objects nor display them in such an efficient and controlled manner. With respect to the current standards, it is a highly conformist interior that is in no way shocking. Mr. Poesiat states that his art "poses a threat [to the viewer] because it comes from a region that is not under the control of the human will." However, it would seem that nothing in the home, other than the paintings, suggests a belief in the liberating power of spontaneity and the unconscious. This is not to say that Poesiat's beliefs are insincere, but judging by the symbolism in this room his role as an artist is more segregated from his personal life than is supposed to be characteristic of a surrealist. His artifactual environment seems to bracket and distance the potential subversiveness of his ideology. Rather than a disguise, the living room is a negotiation with the conventions of his class and time and for that reason it undermines the threat posed by his art.

◆ ◆ ◆

Victoria College's bungling administrators have often been the targets of Paul's needling humour. To poke fun of one female Principal, he cut out pictures of the improbably named television star Victoria Principal from sleazy tabloids like *The National Enquirer*. He makes collages out of photographs and tacks them up on a bulletin board beside his office door. The messages are cryptic, interpretable in positive terms, if one does not give them much thought.

His "dancing Sandy" was made from a styrofoam cup turned upside down. Paul put thumbtacks along the rim of the cup to add weight and cut a small hole in the up-turned bottom. In the hole he inserted a caricature of the principal from a university newsletter which blends her features with those of the widowed Queen Victoria. When the cup is placed on a horizontal air vent, the moving air makes it dance.

◆　◆　◆

Our relationship is not free of bickering and stress. I am not above whining and complaining about the most insignificant things. Our problems include my inability to establish a proper level of independence. At times I think I am little more than Paul's shadow, a complaint which he dismisses as foolish misperception. He lists all of my objects that are displayed in our Toronto living room as proof of my power in our relationship. I feel stupid to complain.

I do not mind being directed by Paul, but I think he sometimes exceeds the role of benevolent guide. I have certainly benefited from his guidance, but being told what to do leaves vestiges of ambivalence. Paul insists on buying milk by the quart rather than the gallon, something I resent because I am always running out of milk. I am the only one who drinks milk. (But not, Paul added when he read this manuscript, the one who carries it from the store with all the rest of the food.) To reduce the number of shopping trips, I prefer large containers. His preference is for freshness and thus smaller sizes. My problems of excess dependence are exacerbated by the fact that as a dual-career couple we live separately much of the year. The mental independence and self-reliance that are required to live alone clash with the compromises demanded by living together.

Paul is more spontaneously creative, self-confident, assertive and optimistic than I am. Better established in his profession, he was fortunate to have begun his career when academic employment was rapidly expanding. To be appointed at the University of Toronto, then the largest French department in North America, in his 20s and without a Ph.D. (which he subsequently earned) is an experience few of my generation share. I behave inconsistently, complain about Paul's domination, but then expect him to have instant solutions for all my problems. It is typical of our relationship that initially this journal was a book secretly written about Paul. Only gradually, and after many revisions, did I claim some space in my own journal.

◆　◆　◆

Stephen Riggins, writing from Sudbury, Ontario, to the Vietnamese-French-American artist and architect Khoa Pham in Paris:

> One night last week I turned on the radio at home in my musty Sudbury basement apartment to discover that the station was midway through Stravinsky's *Pulcinella Suite* (the version that includes vocalists). I love that music; it is one of the pieces I never tire of hearing. It also has some very special connotations for me which you share to some extent since they all involve Hampstead in London. Paul and I stayed there for July and August 1970 in the apartment of two friends, Terry and Roger. *Pulcinella* was among their record collection and I constantly played it that summer. I have been in Hampstead in all seasons of the year and all kinds of weather, but I continue to associate Hampstead (especially the heath) with hot, sunny, summer days.... What sticks in my mind is a mélange of disconnected Hampstead sights and experiences: trudging up that steep hill, reading the *Epic of Gilgamesh* on the heath (because it was one of Jörn Merkert's treasured books), the house where D.H. Lawrence stayed for a while, the whiteness of that Adams country house you liked in its park setting, winning a live goldfish at a carnival on the heath and carrying it home one pitch dark night with a beautiful man I had met earlier, jogging on the heath, being run out of a bush one evening by a park attendant because I was doing shocking things to the man I was with, the eighteenth-century church and cemetery where Constable lies buried and which I crossed daily on the way to and from the subway and finally a merry-go-round with the printed message 'gay, happy and safe.'
>
> My enthusiasm for London is tempered, but not for Hampstead. (July 24, 1984)

◆　◆　◆

Stephen Riggins, writing from Sudbury, to Khoa Pham in Paris:

> Sitting beside me in the empty seat is my sixth and final crop of blueberries. The bus was an oven when we got in and two hours later still not as cool as I would like. I can smell the berries, although the box is closed. Maybe my imagination. But I was not my usual nimble self picking them in the heat and stepped on the

corner of the bag. An older colleague in the sociology and anthropology department, Helen Devereux, was saying this week that when she came to northern Ontario in the 1950s she rode in a train so old-fashioned that it was lit by gas lights. The barrens beside her were a blue haze. That's how many blueberries there are in Ontario.

The passing landscape at this point is extremely rocky—little top soil, scrubby trees. It is a hunters', fishers' and sailors' paradise. This sometimes bothers me when I'm pressured by work. The first year, in fact, I would not even look out the window. The contrast with my own non-stop work was too painful. The lakes and islands are beautiful and we must pass two dozen bays or inlets or lakes. Hard to detect the difference from the bus. Signs at gas stations read: 'ice, pop and worms.' You won't find that in Paris in any language! In this place they fill refrigerators with live worms. Not enough soil to hold telephone poles which are anchored to solid rock and held upright by small boulders. Private driveways are sometimes marked by a row of small rocks painted white or bright yellow. At the end of Labour Day weekend literally every fifth car is attached to a boat of some sort.

The photograph I sent last week is one of my favourite portraits. I am standing outdoors in the Marais in 1978 in front of the closed shutters of a shop. Someone that year went around Paris spraying this artistic graffiti which is behind me. Maybe you remember seeing it? The graffiti appealed to me because of its sexuality—highly stylized human figures, with prominent mouths and genitals, in all kinds of postures, as in an orgy. Paul took the pictures—at my suggestion. There are a series of these "snap dragon shots—poofproof "—some showing more of the graffiti, some in which I am looking rather cross. Paul, with his subversive humour, decided to take two pictures of me, one from the waist up and another from the waist down. Putting the two pictures together, you can elongate and shorten my legs, and make me dance. Or at least so he thought. How could anyone be seriously sexy with such a trying photographer? (August 7, 1984)

♦　♦　♦

Khoa Pham is a graduate of the architectural program at Cornell University in Ithaca, New York. We became acquainted through Ron Bowen, who taught art to Khoa at the American high school in Paris. Ron has depicted each of us in two of his best hyper-realist portraits.

Khoa Pham, writing from Paris, to Stephen Riggins in Sudbury:

The background colours of your last portrait, finished this afternoon, are not what I expected! Except for a black band, the rest is
in shades of browns and greys recalling the colour of your cardigan,
and the overall effect is silvery. The diffused light on the face and
hands no longer have a source in the painting because the background is abstract. As for the face, I can't decide whether it looks
like you or not. Sometimes I recognize the expression, other times
I find everything just slightly off to prevent the resemblance. But
seen upside down the attitude is unmistakably yours! I had not
seen it so restrained, but as it's turned out the painting is still
fantasy-potent! (August 8, 1984)

◆　◆　◆

Khoa Pham, writing from Pornic (Loire-Atlantique), to Stephen Riggins in
Sudbury:

Do not be lenient with my attempts at collage. But I think that
perhaps it is a way for me to begin working with abstract compositions again. My problem has always been to find a "subject" able
to motivate a painting or a drawing; I no longer have the urge to
simply paint a "still life" or a "landscape;" for I do not feel I have
anything "to say" about just any still life or landscape. So there are
portraits. But strict realism is limiting. And my abstractions have
not been motivated by strong desires so I quickly run out of ideas
and they are simply decorative. But if the "subject" of my abstract
compositions (really the initial motivation to create something) is
at once something that I feel strongly about and which allows a
pictorial transposition, such as your letters or your diary, then
perhaps I can begin working in that direction more productively?
(September 20, 1984)

◆　◆　◆

From the coastal town of Pornic, in Brittany, where Khoa is on vacation, he
sent four whimsical, cubist-inspired collages made on the back of postcards. The themes are experiences I recount in my letter about Hampstead.
One is a portrait of me reduced to mouth and mustache. The second, the
beautiful young man depicted in his pinkish phallic dimensions, made

from an ink blotter. The third is the goldfish—gold wishbone lines for tail and head, scales suggested by the border of a sheet of stamps decorated with curved patterns. It swims in blue marbled paper like the old-fashioned paper on the inside covers of good books. The fourth collage is a painted black rectangle, the heath through which I walk carrying my trophy home in its bowl of water. Nothing is seen in the darkness but random dots of gold and a squiggly gold line, the stars and my path illuminated by the fish.

◆ ◆ ◆

Khoa Pham, writing from Paris, to Stephen Riggins in Sudbury:

> Today, the Pont Neuf is half-wrapped [by Christo]. The media have presented the sensational, eccentric and megalomaniac aspects of the project; no one so far talks of its visual qualities, the surprising beauty of it. Earlier in the week I was struck by the technical mastery necessary for its realization, in contrast to the loose and graphically expressionistic renderings of the project. The metal frames, girders and clamps needed to hold the cloth in place have all been minutely designed, their installation carefully planned and organized. This is all the more remarkable in that the people who execute the work are not from a special Christo team but are simply local construction workers, and French alpinists and divers. I am in true admiration of the feat, realizing the difficulty of having anything built as designed in architecture.
>
> But the greatest success remains its beauty, its exciting visual qualities. The cloth used is a glossy ocre fabric which shimmers in the light like gold "lamé" in an haute couture dress. Paradoxically the design of the bridge suddenly becomes more visible covered: the major lines and edges are sharply revealed and defined while the secondary details are covered by the cloth. He plays with blurred and sharp edges as a painter would on a canvas. For more definition he uses the red ropes, strapping the cloth more closely to the covered forms. A humorous note today: several of the draped bronze lamps on the bridge have not been tied with rope and the cloth forms which cover them balloon in the breeze like giant phalli sheathed in gold condoms (September 19, 1985).
>
> Going to the Préfecture this morning, to renew my travel document, I crossed the Pont Neuf, all wrapped. All the barricades have been removed; it's guarded only by the little blue Christo

army. The sensational spectacle of its wrapping is over. Now that the Parisians no longer find it surprising, and after five days accept it as casually as they do the crude slogan that looks down on it: La Samaritaine m'emballe, its extravagant reality is all the more manifest. The cloth is soft underfoot; in the early morning sun it shimmers like some surrealist mirage, questioning the reality of the bridges, the monuments beyond and the four banks it joins. (September 27, 1985)

◆ ◆ ◆

As I lifted my hands from the keyboard at the end of the first measure of Rachmaninoff's "Prelude in C-Sharp Minor," I could see out of the corner of my eye Professor Walter Robert turn to the future dean Charles Webb and shrug his shoulders. It was distracting because I could not imagine that anything could possibly be wrong in my playing of three simple chords. It was a gesture of that ironic humour which I later discovered flavoured his conversations. To find a more professional music teacher I was auditioning at Indiana University's faculty of music in the summer of 1961, playing in Professor Robert's studio.

I had not yet learned that a performer is supposed to serve the composer's intentions. I had taken the liberty of holding the third chord for about half the proper time ruining the pensive drama that is supposed to open the piece. Thus the decision was made that I should study with his wife Dorothy (1904-1998), who was prevented from teaching at Indiana University's faculty of music because of its regulations against hiring husbands and wives in the same department. Mrs. Robert was my instructor for about two and a half years, and she arranged for me to study with a faculty member, Frederick Baldwin, when the Roberts were in Naples during my junior year of high school. These lessons required a considerable sacrifice from my parents because Bloomington is located fifty miles from Loogootee. The lessons were mother's idea. To some degree I was fulfilling her thwarted ambitions. She is surprised that she was bold enough to contact the university. She learned to be more enterprising by working for the Red Cross during the Second World War, gathering information for investigative reports, assisting families in obtaining furloughs and helping to organize fundraising drives.

The ancestors of Mrs. Robert's father were from the small town of Ellwangen in Baden-Württemberg, Germany. Her father, Gottlob Hess, was a well-known bookseller and antiquarian in Munich. Mrs. Robert grew up in Munich and in Vienna in a secular Jewish household. She could trace her ancestry back to a judge who had the distinction of being the first Jewish judge admitted to the Court of the King of Württemberg. After immigrating to the United States, she earned a master's degree in musical education from North Texas State University.[10] Mrs. Robert, who had wavy red hair and spoke English with a heavy German accent, did not perform frequently in public. I am aware of only one occasion when she performed at Indiana University. This was a concert of piano duets, given in collaboration with her husband, that occurred many years prior to my study with her.

Walter Robert (1908-1999) was typical of the central European musicians and intellectuals who fled Naziism and found congenial environments at American universities. He had been born in Trieste when it was the Habsburgs' imperial seaport. At the turn of the nineteenth-century Trieste was transformed from a sleepy fishing village into a seaport for Austria's Mediterranean navy. The travel writer Jan Morris refers to the city as the Capital of Nowhere, although she makes its colourful and polyglot nature seem the epitome of cosmopolitanism. Jews were encouraged to settle there. "In my mind," Morris observes, "Jews and Trieste go together, and the long and fruitful association of the two has made the city what it is— or at least, what it seems to me to be in those moments, ten minutes before the hour, when the idea of it bewitches me."[11] The Jews of Trieste inspired James Joyce to write *Ulysses*.

In 1931 Walter Robert was awarded the Bösendorfer grand piano which was presented to the best student pianist graduating from the Vienna State Academy of Music. He first worked in New York and then Texas prior to being hired as an Associate Professor in 1947 at Indiana University. At some point Walter Robert changed his name, not unusual for ambitious residents of Trieste. His parents were Julius and Pauline (Deutsch) Spitz. To Americans the word "spitz" sounds too much like spit. In German it means sharp. If Professor Robert had looked for a more literal translation of his family name, he might have chosen Wiseman. Walter Robert was a gifted linguist who could speak, in addition to German and English, Italian (the working language of Trieste in his childhood), Russian, French, Greek and Latin. He translated Descartes' *Compendium Musices* into English. In middle age he had the same white hair, square jaw and natural masculinity that I see in photographs of Shostakovich.[12] In my own middle age, now that I have begun playing the piano again, Brahms' "Intermezzos" are some of the pieces which interest me the most. Brahms had been among Walter Robert's specialties. But as an undergraduate I thought that specializing in such a hopelessly conventional composer was tedious. So I never heard Walter Robert play or talk about Brahms.

At my first lesson Mrs. Robert felt that it was necessary to return to music as simple as Clementi's "Sonatinas" in order to acquire solid technical skills and to master the differences between Romantic and Classical styles. She was a dynamic teacher, well-organized and exceptionally good at keeping students motivated. She was exacting about technique but not in a way that students might resent. I do not remember her ever making disparaging remarks about my playing. Certainly I had not yet experienced the way a score can be dissected, sloppy details played at varied tempos and with a different touch, in order to play smoothly and as literally as possible precisely what is printed on the page. It was from her rigorous training in practicing scales, Czerny's exercises, and Hanon's *The Virtuoso Pianist* that I learned playing the piano is as physical as playing basketball. Maybe that's why I find so much satisfaction, even as an adult, in playing Hanon's expressionless exercises that are supposed to make the fourth and fifth fingers strong and agile.

Browsing through the standard repertoire, Mrs. Robert let students pick the pieces they wanted to learn. In my case that meant shunning the composers which I thought were too Romantic: Schubert, Schumann, Mendelssohn and above all Chopin, most of whose music I still dislike. We tended to concentrate on music from the Classical and Baroque eras. Perhaps Mrs. Robert understood best the spirit of classic Viennese music. The tempo is relaxed so the music can sing and the piece is not inappropriately turned into an empty virtuoso exercise. She was critical of the playing of a pianist such as Glenn Gould, which in her mind was too idiosyncratic. Mrs. Robert did appreciate the masculinity of Gould's playing, the way he made Bach's *The Well-tempered Clavier* sound primitive in the best sense of the word. I especially remember Mrs. Robert's ability to play expressively the darker pieces by Bach, for example the sarabande from the "French Suite Number Five." Played mechanically with little feeling, the sarabande sounds like nothing. Someone once said to me that I have an innate feeling for playing Haydn. Certainly Mrs. Robert would know that this is not true. If I ever managed to convey such an impression, it is due as much to her teaching as to my temperament.

In a small notebook Mrs. Robert recorded the instructions that I was supposed to remember when I practiced. Here is some of her advice for playing Mozart and Haydn. Her remarks are by no means original, but they do show her conscientiousness as a teacher and the principles she was trying to convey. We were probably working on Mozart's "Sonata in C Major" (KV. 545) and Haydn's "Sonata in C Major" (Hob. XVI:35). For the Mozart sonata, she wrote over a period of several weeks: "listen to pedalling and phrasing. Light endings. Careful fingering. Expressive. Play all phrasings elegantly. Runs adagio. Not too fast. Lyrical tones. Work for ease. Fortissimo not too heavy." For the Haydn sonata: "Listen if each note is there and for pedal. Pedal less and shorter. Get lighthearted spirit in Haydn style. Know it well enough to make it sound relaxed and gay."

Under Mrs. Robert's guidance, I studied the standard repertoire: Bach, Haydn, Mozart, Beethoven, Brahms, Grieg, Dvorak, Debussy and Ravel.[13] The most difficult compositions I studied with her were Beethoven's "Pathetique Sonata" and Ernst von Dohnanyi's "Third Rhapsody." Percussive twentieth-century music attracted me in particular, which I heard occasionally on the radio stations of Indiana University and the University of Illinois. The Hungarian composer Ernst von Dohnanyi's "Third Rhapsody" was one of the ideal compromises between my interest in banging away at the piano and the more established music Mrs. Robert preferred. Paul compares this with the gratification a motorcyclist gets from revving up his engine. Published in 1902, the rhapsody is alternately humorous, dissonant and powerfully romantic. It is still obvious in this piece why Brahms in his old age would enjoy Dohnanyi's early compositions. Mrs. Robert also helped me learn other pieces from the conservative modern repertoire: Bartok, Prokofiev, Kabalevsky and Norman Dello Joio. If I mention my perception of Mrs. Robert's taste, and I emphasize that this is just my personal perception, it would be relatively traditional music steeped in German/Austrian culture. Among the music that reminds me of Mrs. Robert is Busoni's transcriptions of Bach, music I never actually studied with her.

Mrs. Robert once recalled that in high school I had "played competently for my age," but my emotional reticence resulted in a style that did not have enough dynamic contrasts. Erratic rhythm was one of my worst mistakes. Advice to "count aloud and play in one tempo" appears in the notes from several lessons. My shyness was more difficult to remedy. I was too timid to perform at my best in public. Neither Walter nor Dorothy Robert was opposed to my pursuing a career in musicology; however, they tended to emphasize so much the hardships professional musicians experience that this did not seem an appealing option. In 1964 I auditioned for admission as an undergraduate student in the music faculty of Indiana University and was accepted in music education. Nonetheless, before school began in the autumn of that year I decided not to specialize in music and entered without declaring a major. On several occasions I have regretted that I so thoughtlessly rejected the opportunity of becoming a musicologist. I eventually found myself in the odd situation of writing a Ph.D. thesis on the social history of nineteenth-century French music although I had never taken a single music history course.

From Mrs. Robert's letters I suspect that my vague memory of her personality is due to her tendency to focus on music and to avoid talking about herself. One story she liked to tell is about an experience in Naples. No one except teachers and students was allowed inside the conservatory in Naples. Only toward the end of their year-long visit did Mrs. Robert finally have the first opportunity to meet her husband's students and hear them perform. She arrived at the conservatory, informed the guard that she was the wife of an instructor. The guard took her directly to the door of Professor Robert's studio where his students were waiting to meet her. As everyone watched she opened the studio door, but stumbled in the threshold and fell flat on her face.

Studying with Dorothy Robert was my first personal contact with the arduous but fulfilling demands of academia. Classical music gave me a way to explore domains outside my native environment. Playing the organ at church and the trumpet in the school band did not give me this refuge. It was the piano lessons from Dorothy Robert. Her teaching opened worlds far beyond classical music.

◆　◆　◆

At the age of 92 Dorothy Robert did get to hear my praise for her. I recorded the preceding remarks and sent them to her and her husband at a retirement community in Bloomington. In order to respond Dorothy needed someone's assistance because late in life she had become blind:

> I was very interested and touched by your letter. I was very touched that you think of me after such a long time in terms that may be exaggerated—but I like it very much anyway.
>
> I'd be happy to answer any questions you may have. But if you ask me about my methods, I am at a loss as to what to say because I have no methods. My "method," if there is any, is to work with each student according to his/her needs—technical as well as musical....
>
> I remember you very well in spite of my bad memory and in spite of my being blind.... The thing I do remember is that you sat in my room waiting for your lesson and looked at all the books, and when you realized I came into the room, you took the book you just had and sat on it so I wouldn't know that you were looking at it!

Accompanying Dorothy's note was a letter from Karen Taylor, a professor of piano I had met in Paris, that includes an expanded version of this story as she remembered hearing it several years earlier. Personally, I would explain my actions by saying that it is typical of only children. There are many advantages in being an only child, but one minor disadvantage is that parents, having just a single child to contemplate, spend too much time nervously worrying about its development. Only children perceive this as intrusive. It is not that we have anything of importance to hide from parents or from adults, but we sometimes go to odd lengths to attain some privacy. Mumbling or talking too softly and too fast are good strategies for keeping smothering attention at bay. The people asking probing questions get tired of requesting that you repeat yourself. Here is Karen's version of Dorothy's story:

> …Dorothy said that as a youngster you were quite shy, but had a wonderfully inquisitive mind and a tremendous thirst for learning. She said that after she reassured you that it was OK to browse through the books in the waiting room, you would glance through as many as you could before the lesson. Then, without saying a word you would go to the piano when she was ready to start your lesson and place one book beside you on the piano bench. Only when she asked you if you would like to borrow the book to read it, would you happily admit that such was your desire. The next week you'd return it, and beside you on the piano bench she'd discover *another* book! I wonder how much of the Roberts' music library you devoured this way....
>
> …You were quite right in what you said in your letter: not only is it kind of hard to get a handle on her approach because she always subordinated herself to THE MUSIC, but on top of that she always adopted a modest, self-effacing demeanour that served to keep Walter Robert in the spotlight and herself in the background. Between you and me (et tout en confiance) she is *at least* as intelligent and interesting as he is, but it takes a long time to realize that—at least if one's primary musical contact is with him, as was the situation in my case. It's high time someone paid a little attention to her achievement, which I suspect was considerable at least in the pre-college sphere. I have the feeling that in the '50s and '60s, Dorothy was *the* pre-eminent pre-college piano teacher in Bloomington. I believe that you were only one of quite a few young pianists whom she helped form and enabled to gain admission to college music studies, whether in performance or in academic disciplines.... (November 29, 1996)

◆ ◆ ◆

The television set in my parents' home in Loogootee is decorated with traditional stylistic features. Adorning each side of the screen are pilaster-like wooden shapes resembling furniture legs that have ribbing and spooling. Below the screen are two false wooden drawers with curved Italianate brass handles behind which are straight backplates that end in a fleur de lys. An open book, highlighted by a wooden easel, rests on top of their television set. The volume has been glued shut except for the two opened pages, and pasted on top of them is an extraneous picture and text. The picture is one of the most common religious images in Protestant homes, "The Good Shepherd," by an artist named Plockhorst. It refers to one of the best known parables about God's mercy. On the opposite page is the complete twenty-third Psalm in the King James translation: "The Lord is my shepherd; I shall not want. He maketh me to lie down in green pastures; he leadeth me beside the still waters. . . ." The volume has a false patina of age. The cover and the edges of the pages have been gilded, some of the paint scratched away to create an antique appearance. Paper doilies have been glued to the cover. The Biblical quotations are pasted over a secular book. For my mother this is a significant collective object, a visual affirmation of her membership in a local church. However, from the perspective of medium theory, a specialty in mass communications research which explores the relation between a society's most popular medium of expression and its prevailing values, this juxtaposition of book and television set reveals a transitional anxiety. America's past source of authority, the (religious) book, has been placed atop the contemporary source of authority that has replaced print media, the (secular) television.

In the dining room is a six-foot display cabinet consisting of three glass-enclosed shelves, a drawer, and two shelves hidden by panelled doors. The cabinet functions as both a shrine to the past and to good dining as well as a catch-all. Mother has collected and placed on display traditional objects of femininity: antique china (from my father's family for the most part) and cut-glass (from her family). The contents of the shrine are to me an interactional backdrop, functioning in a way similar to that of my books in the living room in my parents' eyes.

Most objects were given to my mother or they were inherited. The few pieces that were actually purchased tend to be travel souvenirs. Here is the kind of late nineteenth and early twentieth-century fancy china and glassware which was preserved for special social occasions. They carry the standard decorative features of the era: clear glass with stars and thumbprints; hand-painted china with pastel roses, lilies, pansies and fleurs de lys; pictures of deer and gnomes; and, gilded and painted rims. Although the trademarks show that several of the older pieces were manufactured in Germany, this is probably a reflection of conditions in international china and glass industries rather than conscious family identification with German culture. Perhaps the two most artistic pieces are a plate of Haviland china decorated with pictures of red and black raspberries and leaves, and a Ginori cake plate decorated with pink and white lilacs.

Although antiques predominate, the shelves do contain on closer inspection an eclectic mix of styles and types of objects: reproductions as well as genuine antiques. There is memorial china (from my parents' golden wedding anniversary), a cheap blue pitcher decorated with a picture of the child actress Shirley Temple, a real pine cone from Bavaria, a marble pebble (a travel souvenir of unknown origin), a snail shell, an Inuit soapstone carving from Canada, a reproduction of a colonial glass bottle from Jamestown, Virginia and a plastic needle threader whose location in a display cabinet makes it easy to find. There is also a clear-glass beer stein illustrated with figures in relief—people in costumes typical of heroes and heroines in historic operas. Originally sold as a container for food, the beer stein was used by my grandmother as a flower vase. Since it is displayed as a decorative item in a household of teetotallers, its message is ironic: "Drink moderately and sing songs in order to achieve good things." The few pieces of modern tableware were gifts from me: a Delft china flask and vase, and Arabia Ware egg cups. Items for use in social contexts more prestigious than Sunday afternoon family dinners also tend to be from me. An example is a rectangular clear-glass bottle encased in a silver holder of lilies of the valley.

I value most an insignificant-looking item, an obviously cheap mug decorated with a wreath of pansies and a gnome. It was used as a shaving mug by my paternal grandfather, Harve Riggins (1881-1917). For me, this appreciated emblem of masculinity is a sign of a broken bond with the past. It might also steer a conversation toward the topic of gender, documenting my belief that traditional female values are superior to the traditional values of men. My reference would be the literature summarized by the psychologist Lillian Rubin about the difficulty adult men experience in maintaining intimate relationships. Rubin traces the relative social incompetence of men in intimate relationships to the structure of the family during childhood, the fact that mothering or caregiving is the work primarily of women, the same sex for girls, the opposite sex for boys. Psychoanalytically-inspired feminists believe that this pattern of caregiving fosters excessively strong ego boundaries for boys as well as a discontinuous gender development. When mothers push young sons away in order to encourage a male identity, sons misperceive this as abandonment. Apparently, such misperceptions remain lodged in the unconscious and are among the reasons why adult men insist on asserting their separateness and detachment from others.

The shaving mug with the pansies and the gnome belonged to my paternal grandfather, whose political views might be an inspiration to me if I knew more about them. I have spent a considerable amount of time writing about the personal lives and farming techniques of my mother's family. This is not because I identify with the politics of the Ledgerwoods, but because mother, being more psychologically involved with others, remembered so many of the stories about her extended family that she had heard as a child. Even if you are tracing the line of male ancestors, family history is largely women's history because it is women who remember the information they hear. In the case of Harve Riggins selective memory due to gender has reduced the story of his life to a few sentences. Despite being a farmer, he is supposed to have been sympathetic to the labour organizer and socialist Eugene V. Debs and he threatened to become a pacifist if the United States entered World War I. Harve drowned, however, in a fishing accident before he had the opportunity to take a public stand as a pacifist.

♦ ♦ ♦

Walking together in autumn rain showers in St. John's, Newfoundland, Paul makes up variations on the expression "take down the umbrella": cancel the umbrella, retract the umbrella, dismiss the umbrella, take off the umbrella, clear away the umbrella, withdraw the umbrella, do away with the umbrella, close the umbrella, eliminate the umbrella, amputate the umbrella.

♦ ♦ ♦

Ignoring Paul's advice, I got a kitten in St. John's to keep me company. I'm now away from Toronto two-thirds of the year. Paul likes cats but he feels it is not practical for us to own one. A colleague gave me one of the daughters of Spare Cat, the runt of this summer's litter. We rescued a kitten with a really sweet temperament. Although I think she would be called a grey tabby, the veterinarian recorded her as brown. We are told that in Indonesia a cat that has a coat of three colours and four white feet is a sign of good luck.

Paul believes cats which result from chance matings are more vigorous and intelligent than those who possess pure pedigrees. "This cat really hit the jackpot when it found us." In the veterinarian's records the cat is named Durkheim in honour of my favourite sociologist. Paul wanted to give her a pun for a name—Pizzicati, from pizzicato, the plucking of a stringed instrument. Since Paul thought Pizzicati would be a good mother, he imagined we had an obligation to let her breed. But I was more concerned about her inappropriate peeing around the house when she was in heat and had her spayed before she had a chance to have kittens. He also refers to Pizzicati as "the cats" because she is so frisky she unexpectedly appears from every corner of the apartment.

The names Paul coined for Pizzicati's unborn kittens are also jokes. Mandu suggested a kitten that was self-assured and poised. Astrophe, the ugly kitten. Erpillar, the mean one. Egory is supposed to sound old-fashioned and Victorian. All these names are derived from words which have "cat" or "kat" as their first syllable: Katmandu, catastrophe, caterpillar and category.

◆   ◆   ◆

I pay such an outrageous amount of money to heat my apartment in St. John's that Paul suggests this bigger beggar who bugs us, our sleep and dream expert that purrs like a helicopter, must be turning up the heat after I leave for work. Pizzicati also enjoys chewing on the Venetian blinds, much to my irritation. "Does she also eat their white canes?" Paul asks. "Soon she'll be eating the mutes."

Paul goes "fishing for cats," dragging his tie along the floor and across the bed to attract Pizzicati. When she's trapped, she unexpectedly purrs.

He wants to write a serious, academic article titled "What My Cat Knows."

◆   ◆   ◆

Paul's haiku about me and Pizzicati:

Flowers come and go
Wars are won and lost
Nothing like a warm lap for a five-minute nap

◆   ◆   ◆

In traditional Japan there was a ritualized way of confronting death. On the verge of death, the dying wrote a "parting with life" poem. The purpose was to demonstrate indifference to the extinction of the self and to prove that even in the most extreme circumstances it was possible to manage one's emotions. The poems were typically seventeen-syllable haiku with an implied spiritual message. More elaborate forms of poetry would have been inconsistent with the idea that this was supposed to be a ritual anyone could perform. The author of a good parting with life poem was supposed to show appreciation for the natural beauty of the moment in its more humble, transitory forms. The writer was to look for a symbol that helped him or her embrace transitoriness rather than resist it.

The custom resembles Victorian deathbed scenes in Europe and North America when the dying called relatives into the bedroom one at a time for a last dramatic farewell. But the Japanese custom seems more ritualized and more spiritual. "Farewell children, farewell. Be good. Be good," are the dying words of my maternal grandfather, who passed away in his mid-50s in 1913. The last words spoken by mother's sister which the family was able to comprehend in her delirious state was an imaginary dialogue with one of her teenage sons. He often forgot to close the gate of the fence surrounding their home. In the hospital as she lay dying of acute appendicitis, she managed to mutter: "Shut the gate, Wayne."

In 1778, at the age of thirty-nine, a person named Chori wrote the following parting with life poem: "Leaves never fall in vain—from all around bells tolling."[14] Chori's humility is evident through his identification with such an anonymous form of nature as the leaves of unnamed plants. Like them, his body will be recycled. Perhaps actual noises are heard at the time of his death in the autumn of the year that can be interpreted as consoling. But the word "bell" is really a metaphor. There is no deliberate, personal or human commemoration of his life. This does not trouble him.

◆ ◆ ◆

In his "Trio for Piano, Violin and Cello" (Opus 120), Gabriel Fauré embraces life with joy, serenely accepting the limitations of his own sick body. The trio seems more convincingly religious than his famous requiem. Because he had played the organ for so many funerals in Paris, he wanted to write a different kind of requiem. But it is sometimes too charming, other times too languid to be consistently satisfying, however much one might appreciate the composer's humanism.

The years of Fauré's autumnal maturity were approximately 1919 to 1924. It is difficult to date precisely because some of his earlier music has similar qualities. He was seventy-four years old at the beginning of this period, nearly deaf and in declining health. But he composed emotional and joyful music infused with an elegiac spirit which is never self-obsessed, morbid or weary of life. How different from Gustav Mahler. The combination of sensuality and spirituality that Fauré brought to music is rare.

The gradual loss of his hearing was perhaps a blessing in disguise. It was easier to ignore the fashionable frivolity of the *années folles*, as the 1920s are known in France. The voluptuousness of late romantic music is tempered through austerity and mild dissonance in Fauré's music. In the hands of a lesser composer these qualities might have resulted in pale reflections of earlier compositions. In Fauré's case they swept from the page the excessive sweetness that mars his youthful music.

The opening movement of the trio, allegro ma non troppo, begins with a repeating two-note figure in the treble of the piano that creates a pulse, a quiet but energetic background for melodies on the cello and violin. There is nothing the least bit remarkable about the beginning. Fauré often starts his pieces this way. And then after a minute or so the music reaches a state of ecstasy, a whirling exuberance that suggests dance. A melody in the third movement reminded the musicologist Robert Orledge of an accented rustic dance tune.[15] To me, the entire first movement in three-quarter time has this quality. The melodies seem less significant than the rising and subsiding tension. There is an amazing tension in the piano accompaniment that is created through chromatic complexity, syncopation, crescendos and repetition. A feeling of restrained joy is conveyed by the brevity of the climaxes. The euphoric moments, which most composers would have extended, quickly subside and a slow ascent begins again.

Fauré's philosophical wisdom is most obvious in the final climax of the second movement, marked andantino. After the melody has become increasingly chromatic and tense through seven repetitions, there is a moment of suspension which is repeated a second time. This sets up expectations of a rhetorical conclusion perhaps a bit less bombastic than Vincent d'Indy's "Piano Quartet in A Minor" (Opus 7) in which good too obviously triumphs over evil. Instead, Fauré's melody suddenly falters and the music expires in eleven measures. The concluding third movement, allegro vivo, is forceful and animated—no trace of the wistful sadness of the first two movements. Here is the reassurance that at the end of a long life it is still possible to be supremely creative.

◆　◆　◆

When I report to Paul the remarks of the composer and inventor of electronic instruments Serge Tcherepnin, someone he knew in Paris in the
1960s, the subject of the praise responds impatiently: "I said things from
the top of my head and they thought I was a genius. Nobody can take
themselves seriously or they die." It is not easy to struggle against Paul's
opposition to my writing about him. "Futile," he calls it. Luckily, the
encouragement I need is voiced by old friends and acquaintances. In
response to my request for information Tcherepnin writes:

> Paul is indeed a special character in my life, something like the
> block of black granite that features in Stan Kubrick's *2001*, of deep
> influence and meaning, massive, humorous and lasting.
>
> I wish I hadn't been so flighty in my life, and had kept up my
> contact with him. There are big holes in my knowledge of his activ-
> ities, which I have since discovered were filled by him in a brilliant
> manner.
>
> But I do have several favourite memories of his, shall we say,
> unusual…and, perhaps, subversive…presence in France in the
> '60s. I'll be glad to share them with you.
>
> Another of his friends in those years is Jean-Louis Bourgeois,
> the son of Louise Bourgeois, the French sculptor who lives in
> Manhattan.
>
> So…I'll get my whisk to blow some of the dust off my recollec-
> tions, and now that I think of it, even the dust will be sent because,
> in Paul's case, it is so precious and special. (March 12, 1999)

Kubrick had been in the news just before Tcherepnin wrote. Since the
block of black granite is an infuriatingly obscure symbol—worshipped
and feared by violent apes, somehow appreciated by technologically
sophisticated humans—the composer does not really say what Paul
means to him. Tcherepnin used the Internet to locate Paul after having lost
contact with him for over twenty-five years. The praise is beautiful, but I
suspect it may turn out to be unconvincing. Two days later, I received
from Tcherepnin an enigmatic e-mail message. Difficult-to-decipher
messages seem to be his forte. Unfortunately, I don't know my Tolstoy
and I have not looked through the lens of a microscope since high school:

> Stephen, it's imperative you contact Paul ASAP [as soon as possible],
> to warn him, if he knows his Tolstoy, that it wasn't really my
> intention, if I had known, but that it's been out of my hands for a

while now. Who would have known, about jlb [Jean-Louis Bourgeois] and all of that. I'm not a microscope. (March 14, 1999)

Nearly a month passed. I graded examinations and essays, and despite many complaints, finished a grant application. Once again, on April 12, I prodded Tcherepnin, sending a message consisting only of two short and funny entries from this volume. I picked the entry about Paul's father upon his return from a prisoner-of-war camp repressing his son's dancing and the entry about Paul's ability through words to turn a pumpkin into a coach and water into wine. Within hours I received the following:

Thanks for your amusing text concerning the old bear, the old dancing bear i dare say.

Yep that's how i remember old Paul full of fun and pomp, curious admixture wouldn't you say (you can quote me).

More like a bee myself…unlike a lunk-a-lout leery-faced old bear…though we both deal in honey, albeit one steals it from the other, digging with his big fat paws, i have occasionally been buzzing around my sticky hive memory mind looking for tasty tidbits for your story. However more i look, more i remember my dislike of Paul's ugly behaviour: his insensitivity to people's feelings, his somnolent violence which I've always imagined came from the strange vales of the country-side around his native Bordeaux, where screechy creatures live when the fields turn dark: grandfather owls and lots of bats, scrawny old 19th century monster wolves (the Bête du Givaudan), screeching and pawing around cutting people up for their owltime delights, yet also during the day Paul's obvious peasant ancestry sent chills of foreboding up my more urban spine, so natural to think of Paul slitting the rabbit throats, draining them of their blood. Yes, Paul: a werewolf at night, a lunky loutish peasant during the day eating ravenously from the flesh of innocent creatures.

So no honey in my hive; more like a sudden realisation that i'm not as keen on Paul as i previously thought.

For example, from one day to the next, our mutual friend Jean-Louis Bourgeois became a persona non grata for Paul. Something poor JLB did? But what? What was most curious was how seriously Paul took it all: JLB became a "noodle," someone soft and effeminate. No sense of play or fun about these declarations. I realised therefore I was dealing with a fucker who might turn on me…yikes, the horror of it. I became slyly happy to see this pompous arse fall on his face, as he did occasionally, the day of his telling me he had failed his entrance to the École Normale. . . .

Well I'm being mean. But I have my reasons to be truthful. . . .

I have lots more to say about this doggone french lout but my enthusiasm to disgorge this particular abscess has waned...so let this stand until next time, next time being when I get another head of enthusiasm for bashing this bugger of no friend of mine. (April 12, 1999)

Amazing the sorcery some people can achieve with a lowly whisk. I was not willing to just drop the correspondence at that point and I felt obliged to defend Paul but in a manner which recognized the legitimacy— extreme though it was—of Tcherepnin's insights. Let some time pass, I thought. However, in the meantime Tcherepnin replied:

What kind of friend are you—Stephen???

You should be all over me for the mean low stupid regretful incoherent fallacious murtherous items I hauled your way yester- day...was it yesterday, it seems like light years away, light years back on a distant and faraway star at which a monolith and a broomstick must have met, at the time for its own birth, 1938?...no mistaking the light!

Please tell Paul he should know my grudges pass quickly, whereas my gratefulness, when won, is a bedrock, and won.

Please tell him I hope he and you will give me a call when you come [to Paris] in June?—or whenever. . . . (April 13, 1999)

My response begins with my mentioning that I had been collecting information for my personal journal for twenty-seven years and that the project had now reached the stage at which I had been giving it to some acquaintances to read:

...This Christmas it was read by a Canadian novelist and TV per- sonality, David Gilmour, who once studied with Paul. One of Gilmour's comments was that by the end of the book readers cer- tainly have the impression that they understand Paul's character.

What I found so interesting about your April 12th e-mail message was that it fractures my positive and loving portrait. Readers of my book immediately see from your remarks—and maybe for the first time—that it is not Paul as such that has been documented but my personal version of him. Despite your sometimes obvious unfairness,

I see the legitimacy of your reactions. Paul's humour—which in my account tends to be child-like and innocently playful, maybe like Erik Satie—could legitimately be interpreted as aggression by someone he rejected or someone who did not sympathize with his values. Indeed, Paul does sometimes radically change his opinion of people in a manner which I think is unfair.

You must have an excellent memory. You still correctly remember some of his vocabulary despite the passage of over thirty years. He does label some people "noodles." In my journal the word never appears, but I have actually heard him use it. There is also a synonym, some kind of steamed vegetable. I'm not sure which vegetable (he's the cook), but it's probably a "steamed zucchini."

"What kind of a friend are you—Stephen???" Actually, I have been Paul's lover for a few months short of thirty years. In the late 1960s Paul must have been living an openly gay lifestyle in Paris, although he may have been rather closeted in the early 1960s. At least that's my impression. You may or may not know he is gay. I still don't know when in the 1960s you were associating with him.

From my point of view what you have misunderstood is Paul's genuine lack of pretentiousness (not to be confused with lack of opinions), his generosity and his self-perceived marginality which results in a fascinating kind of humour that has a socially subversive edge. In the early 1980s—long after the noodle incident you mention—Paul and I spent a week in New York and visited Jean-Louis Bourgeois. I certainly did not have the impression that there was any animosity between them.

…Your March 12th e-mail message, referring to the black block in the film *2001*, was important to me because it confirmed that my project was in fact worth the effort. It has been confirmed by others as well. All of the criticism in the second message, because it is so cleverly written, also gave me the same impression, oddly enough. Nonetheless, I'm glad to see that you have changed your mind. But I really don't know my Tolstoy. His writings are so vast that I can't see one obvious theme. (April 15, 1999)

Later that night Tcherepnin replied. Given the number of typing mistakes it looks as though he was somewhat drunk. I do not remember meeting him when he visited Toronto in 1972. Certainly, the contact would have been very brief. I may have paid little attention to him in order to avoid speaking French.

...I've always felt good around Paul becoz at his heart is an unfor-giving light....

he's gay, you don't say. I do remember precise the strained feeling of Paul's space when I came visited him up some tower in Toronto and first met you. What a strange Giacometti experience a bit sad for me, much sad for me indeed.

But now ye both live in eternity's sunrise! Hey! And I wish it for both of you!

Yes from the first i knew he was gay—and a bon vivant sort of one.... I remember meeting paramours of his in the 60s....

Vision of Paul introducing me to a sweet circus boy at the Cirque Bouglione in Paris...and later, at the Ile Ste. Louis, meeting flamboyants worthy Jack Smith's Flaming Creatures, all joking and laughing in a setting for Casanova (view of the quais and river, the painted marquetry through the apt....)[16]

Somehow my innocence has carried me into the intimacy of great gays....

oodles of noodles!

Say hi to the noodle himself! (April 15, 1999)

◆ ◆ ◆

Paul's interest in decoding the messages of rock art did not emerge out of the blue. Someone once referred to Périgord as the Manhattan of the pre-historic era. Paul's paternal grandfather worked as a volunteer excavating prehistoric sites at the turn-of-the-century. Paul cannot name the exact location where his grandfather worked, but believes it was near Le Bugue or Sarlat. The grandfather had an amateur's interest in the natural sciences (space, radiation, the structure of matter), and one of his revered authors was the Catholic priest and paleontologist Pierre Teilhard de Chardin. Bicycling as an adolescent around Périgord and Quercy with his friends, Paul visited many prehistoric caves. His eclectic reading throughout his life has included much of the professional literature on rock art which came to his attention as soon as it appeared in print. In addition, his long-term interest in animal behaviour is consistent with an interest in rock art because the spectacular and frequently reproduced prehistoric paintings are of wild animals. Although Paul has not written about the origin of languages, it is a topic that has captivated him for a long time.

The less spectacular prehistoric caves in southern France are some-times in private hands. A visit to these caves can bring one into contact with people who have passionate, sometimes idiosyncratic theories about the meaning and role of prehistoric art. For example, Paul tells a story about meeting a farmer, a resident of a troglodyte house carved into the side of a cliff, who was himself excavating the cave behind his home. Finding many small pieces of bone with drawings on them, the farmer thought that these were models for paintings that had been carried by migrating artists.

In the 1980s when Paul started attending conferences about rock art, he formed the impression that some of the ideas specialists discussed were old-fashioned in comparison to the developments in the other social sciences. The assumption that prehistoric peoples were child-like reminded him of earlier racist beliefs about the inferiority of non-European societies. Experts seemed to dismiss out of hand the possibility that prehistoric peoples could be intelligent enough to express complex ideas or have the desire to write their own language.

Paul was led to the assumption that some prehistoric art is actually a written language. It is not possible that all of the drawings would constitute a code of symbols systematic enough to form a language, but some might have these properties, most obviously handprints because they consist of so many separate components: size, colour, orientation, whole hands or hands lacking fingers and parts of fingers, openness, mode of production, location in the cave, et cetera. It may never be possible to read the language(s), but the hypothesis is easy to test and it has significant consequences for our assumptions about the level of intelligence of prehistoric peoples. If it is found that these elements are purely random, handprints cannot be a written language.

> The case of the numerous hands that are observed among the clearly identifiable patterns that have survived in the caves provides an example of the way in which perceptions are biased by assumptions, and data are constructed by narratives. Hand representations have a particular status because they evoke more vividly than any other traces the physical presence of the humans that once lived in these regions. They indeed appear to be produced either by direct imposition of the painted palms and fingers on the rock surface (positive hands), or by stencil (negative hands) through methods that have been extensively discussed and tested.
>
> However, their interpretation seems to have been comparatively less contentious than any other rock art patterns. They are immediately identifiable—it is well-known that hands and faces are overriding perceptual forms among the primates—and they are perceived as part of intentional gestures. The problems they raise

usually are restricted to the sphere of "deictic" meaning, that is, meaning determined by the context in which the gestures have been performed. This is why their interpretations have been over-whelmingly of a pragmatic or ritualistic nature. These hand impressions are spontaneously related to individual humans in particular situations: appropriating an animal through the magical grasping of its image; asserting tribal ownership of a place; offering to a deity the visual proof of sacrificial finger mutilations; marking the rocks as a gesture of allegiance or as an element of a ritual ini-tiation, and the like.... While there have been interpretations that construed zoomorphic paintings and geometric signs as symbolic representations to be understood in relation to religious codes (myths) or secular systems (kinship, astronomical calculation or even forms of reckoning), hand morphs have not been integrated in these symbolic interpretative attempts except possibly as indi-vidual or collective "signatures."

...It seems that the apparent bodily immediacy of these marks disqualifies them for articulating abstract propositions and symbolic values. It is possible to reconstruct the gestures, postures and artifacts that have made them possible. But, beyond speculating that they may have served as identity marks of distinct ethnic groups (a typical deictic function of the kind "I was here"), our ignorance of the context precludes any credible deciphering of their significance.[17]

◆ ◆ ◆

In the 1980s Paul and I both became professionally and personally con-cerned with Asian societies, in Paul's case, India and Indonesia; in mine, China and Japan. On Paul's first trip to India the city of Mysore reminded him of ancient Rome, although he now admits that his initial response was an illusion. "It's no more than a fantasy. I don't know that there are any grounds for believing this, but I related to India through my knowledge of classical times." As a Frenchman, he thinks England is more exotic than India.

From spending years in school translating Latin and Greek texts, he formed an image of the appearance of ancient Rome. He recalls translating Juvenal's *Satire Number Three* in which there are some passages about traffic in Rome. His first reaction on arriving in Bombay was that Europe would have looked like India, if Christianity had not destroyed local cultures and religious diversity. He imagines Roman temples resembling Hindu temples in spirit, not in detail. Many other features suggest ancient Rome: the sheer numbers of people in the streets, the colourful clothing, the way shops open directly onto the street, men loafing and talking outdoors rather than rushing to appointments, the variety of vehicles and animals. There is evidence of a high level of civilization in India without technology being overpowering as it is in North America.

◆　◆　◆

The young Brahmin who walks a few yards to bring Paul and me tea carries a big stick at night, which he says is to scare away cats. He means tigers. But if you talk about tigers, they are bound to appear. A few days earlier some boys saw the footprints of a tiger near the lodge where we are staying at a warden's post inside Nagarhole National Park in Karnataka. We sleep at the lodge, confined indoors at night because of the animals. A warden offers to drive us into the jungle to see them up close. Since he is drunk, we find excuses to stay put. The men who work domesticating elephants sing all night in order to scare away predators. Even deer come close because they feel safer near people.

The Honey Gatherers, or the Jenukorubas, are a nomadic tribal people who make a living by hunting and gathering and by paid employment in the park. It is these men who do the real work in domesticating elephants. Kikeri Narayan, the linguist who developed a script for their language and recorded their epics and traditional knowledge, takes us to one of their villages near Nagarhole. The village is an attempt by the government to goad the Honey Gatherers into settling down and farming. In December 1987 it is certainly too cold for people to sleep outdoors. Yet, the Honey Gatherers insist on sleeping on bare ground in front of their government-constructed brick houses whose cooking facilities they appreciate. On our arrival some of the men excitedly tell Narayan about seeing a rogue elephant strolling by a day earlier. Traditionally, the Honey Gatherers' only escape from mean elephants was to climb trees because their houses of branches could easily be flattened. They would not be safe even in modern houses. Some of the men show us how to make a fire without matches, a skill they take pride in. As a memento, we pick up off the ground a little mud ball which the Honey Gatherers throw to kill birds.

The next morning we are driven by car a short distance until we encounter a big rogue elephant that is blocking the road. No honking horns to clear the road. No shouting "Hey, look at the elephants!" Adult male elephants respond to loud noises as challenges. It is the elephant which is in control. We are stuck between two cars and have no room to turn around and escape, if it charges.

An incident like this occurred twice. In recounting the other occasion, Paul uses it to illustrate a point in linguistics.[18] Linguists assume that words are artificial. There is no resemblance or relationship between most words and the physical qualities of the object or animal they represent. Paul argues that these linguists are sometimes wrong because they are not familiar with all of the parameters of the situation. In Malayalam, a language spoken in Kerala, the word for elephant is the diminutive "aana." The word seems a contradiction of the size of elephants and the dangers they pose to humans. He speculates that "aana" signifies the necessity of remaining silent and unimposing in their presence. The word captures the structure of knowledge of the local population rather than the appearance of elephants.

◆ ◆ ◆

In his book *Angelic Echoes*, Ralph Sarkonak, a professor of French, writes about creating in his home a tranquil and reverential space for doing research. He decorated the study with a drawing of Michel Foucault and a photographic self-portrait of Foucault's friend the novelist Hervé Guibert. The drawing of Foucault was created for a poster advertising a conference organized by Paul at the University of Toronto in 1994. Sarkonak thought that the drawing captured the intensity of the philosopher's face and the typographical errors in the conference's bilingual title the transgressive side of his scholarship.

In fact, there are more transgressive meanings to this poster than the ones Sarkonak imagined. The poster is a better example of Paul's high-minded but comic attitude to the academic establishment. Rather than following the normal procedures for commissioning a poster for such a prestigious event, Paul gave the commission to an art student, a Korean immigrant who is barely literate in English. When Paul first saw the artist's childish grammar mistakes in the conference title, he was exasperated. But then he had the brilliant idea of adding more grammar mistakes and claiming that it represented some truth about Foucault's philosophy. Even better, he made certain that the esteemed President of Victoria College, who inaugurated the event, publicly complimented the poster for the conference now titled: "MICHEL.F'S & LA;LITTERATURE AND: LITERATURE PROGRAMME? PROGRAMEE="

◆ ◆ ◆

Buddha, Montaigne and Lévi-Strauss—the three are logically related. Lévi-Strauss once said to Paul that Buddhism was to him the most appealing of all the world's religions. And in his office he keeps a bust of Buddha. One chapter in Lévi-Strauss' book *The Story of Lynx* is titled "Rereading Montaigne." From studying ancient Greek and Roman authors, Montaigne seems to have become a radical skeptic who believed that all accepted knowledge would some day come to be rejected. While there are passages in his essays in which he professes to be a Christian, this appears to be an act of convenience in an age of intolerance rather than a matter of faith. Montaigne's radical skepticism might have led to a self-denying philosophy or perhaps to suicide, Lévi-Strauss argues, except that Montaigne found satisfaction in sensory pleasures, living life as though it had meaning when he knew in truth that it did not.

Any philosophy contains contradictory ideas. Since life is short, we should just be patient and live as best we can with our own contradictions.[19]

◆　◆　◆

"Authentic" is the most prominent word on the sweatshirt Christian Marin is wearing when he meets us at the Hamburg train station. I have not seen Christian for an unbelievably long time, twelve years; in Paul's case it has been about six. An early autumn rain storm blows small, confetti-like leaves across the cobblestones in front of the train station.

Christian drives us to the apartment of a friend who lives nearby, absent-mindedly forgetting to turn on the headlights of his white van. Distracted this morning by a telephone call, he burnt the apple pie he was baking for dinner. One corner of the collar of his denim jacket is turned under. Paul and Christian immediately plunge into a conversation about circus managers as though they are continuing a conversation that was halted only a few days ago. Since Paul and I have just come from Lausanne, where we saw the Knie Circus, the Knie family is the main topic. Christian received a letter from the management of the Knie Circus expressing interest in engaging him for one season. He replied quoting Antonin Artaud about the religious nature of the theatre and sent a video of his performance recorded at the wrong speed like a jerky silent movie. He received in response a letter saying that the circus had enough clowns for the coming season. There was some debate between Paul and Christian if the letter from the management was ironical or serious.

Rather than continuing to juggle on the sidewalk, Christian now prefers to work for circuses in Germany. They pay well. But he still thinks the management of circuses everywhere in Europe is archaic. Performers remain slaves to insensitive and unappreciative circus owners who nonetheless profit from them.

"I feel like I'm in Versailles," he said about his friend's small apartment in Hamburg which has separate living and dining rooms. He continues to live alone in his van or less often in a one-room apartment in Paris. However, his ambition is to live on a houseboat in France. When unemployed, he sometimes goes to Mediterranean resorts in France, living in his van, and flying kites for relaxation.

In Christian's pantheon of philosophers, the German Romantic author Heinrich von Kleist has taken a place alongside Genet and Artaud. After Christian explained some of his ideas about authentic circus art, someone suggested that his opinions sounded like the ideas Kleist expressed in 1810 in his essay "On the Marionette Theatre."[20] The term "marionette" is no longer pejorative for Christian. According to Kleist, consciousness destroys the natural grace of spontaneous movements. Lacking a self, marionettes are incapable of affectation and thus superior to the mechanic who controls them.

Christian still claims that the circus should not be confused with the theatre. In his opinion actors are distorting the nature of the circus by making it too aesthetic. Classical music is such a common accompaniment for circus acts that Christian is thinking about returning to the cha-cha. He criticizes actors for their technical amateurishness that is due to their lack of specialization. "A juggler has to know how to juggle." Some circus managers take the exoticism of the circus, play with foreign and ethnic-minority identities and present this in a crude but more artistic manner than was done earlier. The result, though, is artificial and sterile. Another mistake is to copy whatever is popular in the mass media. Christian calls this a "theft of culture, 'une sauce.'" All this belongs in the garbage can. It is not an art which arises out of a sincere desire to express one's self. Although he is not old enough to have had much personal contact with the commercial circus of the 1950s and 60s, he has come to believe that they were not so bad after all.

Like other boys Christian did some gymnastics and played the solitary game with a soccer ball of bouncing it against a wall and passing it around his back, a kind of minimal juggling. At a vacation resort he observed a girl juggling and a boy doing somersaults. He tried to copy them, at first juggling with pétanque balls. One evening at home he overheard a circus program, *La Piste aux Etoiles*, being broadcast on a neighbour's television. Since his parents did not own a television set, he rushed out into the street to find someone who was watching the same program. After a while he did locate a home where a family had tuned to the program but their window blinds were closed. He stood on the street looking through the closed window blinds. Just at that moment Paolo Bedini, one of the most famous European jugglers appeared on the screen. This was the moment when Christian decided that he wanted to juggle for life.

◆ ◆ ◆

On the way to his first operation Paul talks about surrealism. He is more talkative than usual, the unspoken reason being the absurdity of life which the menace of death makes so apparent. It is a minor operation on one of his sinuses for an illness which also afflicted his father when he was younger. The doctor is a pioneer in this type of operation which is not risky. Paul is supposed to recuperate at home. But still he tends to over-dramatize the situation, in my opinion.

We planned to take the streetcar along Toronto's Queen Street West to the St. Joseph Health Centre, but we go by taxi instead. I learn that Paul had the students in his surrealism class walk along Queen Street West looking for surrealist-type events and information, the way Aragon did in Paris in the 1920s. Beside all the personal signs which vandals have recently spray-painted on buildings are politically inspired messages: "Resistance looks like you, forget learning"… "start dreaming, add some colour, freedom = unavoidable pleasure." There is the juxtaposition of such a range of social types: goth people, squeegee kids, wealthy loft owners, the poor from public housing, residents of nearby Chinatown and Little Italy, the customers of trendy dance clubs and restaurants—glitter and squalor. The social diversity reminds Paul of the Latin Quarter in the 1950s. It's the perfect area for an alternative university or a semiotic café where customers can discuss the philosophical problems of communication and representation.

Waiting at the health centre, Paul suggests that I try writing haiku on sociological themes or Goffmanesque haiku on hospitals rather than the more traditional haiku about nature which I am writing. He talks about the actions of hospital employees following a script, a fact he finds reassuring. Some people know their parts better than others, though. St. Joseph's has an excessive amount of religious imagery. In one hallway there are winged angels, but they are presented in a way that does not undermine a scientific world view. We are all one-winged angels who need each other.

Printed on Paul's clothing is "hospital property." "I'm no longer yours," he remarks. "We're all just little bubbles. If the bubble bursts, it's no big deal. Put my ashes in an urn beside Pizzicati's." He is referring to a friend's treatment of the ashes of his mother and cat. (Pizzicati is still alive and well.) He puts his hand over the side of his mouth to send me a secret kiss as the attendant pushes his bed down the hall and into the operating room. The last words I hear him say, speaking to the attendant, as he is about to disappear behind the door: "I feel like a little ant in an ant colony. . . ."

Paul recovers quickly from the operation, although he is weak for a few days and has trouble concentrating. We assume this is caused by the anaesthetics.

◆　◆　◆

A haiku by Paul that refers to me and an angel-wing butterfly that I saw in late October at the edge of Martin Lake. The two lakes in the state forest near Shoals, Indiana, are the places I go to escape and to think:

> Raindrops make circles on the lake
> Autumn foliage among the pines
> A late bloomer shivers

◆　◆　◆

Paul's message for Valentine's Day:

> Time lashes out at the window
> Two seamless lives and a cat
> woven under the lamp[21]

◆　◆　◆

The mother of all haiku, which Paul wrote for my birthday:

> Time flies
> So what!
> This day we make it a wonder

◆　◆　◆

"Yours till the end." The message Paul wrote on his Valentine's Day card for 2002.

♦ ♦ ♦

The evening after Paul finishes reading through the manuscript version of *The Pleasures of Time* we walk home together from my office in St. John's. Along the way he never lets me forget that our differences tend to misrepresent his outlook on life. Characteristically, I live in a house built in 1849 on one of the cherished streets of the merchants who ran Newfoundland at the turn of the twentieth century. Paul reminds me that the influences on his early thinking include popular romanticism, literary romanticism, Catholic mysticism, negative theology and Sufism. These is practically nothing in this book about any of these topics. I do not know a thing about negative theology. As far as I can recall, Paul is mentioning the topic for the first time. My knowledge of Sufism could be summarized in one very brief paragraph. While I do know a lot about romanticism, it is through music, a notoriously imprecise medium for conveying ideas. The only references in this book to Catholicism are Paul's explanations of why he rejected it in adulthood, not what he found interesting and meaningful about it as an adolescent. Out of the blue I unexpectedly hear that Paul "was colonized by the bad Romans." Although he does not dismiss out of hand the forces which shaped my outlook, he identifies them as Protestant utilitarianism and positivism. These differences have resulted in some of the nightmares—and obviously the pleasures—of writing this book.

Paul complains that I tend to "objectify" things. I spell out to everyone something he might say one way to one person and another way to someone else. Everything does not have to be said, he protests. Three times Paul lost all of his books and papers due to moving in Paris and then emigrating to Canada. His possessions were thrown away or sold by the people who were supposed to safeguard them. Consequently, I have not had access to most of the personal letters and the writings of his youth. When he was about 20 and still a Catholic, he read nearly all of the books of the social activist and mystic Simone Weil. I would like to have seen the notes he wrote in the margins of her books. Resolutely self-effacing, he is still proud of the fact that scholars are not familiar with the body of his work because it is scattered in such obscure journals. Unfortunately, my summary of his research on the circus imprisons him in the past. He feels like an ancient archeological site.

He tells a story about finding happiness. Although he does not know its origin, it is a variation of the Lucky John story, which was recorded by the Brothers Grimm. In Paul's version the main character is not quite the numbskull he seems to be in the original. A farmer named John takes a cow to the market. He is looking forward to enjoying the money from the sale. But he is fooled into trading the cow for a goat, then the goat for a pig, the pig for a goose, the goose for a chicken, and so on. With each trade he has something of lower value. Finally, at the end of the day John is disgusted with himself. He is left holding something which is so worthless he throws it into a lake. Then John finds happiness.

Paul insists that when he was young, he and his friends liked to cultivate the paradoxical: "the best way to tell the truth is to lie."

Notes

[1] Frank Rasky, "The Professors' Wonderful Circus," *Maclean's*, June 5, 1965, 19.

[2] *I am Curious (Yellow)* is the title of a Swedish film which recounts the experiences of a female sociologist who is conducting a sexual survey of Swedish society. At the time of its release in 1967 it was quite controversial because of its sexual content and nudity. It was followed by a second film titled *I am Curious (Blue)*.

[3] Romain Rolland, *Musicians of To-day*, Freeport, NY: Books for Libraries Press, 1969 (1915), 247-248.

[4] Family papers record the progress of Paul's grandfather on the Tour de France: Pocé (Indre et Loire), 28 October 1888 to 29 January 1889; Aiguillon (Lot et Garonne), 2 March to 10 April 1889; Porte Sainte-Marie, 12 April to 9 June 1889; Perpignan, 15 June to 14 July 1889; Béziers, 23 July to 18 October 1889; Agde, 19 October to 2 December 1889; Nimes, 6 December 1889 to 28 April 1890; Villefranche sur Saone, 10 May to 2 June 1890 and 15 July to 1 November 1890; Meursault, 4 November 1890 to 7 February 1891; Buzançais, 16 February 1891 to 4 November 1892.

[5] According to family papers, Raymonde Frêne was an "apprentie et ouvrière couturière" in Châteauroux from 1914 to 1920; "un travailleur au magasin de ses parents" at 42 rue Grande from 1920 to 1936; and a "retoucheuse" from 1961 to 1969. The unrecorded years, 1936 to 1961, were spent in a marriage that ended in an early divorce and in caring for her elderly parents. Paul requested the hyperrealist American artist Ron Bowen to make a drawing of Raymonde using a photograph as a model.

[6] Paul Bouissac interviewed by Stephen Riggins, June 12, 1998.

[7] Stephen Riggins' interview with Michel Foucault first appeared in the Canadian magazine *Ethos*, I (2), 1983, 4-9.

[8] Vladimir Nabokov, *Speak, Memory: An Autobiography Revisited*, New York: Vintage Books, 1967, 207.

[9] Jan Juffermans, *Met Stille Trom: Beeldende Kunst en Utrecht Sinds 1900*, Utrecht: Bruna, 1976.

[10] Obituary of Dorothy Robert, *The Herald-Times*, Bloomington, Indiana, December 24, 1998, A2.

[11] Jan Morris, *Trieste and the Meaning of Nowhere*, New York: Simon and Schuster, 2001, 105.

[12] A biographical sketch of Walter Robert can be found in Walter Robert, *Das Klavierwerk von Johannes Brahms*, Vienna: Reden und Schriften No. 2 Hochschule für Musik und Darstellende Kunst, 1997, 2-3; Obituary in *The Herald-Times*, Bloomington, Indiana, June 23, 1999.

[13] To any real musician the information provided by a mere list of composers' names is too superficial. The following are the actual pieces I studied in high school with Dorothy Robert: Bach (*Well-tempered Clavier, Preludes and Fugues Nos. I, II, V; Preludes VI, VII, XV, XVII, XXI, XXII; The French Suite No. Five*), Haydn (*Sonatas in G. Major, Hob. XVI:27; C Major, Hob. XVI:35;* and *D Major, Hob. XVI:37*),

Mozart (*Sonatas KV. 310, 331, 332, 333* and *545*), Beethoven (*Sonata opus 49, No. 2; Pathetique Sonata*), Brahms (*Second Rhapsody*), Grieg (From *Holberg's Time*), Dvorak (*Slavonic Dance No. 1* in C Major for two pianos), Debussy ("La Cathédrale Engloutie," "La Fille aux Cheveux de Lin," "La Sérénade Interrompue"; and the "Sarabande" from *Pour le Piano*), and Ravel (*Sonatina*).

[14] Yoel Hoffman, ed., *Japanese Death Poems: Written by Zen Monks and Haiku Poets on the Verge of Death*, Rutland, VT: Charles E. Tuttle, 1986, 155.

[15] Robert Orledge, *Gabriel Fauré*, London: Eulenburg Books, 1979, 187.

[16] Jack Smith's (1932-1989) *Flaming Creatures* is a classic underground film from 1963. To Susan Sontag in "Notes on Camp," the film is about joy and innocence, and more intersexual than homosexual. Censors noticed the nudity and the evocation of an orgy. The apartment Tcherepnin mentions is photographed in an issue of *La Maison Française*, "Un Grenier Quai d'Anjou," October 1963, 150-154. There is no marquetry in the photographs.

[17] Paul Bouissac, "Dates, Data and Narratives: The Meaning of Hand Signs in Rock Art Research," Paper presented at the third AURA Congress, Alice Springs, Australia, July 10-14, 2000.

[18] Paul Bouissac, "Syntactic Iconicity and Connectionist Models of Language and Cognition," in Marge Landsberg, ed., *Syntactic Iconicity and Linguistic Freezes: The Human Dimension*, Berlin: Mouton De Gruyter, 1995, 405.

[19] Claude Lévi-Strauss, *The Story of Lynx*, Chicago: University of Chicago Press, 1995, 216-217.

[20] Heinrich von Kleist, *An Abyss Deep Enough: Letters of Heinrich von Kleist with a Selection of Essays and Anecdotes*, Philip B. Miller, ed., New York: E.P. Dutton, 1982, 211-216.

[21] This poem would work better in French. The word "temps" means both time and weather in French. Why this distinction is made in one language but not in another is an interesting question. What is the similarity between time and weather that our anglophone ancestors failed to see?

Stephen Riggins doing Taoist Tai Chi, Martin State Forest, near Shoals, Indiana, mid-1990s.
Photographer: Bill Whorrall

Index

182, 191, 198, 201, 301
Mauriac, François, 26
Maximov, Dimitri, 22-24, 113, 249
Maze, Léonie, 18
McLuhan, Marshall, 156-157, 160-161, 174
Merkert, Jörn, 41, 43, 54, 99, 173, 273
Miazzano, Carmelitta, 46-47
Michaud, 100
Millier, Jean, 53
Montaigne, Michel de, 80, 165, 174, 249, 298
Moris, Jesse, 199
Moss, Earl, 88
Nabokov, Vladimir, 61, 266, 304
Nall (Fred Nall Hollis), 117-118, 128, 173
Nay, Jean-Gérard, 68, 73, 78, 100, 113, 164-165, 171, 174, 249-251
Ohrel, Alain, 19-20, 52-53, 150, 249
Pace, David, 207, 209, 227
Pachet, Pierre, 91-92, 105
Paolozzi, Eduardo, 44-46, 48-50, 53, 58
Parkinson, Jim, 32-33, 39
Parmegiani, Bernard, 40, 42, 45
Pauwels, Pepette, 143-144
Pepperberg, I. M., 224
Perley, Maie Clements, 186-187, 201
Petit, Philippe, 44-46, 64, 66-67, 145
Petrassi, Goffredo, 137
Pevsner, Nikolaus, 134, 173
Pham, Khoa, 11, 162, 273-276
Pipo (Philippe Sosman), 253-254
Poesiat, Hendrik, 267
Poesiat, Leida, 270
Ponge, Francis, 74, 100
Potocki, Jan, 110, 173
Poumeyrol, Pierre, 249
Prévert, Jacques, 100
Rasky, Frank, 29, 31, 57, 304
Reich, Steve, 42
Reich, Wilhelm, 89, 104
Riggins, Harve, 283-284
Rimbaud, Arthur, 88, 103
Robbe-Grillet, Alain, 61, 73-74, 98, 103

Robert, Dorothy, 280-281, 304
Robert, Walter, 277-279, 282, 304
Roditi, Georges, 14
Rolland, Romain, 234, 262, 304
Rolly, 45
Ross, Alan, 153
Rouet, Father, 165-166
Routh, Francis, 135
Rubin, Lillian, 285
Sacré, James, 61, 97, 103, 107
Sarkonak, Ralph, 297
Sarraute, Nathalie, 73, 98, 103
Sartre, Jean-Paul, 107-108, 173, 207, 251
Sax, Ursula, 43, 45
Schönberg, Arnold, 133, 144
Sebeok, Thomas, 210-211, 227, 229
Serres, Michel, 66, 103
Sigala, Father Jean, 79-80, 104, 204-206, 227
Stravinsky, Igor, 123-124, 135, 141, 173, 237, 273
Taylor, Karen, 282
Tcherepnin, Serge, 289-291, 293, 305
Tessier, Christian, 91, 93-95
Tinguely, Jean, 82, 104
Tippett, Michael, 133-134
Varda, Agnès, 16
Varèse, Edgard, 136, 144
Vasarely, Victor, 42
Vesque, Juliette, 22, 205, 227
Vesque, Marthe, 22, 205
Viala, Michel, 23, 66-67
Vivien, Claude, 91
Wald, Susana, 157
Weil, Simone, 303
White, Cynthia, 144
White, Edmund, 77, 104
White, Harrison, 159
Whorrall, Bill, 185
Willen, Sarah, 35-36, 38
Windsor, Eddie (Douglas Kossmayer), 45, 47
Windsor, Elizabeth, 267
Zeller, Ludwig, 157
Zoé, 142-143, 245